"Taylor's writing is filled with a richness of place and a precise attention to detail."

—*Cemetery Dance*

Praise for *Nailed*

"*Nailed* opens in a bar, but what happens to the protagonist, Matt Engstrom, is more like a bar brawl. He's assailed from every point of the compass, and author Lucy Taylor has done a fine job of keeping the reader as off-balance as her hero under siege. . . . Genuinely different . . . edgy."

—Jeremiah Healy, author of *Spiral* and *The Only Good Lawyer*

"Fast and furious . . . an entertaining ride . . . [a] sweaty, bloody mess—and the fun is in the mayhem."
—*The Boulder Daily Camera*

"An exciting amateur sleuth tale . . . a nonstop thriller that leaves the audience *Nailed* to their seat until Lucy Taylor's book is finished."

—BookBrowser

SAVING SOULS

Lucy Taylor

AN ONYX BOOK

ONYX
Published by New American Library, a division of
Penguin Putnam Inc., 375 Hudson Street,
New York, New York 10014, U.S.A.
Penguin Books Ltd, 80 Strand,
London WC2R 0RL, England
Penguin Books Australia Ltd, Ringwood,
Victoria, Australia
Penguin Books Canada Ltd, 10 Alcorn Avenue,
Toronto, Ontario, Canada M4V 3B2
Penguin Books (N.Z.) Ltd, 182–190 Wairau Road,
Auckland 10, New Zealand

Penguin Books Ltd, Registered Offices:
Harmondsworth, Middlesex, England

First published by Onyx, an imprint of New American Library,
a division of Penguin Putnam Inc.

First Printing, July 2002
10 9 8 7 6 5 4 3 2 1

Copyright © Lucy Taylor, 2002
All rights reserved

REGISTERED TRADEMARK—MARCA REGISTRADA

Printed in the United States of America

Without limiting the rights under copyright reserved above, no part of
this publication may be reproduced, stored in or introduced into a
retrieval system, or transmitted, in any form, or by any means (electronic,
mechanical, photocopying, recording, or otherwise), without the prior written
permission of both the copyright owner and the above publisher of this
book.

PUBLISHER'S NOTE
This is a work of fiction. Names, characters, places, and incidents either
are the product of the author's imagination or are used fictitiously,
and any resemblance to actual persons, living or dead, business
establishments, events, or locales is entirely coincidental.

BOOKS ARE AVAILABLE AT QUANTITY DISCOUNTS WHEN USED TO PROMOTE
PRODUCTS OR SERVICES. FOR INFORMATION PLEASE WRITE TO PREMIUM
MARKETING DIVISION, PENGUIN PUTNAM INC., 375 HUDSON STREET, NEW
YORK, NEW YORK 10014.

If you purchased this book without a cover you should be aware that this
book is stolen property. It was reported as "unsold and destroyed"
to the publisher and neither the author nor the publisher has received
any payment for this "stripped book."

For my mother, Margery Taylor-Miller

Chapter 1

Dear Cass,

If I had just known I would meet someone as sweet and cute and sexy as you are, darlin', I would never have murdered my wife. (Mind you, I don't remember killing her, but the jury sure seemed certain it was me who did her, so maybe I just forgot.) It's damn funny, tho. If I had'na been convicting of murdering Melinda, I wouldn't be where I am today, and that's how you and me got hooked up in the first place. When you see it from that viewpoint, maybe all of it was meant to be. Was an Act of God. So you and me could meet the way we done and have a Future. Maybe Fate was controling my acktions all the time. The pastor of my church says it was pure evil in my soul, the Devil working thru me that made me lose my head, and I respect the Rev. with all my heart, but still even a Man of God can time to time be wrong, as I know for a fact to have happened. What do you think?

Your picture fills me with happiness and pease and the kind of thoughts that bedevil men when ther're behind bars (and sometimes when they're not behind bars—ha, ha). I know you understand my meaning, even tho your a nice girl. How do I know your a nice girl? Well, only an Angel would take the time and care to write *every week to a guy like me, in prison and accused of killing his wife. And only an Angel could see that photo of me was run in the Denver Post and tell by my looks I'm not an evil man.*

I am counting the days till 2 things take place— till I come up for parole (which my lawyer says won't be for another 15 years, that's a helluva lotta days) and the days till you come visit, and I first set eyes on you (just four days—a whole lot better than the other!!!).

You drive careful. It's a long way from New York City and them truckers can be real buttholes if they see a pretty girl behind the wheel.

All my love and kisses and a whole lot more besides,
Jack

When the steel doors clanged shut behind her, Cass Lumetto flinched and froze as if she were looking down the barrel of a rifle. She couldn't move. The beige pumps with the gold buckles that she'd bought on sale for this very occasion felt like they were nailed to the floor.

Do I really want to go through with this?

The barrel-shaped guard who was striding ahead of her halted, glared over his shoulder, and barked, "You coming or not?"

Cass nodded, following at a pace that suggested she was being marched toward Death Row instead of the visiting room at Canon City Penitentiary in Canon City, Colorado. At that moment, she wasn't sure she could tell the difference. The five minutes she'd been locked up so far in this grim, scary warren of corridors felt like five years. She wanted to bolt, to scream *Let me out! I made a mistake!* and run for the door.

She commanded herself to breathe. Waited for the panic to pass and kept moving.

"This way."

Another set of steel doors. Another guard, this one

dour-faced and female, eyeballing her floral print blouse, the new pumps and powder blue wraparound skirt with the suspicion of one who views clothing as just an elaborate form of packaging for illicit pharmaceuticals. She'd already handed over her sunglasses, leather handbag, and the keys to her car. All she had left with which to incite mayhem were the clothes she had on and whatever might be concealed inside various bodily orifices. Which was undoubtedly plenty, to judge from the way the guards scrutinized all the visitors, even those so small they were still in their mothers' arms.

The visitors' room was narrow, barren, and noisy, reeking of spilled sodas and cigarette smoke and the screamingly sweet fragrance of clashing perfumes. The inmates sat at Formica-topped tables, talking to their visitors or waiting for them to arrive. Vending machines in one corner dispensed candy, cigarettes, and sodas. Bored-looking guards patrolled the perimeters.

The guard who'd ushered Cass in consulted her clipboard. "Jack O'Doul, huh?" She pronounced the name with a West Texas drawl and a faint distaste, as though the name had a bitter tang to it. "Wait here, hon. Pretty Boy's always late. I figure he'll be out when he gets done admirin' himself in the mirror."

Cass seated herself at an empty table. Maybe two dozen adult visitors in the room, almost all women, another dozen or so kids, and a smattering of grumpy-looking teens. Some of the youngest children were racing around, banging into the vending machines, crawling on the filthy-looking tile floor, squawling and yelling while their mothers either tried frantically to make them behave or simply gave up and ignored them. Others huddled close to their moms, vacant and numb-looking as war refugees, like the kids you sometimes saw on the evening news who'd been caught up in a bomb blast, a terrorist attack. Their expressions mirrored what Cass felt in her gut, and her heart ached for them.

To distract herself from the children, she focused on the women. They ran the gamut from twenties to early fifties, gray hair to cornrows, from tattoos and pierced nostrils to Kmart polka dots and spandex tube tops. Most of them seemed like regulars, at home in these surroundings. Cass was a new face, and they checked her out, either subtly or with overt distrust. She tried to imagine their thoughts: *Which one are you here for? Better not be my man, you overdressed slut.*

Two new women strolled in, chatting and giggling, looking as relaxed as if they were browsing the aisles of Wal-Mart. The taller, heavier of the two was a broad-bottomed brunette with flabby arms and jeans a good size too small for her well-padded hips. Her large breasts flopped uncontained under a Harley-Davidson T-shirt. A guard smiled at her, said, "How ya doin' today, Mariah?"

The other woman was scarecrow bony with a bright helmet of red hair and huge, deep-lidded eyes that looked almost cartoonishly large for her narrow, pinched face. She wore madras shorts, an oversized denim shirt, and a baseball cap turned around backward. Like her friend Mariah, she greeted the guards by name and spoke to some of the prisoners. Cass envied them the easy familiarity with which they moved through this place that she found alien, stark, and unnerving.

A short, soulful-eyed Hispanic with ponytailed hair so ebony slick it looked like it had been shellacked onto his skull jumped up and stretched out his arms to the redhead. She rushed him like an NFL tackle and landed against his chest with a hearty *whomp*. They kissed and groped. The one named Mariah, meanwhile, struck up a conversation with one of the guards and leaned against the wall, arms folded under her breasts, watching the door for her man.

Cass crossed and uncrossed her legs, gnawed at a ragged thumbnail, and tried to visualize what Jack looked like. He'd sent her pictures, of course, but some sort of mental glitch was making it hard for her to remember his face—what if she didn't recognize him when he came through the door? Just the hair, she remembered that. Blond like her own wheat-colored hair, but much lighter, almost white. Cornsilk blond, shoulder-length. Hair that should be whipping in the Caribbean breeze in a commercial for men's cologne, not locked up in this grim, dreadful place.

"Cass, darlin'!"

He called out to her as if she were family, as if they'd been meeting like this forever, and she gave a small gasp and jumped to her feet. There he was, Jack O'Doul, flashing youth and vigor and brilliant white teeth.

Jack O'Doul, wife beater, stalker, convicted murderer.

"Cass, honey, I'd know you anywhere. You're even prettier than your pitcher."

"Jack, sweetheart. It's so great to finally meet."

She felt her mouth stretch into a tight, frozen smile as he strode over, breaching the boundaries of her personal space immediately, and enveloped her in a hug. It was a brotherly hug, more or less, but she sensed it could veer into other terrain very easily. He scooped her up in his arms and shook her gently from side to side and let her go and grinned down at her and then hugged her again.

He was tall, maybe six feet, a good five inches taller than she, and wore the same orange jumpsuit as all the other cons, but on him the garish garb looked almost okay.

"Sit down, sit down," he said, letting her go reluctantly. He took the plastic chair across from her and pulled it close. She could see now that his front teeth were slightly crooked, one incisor badly chipped, another missing. There was a hook-shaped scar about the size of a bottle cap at the outer corner of one eye. When he smiled, the scar crinkled raffishly and looked like a laugh line.

He took her hand. "I'm so happy to see you, honey,

you can't imagine. How you been? I was worried about you. That's a helluva drive all the way from New York City—you must be wore out!"

"No, the drive wasn't that bad," she said, tasting the lie like grit on the back of her teeth. Thinking, not bad at all, really, considering she'd flown directly into Denver from La Guardia, spent the night at her dad's condo in the Denver suburb of Aurora, then driven the two and a half hours south to Canon City. She'd wanted to rent a car, but her father, who collected vintage autos, insisted she take one of his.

"I always heard New Yorkers didn't own cars—they took the subway—but you got your own, huh?" Jack said.

"Yeah, she's a '78 mint-condition Eldorado. My dad calls her the Duchess." She considered telling him the story of how her father'd acquired the car for her from a Detroit dentist and car buff who knew a lot more about vintage autos than winning at high stakes poker, but he cut her off by changing the subject.

"So where you staying at, hon?"

"The Mountain View Inn."

"The Mountain View? That's pretty pricey. You go get a room at the Blue Skies. It's a good forty bucks cheaper and they got free coffee and donuts in the lobby."

No kidding, she thought. The Blue Skies was definitely low-rent, a stone's throw from the prison if you had a good pitching arm. A lot of the women who came from out of town stayed there. Cass had checked it out when she first cruised through town, decided no way was she bedding down in that fleabag.

"Actually, sweetie, I kind of like the Mountain View. I feel comfortable there even if it is a little more expensive."

He looked blank for a second, then light blinked on in his eyes. "Oh, yeah, I forgot. You're an uptown kinda gal. Yeah, I been to the Mountain View, but not in recent years. I got in one fight too many at the lounge. They had to call the cops on me, so my ass ain't been welcome there in a while."

She smiled understandingly, as though boozy brawls, angry bouncers, cop cars screeching to a halt at the curb, were normal in the world that she came from. Although the life she'd grown up in—years, lifetimes ago—hadn't been very much different.

He reached across the table and reclaimed her hand, folding it between both of his. She found herself thinking of his estranged wife Melinda and of what those hands, wielding Melinda's own gun, had done to her, and the air in her lungs turned to lead.

This is a killer, she told herself. *Never forget what he did.*

"You are so pretty," he said, staring at her. "I gotta tell you, I usually find myself attracted to darker women. I mean, I know most men fall all over themselves for a pretty blond gal, but most of my women have black hair or brown—my wife Melinda, she was a redhead—'cause me bein' so blond, a blond girlfriend looks like my sister. But you, Cass, you're pretty enough, I don't even care."

She tried to feel flattered, but she was too busy envisioning Melinda. She hadn't known Melinda had red hair. Hadn't known anything about her other than the information gleaned from newspaper clippings. Only that Jack had shot her to death with her own .38 one night after their separation, when she tried to sneak back into their home to retrieve some personal possessions.

Jack squeezed her hand with the same fingers that the jury decided had pulled the trigger of the .38 that blew out the back of Melinda O'Doul's skull. He grinned and said, "Honey, there's only one gal in the whole world might be prettier'n you. Want to see her?"

"Sure."

He reached into his pocket, took out a photo of a little girl, maybe two or three years old. Curly red hair, freckled skin, wearing jeans and a green Tommy Hilfiger sweatshirt.

Jack beamed and handed her the photo. "My little girl. Twyla."

"She's beautiful."

"Yeah, she looks like her mama. Course this is an old picture. She's five now and twice as big as she was when the picture was took. Least that's what I'm told. It's not like I get to see for myself."

"Where does she live?"

"Oh, right here in Canon City with Melinda's sister Angela and her husband Parker. They hate my guts, 'specially Angela. They won't bring Twyla to see me, wouldn't even accept the call when I tried to phone her on her birthday. I know they're telling her awful things about me, and it just breaks my heart."

"Visiting a parent in prison can be tough for a child," Cass said. Her father had been sent to prison when she was close to Twyla's age, and her mother had brought her along once on visiting day. She still had nightmares about that visit—the gray walls topped with spirals of jagged-looking metal, the towers where faceless men, bundled and hooded against the cold, stood cradling long guns in their arms.

She handed the picture back. "Maybe it would be better to wait till she gets older—"

"Till she forgets all about me, you mean? No way, no fucking way!"

His anger took her by surprise. She found herself stroking the back of his hand in a placating gesture.

"Not seeing my daughter," he went on, "that's the worst part about being in here, even worse than having everybody think I killed Melinda, which I still don't believe I did. But I'm trying to practice acceptance. I've talked to my pastor, the Reverend Butterworth, and he says all I can do is wait and pray on it. Maybe Angela will have a change of heart."

She was debating whether to tell him a little more about her history, the trauma of seeing her father in prison, when a sudden commotion a few tables away interrupted her thoughts. A woman's tremulous voice saying, "Please, Luthor, don't get mad!" was followed by the thunderous impact of a fist hitting a Formica tabletop.

Cass whirled around. An enormous, barrel-chested man with a frizzy, salt-and-pepper beard and crude jailhouse tattoos on both biceps was towering over a round-faced woman with bouffant blond hair and pillowy lips. The man's hands were clenched and he trembled as though from the effort required not to attack the woman with his fists. His dark, hooded eyes burned with malice as several baton-wielding guards pinned his arms behind his back.

"This'll be the fuckin' sorriest day of your life," he shouted as he was led away.

"Luthor, I'm so sorry, I didn't mean it," the woman wailed. She started to run after him, but was restrained by another guard and led off in the other direction.

"Wow," said Jack, a trace of awe in his voice, "that's Luthor Shaw."

"You *know* him?"

"Luthor Shaw, sure. I used to run with him and his biker gang before he got sent up for a double homicide a few years back. He's a stand-up guy. His girlfriend there, I don't know her, but I've seen her smilin' at different guys. I think she likes to flirt. Wonder what she said to piss him off."

"Whatever it was must've devastated him."

"She prob'ly broke up with him," Jack said. "Worst thing can happen to a man behind bars is have a woman not loyal to him." He fixed those glittery blue eyes on her. "What about you, Cass? Are you loyal? You're a loyal letter writer, I know that. Twice a week, every week since we started. But what about now that you're here and you met me? Are you one of them just gonna come here visiting a few times, then decide it's too tough and you can't do it no more? Meet up with some guy in the free world and break my heart?"

She put her hand over his. "I wouldn't lead you on like that, honey. You deserve better than that."

"Then you're planning on staying around? You gonna get yourself a place here? Find a job? Maybe some kind of secretarial stuff like you wrote me you did in New York?"

She smiled and squeezed his hand. "Of course I'm gonna find a place and get a job. How else would I be able to see my sweetie every visiting day?"

"Then that means you're gonna be my girl?"

"I came all the way from New York for this, Jack. I'm not turning back now."

"All right! That's what I want to hear!" He grinned, then swiveled in his seat and pointed out the redhead Cass had seen earlier, snuggling in a corner with the Hispanic. "See Frank and Opal over there. They've been goin' together, oh, I don't know how many years. Engaged to be married."

"You mean when he gets out of prison?"

"Well, that remains to be seen. Frank killed a man, so he might get out or he might not. He's up for parole soon. But whether he gets out or not, them two's gettin' married." He focused the full wattage of that country-boy smile on Cass. "Little while down the road, that could be you and me makin' plans for our wedding. That scare you?"

"Yeah. A little bit."

"Good, you gave me an honest answer, and I appreciate that. Wouldn't be normal if it didn't scare you." He slid an arm around her shoulders and kissed her. She felt herself tense. Gently, she pushed him away. "Don't the guards watch?"

"A few sneak a peak now and then, but most of 'em are respectful. They look the other way. After a while, you forget they're even there."

She looked around at the guards, the spartan plastic tables and chairs, at a teary-faced toddler alternately taking bites out of a Snickers bar and whining for his mother, and suddenly, for the first time since she'd come there, said exactly what she was thinking. "How do you ever relax in this place? What's it like living here all the time?"

"Well, if you call it livin'," said Jack, "which I don't. More like existing. You just get by one day at a time, hope your lawyer turns up some kinda grounds for appeal, hope you make parole, hope and pray a beautiful young woman takes an interest in you and comes to visit."

Cass felt the color rise in her cheeks, hated herself for not being able to stop it, and lowered her head.

He laughed. "You're shy, aren't you? I like that. Guess I had this image of New York women being tough and bitchy, lookin' to bust a man's balls, but you're not like that at all."

"Give me time."

"Admit it, though, you musta had a great life in New York. Bet you could probably do most anything, couldn't you? Get most anything you wanted anytime? Drugs, sex—it's all right there."

"No more than here in Canon City or anywhere else. I think people usually find what they're looking for—or it finds them."

"Yeah, you're right. A person can get fucked up on drugs, on alcohol, anywhere in the world. Everywhere you look is an addiction. And with addictions, you gotta be honest with yourself all the time, rigorously honest, or they'll bite you in the ass when you least expect it, drag you right down to hell. That's what the Reverend Butterworth says."

She picked up on the thread this was leading to. "You wrote me you were drunk when you killed Melinda. In a blackout?"

"Dead drunk, yeah. But honest to Jesus, I don't remember doing it. All I know is one minute I was leaving the Dark Horse, headed home, next thing I know I'm home, standing at the foot of the stairs, looking down at Melinda's body, and I'm so drunk, for a second I think it's *my* body I'm lookin' at—that *I'm* the one dead—'cause she's wearing one of my shirts and my jacket. But I got no recollection of shooting her, none whatsoever. I mean, we had our problems, but I loved Melinda. There was times when she pushed me too far, and things got a little hot, I admit that. But I loved her with all my heart. I truly did."

He sighed and reached for Cass's hand, fondling the fingers in the fretful, absent way one might caress a rosary. "You ever loved anybody?"

"Sure. My parents, my brother Tony."

"I mean a boyfriend." His tone turned playful again. "C'mon, bet you had a ton of boyfriends back in New York. Or were you just a heartbreaker?"

"There was one guy, Philip, that I dated for a couple of years. He was a good man, but I just couldn't see myself marrying him."

"You broke up with him?"

"Yeah."

"Then you must not have loved him."

"I loved him, but—to tell you the truth, I thought he was a little bit boring."

"Then that means it weren't love. Couldn't a been." He slid his chair against her, slung an arm around her shoulder, squeezed her to him. The side of his body felt as hard as a support beam of a house, unequivocally male and unyielding. She caught herself wondering what else was that hard.

"Maybe you've never really been in love," he said. "We're gonna change that, Cass. We *are*."

A voice came over the public address system, announcing the end to visiting time. Jack pulled out a piece of paper with a number scrawled on it.

"Honey, you'll need some help gettin' settled, I s'pect. This is Reverend Butterworth's home number. He and his wife Fiona, they'll help you out with anything you need. They're fine Christian people, the salt of the earth." He hesitated a second. "I guess one thing I never come right out and asked you in my letters—I been afraid to ask, I guess, but—you are a Christian, aren't you?"

"I was raised Catholic."

"Still practicin'?"

"I go to Mass now and then."

He frowned. "Yeah, guess I shoulda known. The Italian name and all. But I was hoping I might be wrong." Then he must have realized how rejecting that must sound, and added, "It's okay. The Lord's led you this far, He'll lead you to Jesus soon, too, just like He did me. I know He will. Right now all I want is to praise God for sendin' me this wonderful woman." He paused, seemed to grope for words. "You are the very best thing that's happened to me in so goddamn long. For the first time since I been locked up in this damn place, I got hope for the future."

She reached up and touched his cheek. "I won't disappoint you, Jack."

He kissed her again. "Goddamn, you taste sweet! See you next visiting day, baby."

"I'll be counting the minutes, honey." Her voice had a scraped-out hollowness that she hadn't expected. She tried to smile and wondered if her mouth and eyes were in congruence or if, like a lot of the women she'd noticed here, she smiled with her teeth alone.

A guard led her and some others back through the maze of corridors and slamming doors.

The reaction hit her on the way out.

Beyond the final set of doors, just inside the main entrance to the prison, she found a women's room, ran inside, and locked herself in a stall. Even so, she barely made it. On her knees bending over the commode, she threw up till her ribs ached. Painfully, copiously, as if she'd just ingested a meal of salmonella-infested chicken.

Then, still on her knees, she shut her eyes and

prayed for help. A brief prayer, stark and irreverent, but not insincere: *God, what the fuck am I doing?*

When she came out of the stall, wiping at her mouth with a wad of toilet paper, the redhead Jack had identified as Opal was at the mirror putting on a bright streak of coral lipstick. Cass went to the sink next to hers and started rinsing her mouth.

She felt the other woman's eyes on her. "You okay?"

She spit water down the drain, said, "Yeah, I'm fine."

"You didn't sound so fine a minute ago. You sounded like you were about to upchuck your guts."

"Yeah, I'd forgotten how much it hurts to throw up." She straightened, wiped her mouth on a paper towel, and pitched it in the wastebasket. "I'm better now."

"Hard seein' the man you love in a place like this, isn't it? I still cry my eyes out soon's I get home, and I been comin' here to see my Frank for years." The redhead extended her hand. "I'm Opal Brady."

"Cass Lumetto."

"Pleased to meet you, Cass." She turned back to the mirror, added a final dab of lipstick. "Best way to keep your spirits up is to spend some time with other women who got men locked up, too. You saw that lady whose man made such a scene in there? Her name's CharLee St. John—she and my friend Mariah'n me are headed over to the Black Bear Saloon. Right up the road on Gibson Street, 'bout a quarter mile down from the Blue Skies. Why don't you come on down, have a drink or two, a few laughs. Take your mind off your troubles."

"Thanks, but I feel worn-out. I think I'm just going home."

"To a motel room, you mean?"

"Is it that obvious?"

"Honey, you may not know it yet," said Opal,

going out the door, "but if you love that man, then he's not the only one in prison. You are, too. You need to be alone, I understand, but you change your mind, you know where you can find some sisters in suffering."

It sounded like the title of a romance novel. If she hadn't felt so lousy, Cass would have laughed.

At the front gate, she collected her belongings, exited the main gate, and trudged across the parking lot to where the Duchess sat baking in the midday heat. As she was unlocking the door and lowering herself gingerly onto the seat, the cell phone on the passenger seat started ringing.

She glared at the jangling phone, resisting an impulse to roll down the window and hurl it away like a grenade.

She knew who it was, who it had to be.

Sure enough, when she picked up, Kenny's deep, avuncular baritone boomed into the receiver, "Cass, have you seen him yet?"

"Yeah, I saw him."

"Thought you were gonna call me as soon as you left?"

"I'm just this second getting into my car."

"Well? Don't keep me in suspense! How'd it go?"

"I don't know. Not so well, I don't think."

"What does that mean?"

"I'm sorry, Kenny," she blurted out. "I don't think I can do this."

There was a pause where the only sound she heard was a slight change in Kenny's breathing, an almost audible effort at composure. She was fairly certain he was struggling not to shout.

"I don't understand. When I flew out to New York to talk to you, you sounded like you were going to be fine with this. You even said there might even be some articles in it—'Convicts and Their Women,' that kind of thing. I agreed to take care of the rent on your apartment in Manhattan for as long as you needed, plus all your expenses here in Canon City. You can't just change your mind now. You're *in* this."

"Kenny, there's a big difference in writing some bullshit letters to a guy in prison and sitting across from that same guy, listening to him talk about having hope for the future because I'm in his life. He *trusts* me, Kenny. He thinks I'm his girlfriend, that I gave up a life in New York to be here near him!"

"Which is perfect! It's exactly what we want him to think!"

"It's not that simple."

"What happened, Cass? Did something happen? Did he say somethin' ugly, try to put his filthy hands on you?"

She remembered the hand-holding, the good-bye kiss. "No, nothing happened. We just talked. Had a normal conversation."

"What's wrong then?"

"I feel so guilty manipulating him like this. It's hard to explain."

"Well, let me guess. You didn't expect him to look so normal or so cute or that he'd talk so sweet and soft. He didn't fit your mental image of what a cold-blooded killer's s'posed to look like, is that what you mean?" Sarcasm had stripped away the veneer of congeniality. He sounded now like what he was: a Colorado cattle baron, spoiled and arrogant and richer than God. But something else, too, Cass noticed. Underneath the bluster, he sounded scared.

"Or maybe he convinced you he didn't really kill anybody. That he was framed or it was all an accident and he didn't have a good lawyer and the judge had some kinda prejudice against white redneck scum. Am I getting anywhere with this, Cass?"

"Don't shout at me, Kenny."

He plowed on. "He's good-looking in a faggoty sort of way, isn't he?"

"Faggoty?" Her brother Tony was gay, and Kenny's

use of the word made her instantly furious. "What the hell does that mean?"

"All that blond hair, those pretty blue eyes. I sat in his trial one day, remember? Just studying him, trying to figure him out. I saw all those girls come to ogle him. I think you're afraid you might be vulnerable, too; you're scared you'll find out, push come to shove, he's smarter than you are, that with all your fancy college education some high school dropout poor white trash carpenter can manipulate you like so much toffee."

"I mean it, Kenny, don't raise your voice to me or I'm hanging up."

He paused, seemed to consider his options, then made a strategic retreat. "All right, I'm sorry. I apologize. But dammit all to hell, we got an agreement. You can't back out now. If it's more money you want, money to lie on a couch twice a week when this is over and tell some shrink how you were traumatized havin' to march your high-fallutin', college-educated butt into a goddamn prison week after week then—"

"What you're paying me's more than generous."

"Well, what about *her*? What about my daughter?"

She was silent a moment, remembering. The tears that filled her eyes caught her by surprise. She swiped at them angrily. "I loved Raven, too. She was my best friend in college. And that trip to Europe you and Bonnie sent us on was the best thing that ever happened to me. It changed my life."

"Then help me find out if he killed her."

"I can't, Kenny. Not like this. I'm sorry, but I just can't."

His voice roared through the phone. "Goddammit, Cass, we've got an agreement! We've—"

She hit OFF and held the button depressed with such force that when she finally released it a minute later, her finger throbbed like she'd pinched it. But the only sound issuing forth now was the dial tone, and he didn't call back.

The idea of sitting alone in her motel room seemed less appealing by the minute. *Oh, God,* she thought, *I need a drink.*

She pulled a map out of the car's glove compartment, found Gibson Street, and headed over to the Black Bear Saloon.

Chapter 2

"So how many people did *your* boyfriend kill?" Opal asked. She was staring at Cass over the bun of the chili dog she was about to bite into, dark brown eyes big as dimes, half-moon-shaped brows arched like twin scythes. Cass couldn't tell if she was striving for shock value or if the question had, through repetition, become as banal to her as asking what somebody did for a living.

The four of them—Cass, Opal, Mariah, and CharLee—were sitting in a back booth at the Black Bear Saloon. The band, a trio of lanky, bearded young men who looked better suited to cattle rustling than picking and strumming, were taking a break. Shania Twain was crooning on the jukebox. Above the bar, a stuffed pronghorned antelope head presided lugubriously while a bartender who could be politely described as full-figured slung drinks like a champion shot-putter.

When Opal asked how many people Jack had killed, Mariah, a big-built woman with a face as white and unblemished as a farm fresh egg, rolled her eyes and said, "What is it with you, Opal? You keepin' track? Plannin' to go on *Jeopardy* and win big bucks for the 'Men Who Committed Murder' category?"

"I'm just *askin'* is all," Opal said, munching her chili dog.

"Well, honey, don't answer unless you want to,"

advised Mariah, although her inflection, combined with the gleam in her eyes, implied she hoped Cass would not only respond but give plenty of details as well. "What your Jack did is nobody's business but his, yours, and his public defender. You don't have to tell us a thing."

All Cass had wanted was a drink and some company. She'd forgotten that if she was going to socialize with these women, she was also going to have to continue playing the role of Jack's girlfriend. Now she sipped her beer and said, "Jack was convicted of murdering his wife. He says he didn't, but he was drunk at the time, so he doesn't remember."

"Was that the only time he killed anyone?" Opal asked.

"Yes."

"So far as you know," Mariah said slyly, and Cass glimpsed a craftiness in her watery blue eyes that belied the bovine appearance.

In the silence that followed Mariah's remark, CharLee blotted her red eyes and said, "How'd you and Jack meet?"

"My father lives in Denver," said Cass, repeating the story she and Kenny had invented, "and I was visiting him from New York last summer. I saw Jack on TV after his arrest. Maybe it sounds crazy, but I just couldn't get him out of my mind. I started writing him letters, and he wrote back. One thing led to another, and here I am."

The other women nodded as though this made perfect sense. CharLee murmured, "No, it doesn't sound crazy at all."

"I met Frank when the Reverend Butterworth took a group of us into the prison to minister to the cons," Opal said. "It was love at first sight. I couldn't take my eyes off him."

"Reverend Butterworth, that's Jack's minister, too," said Cass.

Opal nodded. "We go to the same church, the Church of Good Hope. Did go, anyway."

"Jack seems to think the world of Reverend Butter-worth."

"Oh, he's a saint," gushed Opal. "He helped me get my job with the Highway Department after I'd been out of work for six months with a neck injury."

Mariah made a scoffing sound. "Yeah, so you can stand out in the sun or the cold all day holding up a STOP sign. You coulda got disability for your neck—same as I did when I hurt my back in that car accident a few years ago. Haven't worked a day since."

"I *like* my work," said Opal. "When those drivers get mad 'cause of the delay, I give 'em a nice smile and tell 'em God loves 'em. And don't go rollin' your eyes at me neither."

She reached for the ketchup, which was only a shade or two brighter than her hair, and squirted the remains on her chili dog.

CharLee covered her mouth suddenly and whispered to Cass, who was sitting next to her, "Ohmigod, there's a fella who keeps looking this way, and he's headed over here. What should I do?"

The guy had set down his pool cue and came ambling over, longneck in hand. He had dyed-looking jet-black hair and wore a belt with a silver buckle the size of a fist. His jeans looked stiff and newly purchased. Like a tree that had received just enough whacks of an ax to tilt it a bit, he swayed slightly. His unsteady gaze swept from woman to woman, before his glinty gray eyes fixed on CharLee.

"Hey there, young lady, how 'bout a dance?"

"Me?" CharLee asked.

"You're the one!" Like he was a game-show host calling her down from the audience to receive a brand-new food processor, Cass thought, and waited for CharLee to decline.

But CharLee smiled and said, "Sure, why not?" as she wriggled out of the booth.

"She shouldn't do that," said Mariah, when CharLee was out on the floor. "It'll get back to Luthor."

"He's in prison. He can't hurt her," said Cass.

"Don't be so sure," Mariah said. "Luthor's got a lot of friends on the outside. If she's gonna play around, she should be more discreet about it."

"But she told Luthor it was over between them."

"Hon, it ain't ever over with convicts. Not till they say so."

"I would never leave Frank like that," Opal said primly. "No matter what."

"Yeah, well, at least you know you'll always be able to see Frank, one way or another," Mariah said. "Me and Madison are running out of time."

Cass slid a lighter and a pack of Virginia Slims out of her purse and shook out a cigarette. "What do you mean, running out of time?"

"I mean my husband Madison is looking at the needle. Unless his shyster lawyer can get a stay of execution and a new trial, he's scheduled to die by lethal injection on November 8." She plucked a tortilla chip from the basket and began snapping it into bits. "Madison's resigned to it, I guess—this isn't the first time life's treated him unfairly—but I can't accept it. I'll fight it to the end."

"What did Madison do?"

Opal looked up from her beer. "You don't know?"

"No."

"Madison Raines. He's pretty well known."

"Famous is what he is," added Mariah.

Now that she'd heard the full name, Cass's memory was kicking in. "You mean Madison Raines, the serial killer?"

"He's been referred to by that term, but I don't for a minute buy it," said Mariah. "You say serial killer, you mean somebody like Ted Bundy, the Hillside Strangler, a monster like Dahmer. Madison's nothing like that. He's admitted to killing more than one woman, that doesn't make him a serial killer."

It was coming back to Cass now. "I remember now. He was included in an article on serial killers in

America in *Newsweek* a few years ago. He was boastful when they arrested him, gave the cops lots of details. He said he'd hang around a motel until he spotted a room where a single woman was staying, then go knock on the door. When she answered, he'd say he was from security, that a prowler had been spotted in the area and he wanted to come in and check the windows and door locks. Then he'd rape her and strangle her. I remember, too, the police said he took trophies from his victims, but they weren't specific as to what."

"I could tell you what kind of trophies"—smiled Mariah—"but that would be breaking Madison's trust."

"Spare us, please," said Opal. She turned to Cass and said brightly, "You know, Mariah met Madison the same way you met Jack."

"You wrote to him?" asked Cass. "Why?"

Mariah chuckled as though at some private joke. " 'Cause I liked his looks, that's why. I wasn't alone, either. Lotta women wrote to Madison, sent him dirty pictures, locks of their pubic hair. It may be hard for people to understand, but some murderers have a mystique. They're the celebrities of the prison."

She reduced another tortilla chip to crumbs. "I'd seen Madison's picture in the paper and read what he had to say about killing those women. He came across as well spoken, very articulate. Plus those eyes, incredible, almost white-pale blue eyes. I thought, here's a man who can't be all bad. So I started writing and visiting. One thing led to another, and we fell in love."

Opal folded her hands and said piously, "I pray for Madison every night and all those on Death Row. I pray they find Jesus before it's too late."

"Madison don't need Jesus," said Mariah. "What he needs is a damned good antideath penalty lawyer. Or a miracle, like maybe the cops realize he didn't kill all those women."

"Who didn't kill all those women?" said CharLee,

returning to the booth out of breath, fanning herself with one crimson-nailed hand. She slid into the booth next to Cass.

"How was your dance?" asked Opal.

"Oh, not bad."

"I'll say not bad," said Mariah. "I was watching. Dude had his hand on your ass the whole time."

"Well, he *does* move fast, don't he? I told him I could use some cheering up and he told me he got all the cheer I'll ever need, right there between his legs." She gave a tipsy giggle, pulled out a compact, and started reapplying a shade of lipstick that matched her nails. "I'd like to stay here, you know, but I keep thinking about Luthor. Maybe I oughta go back to the motel in case he calls."

"Are you crazy?" said Opal. "Don't even think about accepting a call from Luthor tonight. You're drunk."

"And gonna get drunker." CharLee laughed. She raised her arm to summon the waitress and ordered another margarita. Turning back to Opal, she said, "I'm startin' to feel better. Maybe all I needed was to let off some steam. Maybe I shouldn't've broke up with Luthor at all."

"Don't forget how he acted in the visiting room," Opal said.

"Luthor was upset," said CharLee, "but he didn't hit *me*. He just punched the table."

"Still," said Cass, "that shows he's got a dangerous temper."

CharLee said crossly, "Any man worth his salt's got a temper when his woman just dumps his ass. Jack's like that, too."

"What are you talking about?"

Now that she had Cass's undivided attention, CharLee took her time checking her makeup again before snapping the compact closed. "Luthor's a real good listener. People open up to him, confide in him. He told me Jack said he went crazy after he and Melinda were separated and some woman he was dating gave him his walking papers. He actually broke down and wept in front of Luthor."

"What woman—?" But before she could finish, CharLee's mood changed again. She started getting weepy and dabbed at her eyes with a napkin. "Oh, God, I'm never gonna see Luthor again. What have I done? Luthor's not normally violent. I picked a bad time to tell him it was over, you know."

Mariah snapped a tortilla chip and said, "So when woulda been a good time? When he'd just had a full body massage, a bottle of Bordeaux, and spent a few hours stretched out on the beach?"

CharLee glanced toward the bar, where the cowboy was looking at her the way a man dying of thirst eyes a beer. "What am I gonna do about him? About Willy?"

"Who's Willy?" said Opal.

"You know," said Mariah, giving her a playful nudge to the ribs, "*Willy*, Mr. Got-all-the-cheer-you-need-between-his-legs."

As if on cue, the legs in question strode over to the table, and Willy put a proprietary hand on CharLee's back. " 'Nuff girl talk now, darlin', let's leave."

CharLee shook her head. "I'm not done here."

"Well, when will you be *done*?"

"I think I'll just stay here with my friends."

"That's not what you said on the dance floor."

"I changed my mind."

"Well then, I'm changin' it back." He squeezed CharLee's wrist just as the waitress arrived with a fresh margarita and set it in front of her. CharLee flinched and her elbow hit the glass, which skidded and spilled. Green froth puddled between the women's plates and the basket of nacho chips.

"Oh, I'm sorry," moaned CharLee. "Look at the mess." She grabbed her napkin and started wiping the table.

"Dammit, Willy, that's your fault," snapped the waitress.

Willy glared at the waitress and tugged CharLee's arm. "C'mon, honey, the help'll clean it up. That's what they're paid for. Let's you and me get out of here."

The guy's macho gall made Cass furious. "Hey, didn't you hear her, she said no!" she shouted at precisely the moment the band chose to finish its song. In the comparative silence that followed, her voice boomed. Heads swiveled around.

The bartender, a heftily built blond whose arms and manner of slinging drinks down the counter made Cass think of an aging Olympic discus thrower, yelled, "Willy, you makin' a ruckus over there? Cut it out!"

"Let me alone," CharLee said quietly. The cowboy glared furiously at Cass, then at CharLee. He let go of her hand with a sneer of disgust, as though her fingers were covered in cowshit.

"Hey, forget it, I'm sorry I asked. Who needs a drunk bitch anyway?"

"Asshole," hissed Mariah as he strode away.

"Creep," said CharLee. She squeezed Cass's arm. "Hey, thanks for standin' up for me, honey."

Cass lifted her beer and downed a last swig. The beer was icy and just a tiny bit bitter, but hot by the time the alcohol reached her stomach and spread tinglingly through her bloodstream. Something about the intrusive cowboy made her think of her ex-boyfriend Philip, back in Manhattan—and not in a flattering way. What would Philip do, she wondered, in such a situation? Not much, she decided, certainly nothing involving the expenditure of testosterone. If things got really bad, he'd call the cops on his cell phone. If things got really, really bad, he'd threaten to sue. Jack O'Doul, she thought with a guilty twinge, would probably put the guy through a table. CharLee leaned over and put a hand to her forehead. "Shit, the room's spinning around. I musta drank too much. I think I better go home."

"You can't drive, honey," said Opal.

Cass took a last drag on her cigarette, stubbed it out. "I'll drive you."

"Oh, that'd be great. Way I feel now, I'm not even sure I could find the motel. I can come back and get my car tomorrow."

The waitress came back with a towel to clean up the spill and scrawled out separate checks for CharLee and Cass, both of whom left money on the table and said their good-byes to Opal and Mariah before making their way to the door.

"Your loss," the cowboy called after CharLee as Cass hustled her out the door into the warm, dry summer night. After the noise and smoke inside the bar, the sudden quiet and calm was, to Cass, like total immersion in a healing bath. She took deep breaths of the pine-scented air and sniffed with distaste at her shirt sleeve, which now, like her hair and the rest of her clothes, smelled like a Philip Morris factory.

"That guy, he's not following us, is he?" said CharLee, glancing up into the rearview mirror as they pulled out of the parking lot.

"I don't think so."

"Oh, Lord, my head hurts. I wonder if I did the right thing."

"Are you kidding? He was a jerk."

"No, I mean about Luthor. I wonder if I did the right thing to break up with him."

They pulled up to a red light. Cass said, "CharLee, look at me. You didn't ask my advice and maybe I should keep my mouth shut, but if I were in your shoes, I'd keep going and never look back."

CharLee nodded glumly. Her skin had taken on a sick, pallid shine, like waxed paper, and Cass wondered if she was about to throw up. It wasn't the best time to begin an interrogation, but she had to try.

"Earlier you said something about Jack's having lost it when a woman he was dating broke up with him. Can you tell me about that?"

"Oh, forget it." She dabbed at her eyes, smearing

mascara like black bars from her lashes. "I have a big mouth when I drink. Last thing in the world I want to do is cause trouble between you and Jack."

The light changed. Cass said, "You haven't caused trouble, CharLee. But I need to know, was the woman's name Raven?"

"Yeah, yeah it was. Jack met her at church. Luthor said when Jack first got sent up, he talked about her a lot. Said he missed her more than he did Melinda."

"What else did Luthor tell you about Raven and Jack? I mean after she broke up with him, did Jack stalk her? Did he ever try to harm her?"

The light changed. Cass turned right and headed up Main Street toward the prison and its tawdry lineup of low-priced motels. "Look, CharLee, if you know anything about what happened between Jack and this woman Raven, I need to know . . . for my own safety."

CharLee put her face in her hands. "Oh, God, everything's turnin' around. I'm gonna fix up an ice pack soon as I get to the room and sleep for a week."

They drove the rest of the short distance to the Blue Skies in silence, Cass biting back her frustration, CharLee holding her head as though it might be in danger of slipping off.

When they pulled up in front of the motel, CharLee said, "Thanks, hon, for the ride," and started to get out.

"Wait," said Cass. She pulled out a scrap of paper, wrote the phone number of her motel and her room number on the back, and handed it to CharLee. "Look, anything else Luthor might have told you about Raven and Jack, I want to know. Call me tomorrow when you're feeling better. Whatever you tell me won't get back to Jack, I promise. Will you do that?"

"Guess I could."

"Or tonight, if you're up to it. I'll be home."

CharLee gave a small smile. "Home in case Jack calls, huh?"

Cass couldn't look at her, but lowered her eyes as she said, "Yeah, in case Jack calls."

Except for the adjacent Starlight Lounge, where Jack O'Doul was no longer welcome and where a sign out front advertised LADIES DRINK FREE ON TUESDAYS, the Mountain View Motel wasn't a whole lot better than CharLee's place. Even with the sun down, a few kids were still splashing around in the postage-stamp-sized swimming pool. A van for a whitewater rafting company was dropping off a family in front of the motel entrance—they lugged tote bags presumably full of swimsuits and other gear and looked tired but happily satisfied.

Cass envied them their contentment as she unlocked the door to a room that probably hadn't changed much since the motel opened in the fifties—queen-sized bed and faux walnut dresser, mismatched chairs crowding a small, circular table, several bargain basement prints depicting a herd of buffalo crossing what appeared to be the same prairie in winter, summer, autumn.

The light was blinking on the phone by the bed, indicating she had a message. It couldn't be from Jack, she knew, because inmates were only allowed to call collect.

Against her better judgment, she pushed the retrieve button on the phone. It was Kenny.

This time, though, his tone of voice was subdued, as close to sounding humble as she'd ever heard him.

"I'm sorry I blew up at you, Cass. Please reconsider what you said. Come out to the place tomorrow, and we'll talk this over. Do it for Raven's sake." He gave a list of directions to the house, then said, "Okay then? I'll look for you."

Cass flopped down on the bed, kicked her shoes off, and stared up at the watermarked, plaster ceiling.

For Raven's sake. Wasn't that hitting below the

belt? Why else had she agreed to do this except for Raven?

For the money maybe, her mind immediately retorted. She was paid well for magazine articles on everything from posh Caribbean getaways to self-defense classes, but Manhattan living wasn't cheap, and Kenny was paying her generously for what amounted to a little detective work and some basic acting skills.

And the excitement? Didn't pretending to be Jack's girlfriend offer her a "walk on the wild side" without really risking anything, the way some people went to fantasy baseball camp or took vacations where they pretended to be cowboys? She'd been born in Detroit on the wrong side of the tracks, but she'd never seen it as an adult. Was that it?

Whatever the answer, she was too tired to dwell on it now. Before she went to sleep, though, she reached over and unplugged the phone, guaranteeing herself a night of uninterrupted slumber.

Still, tired as she was, she tossed and turned and flipped chanels, finally falling asleep with Jack's words echoing in her head like the clichéd refrain from some sappy love song: *Cass, you are the best thing that's happened to me in so long, the very best thing.*

Yeah, right.

Chapter 3

Why are kids playing Marco Polo in the fourteenth-floor hall and how the hell did they get past Alexander? was Cass's first thought upon coming awake the next morning.

Nobody got past Alexander, not salesmen or repo men or livid ex-lovers bent on one final scene—not that Cass was particularly likely to be visited by any of the above, but still Alexander's vigilance about who he let into the building on Thirty-third street was one of the reasons she liked living there.

A woman's voice screeched, "Timmy, how many times have I told you—don't *run*?" followed by the splash of someone doing a cannonball into a pool. With a small interior wince, Cass remembered where she was.

I don't think we're in Kansas, Toto.

She groaned, opened her eyes, shut them again. Wished she could shut her ears, too. The sun was barely up, but outside kids were yipping and yelling in the motel pool. Road trippers eager to get an early start at the Royal Gorge or on some whitewater rafting adventure were revving motors and slamming down hatchbacks.

And she was going to drive out to talk to Kenny Sterling.

She'd made the decision last night, sometime after ninety-three cubic zirconia tennis bracelets sold for

$39.95 a piece on the Home Shopping Network, but before a full set of aluminum cookware was offered at the amazingly low discounted price of $115.

Groaning, she got up, threw on jeans and a T-shirt, and set about brewing something resembling lukewarm mud in the small plastic pot provided by the motel.

In New York, she'd be waking up to the dulcet sounds of rush-hour traffic, impatient taxi drivers leaning on the horn while screaming in a dozen foreign languages, ambulances racing toward St. Vincent's. Not a lot better than screaming kids, maybe, but the quality of the coffee would have been better.

By the time she got going, coffee gulped, map consulted, gas tank filled at the Amoco up the block, the day was starting to blister. Sunlight keen and metallic as hypodermic needles pricked her exposed skin and glanced in dazzling fragments off the Duchess's hood.

The Sterling ranch was located southeast of Canon City, at the end of a dirt road halfway between the tiny towns of Rockvale and Coal Creek. Cass headed south on 115, following the directions Kenny had given her in his message.

As she drove, she thought about the first time she'd met the Sterlings, when Kenny and Bonnie had driven up to Boulder to visit their daughter Raven, who was Cass's roommate at the University of Colorado. Cass still remembered the gleaming silver Porsche the Sterlings had pulled up in outside the dorm, the tony steakhouse high in the hills along Canyon Boulevard where they'd taken the girls for dinner. Kenny Sterling had been sixteen years younger then and life was still waiting to deal him its cruelest blow—to Cass, with her lower middle-class background and a father's whose greatest claim to fame was a propensity for winning at dubiously honest games of poker, he epitomized wealth, sophistication, and power. Bonnie Sterling, trim, petite, and bejeweled, could talk with equal knowledge and enthusiasm about shopping trips to

Paris, backpacking in the Grand Canyon, and skeet shooting on the family's ranch in southern Colorado. Like her daughter, she was stunning. Like her husband, her presence was commanding.

Cass remembered thinking them a charmed family. Enjoying the wonderful dinner and conversation, but then going back to the dorm and sinking into the depths of soul-shrinking envy. Feeling like Cinderella being dumped back into the cellar after the ball. Ashamed of her own parents, especially her father, with his tawdry past and dubious associates, and of her working-class origins, revealed every time she opened her mouth by an accent which, even after years of living in New York, was still pure blue-collar Detroit.

"They're not so perfect as you think, my parents," Raven had told her later. "They love me like crazy as long as I measure up. And believe me, I'd better measure up."

To Cass, though, seeing the Sterlings only from the outside, it was hard to be convinced that they were anything but perfect.

Then, in the summer between the girls' junior and senior years, Raven planned a trip to Europe. She wanted Cass to come along, so the Sterlings had made that possible. Cass remembered it as a magic summer, a turning point in her life, when she realized, not just in an intellectual fashion, but an experiential one, the depth and breadth of excellence in the world, the splendor of the Sistine Chapel and the grandeur of the Louvre, the delight of fine music and art and of fine wine and primo weed enjoyed late into the evening with a young woman who had seen and done it all before, and now was sharing it with her.

After college, they'd kept in touch for a few years, then slowly drifted. Cass moved to New York to take an apprenticeship at a travel magazine; Raven went to L.A. to try a modeling career and found out, maybe for the first time in her life, that being tall and gor-

geous wasn't always enough. Cass heard from her occasionally—she wrote once that she'd met someone
and moved back to Canon City—but the information
she provided about her life was sparse and eventually,
even though Cass continued to write, she stopped
hearing from her.

Until Kenny called and said he had to see her, that
he was in New York and needed her help.

Kenny Sterling needed *her?*

Utterly baffled, Cass had agreed to meet him. By
this time, she was freelancing for a number of magazines, mostly features for the women's glossies. Kenny
had found a self-defense article she'd written for a
women's magazine among Raven's things. He'd tracked
Cass down by convincing a less than vigilant aide at
the same magazine that he was a book publisher looking for a writer to do a nonfiction crime book.

The fact that he used subterfuge to get her unlisted
home phone number should have told Cass something.
At the time, she was merely flattered that Kenny
should try so hard to reach her. With what now
seemed to her to have been incredible naiveté, she
remembered asking if he was actually into book pub-
lishing these days. Kenny hadn't laughed.

What he wanted, of course, was something else.

They'd met at a Starbucks near Union Square, and
although she'd recognized Kenny Sterling at once—
the man's height alone made him stand out in any
crowd—she'd also been shocked at how dramatically
he'd aged. And then he'd told her Raven was dead
and what he thought had happened to her and how
she could help him find the man who killed her.

And Cass, appalled and horrified and (admit it, she
told herself) just a little greedy for the money Kenny'd
promised, had agreed to the plan.

Then.

But this was now.

Jack O'Doul was more than just an abstract name
now. He was a person she'd sat down and talked with

and . . . maybe even been a little bit attracted to. She couldn't do it, that was that.

And so she drove, determined to set things straight.

The sprawling, two-story home, about twenty miles beyond the middle of nowhere, looked like no ranch of which Cass could have conceived. It was surrounded by gleaming white walls and a wrought-iron gate through which she could see a pool so blue it might have been filled with cut turquoise glass. In the distance were a barn and horse paddocks where thoroughbreds grazed. Beyond the pool, a bone-white gazebo and a profusion of trees.

Bonnie Sterling must have heard her drive up, because she came out onto the porch and trotted down the front steps to meet Cass. Bonnie must be in her mid-fifties now, but Cass would have had difficulty saying how the Bonnie of today differed from the one she'd dined with in that Boulder restaurant sixteen years ago. Less makeup, for certain, and dressed in what, for Bonnie, must pass as casual: an ankle-length denim skirt accented with silver studs, red and black cowboy boots, a denim shirt with fringe at the collar and bodice. She was still tiny, her hair still a fiery tangle of cinnamon curls framing porcelain skin. The only change Cass noticed was a pained tightness around the lips and eyes, as though either the skin or Bonnie's nerves were stretched to the snapping point.

"Cass, how are you?" She offered a hug that was more a nervous flapping at the air than a real embrace and said, "Did you have trouble finding us?"

"No, not really. Kenny gave good directions."

"Yes, he's good at directing, all right."

Cass was starting up the porch steps, but Bonnie put a light hand on her wrist to stop her. Still smiling, as though to project the image of two women discussing recipes for latte, she said softly, "Kenny told me about your conversation last night, honey, and I just want to say, don't you do anything you're not comfortable with. I don't care whether Kenny thinks you've got an agreement or not, it's nothing morally binding. You can back out right now, and not be doing a thing wrong. Don't let him bully you into doing something you don't want to do."

Cass nodded, while firmly extricating her wrist. "I won't, Bonnie. You don't have to worry about me."

"I know that, honey, it's my husband I'm worried about." From a pocket in the skirt, she produced a pack of cigarettes and shook one out. It was slender and brown, and Cass could smell the aromatic odor of cloves even before she lit it.

"They're called Gudang Garam," said Bonnie, noticing her interest. "Made in Indonesia. The cloves are from Sumatra. Want to try one?"

Cass shook her head. "Thanks, no."

"Kenny says I only smoke them because I prefer things foreign and exotic. I say how can that be when I married him." She laughed harshly and exhaled a breath of thick, fragrant smoke. "But then I guess exotic's in the eye of the beholder."

Something about the clove-scented smoke had an unpleasant effect on Cass's sinuses. She found herself wanting to sneeze.

"This quest that he's on," Bonnie continued, "this obsession . . . it's taking a toll. The doctor told him he's a hair trigger away from having heart problems if he doesn't take some of the stress out of his life." She turned her head to exhale, but a slight breeze blew the smoke straight toward Cass. "So if you choose not to go on with this crazy scheme, you'd be doing not just yourself a favor, but Kenny as well."

"I'll keep that in mind." The first sneeze erupted out of her, then another.

"Gesundheit," said Bonnie.

She kept sneezing, finally dug into her purse, found a Kleenex, and blew her nose. "Sorry, something about that cigarette. It shouldn't bother me, I'm a smoker myself."

"I'll put it out," Bonnie said, dropping the cigarette

to the dirt and grinding it under the toe of her boot. "I don't smoke in our house anyway—Kenny won't allow it—only in other people's."

Cass started up the stairs, Bonnie preceding her like the lead float in a very small parade, all swishing denim and jangling silver.

They entered a colorful foyer where sunlight streaming in the open windows glanced off turquoise Spanish tiles. A gorgeous orange and brown Navajo rug took up an entire wall behind a highly glossed, wooden preacher's bench. A trio of earthenware jugs decorated with vivid black slashes, like tribal markings, enlivened a corner. In another, a carved, hooded saint almost as tall as Bonnie gazed dolefully at his hands cupped in prayer.

"Lovely art," said Cass, but Bonnie brushed off the compliment, saying, "This is nice, mostly things Kenny and I picked up down in Santa Fe—they have the most wonderful galleries—but the real treasures are in Kenny's study."

"I'll look forward to seeing it."

The living room was a larger version of the foyer, replete with massive hand-hewn wood furniture, a vaulted ceiling with exposed cherrywood beams, and cathedral-style windows. A big-screen TV at one end of the room was turned to CNN—the female anchor was reporting a new record for NASDAQ. When Cass and Bonnie entered the room, Kenny Sterling was bent over what Cass thought to be an elaborate cappuccino maker of the kind she'd thus far only seen inside a few posh Manhattan hotels.

"Cass, hello!" The booming voice was even more commanding in person than on the phone, issuing as it did from Kenny's massive frame. An imposing man, at least six feet two inches and well over two hundred pounds, Kenny's deeply tanned face was red, flat, and generally expressionless as a slab of undercooked liver. His mouth was a tiny, tightly smiling gash, and his small, deepset blue eyes glinted like buried ice chips.

Unlike his wife, Kenny was dressed simply, in beige sweats and tennis shoes. His thinning gray hair looked damp from either the shower or a recent workout and while he tried to laugh at his own apparent ineptitude with the coffee machine, an undercurrent of last night's anger still remained—Cass got the feeling he was also considering giving it a punch.

"You ever work in a restaurant, Cass?"

She started to remind him that waitressing was, to a large extent, how she'd put herself through school, but decided not to.

Kenny went on, "I bussed tables as a kid, but that was the extent of my labors in the food industry. But this thing here—this cappuccino contraption that Bonnie wanted—you could get a compact car for what we paid for it, and now I'll be damned if I can get it to spew out a damn cup of coffee."

He twisted a silver dial, which produced a small sigh of steam but nothing else.

"I'll brew some in the regular coffeemaker," Bonnie said. Then, to Cass, "Kenny thinks because you're from New York, you probably start out every day with cappuccino. He doesn't even care for it himself."

"How would I know if I do or not," Kenny said, spreading his hands, "damned machine won't ever make any."

"It's all right," Cass said. "Instant's fine. Whatever you've got has to be better than what I had at the motel this morning."

"Speaking of which, I want you out of that motel," Kenny said. "Find an apartment. You need someplace that feels like home. A place you feel comfortable writing or whatever you want to do—when your time's not taken up with Jack, that is."

Across the room, Bonnie's hands were held primly in front of her, but Cass noticed that her spine went as rigid as the carved saint in the foyer.

"I don't think your hearing's what it ought to be, Kenny. Cass told you last night she can't do this anymore. And here you are making plans just like you never heard her." She turned to Cass. "He does this to me, too, honey. I swear, sometimes it can be like talkin' to a wall."

"Bonnie?" Kenny's voice was softer than before, but underlain with steel. "Will you please go in the kitchen and make us some coffee out of a machine that does more than just *look good*? We'll be in my study."

For a second, Bonnie's delicate features compressed into a scowl that foreshadowed the old woman she would become. Then she forced a tight smile and left the room, skirts swishing. Icicles trailed in her wake.

"I'm sorry if I've upset anyone," Cass said, "either you or Bonnie. But I meant what I said on the phone the other night. Doing this—in person, with a real human being—it's a lot different than just writing letters."

"It's real, you mean," said Kenny.

"Yeah, too real. I'm sitting there with Jack in that horrible visiting room, trying to look all starry-eyed, playing the role of the girlfriend who's been swept away by his charm or whatever the hell and he's saying I'm the best thing that's ever happened to him and I feel like the world's biggest heel, although frankly, another four-letter word comes to mind. I don't mind playing detective—in the beginning, when I was just writing letters, it was sort of a kick, a big difference from the kind of writing I usually do. But now it just feels like I'm using someone, which is wrong, even if that someone is a murderer."

Kenny swallowed and didn't look at her. His voice was hoarse with emotion as he said, "He killed his wife, Cass. He doesn't deserve compassion."

"He was convicted of killing her, yes. Yesterday he told me he doesn't remember a thing about it."

Kenny held up his big hands and shook his head as if he were about to be felled by the sheer magnitude of her stupidity.

"Cass, how many cons have you known in your life?"

She felt herself tense. Had Raven ever told him about her father? "A few."

"Have you ever known a con to say he *was* guilty? They're all innocent. Every last one of those men was framed, set up, abused, and misused. Please. Give me a break. You're too smart a woman to fall for that kind of bullshit."

"All right, then, for the sake of the argument, Jack murdered his wife. That still doesn't make it okay for me to pretend I'm in love with him when all I want is information."

"Information? Christ, it's more than just information, it's—look—before you go any further, come here, I want to show you something."

He got to his feet and Cass followed. They passed through a small atrium decked out in turquoise tile like the foyer, then crossed a breezeway that divided the house into two sprawling sections and entered Kenny's study, a spacious room whose vaulted ceiling duplicated the one in the living area. Cass was immediately struck by the artwork Bonnie had referred to— big, brightly colored paintings that took up most of the wall space not covered by paneled bookshelves. The work was obviously done by one artist and depicted women almost exclusively—sultry cowgirls in glitzy hats and sequined jeans, biker queens who straddled shiny Harleys and whose aggressive stares said *fuck me if you dare*. Come hither with attitude plus.

Her eyes could only remain so long on the paintings, though, before straying to the bookshelves, which were crammed with photographs. All of them of Raven—her life depicted in chronological order from baby snapshots through Girl Scouts to family outings and photos from her high school prom, then on to the years when Cass had known her, as an impossibly svelte and sophisticated college woman who downed martinis with a twist and campaigned for abortion rights at a time when her Catholic parents were attending fund-raisers for a local Right to Life group.

Looking at the photos now, Cass remembered why being Raven Sterling's college roommate hadn't always been easy. On the one hand, she always had dates—there were so many boys hanging around Raven, vying for her attention, a glance, a smile, a chance, that a few of them couldn't help but notice Cass—but there was also the constant reminder that no matter how diligently she dieted or did her hair, no matter how witty or how charming she tried to be, in male eyes she was always second to her striking black-haired, green-eyed Gemini-with-Libra-rising roommate.

"I didn't notice pictures of Raven anywhere else?" said Cass. "Is this room the only place?"

Kenny nodded. "Bonnie seldom spends any time here. She says she can't stand to. I understand, but I can't *not* have these photos where I can see them every day. They're all I have now. The photos and"—he gestured at the walls—"her paintings."

"Raven did these? My God, in school I knew she took a painting class or two, but it seemed like just a casual thing, an easy A—I had no idea that she could paint like this."

"After the acting thing didn't work out in L.A., she got serious about painting. She was making a name for herself. Some of the galleries in Taos and Santa Fe were starting to show her. Locally, people were buying her work."

Cass echoed his unspoken thoughts. "She had so much talent. What a waste."

She took a seat in a heavy, hand-hewn oak chair near the window and waited for Kenny to do likewise, but he paced up and down the length of the room before finally settling himself in his leather desk chair.

"O'Doul killed her, you know."

"But that's the whole point. We *don't* know. For one thing, there's the difference in the killings. Melinda was shot with her own gun, Raven was strangled."

"Because a gun was available in one case and not in the other," said Kenny. "He murdered my daughter. I know it in my gut. The police say there's no proof Jack did it, that all the evidence is circumstantial, and they're tired of hearing from me. I know they think I'm some kind of nut. You're the proof, Cass, the potential proof. With proper encouragement, one day he'll confide in you or brag to you that he killed her. Then we'll know."

"When you came to New York, you told me Raven had dated Jack for a time. While Jack was married to Melinda."

"He told her he and his wife were separated. Which was true, up to a point. Melinda and he were on-again, off-again, with Melinda leaving him to move in with her sister when Jack would get physical with her. That's a matter of record, the domestic violence. The police made, oh, God knows how many calls to the house because Jack would get drunk and start abusing his wife. But Raven thought the marriage had ended."

"And she broke up with Jack because she found out he'd lied to her about his marital status?"

Kenny shifted uncomfortably. "That and because he was pressuring her to have sex."

"And she didn't want to?" It came out a little more incredulous than Cass intended. She hoped Kenny didn't think she was implying that any woman in her right mind would want to have sex with Jack O'Doul. She hoped, on some level, she didn't mean exactly that. Fortunately, he didn't seem to take it that way.

"She wasn't going to sleep with him unless they were married. In the Church of Good Hope, that's considered a sin."

"Wait a minute," Cass said, "they went out together over a period of a few weeks, you told me. But they never had relations?"

"Is that so surprising?"

Actually, Cass found it downright amazing, but something in Kenny's tone of voice warned her to tread carefully. She tried for tact. "In college, Raven was, well, high-spirited. She liked good-looking men. And, understand I don't mean this to be disparaging, but she didn't exactly choose them on the basis of their intellects. Her women friends, yes, but the men, no. She laughed about it—that men were only good for one thing and most of them couldn't even do that right."

"People change," Kenny said tiredly, as though he'd heard the litany of his daughter's wild oat-sowing before.

"Of course they do, but . . ."

"This church that Raven belonged to, the Church of Good Hope, it changed her. They're fundamentalists, and she adopted their way of life. No sex outside of marriage. That was one of the rules."

"But that was Jack's church, too. So you're saying he talked the talk, but didn't walk the walk?"

"People can also be hypocritical. Raven was trying to live up to her new belief system, to make up for some of the indiscretions of her past. I think it disappointed her that Jack belonged to the church, but didn't respect the rule of sex only within marriage."

Cass had to bite her lip to keep from saying that Raven must have changed a helluva lot, because the woman she remembered would accept a no-sex-outside-of-marriage rule about as willingly as she'd champion vivisection.

Fortunately Bonnie appeared in the doorway then with a tray containing two mugs of steaming coffee, a small pitcher of cream, and a sugar dish that she set at one end of Kenny's desk before retiring. Her spine was ramrod stiff, and she made eye contact with nothing but the floor. Her intrusion was so brief and silent that had she not known otherwise Cass might have taken her for an overdressed maid.

She waited till Bonnie left the room and said, "You also told me Jack once tried to rape Raven. When did she tell you that?"

"She didn't tell me. Someone else—"

"Who?"

"An acquaintance of hers—someone she'd confided in during a weak moment, not someone that she'd normally associate with—this person said when Raven told Jack the relationship was over, he told her it wasn't over till he said it was and tried to force her. When she fought him off, he threw her out of his car in the middle of nowhere and drove off. Left her there."

"So who's the acquaintance who told you this story?"

"Former acquaintance. It doesn't matter. I believe this person's story. Violence toward women is O'Doul's M.O. For him to do something like that sounds exactly in character."

"But it doesn't *prove* anything."

"Cass . . ."

"I think I'm wasting your money, Kenny. Even if Jack were to tell me he did murder Raven, that's not going to automatically guarantee a trial, much less a conviction. He'll just deny saying it. It's not like I can go waltzing in there with a wire, either—the metal detector would catch it as fast as if I were packing a Saturday night special."

"You don't understand. If Jack were to admit to you, imply even, that he murdered my daughter, I wouldn't ask for a trial or even for any more time to be added to his sentence. All I want is to know whether or not he killed her. I'm ninety-nine percent sure in my own mind that he did, but I need to be a hundred percent sure. I have to *know*."

Cass sipped her coffee. It tasted strong and bitter as the woman who'd served it. She reached for the cream. "You're telling me if Jack confesses he murdered Raven, you aren't going to pursue it? C'mon, Kenny, don't take me for a fool. You'd make a few phone calls, some cash would change hands, and Jack would have a knife in his neck the next day."

"You're wrong."

"I'm sorry, Kenny, but forgiveness doesn't appear to be your strong suit."

"You don't know me as well as you imagine." But his tone was ice, with no inkling of forgiveness in it.

"All I'm asking you to do," he continued, "is what we originally agreed upon—what I paid you to do. Be Jack's confidante, his girlfriend, his fiancée even, if that's what it takes. You don't have to worry about the physical aspect, because you're not going to marry him and that's the only way he'd be eligible for conjugals." He lifted his mug, took a long swallow, and winced at the strength of it. "You're a smart woman, you shouldn't have any difficulty getting him to open up. I don't care how long it takes. I'll pay all your expenses plus the weekly fee we agreed upon, and I'll add a thousand dollars a week as a bonus on top of that." He paused a beat to let her absorb this. "Now then, are we on the same page here?"

Cass had been dreading this. She set her coffee cup down and stood up. "I can't, Kenny. I'm sorry. I'll put a cashier's check in the mail to you this afternoon for the balance of what you've paid me."

"You can't do that! We have a deal. You can't!" He started to stand, then flopped back into the chair, eyes wide with anguish and incredulity. Looking, for all the world, Cass thought, like a man who'd been shot in the stomach.

She showed herself out.

She moved quickly, too, afraid that Kenny would come after her, offering more money and more justifications, but Bonnie was the only one who followed. She caught up to Cass as she was jabbing the key into the door of the Duchess. Like an aging cowgirl, she tossed that wild mane of red hair and flashed the smile of the Miss America runner-up from Colorado she once had been.

"You did the right thing."

Cass stopped fumbling with the key and turned to face her. "How do you know what I did?"

Bonnie's hand fluttered to her chest. She gave a conspiratorial, girl-to-girl wink and said, "Well, now, no harm in a little eavesdropping, is there? I'm just thankful you had the sense not to let Kenny suck you into his lunacy any further than he already had. It's become an obsession with him, this idea that Jack murdered Raven. His cholesterol's over the moon, his blood pressure's about as high as the Sears Tower—he needs to let go of the whole tragedy, accept that we lost our little cupcake, and move on with his life."

Something clicked in Cass's mind, but she couldn't quite reach it, only knew that Bonnie had teased loose the thread of it from somewhere in the back of her mind. She gave the thought a mental bookmark and resolved to go back to it later.

"So what do *you* think, Bonnie? Are you as certain as Kenny that Jack did it?"

Her face changed so abruptly it was almost as if Cass had asked if *she* murdered her daughter. Her eyes narrowed, and her mouth became a thin little scar. "I don't know who killed my daughter. She's dead, and nothing's going to bring her back. You know something else, I don't even *want* to know who killed her. Because then I'd have to see his face every time I closed my eyes and I don't want that. I'd rather not know."

She shut her eyes for a second, squeezed a tear silently from beneath the tinted lashes.

"Cass, I want to give you something." She reached into her skirt pocket and produced a check, which she pressed into Cass's hand. "Because I know you're losing money walking away from this, honey. And integrity doesn't get rewarded often enough in this world."

"No thanks, Bonnie. Really, no."

"I insist."

"I insist, too." She tucked the check back into Bonnie's pocket in such a way that, for a second, a casual observer might have thought they were engaged in some sort of playful wrestling match.

She fairly leaped into the Duchess, prayed the car would start easily before she changed her mind about the check, and was halfway back to her motel when the thought she'd almost had earlier jiggled loose from her subconscious and whomped her upside the head: Raven and she, drinking one night in their dorm room, talking about life and death and men and the kind of lives they'd left behind and the kind of lives they wanted, then the talk turning to their parents, to mothers, in particular, and Raven, altogether serious, saying, "My mom reminds me of one of those insects on the Discovery Channel—you know, some kinda bright-colored beetle devouring its young. She calls me cupcake. Right. My mom ever tried to give me a cupcake, I'd figure it had cyanide in it."

Cass spent the rest of the drive back to Canon City turning Bonnie Sterling around in her head like a silver-and-denim Rubik's Cube. The woman was awfully eager to get her out of the picture. Was she really that concerned about Kenny's health? It certainly couldn't be the money. Kenny could afford to pay Cass whatever he wanted. Even if she didn't learn anything useful from Jack, if Bonnie could overlook the moral implications—which Cass was pretty sure she could—what harm was being done? Was it possible she saw Cass as a threat? She almost laughed aloud at that one. She knew she wasn't a bad-looking woman, even pretty, but a femme fatale stealing middle-aged husbands she was not. Somehow, too, she knew instinctively that age difference aside, she was no more Kenny Sterling's type than he was hers.

Bonnie claimed she didn't want to know who killed her daughter. Kenny claimed he *only* wanted to know, that if he found out Jack had killed Raven, he wouldn't seek revenge. Did any of that make sense? Cass thought about her own parents. If she were murdered and if they thought they knew who might have killed her, what would they do? She knew before the thought even finished flickering across her mind, without a moment's doubt. Her mother, Hilda, if she were alive, would go to Mass to pray for the soul of the killer. Her father, Johnny, would make a few calls to Detroit and take out a hit. Either way, they'd be appealing to a Higher Power—it was only their conceptions of that Higher Power and how It operated that would differ.

She was still mulling over the Sterlings' behavior when she pulled up in front of the motel and saw two men standing outside the door of her motel. One was tall and solidly built, bulky in the torso without being fat. He wore sharply creased jeans, a pale blue shirt and tan boots, and his face was obscured by a combination of Ray•Bans and a cowboy hat a few shades lighter than the boots. Under his arm, he carried a clipboard.

The other man, the one now knocking on the door, had his back to Cass, but she could see that he was older, stouter, and that his jet hair was so neatly cropped as to almost suggest a military background. He wore a gray suit and dress shoes. A gold ring was visible on one of the knuckles striking the door.

"Can I help you?" said Cass, walking toward them with her room key in hand.

The taller man consulted his clipboard. "Cass Lumetto?"

He pronounced her last name wrong, with the emphasis on the first syllable rather than the second, making it sound like the Latin name of a species of firefly. She nodded.

"Detective Shep Loomis." He removed the Ray• Bans and extended a hand. He had a broad, open face, gray-green eyes deeply etched with crow's-feet, and the kind of fair Nordic skin that begged to blister. A pink, peeling spot on the bridge of his nose seconded that assessment. "This is my partner, Detective Drake Munez."

Cass shook the second man's hand, although a sense

of deep dread was beginning to pierce her. "What
do you . . . ?"

"Ms. Lumetto, do you know a Charlotte St. John?"
Loomis said.

Something about the way his jaw muscles rippled as
he said it made Cass's blood turn to ice. When she
spoke, her voice sounded strange to her, like it was
coming from far away. "You mean CharLee? I drove
her back to her motel last night. What's this about?"

"Well, I'm sorry to tell you," Loomis said, "but it
looks like except for whoever killed her, you might be
the last person to have seen her alive."

Chapter 4

Crammed behind the wheel of his Jeep Cherokee, the Reverend Claude Butterworth fanned himself so vigorously with a folded church program that his wrist began to ache. Sweat streamed down his well-sueted torso and puddled in the folds of fat padding his neck. His thighs itched and his bladder felt as bloated as a water balloon as he clawed at a mosquito bite on the back of one hand.

At six foot three and close to three hundred pounds, Butterworth's appearance combined the unruly white hair and piercing gaze of an Old Testament prophet with the crooked, flattened nose of a professional boxer, which he had actually been—not unsuccessfully—during the years of his angry, violent, often misspent youth.

All long past, of course. He was on the downhill side of sixty now, a thick-bodied, woolly-haired man with a squashed proboscis, a man shaped like a Kodiak bear, all gristle and meat. Arthritis in the left knee gave him a slightly off-center gait, and he carried a heavy mahogany cane, the gift of a gun-loving parishioner who'd modeled the handle after the grip of a Magnum .45. His smile, which was broad and hearty, was wider on the left and the creases deeper, as though there were some deep-seated imbalance in his soul, making his left side more extroverted, the right retaining a greater measure of reserve, preserving secrets.

Not what you'd call a handsome man, the Reverend Butterworth, but imposing and grounded. A Capricorn, like Jesus Christ, born on Christmas Eve. His voice was as big as he was, too, part Billy Graham, part Elvis. When he bellowed fire from the pulpit, people quailed. When he whispered, they held their breath to hear. If you were a person who conceived of God in human terms and thought He spoke with a human voice, then—no doubt about it—God sounded like the Reverend Butterworth.

Now he stared through the grimy windshield at the row of identical motel-room doors and suppressed a growl. *Where is my wife, goddammit!*

So great was his frustration that he was tempted to abandon this ill-conceived mission altogether—to heck with Fiona and whatever wretch she might have lured into her bed of sin this time.

But still he had a stubborn streak. He had to know the truth. Was she cheating on him yet again? After all the sweet words of fidelity, all the promises?

For all his anger, too, he was genuinely worried for her safety. A murderer was loose. He'd heard about it while listening to his favorite radio show, a Christian station where listeners could call in to express their opinions on evils ranging from abortion to sex education being taught in the schools. More evil on the show's midmorning news break: a woman's body had been found at the Blue Skies Motel. Charlotte St. John.

Most distressing of all, Butterworth actually knew the woman. Had met her, anyway. He'd only spoken to her once, when he'd tried to interest her and her boyfriend Luthor Shaw in the weekly prayer meeting he held at the prison, but she'd said thanks, she was an agnostic. He didn't remember precisely what Luthor Shaw had said, only that he'd phrased it less nicely.

Now she was dead.

Burning in hell for all eternity, writhing in agony—all because she wouldn't let Jesus Christ into her life as her Lord and Savior, thought Butterworth. Poor, foolish wretch.

Tragic, he mused. Not so much the fact that she'd been murdered—although that was heinous, of course, and reflected the increasing godlessness and viciousness of the times—but because she'd died without reaching salvation. Without doing the one thing that would have saved her soul and guaranteed her a life everlasting—being born again and taking Christ to be her Savior.

His wife Fiona had accepted Jesus so, for all her tendency to stray, at least he didn't have to worry about the future of her soul. Still, he reflected bitterly that the wretched husband condemned to the earthly torment of jealousy by a faithless wife was damned in a different way.

At the thought of Fiona with another man, he felt rage spreading like a fever through his body, commencing at his genitals, then moving upward, constricting his chest and clouding his mind, erasing all rational thought. If Fiona was cheating on him *again*, he should make her pay for her adulterous ways, he should just . . . He gripped the steering wheel in both ham-sized hands and tried to calm himself by murmuring a prayer.

"Forgive me for spying upon my dear wife, Lord, and for having evil thoughts. Forgive her for compelling me to spy upon her and for engendering those thoughts."

But even if Fiona could be trusted—which Lord knew, she couldn't be—there was still the matter of a killer who could strike again. The radio newscaster had said the police didn't even have a suspect in CharLee St. John's murder yet.

Granted it was only midafternoon—not too many

motel-room murderers likely to be afoot in broad daylight—but still, he wanted to know where she was.

He'd already visited a number of motels. This was
the fourth one, the Super 8 with its tawdry neon and
small, scummy-looking pool. Next door was an out-of-
business taco stand where a couple of drifter types
loitered under a red and white awning. From across
the street, the odor of grease and unsavory spices ema-
nated from the kitchen of some type of ethnic restaurant that featured a tricolored flag in its window.

He had parked near the pool, at the back of the
parking lot, out of range of direct view should anyone
peer from a window. Unless someone was specifically
looking for a watcher, they'd be unlikely to notice
him here.

From his vantage point, he could see most of the
parking lot. He'd cruised it earlier, circling the cheap
glitz-and-sleaze fifties-style motel when he arrived, and
knew Fiona's white Mazda wasn't here. That didn't
surprise him, though. It wasn't over at the middle
school either, where she was supposed to be taking an
Adult Education course, watercolor painting or tai chi
or Spanish for travelers, some fluff thing of the sort
some women liked. Blessed were the husbands of such
women, he thought. Fiona's hobbies were of a different bent, indeed. .

God give me patience, he thought. *And let me not
be tempted to condemn her until I have some proof.*

The door to the manager's office at the far end of
the motel opened and an enormously obese woman
waddled outside. She wore thong sandals and a loose
flowing denim sack large enough to clothe three
average-sized women. She called to some children
splashing in the pool. When they ignored her, she
scrunched her forehead as though confronted with a
deep and complicated dilemma, then ambled back into
the motel.

Fat sow, Butterworth caught himself thinking. Feeling guilty—who was he, of all people, to condemn the corpulent?—he amended it to, *Poor soul. Victim of gluttony*.

Another miserable half hour passed, the heat pounding down like an anvil on the roof of the Jeep. Butterworth was exhausted by now, wondering again if he shouldn't give up. Do something more productive than attempt to spy on his wife. Like get to work on this Sunday's sermon or stop in at the home of the Lomaxes, whose son Judd had just returned from Thailand and brought with him all manner of dangerous ideas. But Fiona had been acting awfully happy lately, he reminded himself, quick to laugh and toss her hair. And Toulouse-Lautrec himself, who specialized in whores, could have painted her makeup.

A late-model Corvette, ostentatiously clean and well kept for this part of town, pulled into the parking lot. A young man—late twenties, auburn-haired, and good-looking in a lean, fox-eyed way—strode into the manager's office while his companion sat in the car. A minute later, Fox Eyes came out with a key and conferred with his companion, while the other man stole a caress across his lover's denim-clad rump.

Had Fiona emerged at that moment, naked in the arms of her paramour, Butterworth could not have felt more disgust. Vile Sodomites! They and all their loathsome kind faced eternal damnation, but were too obsessed with their indecent obsessions to even be aware of the fate awaiting them. Abominations unto the Lord, with their unnatural acts, their vile desecration of the sacred love between a married man and woman.

Damn them all to hell! he thought.

Then the door to the room next to the manager's office opened a crack and Fiona slithered out, looking like an Apache princess in a buckskin skirt and an elaborate turquoise necklace over a fringed blouse. Even from here, he could see her lipstick, a bright slash of crimson in a now otherwise unpainted face. Whore lipstick, the color of lust.

The man, whom Butterworth recognized, was in his mid-to-late thirties, medium height with biceps bulging under a checkered work shirt, shaggy blond hair, and the start of a paunch working its way over a belt buckle the size of an apple. The loopy grin plastered to his deeply tanned face might have suggested either infatuation or stupidity, but Butterworth knew it to be both.

Otis Dawes, a lovestruck roofer. Fiona'd had a fling with him the year before. Apparently he was one of her recyclables.

Dawes put his arm around Fiona's waist as they scurried across the parking lot and got into a black and tan Chevy. They didn't kiss—how could they, without smearing her lipstick?—but Fiona snuggled close to Dawes, whose right arm went around her shoulder, pulling her against him as they drove off.

For an instant, Butterworth's piety was threatened by an impulse so ungodly that only Satan could have inspired it—to run the Chevy off the road, ram it into so much scrap metal, then drive the Jeep over the roof.

But that was not the Christian way, of course. *Forgive me, God*, he thought as he slammed a fist between his eyes, dispelling the despicable fantasy of his wife and her lover reduced to bloody pulp.

At least, he thought, he knew the truth and could deal with Fiona when the time came. But not yet. Better to bide his time for now, and when the guilt grew too great for her, let her come to him and ask forgiveness. He would give it, as he always did, but this time, he'd make her crawl to him and beg for it.

He drove home in a cold and righteous wrath.

Chapter 5

"I need to see some ID," Cass said, while the shock waves of what she'd just heard reverberated through her. She felt stunned and numb, but also wary. Only when she'd seen sufficient ID to convince her the men were, indeed, detectives with the Canon City Police Department did she unlock the door and walk into the room in front of them. She sank into one of the two upholstered chairs across from the bed. Munez took the other.

Loomis removed his hat and laid it on the bed, then took a seat by the window. In keeping with his complexion, he had red hair and a scattering of freckles on either side of the sunburned nose. Muscles bulging against the fabric of his shirt attested to serious time spent in weight rooms.

Cass wiped at a trickle of sweat sliding along her temple. "I can't believe it. I was with her just a few hours ago. When did it happen? Who would do such a thing?"

Munez leaned back, apparently seeking a more comfortable position than that permitted by the lumpy cushion of the chair. He had a thin, dark mustache as neatly barbered as the back of his head and bushy eyebrows that grew in a solid black band across a forehead pitted with the scars of long-ago acne. One of his ears was badly misshapen and drooped from his head like some kind of rotting vegetable.

Having found the chair unyielding, he straightened again and said, "Forensics puts the time of Ms. St. John's death somewhere between eleven p.m. and one. As far as who'd do it, we're hoping you can help us figure that out."

"God, I only met CharLee yesterday, but I mean . . . I *knew* her, I gave her a ride home last night . . ."

"We know that," said Loomis. "The night clerk at the Blue Skies remembers a woman with a car like yours dropping the victim off about nine-thirty. She's exact about the time 'cause one of her favorite TV shows was just going off and she'd got up to go to the bathroom. And she's exact about the car because, well, it's distinctive."

"How'd you find me so fast? Just from the description of the car?" But as soon as she'd said it, she remembered, of course—giving CharLee her phone number, CharLee tucking the little square of folded paper into her purse.

"Oh, damn!" She leaned back from the chair, scrunched her eyes shut.

"What is it?" said Munez.

"She was upset when I dropped her off, so I gave her my phone number in case she wanted to talk later on, but then . . . then I was tired and I wanted to sleep, so I unplugged the phone. I can't believe I did that. What if she tried to call me and she couldn't get through? What if I could have saved her?"

Loomis held up a hand. "Whoa, let's not get ahead of ourselves. I don't know what happened to Ms. St. John, but one thing you can be sure of—if somebody was outside her room, intent on doing her harm, she'd've been dialing 9-1-1, not calling you. So don't for a minute go blaming yourself."

Cass nodded, knowing what he said made sense but still feeling terribly guilty. Guilty because she'd taken the phone off the hook and because underlying her sorrow at CharLee's death was also the knowledge that she'd never know what else CharLee might have been able to tell her about Raven's relationship with Jack.

"For the record, though," said Munez, "it doesn't look like force was used to get in her room. She either trusted the killer enough to let him in or she went out for ice or something and left the door unlocked. The killer could've been waiting for her when she came back in the room."

"Yeah, ice," said Cass. "We'd been out drinking, and she had a headache. She said she was going to soak a towel in ice and put it over her eyes."

She saw Loomis jot something down on the notepad.

"Was it quick?"

Loomis looked up from writing. "Sorry?"

"I asked if it was quick. How did she die?"

He hesitated, glanced over at Munez.

In a flat voice that sounded like he was addressing a press conference, Munez said, "Ms. St. John was hit from behind with the metal base of a lamp that was already in the room and then strangled with some kind of cord. We didn't find it in the room, so the killer took it with him. The first blows were hard enough to put a three-inch fracture in her skull. She probably didn't feel anything that went on after that."

"*After* that . . . are you telling me she was raped?"

"Forensics found the presence of semen," Munez said. "We don't know yet if she was raped."

"I don't understand. If there was semen, then obviously . . ."

"Not as obvious as you might think . . ." Munez trailed off and seemed to focus his attention on a painting of a prairie landscape on the wall behind her.

"The presence of semen doesn't necessarily mean penetration," Loomis said. "Sometimes guys, well, they like to ejaculate on a victim. Particularly if the victim was already dead, he might have felt squeamish about violating her."

"Meaning you can rule out necrophilia?"

"Well, that's one way to look at it," said Loomis, clicking the pen. He looked around the room, taking in the garment bag hanging in an open closet, the computer case and overnight bag, the two large, patterned suitcases on luggage racks by the wall. "You out here on vacation, Ms. Lumetto?"

She was tired of him mispronouncing her name. "Lumetto," she said, stressing the second syllable. "Call me Cass if it's easier. Yeah, I'm on vacation."

Munez reached up and plucked at a fold of his ruined ear, where the lobe would have been if the ear had been normal. "Where you from, Ms. Lumetto?"

"I live in New York. I was visiting my father in Denver."

Loomis stood up and flipped up the metal guard on the air-conditioner controls. She noted that whatever his weight-lifting regimen was, he didn't work on his torso alone. "You don't mind if I turn up the air?"

"Go right ahead."

He fiddled with the controls, sat back down again. Clicked the pen. "What line of work are you in, Ms. Lumetto?" Making sure to pronounce her name correctly this time.

"I'm a writer. Magazine articles, public relations."

"A writer, huh? Anything I might've read?"

"I doubt it, Detective. Unless you're interested in women's fashion and ten herbs to help you through menopause."

She heard Munez stifle a chuckle.

Loomis cleared his throat and pressed on. "Lotta luggage. Doing some sightseeing out West?"

"I'm just visiting Canon City."

"Well, we do have some fine attractions—whitewater rafting, the Royal Gorge, great fishing and hiking. Any of that on your agenda?"

"Actually I'm here visiting someone in prison."

Loomis's brow furrowed slightly. "So was CharLee St. John. Is that where you two met—at the prison?"

Cass nodded. "She was visiting a convict named Lu-

thor Shaw. She broke up with him, in fact, and he
didn't take it very well."

"We know all about Luthor Shaw," Munez said,
"and the fact that Ms. St. John visited him yesterday
afternoon. We also have a roomful of witnesses who
saw him lose it."

"You think he called somebody on the outside and
told them to hurt her?"

"That's the case, whoever it was did a pretty thorough job," said Loomis. He jotted something else
down, then turned back to Cass. His gaze was direct,
but still disarmingly youthful. Except for the etching
of crow's-feet around the eyes, the faint lines bracketing both sides of his mouth that put him in his early
thirties, he had the look of somebody's perpetual kid
brother, the guy who gets fixed up with everyone's
sister.

"You said you and Ms. St. John went drinking last
night. Tell me about that—everything you remember—what was said, who she talked to, her state of
mind when you drove her home."

"Her state of mind when I drove her home was
drunk," said Cass. "That's why I drove her back to
her motel." She went on to describe everything she
could remember about the evening at the Black Bear
Tavern, especially CharLee's misgivings about having
broken up with Luthor and Willy-with-the-slicked-
back-hair who'd turned nasty when CharLee wouldn't
go home with him.

Munez tugged at what had once been his ear again.
"Do you think she told this guy where she was staying?"

"She might have. She was concerned about him following us when we left the bar. If he did, though, I
didn't see him, but somebody at the bar might have
noticed when he left. He seemed to be a regular—the
bartender and wait staff knew him by name."

"Oh, we'll check it out, all right," said Loomis.
"We'll find out who else was there, interview the
whole . . . wait staff." He leaned forward in his chair,

narrowing the space between him and Cass in a way that made the small room seem to shrink even further, creating a false sense of intimacy. "You said you met Ms. St. John and these two other women"—he read from his notes—"Mariah Phelps and Opal Brady—at the prison. Who was it you went there to see? Boyfriend? Relative?"

"Just a guy I've been writing to."

There was a beat of silence that Cass imagined was heavy with reproach. "His name?"

"Is it really relevant?" She realized her reluctance to reveal such an innocuous piece of information might, in itself, seem suspicious, but she hated letting the cops think she was dumb enough to fall for a guy who'd murdered his wife. And she already had an idea of their opinion of prison romances.

Munez shrugged, stretched his legs out. "It's not a problem if you don't want to tell us his name. We can find out easily enough. Who visits who, it's all on record."

They talked a while longer, going over many of the same questions, while Cass tried to provide further details, especially anything else she was able to recall about Willy. When it looked like the interview was at an end, Loomis handed her his card. "Anything else you remember, give me a call. You *are* planning to be around for a while?"

"I'm not sure."

"Well, be sure," said Loomis as both men stood up, "at least for a few more days."

"Are you saying I'm a suspect?"

"Not at all," Loomis said quickly, "only that as we talk to other people, more questions may come up."

"Actually," said Cass, "I have some questions of my own."

Both men looked surprised. After a beat of silence, Loomis said, "Go ahead."

"Does Canon City normally have a high murder rate?"

"Not at all," said Munez, worrying his ear again. "Usually no more than one or two a year. And in the majority of those, victim and killer knew each other—you get a skirmish outside a bar where somebody pulls a gun or a domestic violence situation."

"I heard a woman was murdered here a little over a year ago, and the killer was never caught. I believe her name was Raven Sterling. I wondered if there could be a connection between CharLee's murder and hers?"

For an instant, something dark and mistrustful flickered across Loomis's features. Cass wasn't sure if she'd hit a nerve or if he just disliked being on the receiving end of the questions.

He started to say something, but Munez cut him off. "Ms. Lumetto, I'm sure you mean well, but this isn't really the time to play amateur detective. If there's a connection between the two cases, we'll look into it."

But his tone of voice said clearly that her idea had been dismissed.

"You said CharLee was hit with the base of a lamp and then strangled," she continued. "And some sort of sexual activity took place, since you found semen. Is that similar to the way this other woman was killed?"

She already knew the answer, of course, from newspaper clippings and the information the police had given Kenny. Raven's body bore signs of a violent struggle, but there was no evidence of sexual assault. Her death had come from manual strangulation and it had been prolonged—the killer was apparently a sadist who strangled her a little at a time, over a period as long as half an hour. No one had ever suggested that Raven's death had been either swift or merciful.

"Forgive me," said Munez, "but we've both *been* to the crime scene, so we might have a few more details about Ms. St. John's death than you do. Believe me, there're no similarities between the two killings."

Cass pressed on. "I'm sure I remember reading that Raven Sterling was strangled. And you said that CharLee—"

"No *other* similarities."

"Except in both cases, you don't know who the killer was."

"Where'd you hear about the Sterling case anyway?" Loomis said.

Cass thought quickly and said, "Last night in the bar—CharLee mentioned it. I just think it's kind of a coincidence—two unsolved murders where the women died of strangulation."

"Well, that's all that it appears to be," said Loomis, "a coincidence." He shot a look at Munez that clearly said the interview was over.

Cass started to say something, but Loomis was already on his feet and moving toward the door.

"You forgot your hat," she called to Loomis, grabbing it off the bed. She winced as something cut into the meat of her thumb. "Damn!" She thought at first a bee had stung her, then saw the buglike little thing stuck into the hatband. It was made of tiny brown and orange feathers with a hook protruding near the base.

"Oh, sorry about that," said Loomis. "You okay?"

She looked at the drop of blood squeezing out of her finger. "I think I'll probably avoid major surgery, yeah." She took a closer glance at the thing that had wounded her.

"Dragonfly nymph?"

He looked startled. "You fly-fish?"

"Used to, a little bit."

"Well, you shouldn't mind spending a few extra days here then. We've got some of the best fly-fishing in the state."

"I'll keep that in mind."

She walked the men outside to their car, a late-model black Buick Regal. When the sun hit Loomis in the face, she revised her opinion of his age. The lines were deeper than she'd realized, and she put his age at late thirties, early forties. Which meant married, she thought, or at best hauling serious baggage.

Munez went around to the passenger side of the car and opened the door to give the superheated air inside a chance to escape. Loomis did the same with the driver's side. As Cass started to go back in the room, he said, "You and this friend you got in prison, is that something serious?"

Was he flirting or just asking for the sake of information, she wondered, then felt annoyed at herself to be thinking about the eligibility of a man she'd just met when a woman she knew, albeit briefly, had been murdered.

"Yesterday was the first time I ever laid eyes on Jack in person," she said. "How serious does that sound?"

"Hard to say. Some women correspond with these men for years. First time they meet the guy in person is when they show up to marry him."

"Well, believe me, that's not the case here."

"Then I guess I'd say it sounds casual."

"Casual it is."

Munez had lit a cigarette and was getting into the car. Loomis started to get in, then turned back. "You said Jack?"

The secrecy, at this point, felt ridiculous. He'd find out who she was visiting anyway. "Yeah, Jack O'Doul."

In the eyeblink that it took to say the name, Loomis stopped reminding her of the boy next door grown buffed and middle-aged and started looking like a cop, angry and suspicious and unforgiving. His eyes bored into her like he'd mentally matched up her face with some photo in a Most Wanted poster—a woman who blew up day-care centers, stole from the blind.

"How did you get hooked up with O'Doul?"

"Like I said, we wrote letters to each other," she said, hating herself for sounding rattled.

Loomis rolled his eyes.

"You have a problem with letter-writing, Detective?"

"Only letters to scum."

"Shall I assume you and Jack have a history?"

"Ms. Lumetto, if you lined up all the cops who have a history with Jack O'Doul, they'd reach from here to Colorado Springs."

"Sounds personal to me."

"Ms. Lumetto?" He'd begun mispronouncing her name again and was compounding it now by adding an inflexion of superiority and sarcasm. "I realize it's some kind of weird law of nature that women fall for the worst possible men—I can even live with that if we're talking guys who drink a little too much, get a little rowdy, make life exciting. Women don't like boring, I can understand that, 'cause men don't like boring, either. But a murderer? A cold-blooded murderer? He killed his wife. He killed the mother of his child."

"He says he didn't do it," Cass blurted out and immediately regretted it.

"He didn't do it? Well, then whoa, let's call a press conference, call the governor, get the poor guy released, get *all* of those fine gentlemen released."

"This really isn't any of your business."

"You're right. It isn't. But finding who murdered Ms. St. John is, so when I need to talk to you again, make sure I can find you. Understood?"

A sweating Munez looked over the top of the car at his partner. "You about through socializing?"

Loomis put one leg inside the cruiser, but still didn't get in. Anger burned off him like the heat escaping from inside the car. "And keep this in mind next time you visit O'Doul. He's in prison for what he got *caught* at. Odds are there's three times as many felonies the man's committed over the years that he didn't get nailed for. Maybe even murder. 'Cause much as we hate to believe it, Ms. Lumetto, people get away with murder all the time."

"Is that what's going to happen to the person who killed CharLee? Is he going to get away with it?"

"I doubt it, Ms. Lumetto. I sincerely do. But I gotta tell you that with a woman like Ms. St. John, a woman who hooks up with a convicted murderer, something like this happens to her and you gotta think maybe she brought some of it on herself."

"You're saying Luthor Shaw had her murdered because she broke up with him?"

Loomis waved the question away. "I'm not saying that. All I mean is a person who courts trouble—no pun intended—sometimes ends up with more of it than she bargained for."

For much of that night, she lay awake, turning Loomis's words over in her mind, more troubled by them than she wanted to admit. After all, deep down, didn't she agree with him? That the women she'd seen in the prison the day before were somehow of a lower order, both laughable and pathetic in their blind allegiance to relationships that didn't even exist in any normal sense of the word? Women like Opal, planning a wedding to a man who might never again set foot outside a prison, or Mariah, proudly married to a multiple murderer condemned to death.

She thought about how she'd squirmed inside when she had to admit to the detectives that she was involved with Jack O'Doul.

A painful realization dawned on her. She'd thought it was her ethics that had made her back out of Kenny's offer. That wasn't true. It was her unwillingness to join the ranks of women who, in her heart of hearts, she felt contempt for. To play the role of a woman who, in real life, she felt so superior to.

She'd thought she was being moral by refusing to deceive Jack. In truth, she was protecting her own ego.

By the time she finally fell into a fretful sleep, she'd made up her mind—she'd call Kenny first thing in the morning and tell him she was ready to be Jack's girlfriend again. For Raven. For the truth.

Chapter 6

"After the way Luthor blew up in here the other day and then what happened to CharLee," Jack said, "I was scared you might not ever come back. Thought I might have to bust out of here and come after you."

He sat close to Cass, their chairs touching, one arm around her back and the other gripping her hand. He seemed afraid to let go. The last time she remembered being clutched like this, she and Philip had gone on the roller coaster at Coney Island and he'd practically cracked her ribs.

"Who do you suppose killed her?" Cass said.

"Word on the prison grapevine is Luthor had somebody do it. He went nuts after the C.O.s took him back to his cell, started beatin' his head on the cell wall, tryin' to set his cell on fire. They had to straightjacket him and haul him to solitary."

"If he was in solitary, bound up in a straightjacket, then how was he able to use the phone to call someone to kill her?"

"He was calmed down and outta solitary in time for dinner," Jack said. "He coulda made the call then or got someone else to call somebody for him."

"His being so upset over her leaving him, was that just an act? He really hated her enough to want her dead?"

"No, he *loved* her," Jack said. "I know he was tore up, all right. Heartbroke. That don't mean he wasn't behind it, though. Man with a broken heart's capable of anything."

Like dumping a woman out of his car in the middle of the night because she won't have sex with you, Cass wanted to say. Or maybe coming back a few nights later and killing her?

"Is that what happened with you and Melinda?" she asked. "Did she break your heart?"

Jack disengaged his fingers, began tapping them on the tabletop. "You mean is that why I killed her—*if* I killed her?"

"Well, you admitted that you got rough with her. I just wondered if she'd been seeing someone else and if maybe that was why—"

He seemed annoyed that she'd suggest such a thing. "You saying Melinda might've had another man? No way! Melinda never cheated on me. Nobody cheats on me."

And lives to tell the tale? she thought, but tried to mollify him instead, running a finger down his chest and sitting a little closer. "So you really think Luthor had CharLee killed?"

"I wouldn't put it past him. He's got that kind of mean streak."

"You knew Luthor pretty well on the outside?"

"Yeah. I mean, I wasn't no gang member, but Luthor and I hung together sometimes. Went drinkin' together, shot the shit. You know how it is."

"I guess you lived pretty wild."

"I got around a lot. Seen stuff I wish I hadn't, done stuff I damn well *know* I wish I hadn't." He squeezed her shoulder, clearly proud, despite his words, of the macho exploits he was implying.

"You had a lot of women, didn't you?"

"Not lately. All the sex that I've had lately is right here." He made a pumping gesture.

She slapped his hand away. "C'mon, you know what I mean."

"Well, yeah, I had my share of women. Maybe some

other guy's share, too. But you know what they say"—
his hand roved lower on her back, cupping the side
of a breast—"the best is yet to come."

She wriggled away, repositioning his hand while
glancing over at one of the guards, trying to make him
think that she was modest and not just uninterested
in his adolescent gropings.

"At the bar the other night," she said, redirecting
the subject, "CharLee mentioned Luthor had told her
about a girl you used to date. Said her name was
Raven and she was beautiful." She forced herself to
direct what she hoped to be a lingering, girlish look
up through her lashes. "Is that true?"

From his reaction, she might as well have asked him
if he and Luthor Shaw used to date. His eyes narrowed and the arm grafted onto her shoulder suddenly
wasn't there anymore.

"She was okay-looking."

Cass flashed on an image of Raven: sleek curves
and huge, fawnlike eyes and jet hair cascading down
to her butt. *Okay-looking for the swimsuit issue of*
Sports Illustrated.

"Just okay?"

"She was pretty, you know. Real pretty."

"Were you in love with her?"

He pulled a face. "Just 'cause she was good-looking
don't mean she was my type. Now don't tell me you're
gonna go get jealous or something. I hate it when
women do that. Raven was a long time ago. It's
over now."

"Well, yeah. I guess it *is* over. She's dead."

"Huh?" He jerked back, the pale blue eyes suddenly wary as a cornered cat's.

"Why'd CharLee go and tell you that?"

"I don't know. It just came up."

"Well, she musta had some kinda reason."

Cass forced herself to adopt the kind of high-
pitched, prattling tone she hated to hear in women.

"We were just girl talking is all, honey. It's ironic, though, isn't it? CharLee tells me she knew this girl Raven, who got murdered, then that very night she gets murdered herself. It's scary is all I'm saying."

"Yeah, so? Things happen." He rapped his knuckles on the tabletop and glanced at the wall clock, as if suddenly ready for visiting time to end.

"Sweetie, I'm sorry. I didn't mean to upset you."

He scowled and let out an exasperated sigh. "Look, do me a favor? Don't bring up Raven again. That's done with. You're my girlfriend now, right?"

She nodded.

"Am I *right*?"

"Yes, Jack."

"Another thing," he said sternly, "I know you didn't know any better this time, but don't gossip about me ever again. I don't like to know a couple of women were talking about me behind my back."

"I understand, honey. I won't do it again." She hoped she sounded suitably submissive and meek, but inside she was seething. So this was a glimpse of the man Melinda O'Doul had to deal with before she died? Overbearing and bullying. And *this* man was sober and being watched over by several armed guards.

She reached out, took his hand. "At some point, I want to know all about you, Jack. But we're both new to this. I can understand if you don't trust me enough to talk about certain things yet. I can wait."

"Yeah, well, I can be touchy sometimes. I know that."

"And as a woman—living in a new town, all alone—" she continued, trying to appeal to his protective side, "it scares me when I hear about awful things like what happened to CharLee. That coulda been me."

The strategy seemed to work. He softened instantly, stroking her hair with his free hand. It was as if the anger from a few seconds before had never been.

"Don't worry, hon. Nothin's gonna happen to you. I may be locked up in here, but I can still look out for you."

Oh, great, she thought.

"I don't know what happened to CharLee," he went on, "but I will tell you this, if Raven hadn't broken up with me, I coulda protected her, too. She hadn't broken up with me, she'd be alive today."

"That almost sounds like—"

He held up a hand to cut her off. "Look, I said I don't want to talk about her and I meant it."

"I just thought if—"

"Hey, look who's here!" Jack grinned and leaped to his feet so fast his chair teetered and almost tipped backward, cutting off any hope Cass had of persuading him to talk more about Raven. She twisted around in her chair and saw an enormous man with a broad, beaming face, wearing dungarees held up by bright red suspenders over a checked cotton work shirt steering his huge bulk cautiously among the tables. He had a hand extended, the palm of which looked about as big as a good-sized Virginia ham. Cass pegged him for late fifties, early sixties, and figured, in his youth, he could have made NFL scouts salivate. Even now, he looked to be more muscle than suet, more sinew than lard.

"Reverend Butterworth!" Jack exclaimed, pumping the outstretched hand. "Reverend, I want you to meet Cass Lumetto, the girl I told you about." He turned to Cass. "Honey, this is my best friend, Claude Butterworth. Man of the cloth, man of honor, a true stand-up guy."

Butterworth waved off the praise and shook Cass's hand. "Sometimes I think Jack here ought to be the preacher, such is his gift for embellishment."

"Em-what?" said Jack.

"Pleased to meet you," said Cass.

"He's heard a lot about you," said Jack.

"All of it high praise." Butterworth pulled up a

chair—the girth of his backsides really required two—
and lowered himself gingerly. "Jack tells me you're
going to be settling here in Canon City. Anything I
or my wife Fiona can do to help make your move
easier—whether it's help finding work or the lowdown
on who makes the best pizza—just let us know." He
extracted a card from his pocket and gave it to Cass.
"I won't pry into your religious affiliations, but I will
tell you we have a fine little church and a wonderful
Christian community. Please stop by some Sunday.
We'd love to have you."

"Thank you," said Cass. "I will."

"Belief in the Lord Jesus Christ, that's what saved
my soul," Jack said fervently. "And it was Reverend
Butterworth who introduced me to Him. It was the
Reverend who stuck by me through my trial, too,
when my own family wouldn't so much as spit on me.
Without him, I'd be just another lost soul."

"Give the credit to the Lord, Jack," said Butterworth.

"Yeah, but don't the Lord work through human
beings?" He turned back to Cass. "And I'm telling
you that was the Lord at work using the reverend here
as his instrument. First time I met Reverend Butterworth was right after Twyla was born. I'd got in a
little scrape and ended up doing three months for
drunk and disorderly. Reverend Butterworth and
Fiona would come by the prison to lead the Wednes-
day and Saturday night prayer groups—soon's I got
out, first thing I did was go join the church and tell
Melinda she had to join, too. And we did, too, we
went every Sunday. Melinda volunteered for the
church soup kitchen, put Twyla in Sunday school. I
never forget she gave me a drawing she'd done one
Sunday. A bunch of lambs and birds and piglets and
what all, with Jesus watching over 'em. Damned wonderful art for a little three-year-old girl." His voice
trailed off. "Damn, but I sure do miss her."

He looked at Butterworth, who shifted in his seat

as though he knew what Jack was about to ask. "How'd it go, Reverend? Did you talk to Angela?"

Butterworth drew a deep breath, which compressed the loose flesh beneath his neck into a series of chins. He knotted his big hands on his belly in a stance that was surprisingly Buddha-like. When he spoke, his deep voice resonated with warmth and compassion. "She said no, Jack. I spoke to both her and Parker. They feel it's too soon for Twyla to see you, that she's still adjusting to the loss of her mother without the added stress of—coming here to the prison."

"So she gets to adjust to the loss of her father, too! What kinda fuckin' logic is that?"

"I'm sorry, Jack. I was hoping I could persuade them to let her see you. Maybe in time . . ."

"Fuck, she's my *kid,*" said Jack. "I *miss* her."

". . . they'll see things differently."

"Yeah. Maybe," said Jack, but there was no conviction behind it. He turned to Cass. "The other day you asked me what it was like in here. *This* is what it's like. I can't even see my own flesh and blood."

"Remember things happen in the Lord's time, not ours," Butterworth said. "Be patient and pray for Angela and Parker to open their hearts." He glanced at his watch. "And speaking of time, I'd better be going. I know Luthor Shaw doesn't have much use for what I'm peddling, but I was hoping to speak to him. I heard about what happened to his girlfriend . . . he may not show it, but I know he's hurting."

One corner of Jack's mouth curled bitterly. "Yeah, hurtin' anybody gets in his way. See if you can get him to confess to sending somebody to off his girlfriend." He saw the expression on Butterworth's face, a mixture of shock and distaste. "Sorry, Reverend, I didn't mean to make light of it. I'm just bummed about Twyla and actin' like a jerk. Sorry."

"It's all right, Jack." Butterworth patted him on the shoulder, rose on knees that creaked and popped like old boards. He smiled down at Cass. "I'm so happy that you and Jack found each other. And I meant what I said—anything at all my wife or I can help you do to get settled, let us know. And please, drop by our church this Sunday. We'd love to see you."

He moved off, steering his vast bulk toward the table where Luthor Shaw still conferred with his lawyer.

Cass watched him go. "He *is* a big man, isn't he?"

Jack nodded. "Big in more ways than one. Thing is, the Reverend Butterworth hasn't had an easy life—he grew up poor as dirt in some little town down in Arkansas—yet he made something of himself all the same. Didn't let poverty and lack of education drag him down. Once he found the Lord, he never lost faith. And let me tell you, Cass, he preaches a cracker-jack sermon. Better than anything you'll hear on TV. I want you to go to his church Sunday. If we're gonna be together, we got to belong to the same church. You'll do that for me, won't you?"

"If it means that much to you, honey, sure."

"I gotta ask you one more thing." He clasped her hands and gazed into her eyes, his mouth curved in a broad, loopy grin. He could clearly go through abrupt onslaughts of emotion, from elation to rage in an eye-blink. Such emotional swerves were like riptides in an otherwise calm sea, Cass thought, illusive and deadly. She reminded herself that this man was locked up in prison. He couldn't hurt her even if, someday, he might want to.

"What is it, Jack?"

"Would you go see Angela and Parker and check on Twyla for me? I'll give you their address and phone number. Just see how she's doin', that they're treatin' her right. Then, can you convince them to let her come to see me?"

"I'll do whatever you want, Jack, but if the Reverend Butterworth couldn't persuade them, what makes you think I can?"

" 'Cause you're a woman and women stick together,

which might help with Angela. That's one reason. 'Cause you're pretty, which may hurt you with Angela, but at least'll make Parker listen to what you say. And 'cause you're 'bout the only person I got left to ask."

"You really love her, don't you?"

He looked at her as if it were the strangest question. "She's my daughter. Course I do. Like any father'd love his little girl. Didn't your dad love you?"

"In his own way, yeah, he loved me," said Cass, thinking that Johnny Lumetto's ways of showing love, while genuine, were hardly conventional. Before Jack could pursue the topic of her father, she went on, "I'll do it, Jack, but you have to be realistic. It sounds like their minds are made up, at least for now. Somebody else coming to see them to plead your case may only make things worse."

"You'll do it, though?"

"If it means that much to you, sure."

"Thanks, darlin'."

"But I want something in return," she said. "Not now, but later . . . when you're ready."

"What's that?"

"Full disclosure."

He looked confused. "What's that? It sounds like lawyer talk."

"No, it's my way of saying I want to get to know you. Everything about you, good and bad. No secrets between us, nothing held back. So at some point, after you trust me more, I want you to tell me about Raven and all your other girlfriends, too."

He frowned, clearly not accustomed to such propositions. "That mean you expect me to listen to you talk about your old boyfriends? 'Cause I'll tell you up front, I am a jealous man. You told me about some Philip guy you dated, and that's enough for me to know. Less you just this day first set foot outside the convent, you're better off I don't know about your past. That way I can't imagine stuff, make pictures in my head of you and other men."

"Fair enough," she said. "You don't have to. But I want to know about yours."

He squinted at her, then broke into a wide grin. "How come you never told me you was such a nosy woman?"

"You didn't ask. Now give me the address where Twyla lives. I'll go see her stepparents."

She'd had to leave her purse at the front gate, of course, and he wasn't allowed to carry around pens or pencils, so she memorized the address.

"I'll do my best for you, Jack."

"I know you will, honey."

She got up to leave and he pulled her against him, kissing her hard and deeply. She found herself liking it more than she should have, responding to the heat and hardness of his body with ardor of her own. How long since she'd been kissed like that? *Too long*, she thought.

To break the circuit of sexual energy between them, at least mentally, she first tried thinking of Philip, which didn't work, and then of Detective Loomis, which did. She imagined that she was kissing him, running her hands over his firm-looking denim-clad ass.

"Darlin', you sure can kiss," he said when he released her. "Now you come back here just as soon as you can. And when you see Twyla, tell her Daddy's thinkin' 'bout her."

"I will, sweetie." She turned away.

"And, hon?"

"Yes?"

"Don't *you* forget I'm gonna be thinkin' about you, too. Thinkin' about you plenty."

"Same here, Jack," she said in one of those rare times she could speak the complete truth. "I'll be thinking about you every minute."

Escorted by one of the guards, the visitors filed out through a set of steel doors into a hallway leading to a second set of doors and the front desk where they could reclaim their possessions. At one point, Cass found herself walking beside Butterworth.

"Did you talk to Luthor Shaw?" she asked.

"Well, I tried, but he told me to go to hell," said Butterworth, "so I told him to have a nice day and went on to others more receptive to my ministry."

"Must get frustrating," said Cass.

"No, not when there're so many men hungry for the Lord. Like Jack, for instance, although at this point in his life, I'm afraid God's not enough. He needs a woman who cares about him, Cass, and I don't mind telling you, I truly hope it's you. I don't delude myself into thinking I have any special insight into people I've just met, but I can tell you have a good heart. That could make all the difference in the world for Jack. He has a lot of inner sweetness, but he needs someone to bring it out in him."

They passed through another gate, then reached a small bottleneck of people picking up handbags, keys, and the like. Cass said, "I'm sure you know Jack thinks he didn't kill his wife. Do you believe him when he says that he's not capable of murder? Do you think his being in prison is all a terrible mistake?"

Butterworth sighed. Sorrow, profound and dauntingly personal, seemed to settle over his potato-eater features, giving his face a kind of rough tenderness. "I think Jack believes he isn't capable of murder. But since Cain killed Abel, the whole course of human history has been nothing but bloodshed, has it not? I know Jack's capable of murder, because we all are. The flesh is weak. That's why we can never be saved through our own paltry efforts, but only through the blood of our Lord."

"So even though you're couching it in theological terms, you believe Jack murdered his wife."

"Sadly, yes. Does that mean you can't love him?" He glanced around the room at the predominantly female visitors filing out. "So many of these women believe their man is different, is innocent in the face of every evidence to the contrary. They *have* to believe that in order to make the sacrifices that loving a man in prison requires. Is your love based on needing to believe Jack's innocent?"

"No."

Butterworth's massive head jerked upward as though a weight had been removed. "Then that means I was right about you, Cass. I was right."

His smile seemed heartfelt, almost touching. *If he only knew*, thought Cass. She hurried to retrieve her personal items, bade Butterworth a brief good-bye after promising to appear in church that Sunday, and headed out into the parking lot. A black Harley with an obnoxiously loud motor was behind her for a few blocks after she pulled out of the prison. It turned left with her onto Royal Gorge Avenue and roared past when she stopped at City Market.

There was no refrigerator or minibar in her room, so she had to limit herself to snack foods—some bags of trail mix in case she went hiking, granola bars in various flavors, Ibuprofen, and—God help her—a bag of pork rinds. Outside the market, she slid some coins into the Pepsi machine and held the icy can to her cheeks for a few seconds before popping the top.

She headed back to the motel on automatic pilot, trying to sort through the contradictory feelings she'd felt about Jack's kiss and his reaction to her questions about Raven, when the black Harley reappeared behind her.

Can't be the same one, she thought, but there was a queasy feeling in her gut that argued otherwise. She made an unplanned left turn onto Seventh Avenue, and the Harley followed.

At the next street—Main—she turned right.

The Harley turned right, too.

Shit.

She glared at the guy in her rearview mirror and turned left again, deliberately missing the turn that would have taken her to the motel. He revved his motor and closed the distance between them. The black helmet he was wearing concealed the rider's face, but she could see he was a big man—not in the Reverend Butterworth's category, but definitely near two hundred pounds. He wore jeans and a black tank top with the Harley eagle logo. Some type of ornamentation—a necklace or chain, she supposed—produced an explosion of light on his chest when the sun struck it directly.

Fuck this, thought Cass. She sped ahead, then stomped on the brake and made a screeching U-turn in the center of Main Street. The biker revved his engine to a roar that must have been audible in Colorado Springs and kept going. He gave a mock salute with a hand clad in a fingerless black glove as he continued on up Main Street, turned right back toward Royal Gorge Boulevard, and disappeared.

Thankful that the unknown rider had gone, she turned and drove back to the motel, went inside and started to unpack her groceries. She had torn open the bag of pork rinds and was crunching one when she heard the sound of a motorcycle engine. She dashed to the window, peeking out from behind the shades in time to see the Harley circling the parking lot. The rider slowed as he passed Cass's car, then exited back out into the street and headed east up Main, giving the same sarcastic little salute.

Letting me know he knew I was watching, she thought.

That he knows where I live.

Chapter 7

The day after her visit to Jack, Cass pulled up across the street from Angela and Parker Dunn's house and sat for a moment, appraising the house and wondering about its occupants.

Like a suspect whose distinguishing features were all negative—a missing tooth, cleft palate, or lazy eye, thought Cass—the house sported a number of distinctive, if inharmonious, structural incongruities. The flower boxes under the windows were mismatched and tilted, the roof sported missing shingles, and the peeling, mustard-colored exterior begged for a fresh coat of paint. Slabs of buckling sidewalk in front of the small, boxy house suggested the rumblings of an incipient earthquake, and weeds stabbed arrogantly through cracks in the sidewalk surface.

Efforts at a type of home improvement were visible, though. Three giant plastic butterflies had been affixed to the outer wall between the window and the front door, where they clung like a trio of birthmarks to the face of the house.

As Cass approached, she was aware of a compendium of noises issuing from inside: the familiar jingle for a line of pet products advertised on TV, a woman's beleaguered-sounding voice saying, "Yes, yes, caller number five!" against a background of children shouting and a country-western diva belting out a love ballad in competition with it all.

She reached the door, which was partly open but childproofed at the bottom with some kind of attachable mesh screen that came to Cass's waist.

A little girl wearing green shorts and a Smurfs T-shirt toddled to the door and peered up, waving hello with one chubby hand while, in the other, clutching a Barbie doll like a javelin she was preparing to hurl.

"Hi there," said Cass.

The little girl grinned, glanced back as if to make sure her mother wasn't watching, and started thwacking the doll's feet at the latch in an effort to open the screen.

"Reba, quit that!" shrilled a voice.

A squat, heavyset woman with dark hair and pale, pimply skin rushed to the door. She wore denim shorts and a tight blue top that squashed her breasts into doughy ovals and unflatteringly emphasized her round shape. She held a cell phone in one hand in much the same manner as her daughter wielded the Barbie, but her nails were long and varnished and accented with sparkly little half-moons and stars.

"Get back, Reba, honey. You're under Mom's feet." She looked at Cass. "Yeah? You here about the new carpet?"

From somewhere farther back in the house, a baby added its squawl to the rest of the chaos.

Cass said, "No, sorry I—"

The woman was unhooking the childproofing gate and firing words into the cell phone at the same time. "What I'm *saying* is am I caller number five? I am! Shania Twain—that song's by Shania Twain!" She gaped at the phone as though unable to comprehend what the deejay was telling her. "It's not Shania Twain? You're sure? Well, okay then—yeah, I love your show. You have a nice day, too!"

She shook her head apologetically and stuck out a hand. "Angela Dunn. Sorry about the mess. You come on in. If you got samples or something out in the car, though, you might want to bring 'em in." She looked at the forlorn, once-upon-a-time blue carpeting at her feet. "I was thinking, you know, teal maybe or dove-gray. Something can take spills, but thick and soft, so it feels good underfoot, plushlike, know what I mean?"

Quickly Cass introduced herself. "I'm sorry to barge in on you like this, Mrs. Dunn, but the phone's been busy whenever I called, so I thought it might be better if I came in person. I'm not from the carpet company. I'm a friend of Jack O'Doul's."

At the sound of the name, Angela jerked and stiffened as though someone had poured ice water down the back of her neck.

"Jack O'Doul doesn't have friends. He uses people and manipulates them to get what he wants. He takes hostages, but he doesn't have friends. So if you think you're one, then you must be either his girlfriend, his lawyer, or his parole officer or some of them three combined?"

"Like I said, I'm his friend," said Cass. "When I visited him the other day, he told me how much he misses Twyla. He asked if I'd stop by and see her."

"He did, huh?" Angela squinted, exhaled hard through her pursed lips, and propped her arms on her hips. "He's got his damn nerve. First he sends over that pompous preacher, Buttermilk whoever he was, running his big mouth about forgiveness. Sure, he can talk about forgiveness, it wasn't *his* sister Jack murdered."

In the background, the baby continued to cry. Angela turned around and Cass stepped past her into the narrow little hall.

"Please just let me come in for a minute."

Angela glared. "Looks to me you already are."

"Jack told me how you feel about him—"

"Oh, I doubt it. Jack couldn't even begin to imagine how I feel. Eternity's not long enough for that man to rot in hell. Forever's too short a time for him to suffer."

"He loves his daughter very much."

"Yeah? Then how come he"—she lowered her

voice and lip-synced the next words—"killed her mother in cold blood?"

Reba came over and started stabbing Angela in the quads with Barbie's pointy-toed feet, gurgling and giggling. *Bam, bam, bam.*

Angela bent down, smoothing the child's hair back, and said matter-of-factly, "Baby doll, if you don't stop hitting Mom's varicose veins with Barbie, I'm gonna give her to the neighbor's dog for a chew bone."

Reba did a pirouette and popped Mom in the knee. "No, you won't. You said the same thing yesterday."

"Then I'll give Barbie to your sister who knows how to care for her things. I *will* do that."

Reba's face knotted up. "She's *not* my sister!"

"Kids," said Angela, lifting thick shoulders and pencil-thin brows simultaneously. Her head jerked around as a new song came on the radio. "Oh, gosh, I know that one. Hold on a sec, I gotta try and be caller number five. Prize money's up to two hundred bucks."

Angela began punching numbers into the phone and moved away from the door, allowing Reba to dash outside and Cass to sidle farther inside the house. The short entryway opened into a cheaply furnished living room dominated by an expensive-looking big-screen Panasonic with built-in stereo where a tear-streaked blonde was confessing to having sex with her father-in-law. The TV set was flanked by speakers taller than Reba and a CD holder and DVD player that must have easily contained over a hundred disks.

A little girl whom Cass recognized from her photo as Twyla came into the room. She was blond and ski-pole skinny in her tank top and shorts. She stared at Cass, emerald eyes sparkling with an impish intelligence.

"Who're you?"

"My name's Cass. And I'll bet you're Twyla?"

She beamed. "How d'you know my name?"

"Damn, I got cut off," said Angela. She turned to Twyla and shouted, "Hon, Reba just run outside. You

go keep an eye on her. This lady was just leaving."
She turned back to the phone, started to redial, then
yelled to Twyla as she went out the door with Reba,
"Keep an eye on her now. Don't let her get near
the street!" She turned to Cass. "People use this as a
shortcut, they drive like it's the Indy 500 out there."

A voice on the radio was announcing a special five-
hundred-dollar grand prize to whoever could identify
the snippet of song that was jingling. Angela's face
knit with the intensity of concentration.

"I know that one, oh, darn it, I *know* I know that
one!" she cried, slapping a palm to her forehead and
dialing again.

Cass used the distraction as an opportunity to seat
herself in a chair by the window while she puzzled
over the room's dubious decor. The furniture and
most of the bric-a-brac was well worn and deter-
minedly tacky, but the electronic equipment looked
high-end state of the art. Was Angela better at winning radio giveaways than she appeared to be? Cass
wondered. It didn't appear so.

"Well, dammit all, I got rattled and forgot the name
of the song," she was saying, raising gelatinous arms
in dismay. "And I *knew* it, I really did." She looked
surprised and a little dismayed to find Cass was not
only still there, but now ensconced in her living room.

"Look, I'm sorry if I caught you at a bad time,"
Cass said.

"Like there's ever a *good* time," snorted Angela.
She leaned past Cass to peer out the window. "Those
two better stay out of the street or Parker's gonna tan
their little butts."

Cass took the cue. "Having three kids to raise now,
that's got to be a handful."

"Yeah, well, whattaya gonna do?" Frustrated with
her lack of luck with the radio, Angela's gaze turned
to the TV screen, listening so intently to a commercial
for a new improved brand of dog food that she might
have been trying to memorize it. Finally, with a deep

sigh, she sat down on the sofa and turned back to Cass. "So look here—what did you say your name was?"

"Cass."

"Listen, Cass, since you're here in my home, I'm gonna ask you the same question I asked my sister a few years ago: How'd a nice-looking woman like you get mixed up with scum?"

Cass told her about being penpals with Jack, then meeting him for the first time when she moved to Canon City, although she neglected to say how recently that move had been.

"And he's already got you running errands? I tell you, for a guy I always thought was more or less a walking dumb blond joke, he sure can work women. Pretty ones, too. My sister was pretty—till about a year or so before she died. Then she went all to hell. Lost weight, stopped doing her hair, her nails, just didn't give a shit anymore. Who can—when they're being beaten up all the time."

"Melinda was actually living here with you, though, at the time she was killed?"

"Yeah, she went back for some of her stuff and he got her. That's the most dangerous time, too, for a battered woman—not when she's there with the guy but when she leaves him. I told Melinda to take Twyla and go upstate—we got cousins up in Ft. Collins she coulda stayed with—but she was stubborn, said she wouldn't let Jack run her out of town. I guess she still loved him, God only knows why."

"I know he'd been cheating on her with a woman named Raven," said Cass, "but she wasn't in the picture anymore. Maybe Melinda thought they could patch things up."

Angela's thinly plucked eyebrows arched. "Jack *told* you about that Raven woman?"

Cass nodded.

"And did he get around to mentioning *she* was murdered, too? He murdered my sister on July 31. The cops said Raven Sterling died on May 2. Pretty goddamn suspicious, if you ask me, but the goddamn police say they can't prove anything."

"You think he killed Raven, too?"

"Well, I didn't *say* that. But she's dead, right? And my sister's dead, and he *did* kill my sister. Two plus two equals four, know what I'm saying?"

"Jack says he didn't kill Melinda."

"Says he can't *remember* killing her—not the same thing. He's a drunk, Cass, an alcoholic, and you've never seen him but when he's sober. Take it from me, when he drinks, he's a different person. I mean, anybody gets shit-faced, of course they act different than they do sober, but I'm talking a complete switch. You meet Jack sober, he's no ball of fire in the brains department, but he can be sweet, playful, good with kids—you start to think, hell, he's a big kid himself. You get him drunk, though—he's the devil. Just plain *bad* through and through. If you can't see that for yourself, all I can say is, you're pretty damn dumb or pretty far gone in love with him, which amounts to the same thing."

"Are you talking about my daddy?"

Cass's and Angela's heads both swiveled in the direction of the front door, where Twyla was standing, one hand clutching Reba's, who was struggling to break away from her.

"How many times have I told you not to listen to other people's conversations?" Angela said.

"You *were*, weren't you?"

"I oughta smack you for snooping."

"I was not snooping," said Twyla. "Reba ran out into the middle of the street, and a *car* almost hit her. I *thought* you'd want me to bring her in."

"Well, how'd she get away from you?" said Angela. "You were supposed to be watching her."

"You *were* talking about my daddy!"

"What this lady and I were talking about is none of your business. Go take your sister out in the back-yard and this time do a better job of watching her."

Twyla and Reba both glared and said, almost in sync, "She's not my sister."

"Go!" yelled Angela. "You're making my head hurt." When the girls were out of the room, she said, "I don't mean to be rude, because I don't think you're a bad person, but I don't want anything remindin' Twyla of her father."

"Look," said Cass, "you have every reason to hate Jack, I understand that. But this is about Twyla, too. He's her father. If she doesn't want to see her father, then I say more power to you, keep her away from that prison. But if she does want to visit him and you don't want to have to see him, then I'd be happy to take her. That's all I'm offering."

Angela's eyes zapped back to the TV screen like little magnets. "She don't want to see him."

"You're sure?"

"Sure I'm sure."

"She said that?"

"She's a kid. She says one thing today, ten other things tomorrow, none of 'em the same. But no, take my word for it, she don't want to see him."

"If your sister were alive," said Cass, "don't you think she might want Twyla to have some contact with her father?"

"She sees her father every damn night," said Angela, "at the dinner table. His name's Parker and he's right here."

As she spoke, Cass saw a late-model, pewter-colored Suburban pulling up to the curb outside the house. A scrawny guy with lank brown hair tied back in a ponytail got out and slouched up the front walk. He had the kind of ropey, all sinew and tendon body that hinted at childhood malnutrition and the opaque, lightless eyes and grimly set mouth that told of a different kind of undernourishment in adulthood.

He eyed Cass rudely. "You the lady from Billingsley Carpet Shop?"

"No, she's not, Parker," said Angela. She nodded to Cass. "This is my husband Parker, Twyla's Dad now. Honey, this lady's name's Cass. She's Jack's girlfriend."

Parker's eyes narrowed and he shook his head as though Cass's presence there were an unutterable inconvenience. "Jack's girlfriend? What's she want?"

"She come to see would we let her take Twyla to visit Jack."

"When they're holdin' ice hockey matches in hell," said Parker and snorted at his own wit. He turned to Cass. "You in cahoots with that preacher come by here the other day, fat guy with a cane and a Bible?"

"He was just big, Parker," said Angela, trying to mollify, "not fat."

"The hell you say, he damn near broke through the porch. And you," he said, directing his anger at Cass, "tell Jack to leave me and my family alone. Twyla's being took good care of. She don't want for nothin'. We didn't ask to have her come into our lives, but she's here now and I'm lookin' out for her."

Cass hoped the little girl was out of earshot. She said, "What do you do for a living exactly, Mr. Dunn?"

A vague look of perplexity, then annoyance, passed across Parker's features. "I'm a 'lectrician."

Angela said, "He got laid off a while back, but there's plenty of work out there." She shot her husband a look. "Plenty of work."

"No doubt," said Cass. "Well, thanks for your time. I'll be going now." She paused, looked at Parker. "Nice Suburban."

He seemed to puff up noticeably. "Paid for, too."

On the radio, the deejay was playing another snippet of song to be identified for two hundred dollars, and Cass left Angela and Parker bickering over the title.

Outside she headed for her car, wondering again at what kind of illegal activity Parker must be involved in that would explain the Suburban and the stereo gear, when a small voice said, "Hey!"

Cass turned around as Twyla came running from around the corner of the house. She must have ditched Reba, but at least the younger girl wasn't playing in traffic, which Cass figured was probably the best one could hope for around here.

"That's not true what they said about me," Twyla said.

"What's not true?"

"That I said I don't want to see my dad. I do too want to see him, but they won't let me go. They say I should act like he's dead. I miss him, and I want to see him. You tell him I said so. Okay?"

"I sure will."

"Will you take me to see him?" She glanced toward the house. "I could sneak out. We don't have to tell *them*, do we?"

Cass felt her heart sink. "I can't take you without their permission, honey. I'm sorry, but I can't."

Twyla's features bunched toward the center of her small face. "Well, fuck you then," she said and dashed back toward the house.

Jack's daughter, thought Cass, *through and through.*

Chapter 8

Heads turned when Cass walked into the Pioneer Café, but she attributed that more to the fact that she was a new face among regulars, most of whom happened to be male, than any suddenly acquired sex appeal, especially since she was wearing her baggiest jeans and an oversized T-shirt that did nothing to flatter her figure. Still, after the disheartening visit to the Dunns' chaotic home, it felt good to be in a place where the people seemed friendly and the atmosphere calm.

The café was packed with the weekday lunch crowd, groups of guys who might have been construction workers or mechanics, tourist types with kids, a haggard-looking woman in the corner trying to quiet a fractious toddler. Already Cass had come to recognize that look—odds were good that the woman was in town to visit someone recently incarcerated.

The booths and tables all seemed to be taken, but there was space at the counter, an empty seat next to a unkempt-looking, bushy-faced man in tattered slacks and a heavy pullover sweater that might have served him well in the spring, but were much too warm for a hot summer day. Cass steered away from him and found another seat farther down the counter. A middle-aged waitress with a bouffant bubble of ash-blond hair and a name tag that read Muriel affixed to her pink uniform handed her a menu and rattled off the day's specials as she poured coffee for the man at the next stool, who was digging into a steak and eggs platter.

"Know what you want, honey, or do you need a minute?"

Cass ordered a steak and iced tea, opted reluctantly for the salad instead of French fries, and promised herself dessert as a reward for virtue in ordering the salad. She was thinking about the Dunns' depressing little house and the few incongruously expensive items—the TV set, the new Suburban—when she became aware of the man to her left, the steak-eater, saying to the waitress, "You ask me was prob'ly an inmate got out, killed that woman, then snuck back inside."

Hoots of derision from others seated at the counter greeted the remark.

"What'cha think it is over there, a Days Inn?" said the waitress. "They check out when they want to, do a murder, check back in?"

"Naw, it was an inmate who killed her all right, but he *had* one of his friends do it," came an opinion from the far end of the counter, a lanky kid with peeling, sunburned shoulders who was forking a piece of blueberry pie up to his mouth.

"What I heard was she'd brought drugs on her to smuggle into the prison and somebody murdered her for them," said a man several stools down from the steak-eater. He had long black hair under a cowboy hat, a handlebar mustache that drooped toward a sharp chin, and looked, to Cass, like a probable yuppie in search of his inner Wyatt Earp. All he needed was a six-shooter and spurs to complete the gunslinger facade.

Muriel pulled a face, set a glass of iced tea in front of Cass, and refilled the pie-eater's coffee. "She'd been visitin' her boyfriend the day she was killed. She'da had drugs on her, she'da already *gave* 'em to him."

"How you know he didn't give the drugs to *her*?" said the steak-eater, jabbing his knife for emphasis.

"Smuggling drugs *out* of prison, now there's a good one," said Wyatt, whose sleeves were rolled up to just under his elbows, exposing tanned skin and veined, brawny forearms. He glared at the steak-eater. "Buddy, you don't know what you're talkin' about. Sounds like you never even been *in* prison?"

"Meaning you have, I suppose?"

Wyatt grinned so that the mustache twitched like a couple of itchy trigger fingers.

The steak-eater pointed the knife and made a jabbing motion that reminded Cass of Reba and her Barbie doll. "Hey, fella, I done time. I done *plenty* of time."

"Where at?" retorted Wyatt.

"Uh . . . Alcatraz," said the steak-eater.

Muriel suppressed a grin and a passing busboy, who'd overheard the exchange, almost dropped an armload of dishes.

"What, you worked there as a tour guide?" Wyatt said. "Or maybe you had a job shovelin' birdshit off the rocks? Man, the closest you ever come to doin' time is stepping inside a cell to get your picture took in the Territorial Prison Museum."

"Well, it's nothin' to be *ashamed* of," complained the pie-eater, although no one was listening. "Man ain't done time don't mean he's less of a man."

Spoken, thought Cass, like a true virgin to the Department of Corrections.

"Well, somebody's gonna do some serious time for killing that gal," said Muriel, scooping tip money off the counter. "What was her name? Carol?"

"Carlie," said the pie-eater. "Like Carly Simon."

"That don't sound right," said Muriel. "I think it was Carol."

She went to the window and lifted out a steak and salad plate, which she set before Cass. "It was CharLee," Cass said.

"CharLee," yelled Muriel, as though placing an order. "This gal says her name's CharLee."

"Naw, it was Carly," said the pie-eater.

The waitress looked at Cass, said loudly enough to be heard at the end of the counter. "He don't know nothin'. Been comin' in here for years and still calls me Miriam."

"I know this," said a voice so cracked and gravelly it could only have come from a chain smoker's ruined larynx, "whoever killed that woman, ain't gonna do time." It was the bedraggled man at the other end of the counter, the one Cass had avoided sitting beside when she came in. He was dunking the last of a bear claw into a cup of coffee. The stool next to him was still empty, although people occasionally cruised past looking for seats.

"Box Car, you want some more coffee? 'Nother bear claw?" said Muriel kindly, approaching with the pot, but the bushy-faced man waved her off with a scowl. His tortured voice rose. "Only people do time in this town are those that don't have money to pay off the law. The law's fucked up in this town. Crooked as an L.A. lawyer. Fucked. Up."

The pie-eater, who was nearest the speaker, wiped his mouth with a napkin, slapped some money on the counter, and stood up.

"Box Car, what've I told you about that kinda rough talk?" Muriel said. "You gonna talk like that, you gotta take your dirty mouth elsewhere."

She might as well have said have a nice day.

"In this town, the law thinks it's God Jehovah all-fucking-mighty," the shaggy man raved on. "The Lord giveth and the Lord taketh away. The Law don't like the way you look, the Law don't like the way you smell, then the Law gonna beat the shit out of you. Whether you done nothin' or not, the Law gonna fuck you *up*."

"That's it, Box Car, you're outa here," said Muriel.

"You don't owe me for the coffee and the bear claw, just go."

"No, ma'am, I pay my own way." He began digging in his pockets for change. He threw a few coins on the table and grinned, showing chipped and missing front teeth. "Don't have no money for the tip, Muriel. Maybe I oughta stay and work it off, huh? Wash dishes?"

She shook her head, bubble hair bouncing vehemently, her hands loaded with plates. "You don't owe me nothin' other than an apology, Box Car. Just go."

"Won't lemme wash dishes for my food? Whatsamatter, scared I'll piss in the soup when your back's turned?"

"Goddamned drunk," the steak-eater muttered to Cass. "Lives on the streets. Hassles people for change. Can't believe in a town where the big industry is prisons they don't have a cell for this guy."

"Box Car, you listening to me?" Muriel set the plates down so hard a couple of French fries flipped in the air. "You leave right now or I'm calling the cops."

"Cops?"

"That's what I said."

"I'll call 'em for you," said Wyatt, brandishing a cell phone instead of a pistol.

"The hell kinda place is this a man can't speak his own mind?" Box Car slid off the stool, stuffing the remains of the bear claw in his mouth and washing it down with the dregs of his coffee, most of which sloshed into his beard. He gave the empty coffee cup a push that sent it careening down the counter, where it collided with the steak-eater's coffee cup and turned it askew. Both cups fell to the floor. Crockery shattered at Muriel's feet and cascaded across the countertop while Box Car stormed toward the door.

"Shit," said the steak-eater, leaping up before the hot liquid could reach him.

Cass grabbed a handful of napkins from the dispenser

and started sopping up the mess while a busboy came out of the kitchen with a broom to clean up the floor.

Muriel grabbed the cell phone from Wyatt's hand. "Don't call the cops on him, hon. He's gone now, no real harm done."

"You sure?" said Wyatt, disappointed. "Seems to me he was drunk and disorderly."

"Yeah, but he's a sick man. Cirrhosis of the liver's gonna take him out before long anyway," said Muriel. "I don't want to cause him more trouble." She turned to Cass. "Here, let me get you another salad. You hardly touched that, and now it's all full of coffee."

"Appreciate it," said Cass, sliding off her stool. "Don't clear my plate away, I'm coming right back."

She hurried outside, realized as soon as the dazzle of sun struck her retinas that she'd left her sunglasses on the countertop next to her plate. Holding a hand over her eyes, squinting, she scanned the parking lot and the sidewalk beyond it, then turned in the other direction. Box Car was ambling across the alley behind the café, heading for a spot of shade under an elm tree in a nearby backyard.

"Hey there!"

His head jerked around and a look of trapped agitation, the uncertainty of whether to flee or fight or try to charm his way out of harm's way, flickered over his ruined features. It was a look Cass knew well. As a child, she had seen it on the faces of some of the men who had gambled—and lost—to her father. The look of a debtor when he saw Johnny Lumetto drive up in his sparkling red Cadillac convertible or when, in the midst of a meal, that same debtor saw Johnny walk into Luigi's on Detroit's east side with his little daughter and son—a dozen emotions vying for supremacy in an effort to hide the one overriding reaction which was fear, cold and primitive.

"They were pretty rough on you in there," Cass said, establishing at once whose side she was on. "You shouldn't have had to leave."

His piercing black eyes bored into her from beneath one long band of eyebrow that thinned only slightly above the nose. As she approached, he hugged his sweater more tightly around himself, his hands groping around inside the pockets in ways Cass found both unsavory and unsettling. Despite the fact that it was bright daylight and she was within sight of the guard towers of one of the state's largest prisons, she felt very alone.

Digging into her shoulderbag, she produced a five-dollar bill. "Here, the next coffee and bear claw's on me."

"You know I'll just go get drunk with it." He grinned as if daring her to rescind the offer.

"Up to you."

His hands stayed in his pockets while he glared at the money. "You think I'm just an old bum."

To say no would be patronizing. To say yes was a trap. "Hey, you don't want the money, fine," said Cass, pocketing the bill. "You said the law here is fucked up. I want to know what you meant."

"You better be careful, you asking this kind of question. They'll fuck you up, too." His right hand came out of his pocket with startling speed, revealing a pint bottle with an inch of clear liquid inside. He unscrewed the cap, tilted it to his chapped lips.

She thought about Jack's uncertainty about whether he'd killed Melinda. "Have you ever known anyone who's been framed? Or maybe the opposite—someone who got away with murder?"

He gaped at her as if she were the one wearing a trench coat in the middle of summer, filthy and stinking of perspiration and piss, before wiping his mouth with the back of one soiled-looking hand. "Law don't like you, they don't come arrest you," he said. "Law catches you alone and beats your face in. *That's* what I mean, lady. That specific enough for you?"

"No, it's not," said Cass. "Who are you talking about?"

He turned away from her, eyeing the tree and its offer of shade, and started stumbling toward it. "About that money?" he said.

Cass's fingers scooted into the pocket and produced the five-dollar bill. "Here you go."

He snatched it like a hungry animal taking food from fingers it doesn't quite trust, then added, apparently having already forgotten his earlier comment, "Bear claws gettin' to be expensive these days."

"Oh, really?" She found another five-dollar bill and gave it to him. "That should keep you in bear claws for a while. Now tell me what it is you're talking about."

"No, ma'am, I don't think so." He grinned. "I ate, I drank, now it's gettin' to be my nap time."

Grinning, he shambled over to the tree, leaned against the trunk, and eased his way down to the grass where he sat blinking up at Cass with liquor-dulled eyes. "Gotta sleep now," he said, waving her away.

"Hey, what is this? I just gave you ten bucks. Now I want something in return. Come on, you're a fair man."

He gave a drunken snort. "Now where the hell'd you get that idea? I'm not a fair man, no, ma'am, not by a long shot. Ask my ex-wives."

"Fine." She shrugged, turned away. She was still hungry and anxious to get back to her steak. This had been a wild goose chase.

His gravel-against-slate voice came after her. "You want *fair*?"

"For ten bucks? Yeah. I sure as hell do."

"Loomy-bastard."

For a second, she thought he was saying *loony*. Then she got it—Loomy. "Loomis? Are you talking about a detective named Shep Loomis?"

He sucked from the bottle, then giggled uproariously. "Piss on his boots. Loomy-bastard got piss on his boots."

"Piss on his boots? What does that mean? What are you talking about?"

His head dropped onto his chest so quickly that she

was sure he was faking in order to avoid further questions.

"Hey, I asked you a question."

He expelled air from his lips, making a blubbering sound that was followed by the rattle of snoring.

She stood there a moment, frustrated and perplexed, while his snoring deepened and the empty bottle slipped from his hand, pouring a few drops onto the lawn.

Shep Loomis? Piss on his boots?

She started back toward the café and was going up the short flight of stairs to the double glass doors when Wyatt came out. He was cupping and lighting a cigarette, a small action that showed off the bulge of his biceps to advantage.

"Hey, I wondered where you'd run off to. Hope you didn't let the town drunk scare you off."

"I'm from New York," Cass said. "If that's all you've got in the way of a town drunk, I'd say you're doing pretty good."

"New York, huh? What're you doing out here, sightseeing or what?"

She berated herself for having opened the door to chitchat with the line about New York. Or maybe her subconscious had been speaking for her—the guy needed to lose the mustache but he did have great arms.

"I've got friends in the area," she said vaguely. Despite the heat, she felt a kiss of cold on the back of her neck. Started to turn around.

"Not that area over there?" Wyatt said, exhaling smoke as he gestured toward the tower of the penitentiary that was just visible over the tree line. Behind the glass, Cass knew, a guard was standing, gun in hand. Did that account for the momentary feeling of being watched?

"Look," he said, "how 'bout I take you out to dinner tonight. Then I'll take you around, show you some sights tourists don't get to see."

"And I'll bet you could, too," said Cass in a voice
that, to her own ears, sounded surprisingly syrupy. She
was suddenly, uncomfortably, reminded of how CharLee
had sounded flirting with Willy in the Black Bear Saloon. Of how Opal had sounded when she gushed
about her upcoming wedding to Frank. *Am I starting
to mimic these women?*

"How 'bout it then?" said Wyatt.

"Thanks, but no, I gotta go now," she said quickly.
She went back inside, feeling flustered, wondering
what had possessed her to flirt with a complete
stranger.

By the time she got back to the counter, the conversation had switched from CharLee's murder to the
Av's chances for a Stanley Cup win over the Detroit
Redwings. The steak-eater to her left had been replaced by a grumpy, soup-gobbling little old man, and
Cass finished her meal in silence. She decided to pass
on the blueberry pie—the conversation with Box Car
had diminished her appetite—paid her bill, and lit up
a cigarette as she strolled back outside to see if by
any chance the vagrant was awake and willing to talk
to her some more.

He was gone, though, a patch of grass flattened out
beneath the tree where he'd been sleeping the only
evidence that he'd ever been there.

She took a deep drag on her cigarette, exhaled a
small, satisfying cloud of toxins, and headed back to
her car. She was reaching into her purse for the key
when, only a few feet away from the Duchess, she
stopped cold. The driver's side door was ajar and a
deep jagged scratch extended from the front fender to
the rear of the back door.

"Jesus!" She threw down her cigarette and grabbed
the driver's side door. She'd left the car locked but
now, to her dismay, the door opened, revealing the
glove compartment in front of the passenger seat was
agape. She'd left some change and a couple of twenty-
dollar bills inside—that was gone now except for a

few coins scattered on the floor that the thief hadn't bothered to take. Much worse was the fact that her cell phone, which she'd left on the seat next to her, was gone, too.

Whoever'd jimmied the car door had known what they were doing, that was for sure. The lot was crowded and people were coming and going from the café all the time—he'd had to work fast.

But the worst was when she walked around the car, checking for more damage, and saw what had been scrawled on the passenger door, crudely printed and hastily done but unmistakable, the word *cunt* keyed into the paint job.

Chapter 9

On Sunday morning, knowing she'd be going to the eleven o'clock service at the Church of Good Hope, Cass got up early, went for a five-mile run, then came back to her room to shower and change. The maid, a petite, talkative Hispanic with intricately braided hair, came by with fresh towels. On a whim, Cass asked if she knew of any Catholic churches nearby. The maid said there was a nine a.m. Mass at the Holy Abbey, only two miles away, so Cass changed into a cotton skirt and sleeveless silk blouse and drove there in the white Caprice she'd rented while the Duchess was in the shop being repaired and repainted.

The mechanics at the shop where she'd taken the car had seemed more outraged by the vandalism than the cops she'd reported the crime to. A patrol car with two officers, a stout, bored-looking woman named Conners and a dark-skinned man named Turel, had finally shown up and the facts, such as they were, taken down, but little hope was held out that the perpetrator would ever be found. She'd described the motorcycle rider who'd tailed her the day before, but without a license plate number or a witness putting him at the scene, the cops made it clear there wasn't a lot they could do.

"Call your insurance company," Turel had said, and Conners recommended the body shop where the car was now being repaired.

The frustrations of the previous day still lingered as she drove the Budget Caprice toward the Abbey. She kept thinking about the Duchess. Even though it was actually her father's car, she always drove it when she visited him. It was the car she'd learned to drive in as a teenager, a classic car that she knew would someday become hers. Thinking about what had been done to it made her seethe.

She hoped going to Mass would provide a soothing transition between her irritable mood and the obligatory visit to the Church of Good Hope later that morning.

Built in 1924, the Holy Abbey was a spectacular Tudor Gothic cathedral that Cass had first seen when she passed by it on her way into Canon City on Highway 50. Although her attendance at Mass was sporadic—in New York she occasionally frequented a small Benedictine Abbey in Chelsea where the monks were welcoming and the coffee shop brewed up an excellent Colombian blend—there was something she found reassuring in the traditional Mass, the exotic scent of the incense, the priests in their robes and vestments, the ritual of Holy Communion.

She arrived at the Holy Abbey a few minutes late and enjoyed a Mass conducted by an elderly priest who kept the sermon both brief and heartfelt. She tried to muster some willingness to pray for the person who'd keyed her car, but ended up praying for something else entirely: the knowledge of who had done it and why and, once she found out, the wisdom to know what to do about it.

Then, once started, she found herself on something of a roll. She prayed for Twyla, that she might get to see her father, and for her own father, that he might be relieved of the lust for gambling, and for her brother, wherever he was and whatever he was doing, that he might be safe and happy. She'd been told once by a priest that there was no need to pray for the souls of the dead, that they were either with God or they weren't, but praying for the dead was something that seemed natural to her, that felt right, so she prayed for the soul of her mother.

Finally, she asked forgiveness for herself and for the lie that she was perpetrating. *Forgive me for letting Jack think I'm in love with him. If he murdered Raven, then let him tell me the truth soon. And if he didn't, then please God, let me find out who did.*

She was feeling better when she left the cathedral, although not especially thrilled at the prospect of a second service at the Church of Good Hope, but she'd promised Jack she'd attend. Besides, this had been Raven's church, too, at least at the end of her life. She thought that understanding what the attraction to fundamentalist religion had been might provide her with some clue as to what kind of life Raven had been leading at the end, what sort of person she'd become that was so different from the free-spirited, highly sexed woman Cass remembered.

She was crossing the Abbey's beautifully manicured lawn and had stopped to admire a small statue of Mary when she heard her name called and turned to see Detective Loomis striding toward her. He wore a crisply starched white shirt, gray trousers, and cowboy boots so black she was surprised they didn't leave smudge marks on the grass. The expression on his face suggested he was making a concerted effort to project amiability and goodwill.

"Well, this is a surprise," said Cass, trying to keep her voice and face neutral, not indicating what sort of surprise she took this to be. Since he appeared to have come from the Abbey, she assumed he, too, had attended the service. "For some reason, Detective, I wouldn't have pegged you for a churchgoer."

"Good instincts," he said, " 'cause I'm not."

"Gave it up or never were?"

"I was brought up Baptist, but it didn't take. Now I guess you could say I'm agnostic."

"Meaning all you believe in is that you don't know what to believe in?"

"You could say that. Least I know nothing I believe in or don't believe in is worth ramming down anybody else's throat." He tried to smile as he said it, but there was an edge of bitterness to his voice that belied any lightness of tone.

"Spoken like a man whose parents dragged him to church kicking and screaming."

"My parents didn't much care if I went to church or not—I wasn't the best kid and I think they just hoped I'd stay out of jail. But I've met people who have got me convinced that religion goes to some people's heads like a drug. It's like trying to sit down for a drink with a practicing alcoholic and ordering a Coke—they give you a look like you just spit on the flag. When it comes to God, it's their way or the highway."

"So what *does* bring you here," said Cass, "if not the stirring sermon?"

"I was looking for you."

"Me? How did you know where I was?"

"Relax," he said, "I'm not a stalker, and I'm not into the psychic hotline. I stopped by your motel room just now. The maid's a chatty type—she told me you'd gone here to the nine a.m. Mass without my even having to ask."

Somehow Cass doubted that, but she let it slide. "So what's up? Any news about CharLee?"

"Unfortunately no. There's some reason to think whoever killed her may have murdered before, though, so you know the precautions—keep you door locked and don't open it for anyone you don't know. Plus I'd give some thought to moving out of that motel."

"It's convenient to the prison," said Cass, although Loomis was now the third person who'd advised her to move out of the Mountain View, Kenny and Jack being the others.

"The place CharLee St. John was staying was convenient, too."

"Don't worry, I'm careful. But thanks for your concern."

"Meaning it's none of my business, right?" he said good-naturedly.

She smiled in spite of herself. "Something like that. So tell me, Detective, why *did* you come looking for me?"

"I saw you'd called in a report yesterday that your car had been broken into and vandalized in the parking lot of the Pioneer Café. The officers that came out filed a pretty thorough report, but I wanted to check it out personally. And, to tell you the truth, I wanted to apologize. My attitude the other day was way out of line. Your personal life is nobody's business but your own. I was being judgmental because, well, 'cause I know Jack O'Doul and I don't like him, but I shouldn't have unloaded on you. I'm sorry."

Cass thought for a moment, then said, "Apology accepted. Now let me ask you a question. Do you know anybody named Box Car?"

"Box Car? Sure, everybody in town knows Box Car. He used to be a good jazz musician, believe it or not, before the booze made mush of his brain. How the hell did you meet *him*?"

"He was in the parking lot of the café the other day. I didn't say anything to the officers who came out, but I wondered if you think he could have been the one who broke into my car and vandalized it."

"I'd say not likely. First off, whoever broke into your vehicle knew what they were doing and worked fast and efficiently with some kind of tool. The Box Car I know, he'd have trouble unlocking a car if you gave him the keys. Second, the word that was scratched into the paint job, that's not his style. He's a drunk and a public nuisance, but I've never known him to be vicious."

"Have you ever arrested him?"

Loomis grinned, laugh lines crinkling white against his deeply tanned skin. "Sure, lots of times."

"Enough for him to have a particular dislike for you?"

"Why? Did he say something about me?"

"He thinks the law in Canon City is . . . well . . . corrupt. And he said something peculiar about you."

She waited for a reaction, but the only look that crossed the detective's face was one of what appeared to be genuine puzzlement. "What was that?"

"He said you have piss on your boots."

A deep crease indented the space between Loomis's eyes. For just a second, Cass thought his gaze wavered, that his pupils darted sideways toward the statue of the Virgin that stood serenely, palms and face turned upward, a few feet away. He seemed to be thinking. Then he shrugged, shook his head as though to clear it.

"Piss on my boots? You got me. Only thing I can figure is maybe he'd *like* to piss on 'em—he's not a big fan of law enforcement, to put it mildly—or maybe he's got me confused with some of the legions of cops who've arrested him for public urination at one time or another."

"That must be it," Cass said, wanting to feel relieved but secretly wondering if the explanation wasn't a little too glib.

"So you don't lead a secret life as a vigilante, going around beating up vagrants who then take out their frustrations on your footwear?"

She'd been making a joke, but Loomis didn't look amused. There was an edge to his voice as he said, "Believe me, Ms. Lumetto, I wouldn't last long as a detective if that was the case."

"I'm glad to hear it. And while we're at it, why don't you call me Cass?"

"Cass, it is. About your car, though, I'll ask around, see what I can find out. The b and e part, that's not uncommon, especially since your cell phone was in view, but a word scratched into the door, that's a little more off the wall. It's not like you've been in town long enough to make enemies."

"I work fast."

He grinned and looked at his watch. "Have you had breakfast yet? I know a place up the road, and I promise I'll keep an eye on your car."

"I'd like that," said Cass, "but believe it or not, I'm on my way to another church service."

"Whoa, what are you, in training for the convent?" He put a hand on her arm, a touch that was brief, tentative, but still intensely pleasurable. She was aware of his cologne now, a woodsy aroma she associated with campfires and ski lodges and sex in hot tubs with steam rising up out of the water.

"A convent? My mother would have wished, but not likely."

"Glad to hear *that*," said Loomis. "You were scaring me with all this talk about churchgoing."

She decided to tease him a little. "And why would that be, Detective?"

He seemed caught off guard, maybe not expecting such forwardness from a woman he'd intercepted leaving Mass. "Well, for starters, I was thinking I'd like to take you fly-fishing sometime. Any woman who can identify a dragonfly nymph on sight, now that's something special. I'll even throw in a supply of my own hand-tied flies."

"I think I'd like that." She began to walk toward her car. "Now I'd better get going. Give me a raincheck on breakfast?"

"Anytime."

"Great." He could have left it at that, but instead apparently felt compelled to add, "If we go fly-fishing, you sure your boyfriend won't mind?"

She bit back the urge to say something sarcastic, decided to play it straight—more or less. "Like I told you the other day, Jack and I are friends. I don't report to him with everything I do nor does he expect me to. And even if he *did* expect me to, that doesn't mean I would."

"Good. Then how about if I call you, say, middle of next week?"

"I've got your card, Detective," she said. "How about I call *you*?"

Although only about ten minutes away from the Holy Abbey in drive time, the Church of Good Hope was eons away in terms of grandeur and sublime spiritual architecture. Occupying a half block in a modest residential neighborhood between Tenth and Eleventh Streets, the church's brick and cinder-block facade was one of austerity and resolute, almost deliberate plainness. Once inside the simple wooden doors, though, Cass found the interior much more warm and welcoming, due in no small part to the delicious odors of food cooking that wafted up from the basement.

When Cass told the white-haired greeter at the front door that she wanted to help with the soup kitchen, she was shepherded downstairs to where a dozen or so parishioners, Opal Brady among them, were busy preparing a hearty-looking brunch of scrambled eggs, bacon, hashed browns, and biscuits and setting out a variety of baked goods. Opal left her post frying up hashed browns long enough to give Cass a hug and a welcome and to commiserate with her about CharLee. Butterworth himself, imposing in a billowing white apron that looked large enough to power a sailboat, hovered over the stove, frying bacon. Others were spreading red and white checkered oilcloth over the cafeteria-style tables.

Outside a partially opened side door, Cass could see a line of people snaking around the side of the building, waiting to get in.

"Cass, great to see you here!" boomed Butterworth. "We can always use another pair of hands."

A pretty, curly-haired woman with soft-looking lips and an infectious smile handed Cass an apron. "I'm

Linda Lomax," she said, "you can help me over here with the serving when people start coming in." She then introduced Cass to the tall, ropey fellow making coffee as her husband Jim and to an even taller, ganglier version of the father, their twenty-three-year-old son Judd.

"Judd just got back from Thailand," said Linda proudly. "He was in the Peace Corps over there helping people build schools."

"Terrific," said Cass.

"I loved it," Judd said. "I want to go back."

Linda said pointedly, "Well, it was fine Christian work, but his dad and I sure are happy he's back home safe and sound. We're hoping he'll find a job here in town."

His mother's comment obviously didn't sit well with Judd, who turned away and started banging canisters of salt and pepper down on the tables as though he were hammering nails.

"He wants to go back and *live* over there, can you imagine?" Linda whispered to Cass. "Helping out for a couple of years, that's one thing but to go back to live permanently—his dad and I are just sick about it."

"He's young," Cass said, "it's his time to have adventures."

"You don't understand," said Linda, tears forming in the corners of her eyes, "those people over there where Judd was, they aren't Christian. They're Buddhists. They haven't found the Lord."

"Oh, really?" said Cass.

She was glad when the conversation was interrupted by someone opening up the side door, allowing those lined up outside to file in. She was surprised at the number of women and children, whole families down on their luck. She kept looking down the line, hoping to spot Box Car—surely he wouldn't let a free meal slip by—but she saw no sign of him.

For about twenty minutes, people kept filing past and Cass served up helpings of scrambled eggs. Many people wolfed down their meals and left immediately, causing Cass to ask Linda why the free meal wasn't served after the sermon—and used as an incentive to get people to come to church.

"Oh, that's the way it *used* to be before the Reverend Butterworth and his wife Fiona took over the ministry here," said Linda, her admiration for the couple shining through. "The reverend doesn't want hungry people to have to sit through a service they don't want to listen to just to get food. We feed folks, no strings attached. If they want to stay and hear the message, they'll listen better on a full stomach than an empty one." She nodded in the direction of a slender, brightly dressed woman with waist-length black hair who was crossing the room carrying a tray load of dishes. "There's the reverend's wife now. Fiona Running Bear."

The woman Linda pointed out didn't just walk across the room—she flowed, ankle-length skirt eddying in swells of forest-green above moccasin-clad feet, bangles clanking at her wrists, elaborate beaded earrings swishing out from beneath the sleek hair. She wore a fringed and beaded leather medicine bag across her chest.

"Running Bear?" said Linda. "I didn't realize the reverend's wife was Native American."

Linda gave a small smile. "She's not. She's from somewhere in upstate New York and her maiden name, I think, was O'Roarke. She adopted the name Running Bear when she was living on a commune out in California. She was, you know, a hippie. This was years ago, of course, before she found Christ."

"Or her husband?"

"Him, too."

"Well, the Native American look becomes her," said Cass. "She does a good job of pulling it off."

"I think she has a background in acting," said Linda, as though that explained it. "She's a bit flamboyant, but she has a wonderful spirit." She grinned.

"Anybody who thinks Christians are all solemn and serious Bible-thumpers has only to look at Fiona."

As though to add emphasis to Linda's remark, a teenage boy who was wiping down tables passed by them and Cass got a glimpse of his T-shirt.

"Did that say what I think it did?"

Linda laughed. " 'Born to Raze Hell'?"

"Eyecatching, I'll give it that."

"Some people thought it was scandalous—to have the word hell on a T-shirt—when Reverend Butterworth came up with the idea, but the youth group loved it and pretty soon the parents did, too, when they realized it meant a commitment to not drinking, not lying or stealing, not having sex outside of marriage, and encouraging friends to hold to the same high standards."

"So 'razing hell'—demolishing hell—is their way of saying they aren't going to give in to temptation?"

"Plus the other side of the coin, which is not just avoiding sin but actively engaging in acts of love." She spied a woman she knew moving down the line with a toddler. "Hi, Maggie! How you doin' this week? How's CherylAnne?"

The woman's face brightened and she and Linda talked for a few moments before she got her food and moved on.

"Anyway," Linda continued, serving up some more hashbrowns, "Judd was leader of the church's youth group for three years straight before he joined the Peace Corps." She lowered her voice. "I know the idea behind the Peace Corps is a good one, but I think it's confused him terribly about his faith. His dad and I are at our wits end." She took advantage of a lull in the line to ask, "What about you, Cass? The reverend said you're a friend of Jack O'Doul's, God bless him. Does that mean you're a Christian or just trying to make up your mind?"

She had an answer already prepared for that. "Let's just say I'm searching for answers."

"We'll sit down sometime and I'll tell you how I came to know Jesus," Linda said. "Because you know it isn't really how long any of us lives or how well we live or even how often we give in to temptation—everyone sins—but how well and truly we love the Lord. That's what counts. And by the way, when you see Jack please tell him my whole family sends our regards. We miss him and keep him in our prayers."

"Thank you, I'll do that."

"What a tragedy that was when Jack's wife died," Linda went on. "I only met her a few times—after she and Jack separated, she stopped attending—but what a sweet woman she seemed to be. And what a dear little girl."

"This church has had some hard times all right," Cass said. "Jack told me another woman was killed only about six months before Melinda. Raven somebody."

"Raven Sterling?" Linda directed a dollop of hash browns so hastily that they almost missed the plate they were aimed at. "Oh, heavens, now *that* was another tragedy. What a beautiful woman Raven was, just striking-looking, tall and slender—the young men, Judd included when he came home for Christmas, couldn't take their eyes off her. I've thought about Raven a lot since her death, about how thin the line is between souls that are saved and souls that are lost. I've even talked to Judd about her."

"I don't understand," said Cass. "It sounds as if you're saying Raven's murder was even more tragic than Melinda O'Doul's."

"Well, it *was*," said Linda. "Melinda O'Doul died a Christian, so her soul went straight to Jesus. Raven came here to this very church and renounced her faith before she was killed." For a moment, all the merriment drained from Linda's eyes. She looked stricken and profoundly afraid. "She died a non-Christian, Cass. She's burning in hell."

Cass mumbled something and turned back to her

serving, but not without her eyes first flashing to Butterworth and the bacon strips sizzling and curling in a
pan full of grease. She had a vision of damned souls
as bacon strips—an image at once so horrific and ludi-
crous that she had to bite the inside of her cheek to
keep from erupting in hysterical giggles.

A few minutes later, the line petered out, still with
no appearance by Box Car. Disappointed, Cass helped
Linda and the others clean up while Reverend Butterworth shed his apron and disappeared upstairs to pre-
pare for the eleven o'clock service. Opal stopped her
on the way upstairs, wanting to share the latest news
about her upcoming wedding to Frank and his chances
of being paroled, but Cass listened only half-
heartedly—she was thinking about what Linda had
said, wondering not so much why Raven had changed
her mind about her new religious beliefs but why
someone Cass remembered as seeming so ill-suited to
fundamentalist religion had embraced such beliefs in
the first place.

Well, people change, she thought as Opal babbled
away.

They walked upstairs and were deciding where to
sit when Cass felt a hand on her arm.

"You're Cass?" the dark-haired woman said, flashing white teeth framed in meticulously painted crimson lips. She extended a hand. "I'm Fiona
Butterworth. Claude told me he met you at the prison
the other day."

The two women shook hands. Fiona said, "I know
the service is about to start, but frankly I've heard all
Claude's sermons before. What I'd really like right
now is a chance to get to know you better, take some
time for girl talk." She put a hand on Cass's forearm.
"After all, we have a lot in common."

"We do?"

"Of course we do." Fiona's hand moved a little
higher up Cass's arm. "His name's *Jack O'Doul.*"

Chapter 10

The choir had already begun the introductory hymn when Butterworth heard a timid knock on the door of his study. He went to the door, assuming it was Fiona stopping by to hurry him along, but instead he found Judd Lomax. The tall, lanky young man wore gray dress slacks, a short-sleeved blue shirt with the start of sweat stains under the arms, and a slightly darker blue tie. A gold earring gleamed in his left lobe. His dark eyes met the minister's for only an instant before he looked away, focusing on some imaginary vista at Butterworth's back.

"Reverend Butterworth?" He cleared his throat in a manner that suggested some large obstruction blocking his windpipe. The words seemed to come hard. "Can I speak with you a minute?"

Butterworth felt both disappointed that the person at the door hadn't proved to be Fiona and annoyed that Judd would try to catch him at so inconvenient a time.

But he genuinely liked Judd, and he admired Judd's parents, whom he knew had grave concerns for the boy, so he put on his best avuncular smile and said, "I've been wanting to talk with you, too, Judd, but can it wait just a bit? The Lord may be patient, but the parishioners aren't, and I've got a service to lead. How about you come back afterward when we won't be so rushed?"

The boy's Adam's apple bounced in his neck. "I can't do that, Reverend. I'm not going to stay for the service. I'm going home."

"But you're supposed to be reading from the Psalms."

"I'm sorry. I can't do that."

"Is something wrong? Are you ill?"

Judd finally tore his eyes away from whatever he found so compelling at Butterworth's back. Eye contact finally established, he set his chin and pressed on. "I can't do the reading, Reverend, because it would be hypocritical. I can't be a member here any longer, because I'm no longer a Christian."

Butterworth was aghast. "You can't mean that, Judd. You don't understand the consequences of what you're saying."

Butterworth knew instantly that it was the wrong thing to say, that belittling the boy's understanding of his own words would only enflame his misguided zeal, but he couldn't seem to stop himself. He wanted to say something caustic about the earring as well, but fortunately held back further comments.

"All paths lead to God and maybe this one is right for you," Judd persisted, "but it's the wrong one for me. I think Jesus was a great man and a holy man, like Buddha, but your preaching distorts what he said."

He had to force himself not to grab the boy by the shoulders and shake him. "In what way, Judd?"

"Jesus taught tolerance and acceptance and love for everybody, not just the people in your own little group. His God wasn't a punishing tyrant that had everybody scared shi—scared to death. I think Jesus would be totally bummed out if He could hear you up there every Sunday."

Butterworth felt his face flush. "Have you shared these ideas with your parents?"

"My parents, right." Having gotten past his initial fear of the reverend, the boy was now gaining momentum. "What I figure, you know, me being born to my parents, is some kind of karmic punishment. Either that or I had a connection to them in a previous life and now I'm supposed to lead them to a higher form of spirituality."

"My God, Judd." Butterworth reeled at such blasphemy. He felt as stunned as if he'd been slammed face first into a wall. "How long have you felt this way?"

"Since I got back from Thailand, I've been doing a lot of reading. Books on Buddhism, Hinduism, the Perennial Philosophy. A lot of things I never questioned before, I do now. I see that what you and my parents believe is narrow-minded and wrong."

"Stop," said Butterworth. "I don't have time to discuss something of this importance now, but after the service we'll sit down and hash it out. I assure you it's normal for young people to ask questions, but you're way off base on this, Judd. You need guidance and I can give it to you. Just let me explain a few things—"

"No," said Judd, holding up a hand. "There's nothing to explain. I respect your right and my parents' right to believe what you choose, but I've found the only way that makes sense to me, and that's the Noble Eightfold Path of Buddhism."

"That's the Devil talking," Butterworth said. "You're a bright young man, and the Devil knows that, so he appeals to your intellect. God knows he's tried it with me. He tells you there're a variety of paths to God, each one equally valid, but that's a lie. There is no other path but Jesus, no other path but the one true way of Christ. All other roads lead to damnation."

"Bullshit," said Judd, rolling his eyes. "You're just like my parents. You don't hear me. It's like your mind's frozen in cement."

The disrespect, the earring, even the mixed metaphor—all combined to make Butterworth furious. The ledge Judd was perched on was narrow and crumbling. His tragic plummet was all but assured.

"Please, Judd, you're wrong. Hear me out—"

"No, I should go now. I've said more than I meant to. Plus I'm making you late for the service."

"Wait, boy, *please,* your soul depends on this, your immortal soul . . ."

But Judd strode away, head down, shoulders hunched as though the minister's words fell over him like invisible blows. Butterworth stood there for a second, his hands clamped to the doorjamb, his breath coming in gasps. A clammy sweat poured off his forehead.

The choir was finishing the last verse of the opening hymn for the second time, ending with a rousing crescendo that all but implored Butterworth to make his appearance.

Showtime, whether he liked it or not.

And no sign of Fiona, either.

Feeling profoundly battered, as if he were trudging off to go to war for the souls of infidels whose need for salvation was equaled only by their profound ingratitude, Butterworth hefted his Bible and marched off to do battle from the pulpit.

Although Cass hadn't been able to see it from where she'd parked, around the corner from the church was a tiny, triangular park dotted with oak trees and small shrubs. A duck pond where a couple of mallards floated shimmered in its center. It reminded her of the parks one sometimes found in New York City—little jewels of green appearing unexpectedly in the middle of a cluster of brownstones or office buildings.

"I love to come here sometimes while Claude's preaching," Fiona was saying. She had a light, lilting voice and crystal-clear, tinkling laughter that seemed to belong to a much younger woman. "It's my little oasis. I bring my Bible and some bread to feed the ducks and I just . . . escape into my own mind."

"And your husband doesn't mind that you don't stay for his sermons?"

"Oh, I get enough of his sermons at home," said Fiona, laughing, and although her smile seemed genuine enough, Cass got the sense of hidden rancor.

Fiona selected a grassy spot near the edge of the pond, tucked her long gypsy skirt underneath her, and sat down. Cass, feeling a bit uncomfortable but not knowing what else to do, did likewise.

"So you're Jack's latest conquest," said Fiona, smoothing her skirt out, all girlish smiles.

"Conquest isn't the word I'd use. Let's just say we're good friends."

"Claude tells me you're from New York City. That's about as far removed from Jack's world as Mars. How on earth did you and he meet?"

Cass tried to conceal her discomfort at having to repeat the "official" story of her and Jack's meeting, how she'd been so smitten with his good looks that she started writing to him in prison on the basis of a photo in a newspaper. Each time she repeated it, the story sounded less plausible, but Fiona seemed to accept it. Maybe, with women like Opal in the congregation who visited and fell in love with convicts, Fiona saw nothing unusual in this scenario.

"So tell me, how *is* Jack?"

"About as well as can be expected under the circumstances. But I thought you and Reverend Butterworth both ministered to the inmates. You must see Jack yourself from time to time."

Fiona gave an enigmatic smile. In the bright sunlight, her heavy eye makeup looked troweled on and her lush mouth too thickly painted. "I don't visit Jack when I go to the prison. Claude isn't comfortable with it."

"I don't understand."

From the look on her face, it was obvious Fiona had been waiting for the opening Cass had just provided.

"Well, surely you've noticed that Jack's a very physical person, very sensual. There's an aura of sex that radiates from him so strongly it's like an intoxicant." She turned onto her side and brushed hair from her eyes, a gesture so languid and theatrical that Cass had no trouble believing she had performed onstage. Some kind of stage, anyway. "It must be dreadfully hard for you to visit him, sit with him, touch him, and yet not be able to make love with him."

Cass thought Fiona must be testing her and gave what she understood to be the approved reply. "It wouldn't matter even if Jack weren't in prison. We aren't married, and sex outside of marriage is a sin. Anyway," she added, "there are other ways to be intimate besides sex."

"Of course," said Fiona, "no one knows that any better than I do. In a way, you're fortunate. You have to rely on your fantasies to imagine what Jack's like, not real memories."

Cass, who had been leaning back on her elbows watching the ducks, sat up straighter. "Are you telling me that you and Jack were lovers?"

"For a time," said Fiona, clearly pleased with the idea that she'd shocked Cass. "It was during one of those periods when he and his wife had separated. Jack's a very needy man, sexually and otherwise."

"Not to cast the first stone, Fiona, but isn't that playing a little fast and loose with the Ten Commandments?"

"Being a Christian doesn't mean you're perfect," said Fiona. "Even the strongest Christians sometimes give in to temptations of the flesh."

"Apparently Raven Sterling didn't give in. Isn't that why she told Jack to take a hike?"

For the first time, Fiona's perfectly painted mask of a face betrayed what Cass took to be real emotion. "How do you know about Raven?"

"Jack told me he met her when they were both

attending church here. Sex outside of marriage may be a sin, but that didn't stop him from trying to sleep with her any more than it stopped you from sleeping with him."

"I'm surprised Jack told you that. He's usually not so forthcoming about his . . . past," said Fiona, though she didn't seem to be questioning whether Cass's information might have come from other sources.

"He's opened up to me quite a lot. As time goes on and we get to know each other better, I hope he'll tell me more."

Fiona twisted a garnet ring the size of an olive on her middle finger. "Raven was all wrong for Jack," she said, and there was an undercurrent of spite in her tone that Cass assumed to be jealousy of the younger, more beautiful woman. "I knew it wouldn't last."

"It couldn't very well have lasted, could it? She was murdered."

Fiona smoothed her long black hair, revealing a gold hoop earring big enough to encircle her wrist. "Jack told you that, too? I'm surprised. He used to find her death too painful to talk about. I hope that means time's eased his loss."

"Or *doing* time."

Immediately she regretted being flip, because it gave Fiona an opportunity to feign shock. "Being in prison magnifies grief. He has nothing to do but think—about all he's lost, all he's missing."

"About Raven," said Cass, "did you know her well?"

"Not really. She only attended church here for a few months, but she was distant, not what you'd call friendly. She lost interest in the church about the same time that Jack lost interest in her. Which tells you how sincere she was about her faith."

"That's a harsh judgment, wouldn't you say?"

"Not harsh, just truthful. Claude and I were terribly

saddened by her death. We offered to have the funeral here at the church, but her parents wouldn't hear of it. They're Catholics, I understand. They hate Christians."

As someone raised Catholic, Cass figured she'd have scars on her tongue when this was over, but she said nothing.

Fiona went on, "Raven was a beautiful girl, perhaps too beautiful for her own good. I got the impression she really didn't like men at all, that she used them. But I can understand why Jack was willing to overlook that, why he felt he had to have her no matter what."

"Or maybe he felt if he couldn't have her, then no one else could?"

"You're not implying—? Oh, God, not that lame theory that Jack murdered Raven in some kind of jealous fit? The cops thought that, too. But I can tell you, it's ridiculous. He didn't murder Raven. Personally, I don't even think he killed Melinda. He says he didn't and I believe him." She raised a thinly tweezed eyebrow. "Don't you?"

"I don't know what I believe. But I'm curious, how are you so sure he didn't have anything to do with Raven's death?"

"Because, as I told the police, the night she was murdered, Jack was with me."

"The whole night?"

"Of course not. I'm a married woman, I couldn't stay out the entire night."

"Of course not," said Cass. "What was I thinking?"

"But the police said Raven died no later than midnight and Jack was with me until then. What he did after we parted company, I don't know, but believe me, I know what he *didn't* do was go look for another woman."

Fiona shielded her eyes from the sun and stretched sensuously. She seemed to be enjoying this, and even though Cass knew there was no reason for her to be jealous—what did she care who Jack had slept with?—

when she spoke again, there was an edge of ice to her voice.

"So tell me, Fiona, how do you reconcile being a Christian, married to a minister no less, and having an affair with a married man?"

"Christ doesn't expect perfection," said Fiona. "He only expects us to accept Him as our Lord and Savior and to try to keep His commandments as best we can."

"Sounds like you haven't been trying very hard."

"Don't be so quick to judge. I love the Lord, but that doesn't mean I'm not a human being cursed with having a human body. Christian or not, I have needs."

"Evidently."

Fiona sat up, stretching her bangled wrists out in front of her, and laid a hand over Cass's. "Look, I'm sorry. I seem to have gotten us off on the wrong foot here, and that wasn't at all my intention. I didn't mean to be flaunting my former relationship with Jack or trying to make you jealous. Quite the contrary. I was hoping the fact that having Jack in common would be the bridge to a new friendship."

Her fingers lingered over Cass's wrist. "As soon as Claude told me Jack had a new girlfriend, I wanted to meet you. I'm sure you love Jack—I do, too—but neither one of us can have him, not really. What we do have, though, is a mutual affection and desire for the same man, but the man isn't here—only us."

"You're suggesting *what* exactly, Fiona?"

"Nothing ugly or sordid. Only that at some point some of the love we both feel for Jack might be expressed in other ways." She folded Cass's hand inside hers and gazed into her eyes. "Just because I'm married to Claude doesn't mean I take the Bible as literally as he does."

"We should express our desire for Jack with each other, is that what you're saying?"

"Does that shock you? It shouldn't. I'm not stupid, Cass. I know you're here because Jack asked you to attend his church, and you want to please him, not because you have some burning desire for Jesus."

Her face was inches from Cass, lips parted, eyes bright with something akin to lust, but tainted with an even greater passion, the desire to control and manipulate, to seduce for the sake of seducing.

Cass wanted to recoil from her as though she were riddled with plague, but she said, "You have a point, Fiona. In all honesty, given the choice between a burning bush-type encounter or a roll in the hay with a flesh and blood man, I'm just shallow enough I'd probably take door number two. As far as whatever else you've got in mind, though, forget it. Now please take your hand off my arm."

She stood up, brushed the grass off her skirt. "I'm going back inside the church and try to catch the rest of the sermon. I'm sure whatever the reverend has to say will be stirring enough to erase this little incident from my mind."

For an instant, anger came over Fiona's eyes like a red veil. "You'll be bored silly."

"I'll take the chance."

Butterworth leaned forward and slammed his fist down on the pulpit so hard that it shook.

"The Devil *exists*, my friends, he lives and thrives *in us*. Oh, the non-Christians would have you believe otherwise, but mark my words, it's those who mock the reality of Satan who most please him!"

The words seemed to spill from Butterworth's lips beyond his control. He'd planned a moderate, somewhat upbeat sermon, focusing on the biblical injunction to "be like the lilies of the field" and the difficulty of doing so in today's materialism-infested world. Instead he found himself bracing his hands on the pulpit, spewing out words like rounds of ammo, imploring his audience to beware the Great Deceiver who endangered their very souls.

"I spoke recently with a young person who assured

me that all paths to the Lord are equally true, that
Satan is but a myth, that Christianity is only one
choice at the great buffet table of spirituality. In the
same way that some would have you believe that homosexuality is just a *choice,* just a"—he spit the words
out with contempt—"*lifestyle option* and abortion is
just a *lifestyle option* and fornication outside marriage
is just a *lifestyle option.*

"Well, I'm telling you who believe in these *lifestyle
options*, you are walking the road to damnation. You
are sending your souls straight to hell!

"There is no other path but that of our Lord and
Savior Jesus Christ—to choose otherwise is to choose
to burn in the fiery pit for all eternity!"

On that last note, the breath roared out of him and
he had to pause to collect himself.

He scanned the audience to see if Judd Lomax was
there to be impressed by this, but didn't see the young
man. Jack's lady friend—Cass—was slipping in late,
trying to be unobtrusive by taking a seat in a back
pew. And what about Fiona—why wasn't *she* here?

His vision fogged, and he gripped the pulpit with
white-knuckled hands as the floor seemed to fall away
from under him.

Fiona?

He knew she wasn't here, because, from his new
vantage point up near the ceiling, he had an unob-
structed view of everyone in the church.

Everyone, including himself, standing there at the
pulpit, red-faced and sweating and panting for breath.

The Butterworth watching this display was neither
appalled nor amused, but full of love and sadness.
Like when, as a kid, he'd watched the father he
adored have too much to drink and make a fool of
himself at a picnic. His father was normally a reclu-
sive, rigidly proper man. To watch the spectacle he'd
made of himself on that one occasion had nearly broken Butterworth's heart. That was similar to what he
felt now—a profound and heartfelt sorrow at this pa-

thetic spectacle of a man—himself—ranting and raving like the lost soul that he was about things he knew nothing about. Deceiving and misleading the people listening to him as he spouted lie after lie, to them and to himself.

Then, to Butterworth's shock (or whatever or whomever it was that was watching this madness), the Butterworth-behind-the-pulpit rallied himself and railed on. Us versus them, good versus bad, the godly versus the ungodly, the sinners versus the pure at heart, with no awareness, no inkling, of the monstrousness of the lies that he was propagating.

It's all One, silently spoke the Butterworth up near the ceiling. *It's all God. Christians and Jews, Hindus and atheists, gays and straights, black and white—all manifestations of the one God. Which includes you, Rev. Butterworth, if you'd ever shut up and be silent enough to hear it.*

Then, with a violent tilting and whooshing, the floor cracked apart under Butterworth's feet and a great lamentation, biblical in its force, rose up all around him. Faces—the faces of the damned?—hovering over him like monstrous blooms, and he came back to himself, back *inside* himself, just long enough to think, *Satan, Evil One, get away from me!* before darkness converged on him like a horde of flapping insects and chased away the light.

"My God, what happened?" said the woman next to Cass. "Did you see what happened?"

In the back row, Cass had been so distracted by the memory of Fiona's bizarre behavior that not even Butterworth's strident sermon had completely captured her attention. Hell and damnation and brimstone was the gist she had gotten before tuning him out. The next thing she knew, the minister had slumped to the floor in midsentence, leaving a second of stunned silence, before people in the front pews started rushing to his aid.

A small group formed around Butterworth while someone called for an ambulance. Others went in search of Fiona. A woman from the choir brought water and splashed it in the minister's face. The whole drama took only seconds before Butterworth started coming around, shaking his leonine head and struggling to sit up. Cass noted that even coming out of a faint his strength was such that three people trying to restrain him from rising too quickly were unable to hold Butterworth down.

"Thank Jesus," she heard someone say, "I think he's all right."

Moments later, Butterworth got to his feet and, aided by the burliest of the male choir members, was helped to a chair. In the distance, the keening of an ambulance could be heard. Deciding that between Butterworth and Fiona she'd had all the drama she wanted, Cass slipped quietly out the back way.

Enough of churches and sermons for one day, she thought, driving quickly, almost recklessly, back to her motel. She'd decided to change into outdoor clothes and go for a hike, clear her head, try to sort out the events of the morning.

When she got to the door of her motel room, a package wrapped in brown paper was waiting. She picked it up, turned it over. No return address, just her name, Magic Markered in thick black letters, the last name misspelled.

She unlocked the door, carried the parcel inside, and set it on the table next to the window. No address, so it had been hand-delivered. Not from Kenny—she'd recognize his handwriting and, besides, he wouldn't misspell her name. From Shep then—hand-tied flies maybe? She dismissed that idea as unlikely—he'd hardly leave a box sitting there at her door. He'd drop it off at the motel office and the manager would slip a note under her door saying she had a parcel to be picked up.

Who then? Who else knew she was here?

She unwrapped the package and dug through some wadded-up newspapers to find what was inside. So mangled was the object she pulled out that at first she didn't recognize it. Then a thread of fear slid along her spine as she pulled out the cell phone that had been stolen from her car in the parking lot of the Pioneer Café the day before—smashed so badly that its metallic innards dangled, crushed as though it had been run over by a car.

Chapter 11

The ride in the ambulance, with the paramedics probing and prodding him and barking commands at each other, so sure that he was just another overweight, older man having a heart attack, had frightened Butterworth badly, but not nearly so much as the experience he'd had in the church. Now, near midnight, he still sat slumped in his favorite armchair, a sagging-bottomed thrift-store relic that occupied a corner of the bedroom in the house that he and Fiona rented across the street from the church. He was thumbing through a well-worn Bible, trying to find some clue as to what had taken place.

Job and Moses and Samson and Saul, all had been tested in terrible ways—but this?

So absorbed was he that he barely noticed when Fiona came in, carrying a mug of tea. He didn't even look up until she was standing almost in front of him, her body blocking the cone of light that fell across the page.

Then he *did* look, though, and a great sigh rippled out of his chest. She wore a sheer white, ankle-length gown with gold stitching at the neck and sleeves. Her long hair poured down her back like a slab of obsidian, and he could see the outline of her body through the fabric, the slender torso and heavy, sagging breasts, the endearing curve of her hips. She held the tea out to him.

"Time for bed?" he asked, setting the Bible on the nightstand and taking the tea.

"Past time. You've had a long day. You need to sleep."

She sat down on the arm of the chair, massaging the back of his thick neck while he sipped the tea. "I was so scared this morning. I thought you'd had a heart attack."

"Me, too," he said, although that wasn't true. Before he'd passed out, he'd known something terrible was happening to him, that he might possibly be dying, but that it wasn't a heart attack at all. He hadn't known how to get back into his body. More horrifying, he hadn't wanted to. He hadn't liked what he'd seen—that fat, sweating man spewing out what, at the time, had sounded like the grossest obscenities. The part of him that had been watching that man had deemed him pathetic, delusional, not a soldier in the righteous army of God but a narrow-minded crusader for ignorance.

He was trying to frame a mode of expressing this when she said, "We need to talk, Claude. There's something I need to tell you."

"Actually there was something I wanted to say to you, too, Fiona. About what happened today."

"Let me go first." Her hand slowly stopped massaging his neck. Her arms slid around the meaty pad of his shoulder.

"Please, Fiona," he said tiredly, "I need to speak now."

He felt her stiffen. "I think I know what you're going to say."

"No, you don't. You have no idea."

"What's wrong?" There was an urgency in her voice as she took a seat on the edge of the bed. "Did the doctor say something besides what you told me?"

"No, no. But I need to ask you something important. And I want you to answer honestly."

He paused, framing his words carefully. "Do you

think it's possible that God has chosen me for some
reason? That before He lays out His plan for me, He's
testing me to see if I'm worthy? Or even, on the other
hand, that He's trying to drive me mad, because He
sees into my soul and has judged me evil?"

"Are you saying God's spoken to you directly?"

"God—or Satan—I don't know. I'm not sure what
to think."

He was testing the waters, almost ready to take the
risk and confess it all, to tell her not only about what
had happened to him that morning but also what desperate means he'd used to combat Satan, when she
said, "Do you know what I think, Claude?" and a
laugh trilled out of her, low and lilting, a laugh that
once had the power to melt his heart, but that now,
under these circumstances, turned it inside out.

"I think your spirit's shrunken and your ego's
bloated with self-importance. You're spouting the kind
of gibberish you denounce from the pulpit every Sunday—trying to convince yourself God's talking to you
or Satan's tempting you. Get real, Claude, in either
case—God or Satan—they've better things to do than
worry with the likes of you."

Her words sank into him like sharp, stinging teeth,
but he bore the pain she brought him stoically, as
was his habit—acknowledging in his heart of hearts
that he undoubtedly deserved it. Who was he, after
all, to think God spoke to him? Likewise, surely, there
were souls the Devil coveted more dearly than his
own.

"I suppose I'm just a foolish old man," he said.
"And I was angry when I got up to give the sermon
today, and that may have overstressed me. Judd
Lomax had stopped in to see me. The boy's terribly
confused. I fear for his immortal soul, I truly do."

"Then work with him, Claude. Focus your mind on
helping Christians who've strayed from the fold—
that's where your calling lies."

"I suppose you're right, my dear." He stood up,

ponderous in his robe and slippers, and started to switch out the light, then thought of something else that had been bothering him. "Where were you today at the service anyway? I didn't see you."

"I was having a little chat with Jack's new girl-friend."

At the thought of the two conferring, he felt a new weight descend. "My God, Fiona, aren't you over O'Doul yet?"

"Of course, I'm over Jack. That doesn't mean I don't have concerns for him, though. And I was curious to see what kind of woman he's taken up with."

"Given his circumstances, Fiona, it's not as though he has a lot of options. Anyway, she seems like a nice woman. My gut feeling is she came to worship here more to earn points with Jack than with the Lord, but that's often the case. Over time, she'll start to come here for herself. I like her."

Fiona gave her lavish hair a toss. "She doesn't love him, you know. I don't know what her game is—maybe she's another one like Opal Brady, one of those professional virgins who finds it romantic or convenient to have a boyfriend behind bars."

"Perhaps she's reticent about her feelings," said Butterworth. "After all, she doesn't know you." He removed his robe and folded it, laid it neatly over the back of the chair.

"Suddenly I'm feeling very weary," he said. "I need to sleep."

"Not yet," she said, coming up behind him, pressing herself against him. The warmth of her breasts and belly traveled down his spine, a balm for his tired back and aching knees. "I need to tell you something."

He'd been dreading this moment, knowing it was coming. The cycle of Fiona's infidelity—remorse followed by repentance, before the start of the next adultery—was coming around full circle once again, and he looked for his cane where it was propped against the nightstand, so weary now, so full of woe, that he thought he actually might need it to travel the few feet from chair to bed.

He leaned upon Fiona and let her help him to the bed. "I've been seeing Otis again, Claude."

"I know."

"How? Did someone tell you?"

"Just a feeling I had. You've seemed different lately. You're not as good an actress as you think."

"I never meant to hurt you, Claude."

"I know that," he said tiredly. He was looking at the cane, wondering if he had the energy to get to it, put his robe back on, and go outside for some air, maybe dress and walk over to the little park behind the church.

Instead, with a dispirited grunt, he plopped down upon the bed.

"When you collapsed this morning," Fiona said, "I thought you'd had a stroke or a heart attack. I thought you might be dying. And I realized I can't go on like this, living this lie. I have to tell you the truth."

"In case I kick the bucket tonight?" he said, trying for levity, failing.

"Because I know I'm weak, and I've sinned. I need your forgiveness."

Her hands meandered down his chest, plucking at the tufts of graying hair.

"It's not my forgiveness you need, it's the Lord's."

"But you're my husband, Claude."

"Why can't you remember that when you're jumping into bed with Otis then?"

She drew back as though he'd struck her. He felt a hard, painful pang of guilt pierce him and, just as quickly, a flash of righteous rage. How dare she act aggrieved when she was the guilty one?

He realized his hands had clenched into fists. He opened them, rubbing them over his thighs as though to stretch cramps from his fingers. "You test me, Fiona. It's not as though this hasn't happened before."

"I didn't mean for it to. It just—"

"Happened," he said, his voice heavy with sarcasm.

"Otis called me, said he needed to talk. He wanted to meet me for coffee. One thing led to another and—"

"Of course. Coffee followed by a carnal encounter in a sleazy motel. That's the nature of such assignations, isn't it?"

"Otis told me he's started reading the Bible. He's thinking of becoming a Christian."

"How convenient. The two of you can pray together after you've finished fucking."

She jerked backward. "Don't be crude."

"I'm sorry."

"Will you forgive me?"

His hands clenched again, remembering how he'd fantasized about making her beg. Instead he said, "Is it over this time, Fiona? For good?"

"I'll do my best to end it."

"That's not enough. If you want forgiveness on that basis, ask it of God, not me."

"I'm sorry you feel that way, Claude."

He switched the light off and lay back. Fiona slithered out of her gown and crawled in next to him.

He waited for sleep, but what came instead were images of his wife and her lover—repulsive, venal, carnal. What horrified him most, though, were not the images, but the curiosity they piqued.

Better to hear it from her own lips, he decided, than suffer the torment of his own imagination.

He cleared his throat. "Fiona?"

"Yes, Claude?" She sounded wide awake, as though she had been waiting for this.

"For the sake of your immortal soul, for the sake of harboring no secrets between us, perhaps you should confess to everything. The details, I mean. Tell me the worst so I don't imagine things even more awful. It can help you as well. Looking at the specifics of your sins may disgust you, may make it easier not to repeat them."

She curled against him with her lips brushing the back of his ear.

"Well, Claude," she purred, and he felt himself stir, "if you really want to know everything that Otis and I did, if you think it will help to describe our sins to you, then I suppose I could do that. I suppose I could tell you . . . everything."

Chapter 12

On Monday morning, Cass put on a denim skirt, white short-sleeved T-shirt, and denim vest, stoked herself with enough coffee to wire a football team, and forced herself to make the short drive to the prison. When Jack had called the day before, sounding annoyed because she hadn't shown up during visiting hours, she'd used apartment hunting as an excuse. She didn't mention the cell phone incident, feeling strongly that there must be a connection between Jack and the guy who was following her.

On the other hand, she thought, reaching over to take a sip of coffee from the foam cup in the plastic holder next to the dash, if Jack knew she was being harassed, wouldn't he find it odd that she never mentioned it to him?

She decided not to say anything and see if Jack gave himself away by the kind of questions he asked.

She was slowed going into the prison by a group of several dozen antideath penalty protesters carrying signs and shouting slogans. As the next man scheduled to die by lethal injection, Madison Raine's name and photo were displayed on many of the posters. Cass searched the crowd for Mariah, figuring surely she'd be taking part in the demonstration, but didn't see her.

A small man with receding gray hair, tanned, deeply wrinkled skin, and a red, wattled neck, thrust a pen and a yellow legal pad at her. The pad was divided into three columns and was half full of signatures. "Can I get you to sign this, please?"

"What is it?" said Cass automatically, although she was sure she knew.

"We believe the death penalty is barbaric. We're seeking a stay of execution for Madison Raines."

"I'm sorry, I can't sign that."

The little man's wattled neck corded. "You mean you support legalized murder?"

"It's not—look, I'm not going to debate this, but something has to be done to stop people like Madison Raines."

"He's a human being, just like you, and—"

"He's getting what he deserves." She waved off further discussion and strode toward the door of the prison.

By this time, she knew the drill: surrender possessions, pass through metal detector, wait for a corrections officer to show up, and then follow him or her through a series of bare, brightly lit hallways that always ended in an ominously clanging metal door. Surely the passageway to hell itself could be no bleaker, she thought, wondering if Madison Raines wasn't really the lucky one—better to die than live out a natural life span in such brutally inhospitable surroundings.

She waited half an hour for Jack to show up in the visiting room and was on the verge of leaving when he finally sauntered over to the table where she sat alone, filling the ashtray in front of her with half-smoked butts.

"Hi, honey," she said, getting up to give him a kiss, which he returned with all the enthusiasm of a small boy getting a smooch from his aunt.

For a man locked up in prison with little to do, Jack looked like he had at least a half-dozen things more important to take care of than spending time with Cass.

"Where were you? I thought maybe the C.O. on your cell block forget to let you out."

He seemed to take that as a challenge. "No C.O.'s gonna forget about me, not if they know what's good for 'em."

"Oh. Well, it's just that . . . Opal told me that's happened a few times with Frank."

He shrugged, looking bored and put-upon. His eyes were focused, not on her, but on the tight cotton skirt working its way up the thigh of a woman necking with her boyfriend a few tables away.

Cass felt an irrational surge of jealousy, which she quickly suppressed. "What's wrong, Jack? Don't I get a hug?"

"There was a new C.O. on my floor and he fucked up." She was trying to figure out how the incompetence of a guard could translate to her not getting hugged, when he went on, "Prisoners are supposed to get a shower when they get a visitor, but this asshole don't know that or he gets so behind letting other guys out to get their showers that he was late gettin' to me. So I didn't get to clean up. Better if you don't touch me."

His eyes drifted back to the short skirt in the corner. Another half inch and it would cross over into pubic hair territory. "Look at that, would you, she's half-naked in a room full of people. Fucking slut."

"Do you know her?" asked Cass, trying to understand where all this hostility was coming from.

"Fuck no. Glad I don't."

"What's wrong with you today? Are you upset because things didn't go so well with Angela and Parker? I thought I explained all that to you on the phone."

And she reminded him again, thinking it would cheer him, how Twyla had followed her outside to say in no uncertain terms she wanted to see her dad. When Jack seemed indifferent to that, too, she filled the void in the conversation by updating him on Butterworth's condition after his collapse in front of the congregation the day before.

"Apparently it was nothing serious, though," she

added quickly. "I called the hospital later that day. They only kept him a couple of hours for observation and then sent him home. They said it was just low blood sugar or something. He's fine."

"Course he's fine," Jack snapped, "Reverend Butterworth's a man of God and the good Lord's taking care of him." He sighed and rapped his fingers on the tabletop. If he was trying to communicate profound boredom, he was doing a good job of it.

Gesturing toward the candy and soda machines in the corner, he said, "You got any change?"

"Some."

"Get me a Mars bar and a Coke. And some chips. Lunch was for shit today. I couldn't get it down."

Although she found his insolence infuriating, Cass bit back her anger, counted out the change she'd transferred from her purse to the pockets of her jeans, and went to buy the food, but when she returned a minute or two later with the snacks, Jack brushed them away.

"What's wrong now?"

"I'm not hungry."

"But . . . you just said . . ." *Let it go, let it go*, she told herself.

"So what kinda apartments did you look at?"

"What?"

"On the phone, you said the reason you couldn't come see me yesterday is you were out looking for an apartment. So where'd you look? North end of town, southside of town, downtown?"

"I cruised around."

He propped his elbows on the table and leaned toward her. "Name me some names."

"Well, there was Eagle Crest," she said, thankful to remember the name of a subdivision advertised in yesterday's real estate section of the paper.

"Eagle Crest? Where's that?"

She visualized the ad, a pen and ink sketch of a couple jogging in front of a row of duplexes accompanied by a text heavy on the exclamation points. "Out on 115. It's brand-new. Condos with individual balconies and little gardens. There's even a jogging track."

He frowned. "Never heard of it."

"Of course not, like I said, it's brand—"

"Where else you go?"

Her capacity for improv was running low. "Well, let's see, I can't remember all the names. I think there was—"

He glared at her. "I don't think you looked at no apartments. Where were you yesterday? I mean, *really*."

Cass was taken aback. "I told you how I spent my day."

"Yeah, looking at apartments, but so far, you just told me about one."

"Look, a big part of my Sunday was taken up with church and—"

"The whole day? Reverend Butterworth preached a sermon lasted the whole fucking day, that what you're telling me?"

"No. And I don't appreciate your speaking to me like that, either." She debated telling him about the vandalism to her car, the shattered cell phone left at her motel door, but decided not to. How would she explain telling him about it now when she hadn't mentioned it on the phone yesterday? Besides, she rationalized, Jack seemed to be the type of man who'd figure that if someone was out to get her, then she must have done something to cause it.

"I was tired, so before I went apartment hunting, I took a nap," she said. "When I woke up, there was only time to drive out and see the one complex."

He sneered. "Yeah, going to church, that's real exhausting."

"Jack, there's no need for this."

He leaned across the table, in her face, looming over her, and shouted, "Where the hell *were* you yesterday?"

And in that moment she thought, *You did it. I know*

you did. You killed your wife, and you probably killed Raven, and right now you'd like to kill me, too. Oh, you murdering bastard.

A C.O. who Cass recognized from previous visits, short, much slighter than many of the inmates, came over and told Jack to keep it down or he'd have to go back to his cell.

"Hey, mind your own business, C.O. I'm talking to my girlfriend."

"Well then, talk *nice*."

"No, it's all right," Cass said to the guard. "I'm leaving."

"Hey, you don't go nowhere," said Jack. "I'm not done talking to you."

She shoved back her chair. "I haven't done anything for you to be angry with me, and I'm not going to stay here and take this abuse."

She forced herself to meet Jack's eyes. It was like staring down the twin barrels of a shotgun. He started to come around the table, but then the guard stepped between them, said something Cass couldn't make out, but which she was sure reminded Jack of the precariousness of his position. He whirled away, swearing softly. Cass joined a small group of others who were cutting their visits short, awaiting an escort back outside, back to the free world.

To her surprise, Mariah—who always visited with Madison until the last possible moment—was leaving, too.

"What happened?" asked Mariah, glancing toward Jack, who was being escorted out of the room by a guard.

"He's pissed 'cause I didn't come to see him yesterday. I didn't know I wasn't allowed to skip a day."

"He'll get over it," Mariah said. "You gotta remember these guys are just like any other men, like little boys, only much worse because they're locked up and helpless. Visits from their women are all most of 'em got to look forward to."

"So why are you leaving?" asked Cass.

A lean, haggard-looking female C.O. came by to escort the women outside. Mariah shot the woman a look that could shatter stone and said in a loud voice, "The fucking C.O.s won't tell me what happened. They just decided to deprive Madison of his visit."

The C.O. lifted an eyebrow, but didn't rise to the bait.

Mariah wouldn't give up. "Bunch of pathetic, power-hungry, Nazi wanna-bes, you ask me. Sadists all of 'em. They get their kicks tormenting the men."

Cass was finding her rant embarrassing, wishing she'd shut up, when the C.O. stopped in her tracks, turned around, and said as coldly as if she were testifying before a grand jury, "Madison Raines was deprived of his visit because he threw something through the bars at a C.O. who was going off duty. An unidentified liquid."

"Water?" asked Cass.

The guard shrugged. "I said 'liquid.' Coulda been spit or piss. Or worse." She looked at Cass, but her words were for Mariah. "Ever been walking along, mindin' your own business, and get hit in the face with two weeks' worth of jism some asshole's been hoarding for just the right moment to throw?"

"Jesus, they *do* that?"

The guard chuckled. "And worse."

"Madison wouldn't do that," said Mariah.

The guard said, "Sure he wouldn't, he's a prince among serial killers," and started walking again.

When they reached the outside, Mariah was still fuming about the guard's remark. "Did you hear her? The bitch has no respect for Madison. For any of the inmates. The C.O.s treat them like animals and then act surprised when it's payback time." She fished a pack of Marlboros out of her purse, offered one to Cass, who accepted, and lit another. "The conditions Madison has to live under—it's inhuman."

Cass took a drag on her cigarette and watched the little knot of protesters who had broken off from the main group and gathered under one of the guard towers. They were chanting something and she listened, trying to make it out, until the words became clear to her. They were chanting, "Justice! Justice for Madison Raines!"

Given the butchery that Raines had confessed to, Cass found it hard to work up any sympathy for his plight. She hoped no one would ask her to sign an antideath penalty petition when Mariah was standing right there. She still wouldn't be able to add her name to the list, but hated the idea of refusing in front of the condemned man's wife.

"They're demonstrating on behalf of Madison. How come you're not taking part?"

"Because I don't believe in that bullshit. They're wasting their time. Madison's not gonna be saved from the needle by a bunch of menopausal housewives and retired clerks waving around a few signs."

"You're saying it's hopeless?"

"Not necessarily. But I am saying it's gonna take more to save Madison than some catchy slogans and thirty fucking seconds of airtime between sports and the weather on the ten o'clock news."

They headed for the parking lot, going out of their way to avoid the protesters, who were now handing out leaflets to anyone coming or going, much in the manner of Hare Krishnas waylaying people at airports. A man exiting the prison put his fists on his hips and screamed, "They should fry every goddamned one of 'em!" A shouting match ensued. Mariah and Cass hurried on.

"Mariah, can I ask you something?" said Cass when they were outside the main gate.

"Shoot."

"Madison confessed to murdering and mutilating half a dozen women. He *confessed* to it. And you met him and married him *after* that. How is that—possible? To know a man's done these unspeakable things and fall in love with him anyway?"

Mariah laughed like she'd heard this question a hundred times. "Believe it or not, I didn't have a choice. Something just resonated between us when we met. I fell in love. I didn't choose to. It just happened." She pushed the lank brown hair out of her face, wiping at the sweat trickling off her forehead with the back of her hand, and looked off into the distance as though expecting help to arrive. "Time's running out for him, you know. He's got less than three months."

"The lawyers will keep appealing till the last moment," said Cass.

"Yeah, and the governor will keep turning down the pardons, too. That's how it goes these days. The public's hungry for executions. Give it a few more years, it'll be like Europe in the Middle Ages. Public hangings for popular amusement. Decapitations at Disney World, electrocutions in Times Square." She sighed as though envisioning it all, then squinted down a row of cars to a maroon Ford Taurus with a bumper sticker that read: FIGHT CRIME. SHOOT BACK. "I'm over here."

Cass started to make a comment about the sticker, then decided against it. "See you next visiting day then."

"Yeah, see you." Mariah's glum face suddenly split into a grin. "Hey, you know what? I could sure use a drink. Why don't we go someplace?"

"It's a little early for me."

"Never too early for a beer and a chance to pick up some pretty boys."

"What about Madison?"

"Oh, I was just joking," said Mariah, making a shooing gesture with her hand that Cass didn't quite buy.

"So how about lunch then?" she persisted. "You can eat, and I'll do the drinking for both of us."

"I don't think so. It's such a nice day, I thought maybe I'd go for a hike."

"Where at?"

"Well, actually I'm not sure," Cass admitted, regretting now that she'd ever opened up this line of conversation.

"I can tell you a great place," said Mariah. "You just take Field Road straight north to Red Canyon Park. There's all kinds of trails there."

"Have you hiked it?"

Mariah patted her substantial midsection. "Honey, the only hiking I do is back and forth to the refrigerator. But I do live right on Field Road, and the park's just a couple miles up from my house. You'll go right past my house—it's the blue bungalow with a white fence and statues of gnomes in the front yard." She saw Cass's expression and laughed. "You know, *gnomes*? Little men? I collect 'em. Like I'm Snow White and those are my dickless dwarves."

"I'll look for it," said Cass. "And thanks for the suggestion for the hike."

She headed off toward her car. Mariah called out, "Hey, aren't you afraid to go alone? Weekdays there may not be many other people out hiking."

"The fewer the better," said Cass. She looked back toward the stark stone walls of the prison and murmured to herself, "Right now, I've had about all the people I can stand."

After leaving the prison, she stopped at a convenience store to buy bottled water and a sandwich and found a small guidebook to local hiking trails, which included Red Canyon Park. At the counter, the salesgirl who rang up her purchases confirmed what Mariah had said, that the canyon was a great place to hike.

About a mile and a half from the park, she spotted

Mariah's remarkable house—the yard peppered with stone gnomes popping up from the ground like petrified prairie dogs—then continued on to the canyon, where she parked the rental car in a dirt parking area next to the trailhead. She put her water and food into the fanny pack she'd thrown into the car that morning, slipped a baseball cap on her head, and set off along the most interesting-looking of several different trails.

Unfortunately, her mind wasn't something she could lock away in the trunk of the car along with her purse, but came with her, making it difficult to fully appreciate the canyon walls rising dramatically around her. Why was Jack so angry with her today? Surely not just because she'd missed one visit? On the other hand, he'd told the guard she was his "girlfriend." Maybe thinking of her in that light made him feel it was okay, even normal, to bully her. Or maybe he was blaming her for the fact that Angela and Parker wouldn't allow Twyla to visit him. Anything was possible, Cass thought, for a person confined much of the time to a cell and all of the time to one building, a man whose mind had nowhere to go but around and around, spiraling in on itself, brewing up a dangerous stew of resentment and paranoia.

But how to get him to trust her enough that he'd confide in her, maybe even boast to her, about Raven?

And even if he confessed to killing her, what good would that do, she reminded herself, if the confession was made to her alone, not to the police? Kenny had said it didn't matter, that all he wanted was to know the truth about what had happened to his daughter, but she wondered if that would be enough for her, were she in similar circumstances. Decided that it might not, that the desire for revenge might be too strong.

In spite of what he'd said, what made her think that if Kenny found out Jack had murdered Raven, he wouldn't try to get revenge? Make a deal with someone on the inside, maybe a corrupt C.O. who'd look the other way while someone stuck a homemade knife in Jack's back?

How could she run the risk of something like that taking place?

But what if, despite his terrifying temper, Jack hadn't killed Raven? And what if she could somehow prove it? Fiona'd said he was with her that night, at least during the crucial time frame when the police thought Raven had been murdered—what reason would she have to lie? If anything, she'd have every reason *not* to give Jack an alibi, a married woman, a minister's wife, no less, shacked up with a boozer and wife beater?

Damn, he must be great in bed, she caught herself thinking, then remembered that, presumably, Raven hadn't even slept with Jack—it was the reason for their breakup. As for Fiona, well, she gave the impression she'd go to bed with anything that breathed.

Poor Reverend Butterworth, thought Cass, *with a cross to bear like Fiona.*

She hiked on, the trail and her thoughts growing increasingly more convoluted, then turned back when her water started running low and her feet began to ache.

High, pewter-colored clouds were banking over the western sky, a late-afternoon thunderstorm brewing, by the time she got back to her car. She unlocked the door, threw her fanny pack on the passenger seat of the rental car, stuck the key in the ignition, and—nothing.

Jesus, not now. This can't be happening.

The Caprice wheezed and kicked, gave a metallic-sounding death rattle, then fell silent. Cass tried the engine a couple more times, but she knew it was hopeless. The car wasn't going anywhere.

Automatically she reached into the glove box for her cell phone, thinking to call the rental company to send a tow truck and a replacement car, then remembered she no longer had a car phone—it had been smashed to bits and left at her front door.

Shit.

She sat there, debating what to do, while fat drops of rain began to splat against the windshield. There were no other cars in the parking area and no reason to think anyone else would show up this late in the day. And as much as she didn't relish the idea of hitchhiking, she thought maybe, if she got lucky, she could get a ride into town now and avoid being trapped in her car in a thunderstorm. Pulling the brim of the baseball cap down over her eyes, she hopped out of the car, walked to the road, and took up her stance.

It wasn't exactly the expressway, this road. She soon realized her thumb could fall off before anybody came along who might stop for her. Rain was starting to fall steadily now, and the one car that did pass her sped by without even slowing.

She was thinking about jumping back into her car before the storm really hit or maybe trying to walk to Mariah's house, when a white Camaro—vintage issue, mid-eighties—crested the hill and came toward her. She stuck out her thumb and the driver slowed and pulled over, reaching across to unlock the passenger side door.

Before getting into the car, she leaned over to take a look at the driver. He was a thick-waisted guy, late twenties, early thirties, with a broad torso that strained the buttons of a green plaid work shirt. He had the beefy thighs of a onetime high school football star and the protuberant gut of a current couch potato.

He smiled. "Where you headed, ma'am?"

She could feel the rain on her back. "Just into town."

"Well, hop in." When she hesitated, he kept the smile on his face, but a touch of irritation crept into his voice. "C'mon, honey, the seat's gettin' wet."

He sounded a lot like Jack—cajoling her to do something, but with that undercurrent of insistence in his voice—and she reacted almost automatically, as if it were Jack speaking. She got into the car.

"Thanks for stopping. My car won't start. Can you drop me off at a gas station?"

"Sure thing."

"The Amoco on Main would be fine. They do towing."

"Okeydokey."

He reached over and turned on the radio. Country-western blared from speakers in back. "So what's wrong with your car?"

"I don't know. It just conked out on me."

"Bummer." He gave her a sideways glance. "You out here all by yourself?"

"I was hiking."

"Hiking?" He made it sound like she'd been doing it naked. "In this kinda weather?"

"It was nice when I started out."

"Yeah, well, we always get thunderstorms in the afternoon this time of year," he said in a scolding tone. "Lightning can be bad. Y'oughta be careful."

"I'll remember that."

They drove on, and the rain came in earnest, pounding the windshield. In spite of the loud radio, the absence of conversation made the car seem strangely quiet.

"So, you from around here?" he said finally.

To say she was might invite further questions. "Just passing through."

"What's your name?"

She didn't feel like telling this guy her name. He was just giving her a ride, for God's sake, not asking her to the prom. "Anna," she said.

"Anna." The way he said it made Cass wonder if Anna was the name of someone he loathed. He slowed to twenty miles an hour, then ten. Cass could have run faster. She wanted to ask if he'd like her to get out and push the car.

Suddenly, he twisted the wheel with both hands and swerved off onto the shoulder of the road. Cass was slammed against the passenger side door.

"Rain's coming too hard," he said. "I can't drive in this."

She was appalled. "Hey, you're not gonna let a little rain stop you?" she said, hoping to appeal to his macho side. "I really need to get into town."

He cut the ignition. For a long moment, he stared straight ahead, scrutinizing the rain as though trying to decode a message the falling drops made on the glass. When he spoke, his voice was freighted with bitterness, the memory of a lifetime of slights and insults, real or imagined, all of them hoarded like coins.

"What am I, *Anna,* your fucking chauffeur?"

"What are you mad about? If you didn't want to give me a ride, you shouldn't have stopped."

"Oh, first you want a ride, now you changed your mind? You wanna get out?"

"Yeah, I think that's a good idea. I'll get out."

She reached for the door. His right arm came out straight to the side, pinning her to the seat.

"Hey! What are you doing?"

She twisted around to strike at his eyes, but she was off balance and he grabbed her wrist, twisting it and forcing her down on the seat. She could see flecks of food in his mustache and an angry, raised scar that ran like a red worm under his chin. The sound of the rain battering the car sounded like an avalanche of stones.

He glared down at her with eyes cold and dead as a shark's. "You get out of this car when and if I say you can. But first we got some talking to do. And don't fucking lie to me anymore, Cass Lumetto. Don't fucking lie."

Chapter 13

About the time that Cass was getting into the white Camaro, Butterworth had been finishing up the sermon he was working on at his desk in the church office. Pausing to lower his head, he said a short, heartfelt prayer, then picked up his cane from the canister. After checking to make sure Fiona's car was still across the street at the house, he headed out to his vehicle.

To the east, clouds were gathering. He felt weary, and the arthritis in his hip was paining him—harbinger of rain. He leaned more heavily on the cane than usual, sounding, to his own ears, like an old steam engine chugging toward the scrap heap.

He drove east out Main Street to a new subdivision that was going up outside town under the pretentious moniker of Dakota Ridge Estates, faux Victorian two- and three-story homes on postage-stamp lots whose Easter egg colors looked like they'd been selected by four-year-olds. The only trees were recently planted saplings. Dust from the construction going on swirled in the air, creating the feel of a ghost town in the making.

Wincing as a knot twisted his stomach, Butterworth cruised the unpaved streets and cul-de-sacs until he spotted a gray pickup truck with the name Dawes Roofing Company and a phone number stenciled on the side. The roofing truck and a couple of others were parked in front of a glaringly cheerful, daffodil-colored house with a gray shingle roof about two-thirds complete. He craned his neck out the window and saw several hammer-wielding men working on the steep shingle slope as casually as if they were at home in their garages.

He parked next to the trucks, eased his bulk out from behind the wheel, and trudged ponderously across the dust-bowl front lawn until he heaved himself up onto the pukingly pastel porch. He cleared his throat and coughed, eyes tearing against the dust.

"Otis Dawes?"

The hammers continued to fall, and he shouted again. Somebody yelled down, "Hey, boss, somebody to see you."

He'd assumed that Dawes would be one of the men on the roof, but then, maybe if you were the guy who owned the roofing company, you played it safe and stayed on the ground.

"Help you?" Otis Dawes emerged out a side door. He wore a baseball cap turned backward over a dirty blond ponytail and a paint-speckled T-shirt that might have been pulled from a rag bin. A heavy tool belt sagged down around a waist amply padded with love handles. An odd fragrance, one that Butterworth at first was at a loss to identify, mingled with the harsher odors of sweat and cigarettes that clung to him.

He squinted at Butterworth through dry, sleep-deprived blue eyes and said in a bored tone, "You from the Zoning Board?"

"No, no, I'm . . . is there somewhere we might speak in private?"

Dawes's laconic eyes narrowed in irritation, but he shrugged, gestured *this way* with his head, and sauntered into the house. "This is as private as it's gonna get, buddy."

They entered a cavernous living room with a high, vaulted ceiling and maple floors polished to such a cold gleam that Butterworth thought of an ice rink.

He clutched his cane and moved gingerly, fearing a slip, while Dawes preceded him like a bored, sated panther. "If you're not from the city, then what—"

He stopped, light dawning in the stoned-looking eyes as he looked Butterworth up and down. A lightbulb seemed to come on over his head as he said, "Oh, I got it now. I seen your picture once. You're the preacher. Fiona's old man."

"Fiona's husband, yes," said Butterworth, putting an emphasis on the word, trying not to become distracted ruminating on where Dawes might have seen his picture. His face appeared in the local paper from time to time, officiating at some ceremony or other or advocating against the dangers of Darwinism or other social evils. That had to be where Dawes had seen him. Surely Fiona wouldn't have brought him to the house?

"So what d'you want?" He looked upward, toward the rhythmic banging of the hammers overhead, and when Butterworth hesitated, added, "Times a'wastin', fella. Spit it out."

"Only to make a simple request that any decent man should be able to respect . . . that you leave my wife alone."

"Wellll," Dawes drew the word out, toying with him—"I don't know as I can do that."

"Why is that?"

"Well, first off, I'm fond of the lady. Enjoy her company. Think I might be in love with her." He drew himself up, the hint of abs visible in the holes in the T-shirt, impressive even under a layering of fat. "One of these days, might wanna take her away from here."

Oh, Lord, thought Butterworth, *it's worse than I thought. The man's besotted.*

"Well, you can't have mentioned any of this to my wife. If you did, she'd laugh you out of town."

"Don't be too sure. Fiona knows how I feel." Defensive now. "She know you're here?"

"No. I thought we could keep this between us. Like gentlemen."

"I ain't about to give her up."

"You already gave her up once. Wasn't it only a year ago that you first had an affair with her? Then she got tired of you or she found somebody who pleased her more and she dropped you. Can you have forgotten that already, Otis? The pain and humiliation you must have endured? Can you possibly have convinced yourself she isn't going to do it again?"

He could feel the sweat traveling in lazy zigzags along his temples, meandering along the rutted contours of his cheeks. "She's already told me it's over, Otis. She's not going to see you again."

"I don't believe that." Dawes held up a filthy palm, looked toward the ceiling again, and gestured for Butterworth to wait. He walked outside, glanced at the sky, and then yelled up to the men on the roof. "Hey, looks like it's gettin' ready to rain. You guys go on home."

No one argued, and the activity on the roof seemed to increase appreciably as the men scurried to gather their tools and leave.

Dawes lit a cigarette and watched them depart. Butterworth, meanwhile, took a seat on the stairs leading up to the second floor, his hands folded on the grip of the cane, wishing that none of this were necessary.

When the roofers were piling into their vehicles, Dawes came back inside. "I been thinkin' about what you said, Preacher. You're tryin' to rattle me, and it won't work. Fiona loves me. She went back to you last time because she felt guilty about what we were doing. Now she realizes love's greater than guilt."

"Poppycock," said Butterworth, who had trained himself to eschew harsher language even when the situation called for it. When he saw the smirk on Dawes's face, though, he regretted his choice of a word that, to the other man, must clearly mark him as a prissy fool.

He cleared his throat and said, "She's playing with

you, my friend. She's finished with you. She as much as told me so."

"Well, maybe she lied. Maybe you're the one should be finished with her, ever thought about that?"

Butterworth hesitated. Although at his lowest points he'd considered asking Fiona for a divorce, he would never admit that to Dawes. "Let me tell you something about Fiona," he said. "When I met her, she was a drugged-out young woman sleeping on the streets of the Lower East Side, giving herself to whoever'd supply her with heroin. Before that, she'd been living on a commune in California, hoping for an acting career, but Satan got to her first and made a mockery of her hopes. I saved her, Dawes. Not just her life, but her soul, her immortal soul. I would never abandon her now. It was because of *me* that she came to know Jesus."

"Jesus, yeah," said Dawes, "she yells out for him when she comes." He cocked his head as though he were remembering and relishing the sound. "But you already knew that, right? Or then again, maybe you didn't?"

Butterworth refused to be goaded. "My wife is a Christian," he said, "but she's weak and easily tempted. I think so many drugs, so much debauchery when she was younger, it had an effect on her mind. The Lord will forgive her sins, but not you for corrupting her."

"I think," said Dawes, who seemed a good deal less stoned now than when the conversation had started, "you might give the woman credit for knowing her own mind. She wants me. She thought she could give me up, but she found out differently."

"Oh, I see. First you say she loves you, but now you've amended it, she only wants you."

"With some women," said Dawes, rearranging the tool belt in a way that made it look as though he were repositioning his dick, "it's the same thing."

"Lust is fleeting," Butterworth said.

"So's life," said Dawes. "So's everything." He took a step toward Butterworth, who was still sitting on the stairs, gripping the cane with knuckles turned ashen.

"Leave her alone," said Butterworth. "She doesn't need you in her life. We took vows together."

"Hell, what if she won't leave me alone?" He slung one booted foot up onto the stair Butterworth sat on, leaning forward so that those dry rattler's eyes fixed on him. "What if she knows good lovin' when she beds it? What if she's the kinda woman looks best bent over a chair with her skirt over her head?"

Butterworth could feel the lunch he'd eaten a few hours earlier curdling in his belly. Rage seemed to be crushing his chest like a mountain of stones. "Let me ask you something, Otis, purely rhetorically as I'm already sure of the answer. Are you familiar with the paintings of Heironymus Bosch?"

Dawes blinked and scowled as though the complexity of the name hurt his head. "Hi—who?"

"As I thought," said Butterworth. "He was a fifteenth-century Flemish artist renowned for his paintings of hell. He created what might very well be the most breathtakingly graphic rendition ever of what the damned have to look forward to. The words *loathsome* and *hideous* don't do Bosch's work justice, my friend. And I have no doubt but that it pales in comparison to the real thing."

"Oh, I get it—this is how a preacher handles it when another man's boinking his wife. You don't threaten to beat me up or pull out a gun, you sic God on me, that it?"

"Not God—Satan. And you've sicced him on yourself."

"Yeah, well, I'm fucking shaking, I'm so scared."

"Revile me all you want," said Butterworth. He rose to his feet, knees creaking. Dawes might not be shaking, but *he* was. "I came here in the hope I could save you, as in the past I've done my best to save others, but now—"

Dawes bristled. "Oh, it's that easy, is it? You got a direct pipeline to Jesus, is that it? Well, ain't that nice? Why don't you tend to Jesus and while you're doing that, I'll take care of Fiona?"

"Shut up!" roared Butterworth, thumping the cane on the floor. "This minute! Shut up!"

The very walls of the house seemed to bend away from the power and thrust of his voice and the air pulsed with an ominous energy. Dawes's mouth dropped open and stayed that way as he tried unsuccessfully to muster a comeback. He stared up into the blazing Old Testament wrath of Butterworth's eyes while the echo of the voice pulsed in the air like a prophet's invective.

"I could have saved your immortal soul, I came here *intending* to save it, but no, I think not. I think *not*. Live out the rest of your paltry, sinful life here on this earth, bereft of Christ, bereft of hope, and when Satan comes to claim your soul, remember I could have saved you here and now, as I've saved others. As I wanted to save you."

"Hey, save away," said Dawes, opening his arms in a sarcastic gesture of welcome. "Who the hell's stoppin' you?"

"There are some who don't *deserve* to be saved," said Butterworth, reducing his voice to the harsh, tortured whisper he used for maximum effect from the pulpit. "There are some who deserve to writhe in eternal agony in the pit of fire and filth that awaits them. You, Otis Dawes, are such a one. Not even Bosch himself could have done justice to the tortures that await you in the hideous hereafter. And I, God forgive me for my lack of humility, have no desire to save you from yourself."

Breathing heavily, the pulse pounding at his temple like a bee sting, he marched toward the door. He forced himself to keep going, exerting all his willpower not to look back at Dawes, even when the man—like a monkey who sees its enemy retreating and hurls rotten fruit, oblivious to the jaguar getting ready to pounce from behind—continued to taunt him.

"She told me you wanted her to stop seeing me, but she didn't know if she could do it or not. Well, I can answer you that one—she *can't* stop. She's too hooked on what it is I got here." He patted his crotch. "She told me some other stuff, too—that you're loony as hell. You think Satan speaks straight to you, tries to tempt you. Gives you fucking visions. Well, next time you hear from Old Nick, Reverend"—Dawes made a fist of his right hand and used the left hand to drive it straight up—"tell him to take it like I give it to Fiona—up the ass."

Butterworth felt all restraint and composure depart him. He halted in his tracks and turned, not hurrying, but raising his hands as though getting ready to drive home a point. Instead, he thrust the handle of the cane up under Dawes's ribs, bull's-eyeing the solar plexus. Dawes made a gagging sound. His face went as white as a bled-out corpse, his knees buckled, and he started to fall.

Butterworth flipped the cane so the hooked end was aimed at Dawes and slammed it up between the man's legs. From the screech of agony that resulted, he knew the man wouldn't be putting his equipment up Fiona's ass—or anywhere else—for a while.

Dropping to his knees, he straddled Dawes, whose eyes were rolled back and whose skin had taken on a sweat-sheened, greenish tint. He wasn't sure if Dawes could hear him, but he put his mouth inches from the man's face and spoke anyway.

"You're going to call up my wife and tell her it's over. You can't go on with it. Tell her you're sorry—I don't want you to hurt her more than you have to—but make it crystal clear. It's over between you. Forever. And if I ever catch you near her again, so help me God, Otis Dawes, I will kill you. Understand?"

Dawes groaned and started to wretch. Butterworth helped him flop over onto his belly. As soon as he did so, Dawes vomited copiously and lost consciousness.

Butterworth left him with his cheek pressed into his own puke and trudged back to his vehicle. He felt no sense of victory. In fact, he felt beset by withering defeat, too stricken with guilt to even beg God's forgiveness.

What in God's name have I done?

Like a man in a dream or under the influence of some powerful narcotic, he got into his Jeep, turned the key in the ignition, and started for home.

Half a block from his house, he saw a woman sitting on the front porch steps, holding an umbrella over her head and glancing up and down the street as though she were waiting for someone. With the rain coming down, he couldn't see the woman clearly, could only make out that she wore a colorful ankle-length skirt, so he assumed her to be Fiona. His heart dropped like a stone. For Fiona to be sitting outside waiting for him could only mean one thing—that Dawes had called her and told her what had transpired, that she was furious and awaiting his return so she could unleash her rage on him.

He parked the Jeep Cherokee so rapidly that one front tire was halfway up on the curb and came striding around the corner of the house.

"Oh, Reverend," said Linda Lomax, getting to her feet. "I'm so glad you're home. I went to the church first, but no one was there, and Fiona must have stepped out for a minute. I didn't know what else to do, but wait for you—I hope it's not a bad time, but—"

"Of course not, Linda." He extended his hand, struggling to get control of his face so the relief wasn't visible. "You know you're always welcome here—"

He took in the red-rimmed, puffy eyes, the strain lines around the mouth. "What is it? What's happened?"

Her thin mouth turned down at the corners. She started to cry. He folded her against his chest, sorely self-conscious of the fact that he was in need of a shower and that his deodorant had worn off about the time he laid eyes on Dawes, but Linda didn't seem to mind as he patted her back consolingly.

"Oh, Reverend, it's Judd! He and his father had a terrible fight about Judd's new religious beliefs—his insistence that he's going to turn Buddhist—and Jim ordered him out of the house. He took his camping gear with him, that's all I know. Please, Reverend Butterworth, what should I do? He's my only boy. What if he never finds his way back to Jesus again? Please, Reverend, you've got to help him."

Chapter 14

"Now don't freak out. I just want to talk," said the man with his hand across Cass's throat. "I'm gonna let you up, but if you try anything, we'll have to go another round, and I won't hold back next time. You won't like that, believe me. Okay?"

She nodded as much as she could, given her position with her head wedged between the car door and the back of the seat.

"Okay then, but don't disappoint me or you're gonna get hurt."

Slowly the man lifted his smelly bulk off her. He hoisted himself back over the console and into the driver's seat. She sat up, rubbing her arm, trying to think what to do. The sound of the rain on the windshield and hood was thunderous, but her heart seemed to be beating as loudly. When she glanced toward the door handle, his eyes went there, too, almost daring her to try it. As if he wanted her to.

"All right," she said, "you want to talk? Let's talk. For starters, who are you?"

He leaned back, extracted a crumpled pack of Marlboros from inside the grimy console, tapped one out, and lit it. "Doesn't matter who I am. We're here to talk about you, *Cass*," he added, drawing the name out into two sarcasm-laden syllables.

"How do you know my name?"

He drew on the cigarette and exhaled a mouthful

of smoke that immediately combined with the sour odor of lunch meat that already permeated the car. Cass fought the impulse to gag.

"I know a lot about you—where you're staying, what kinda car you drive and how you drive it, what brand of tampons you buy." He seemed to find this last comment uproarious and grinned heartily.

A feeling of sick dread roiled in her stomach. "You're the guy who followed me on the Harley. The same asshole who fucked up my car and ripped off my cell phone."

"Whoa, you got a mouth on you, don't you? Somebody needs to teach you some manners."

"Did you do something to my rental car, too? Is that why it wouldn't start?"

He chuckled. "First off, you don't get to ask the questions here, I ask them. Second, me doin' something to your car, that would be illegal, wouldn't it? And I'm not doing anything illegal. You put out your thumb for a ride, and I gave you one. Now I'm just waiting for the rain to let up before we go on our merry way. In the meantime, we're making conversation. That okay with you?"

"Except for the fact that you're holding me inside your car against my will. That's kidnapping."

"Hey, I'm supposed to let you get out and walk along the road in the middle of a thunderstorm? And let you maybe get hit by lightning? I couldn't let you do that. I'm lookin' out for your best interests."

Cass edged a little closer to the door. "Okay if I roll down the window? I can't breathe."

"Roll away."

She lowered the window a few inches, enough to get a few cooling drops of rain on her face. "How long have you been spying on me?"

"Long enough that I feel like we're practically fuck-buddies. And I'm not spying. I'm just keeping an eye on you. Trying to get a feel for what kinda woman you are, how you operate. Gotta tell you, Cass, so far,

I don't like what I see. You act awful goddamn friendly with men you don't know."

"What are you talking about?"

"Practically wiping the wall with your ass in the Pioneer the other day, trying to get that guy with the mustache hot."

"I don't know what—" She stopped short, remembering the conversation she'd had with "Wyatt" that day after she'd gone outside to talk to Box Car. Wyatt hitting on her and her brush-off must have taken all of two minutes. This jerk had been watching her and interpreted what he saw in typically misogynistic fashion—if a man was coming on to a woman that meant the woman must be asking for it.

She was suddenly furious. "Jack's put you up to doing this, didn't he?"

He leaned back, puffing smoke in her face. "Jack who?"

"You know damn well Jack who! Jack O'Doul. He's in prison, so he thinks he's gonna use *you* to control me."

The man smirked. "Never heard of no Jack O'Doul."

"You're lying."

He looked her up and down with frank hostility. "Honey, all you need to worry about is how you behave here in Canon City. You got a boyfriend in the can, that ain't my concern."

"And what if I go to the police and tell them you're harassing me?"

"What harassing?" He held his palms in the air, all innocence. "Lady, you don't even know who I am. All I did was stop to give you a ride 'cause it's rainin' and I'm a nice guy. You wanna waste the cops' time bitchin' about that, go ahead. See how serious they take you. But I want you to know, I got my eye on you. S'long as you're in Canon City, I'll be watching every move you make. You understand?"

"I hear you."

"Good. Then maybe I'll drive you on into town—by a slightly longer route." He winked. "Like a gentleman."

"You were a gentleman, you'd've offered me a cigarette."

"Huh?"

"I'm nervous. I need a smoke."

He laughed. "Why not?" He shook a cigarette out of the pack, put it to his mouth to light it, then passed it to her.

She took a puff. "Thanks. I needed this."

"You gonna be nice now?"

"You gonna be a gentleman?"

"That what you want? A gentleman?"

She leaned forward, dangling the cigarette. "Tell me the truth. Jack's behind this, isn't he? He's worried I'll cheat."

"Hey, honey, you got a problem with your boy-friend, you take it up with *him*."

"Oh, don't worry, I will. And just what did you do to my car? What was it, sugar in the gas tank? Something else?"

He grinned. He was actually *proud*.

"Something like that."

She drew on the cigarette. "Whoa, clever boy."

From the way his grin broadened, she could tell he hadn't heard the word *clever* used to describe him lately.

Nor, from the way his eyes bulged with shock when she stabbed the lit end of the Marlboro into the back of his hand, had he been burned with a cigarette recently.

"Bitch!"

He lunged for her, but she was already half out of the car and managed to slam the door on his hand, eliciting another scream, before she scrambled into the ditch next to the road and into the field beyond. The rain was coming almost vertically now. She hoped that it cloaked her. She didn't dare look behind her, but dashed into a stand of trees and kept running, thrusting branches out of the way with her hands, half-blinded by rain but confident that the roar of the storm would drown out any noise she was making.

Skidding downhill, she tripped and went sprawling into a gully. She lay still, listening for the sound of his pursuit, unable to hear anything but the din of the rain.

Finally, she heard a car door slam and the sound of an engine revving. She waited another five minutes, then risked moving on, staying close to the trees but paralleling the road.

Twenty minutes later, soaked and shivering, she jogged up the walk to the gnome-infested bungalow and rang Mariah's doorbell, then banged with her fist when several long rings brought no response.

"Yeah, coming," Mariah finally barked out from somewhere inside, but to Cass it felt like another five minutes before she opened the door and stood there gawking.

"God, what happened to *you*?" She was barefoot, wearing a burgundy robe patterned with small butterflies. Her normally stringy-looking, lackluster hair looked frowzy and disheveled. "That must've been one helluva hike."

"I need to use your phone," Cass said, trying to contain her annoyance. "Can I come in?"

After a second's hesitation, Mariah said, "Sure. Of course," and stepped back from the door.

Cass caught a glimpse of herself in an oval mirror and realized why Mariah might have been reluctant to let her in. She was drenched head to toe, her hair matted to her head like a cap, muddy and wild-looking from hiding in the ditch and her subsequent slog through the trees. She looked like the loser in a serious mud-wrestling contest.

"It's a long story," Cass said. "My car won't run and I need to call a tow truck—and the cops."

"Good Lord!" exclaimed Mariah, and Cass thought

she was reacting to what she'd just said until she saw Mariah's eyes were on the carpet—where a puddle was slowly forming around Cass's feet.

"Shit, I'm dripping on your carpet . . . sorry." She reached down, unlaced her shoes, and worked them off over her socks, then removed the wet socks and stuffed them into the shoes.

"Never mind that, honey, you're soaked. Come on in the kitchen. If you didn't want a drink before, I'll bet you could use one now."

"Make it a double."

Mariah led her through a small, lavender-papered living room whose decor appeared to be inspired by the "It's a Small World" ride at Disney World. Purple and lavender were the dominant colors and munchkin-type figurines the decoration of choice. Gnomes, elves, dwarves—they perched on every horizontal surface. A couple even hung from wire attached to hooks to the ceiling and spun lazily, like grotesque Peter Pans with bulging eyes and misshapen features.

No photographs that Cass could see, but in an alcove containing a fireplace, there was a striking portrait of Mariah and Madison. Madison wore a blue suit and dark red tie and sat in front of Mariah, who rested her hands on his shoulders and gazed out at the viewer with a look that seemed both smug and subtly amused. She wore a green velvet gown and emerald earrings that dangled to her pudgy shoulders and, if the portrait painter hadn't quite succeeded in making her look pretty, she did have a look of threadbare royalty, like the exiled queen of some bankrupt and squalid monarchy.

Madison, on the other hand, despite the artist's obvious effort to inject life into his searingly dark eyes, remained stiff and soulless-looking with the hint of the embalmer's art to his waxy, pallid skin. He looked both anemic and yet dangerously vibrant, as though preparing to leap to life and rip free of the confining canvas at any time.

Cass found the portrait creepy and yet somehow familiar, but she assumed this was because she knew Mariah and was familiar with Madison's likeness from the posters waved by the protesters outside the prison.

"This way," said Mariah, glancing worriedly at the white shag carpet and hurrying her along to the kitchen, where she seated Cass at the butcher-block table by the stove. Briefly Cass filled Mariah in on what had transpired between her and the man in the Camaro, including the fact that, in her opinion, he was undoubtedly acting on Jack's behalf. Her adrenaline was still racing. She was almost babbling. While she talked, Mariah moved about the kitchen, mixing up a blender full of Bloody Marys with the panache of a professional bartender.

"Jesus, you poor thing!" She mixed Stoli vodka and Bloody Mary mix in a blender, then poured the contents into two highball glasses and gave one to Cass. "You musta been scared out of your wits."

"Yeah, well, it wasn't exactly the relaxing hike I had planned. I need to call the cops, though. If they find the guy, he should be easy to identify—I couldn't get his license number, but I can describe him, and I think I marked him pretty good with the cigarette."

"You really think Jack told him to follow you?"

"Do you have a better explanation?"

Mariah thought about it a moment. "Well, maybe he saw you someplace, liked your looks, and decided to stalk you."

"Mariah, he knew my *name*. What does that tell you? Jack *has* to be behind this. I'm sure of it." She took a sip of the Bloody Mary, found it potent as a kick to the chin. "It makes me furious to think he'd pull this, act like he owns me—that controlling chauvinistic scumbag—he's lucky he's in prison or else I'd—" She stopped, realizing Mariah was looking at her as though she were confessing to child abuse.

"Honey, think about what you're saying. Remember the most important thing is that you love this man.

Whether he's behind this or not, getting a friend of his arrested is only going to put distance between you two. And I'd say prison bars are about as much distance as any relationship can stand. Don't go adding to it."

"But this creep vandalized my car—twice! Not to mention kidnapping me. God only knows what else he might have done if I hadn't gotten away."

"I agree, it sounds horrible," said Mariah. "And I'm not telling you not to call the law. All I'm saying is think what effect this could have on Jack—and on your relationship. These men stick together, in and out of prison. If this guy is really his buddy and you have him arrested, Jack might just cut you off. He might refuse to ever speak to you again."

In which case I lose my only chance to find out if he killed Raven, Cass thought.

She took a hearty slug of her drink.

"Ready for another?" said Mariah.

Cass held out her glass. "Yeah, why the hell not?"

There was a crash in another part of the house. Mariah spun around, eyes wide.

Cass jumped to her feet. "Jesus, that's him!" All she could think was that the thug Jack had sicced on her had followed her here to Mariah's house and was in the process of breaking in. She looked around the kitchen for a phone but what she saw was a rack of steak knives next to the sink.

Mariah saw Cass heading for the knives and yelled, "Wait, it's not what you think. Let me deal with it."

But before she could do anything more, the doorway from the kitchen was suddenly filled by a sinewy young man with a dark buzz cut and a white, short-sleeved shirt flapping open over a pale, hirsute belly and a grubby-looking pair of Levi's. He looked sexy in a grungy sort of way. If Cass hadn't realized he must have been in Mariah's bedroom, she'd have taken him for the yard man. He managed to sound both sheepish and petulant as he said, "Hey, look, I'm leaving. I can't wait in there for you all fucking day."

"What was that noise?" said Mariah. "Did you go and break something?"

"I was looking for my keys, and I knocked over one o' them elf statues you got on the bureau."

"Shit," said Mariah, "not one of the Hummels."

He frowned. "What the hell is a Hummel? Some kinda car?"

"Never mind, Danny. It's okay." She softened her tone and lifted her glass in a toast-making gesture. "I was just getting ready to mix up some more drinks. Why don't I bring one back to the bedroom and get you all nice and relaxed again?" She glanced meaningfully at Cass. "I promise no more interruptions this time."

"I don't think so. 'Sides I don't wanna wear no condom. It interferes with my hard-on."

Mariah made her voice saccharine sweet as she said, "No, dear, your pitiful lack of testosterone interferes with your hard-on."

Danny blinked a couple of times while this sank in, then shot back, "Fuckin' bitch. I don't need this shit. I had better lays from women who were passed out drunk."

"Then get the hell out of my house."

Danny retreated toward the back of the house. Mariah went after him.

Not sure whether she was more appalled or amused by this spectacle, Cass poured herself another drink and debated whether or not to call the police. Without a doubt, she wanted the thug to pay for harassing her, *especially* for fucking with the Duchess, let alone the rental car, but Mariah might be right—if she called the police and they found the guy and arrested him, Jack would be even more pissed than he currently was. If she let the incident go, because it was *Jack's buddy* and she "wouldn't want to hurt a buddy of

Jack's," she might win considerable points in Jack's eyes. Maybe even enough that he'd start trusting her more, confiding in her. She could even the score later. After this was all over.

Having made the decision, she found a phone book and was giving directions to the rental car company, explaining that her car wouldn't start, when she heard a door slam. Looking out the window, she saw a red pickup jounce around the corner of Mariah's house, buck the curb, and roar westward. Danny boy, making his departure.

A moment later, as she was hanging up, Mariah came back into the kitchen. As casually as if she were offering a plate of hors d'oeuvres, she laid a pearl-handled .22 Colt on the table.

"Jesus!" said Cass. "You didn't use that on Danny, did you?"

Mariah gave that sly, inscrutable smile. "Naw, I don't need a gun to run off the likes of him. I just wanted to show it to you. Might think about getting one yourself, you know, for protection."

"My father was into guns. I don't like them."

"Suit yourself," said Mariah, removing the Colt from the table and sliding it into a kitchen drawer, "but a gun would've come in mighty handy for you today. I never leave the house without this one in my purse. Look at poor CharLee—you just never know what can happen."

Cass couldn't think of a way to respond, and an awkward silence hung between them. Finally she broke it by explaining that the rental company was sending a towing service for her car in forty minutes. Could Mariah give her a ride back to her motel?

"No problem, s'long as you don't mind being driven around town by a known hussy."

The use of such an old-fashioned word caught Cass by surprise. She hadn't heard it since she was a kid and an elderly aunt used it to describe the wanton girls of the sixties who burned their brassieres. Maybe because of the drinks or in reaction to the adrenaline still in her bloodstream, she started to giggle. In another moment, Mariah was giggling, too.

"So what happened in there? He blew out of here like his hair was on fire."

"Asshole. I told him up front he had to wear a condom or forget it. I even got a drawerful of 'em back there for him to choose from. Said it interferes with his pleasure. Like I give a shit about his pleasure."

"Guess I showed up at an inopportune time. Sorry."

Mariah shrugged and finished her drink. "Did you hear him whining like a two-year-old? Saying he'd had better lays from dead women?"

"Dead *drunk*, I think is what he said."

"Yeah, well, all he's got for comparison is his right hand."

Cass couldn't stop laughing. "I shouldn't have had that second drink or I wouldn't be asking this, but . . . oh, God, were you really that bad?"

"If I was, chalk it up to lack of inspiration. 'Sides, we were arguing the whole time over whether or not he was going to wear the fucking rubber." Her laughter trailed off and she added, "So now you know the awful truth about me, Cass, my sordid little secret. I fuck around. Make any difference to you?"

"Look, Mariah, whatever you do or don't do is entirely your business. I'm not judging you. Madison's on Death Row, and however much you love him, you've got normal sexual needs." She found herself tempted to laugh again. "Although, that guy did look like he was ridden pretty hard . . . where the hell did you find him anyway?"

"The Dark Horse. It's a biker bar over on Peoria Street. From your description, I'd say it's the kind of place your friend in the Camaro might hang out."

"Good idea," said Cass. "I may check it out."

Mariah suddenly looked worried. "Me having a guy here, you won't mention it to Jack, will you?"

"Of course not."

"Because Jack and Madison don't know each other, but it still could get back. Cons got nothing to do but gossip all day. It would humiliate Madison if he thought anyone else knew."

"Anyone else? You mean Madison knows you see other men?"

Mariah seemed to find the question unaccountably amusing. "Yeah, as a matter of fact, it was his idea. You could say we have an understanding."

"Pretty open-minded of Madison. Don't worry, I'd never say a word."

Maybe the drinks were getting to Mariah, too, or maybe she'd gotten a headstart at the Dark Horse, because suddenly she turned maudlin. "Shit, what difference does it make who knows at this point. Madison's gonna die, and I can't do anything about it. God, I love that man so much. I'd die in his place if I could. Come here, let me show you something."

They walked up a short hall to Mariah's bedroom, dominated by a large oak-hewn four-poster whose magenta silk sheets and pillows spilled across the floor along with fragments from the shattered figurine.

"Look at this," said Mariah. She showed Cass a huge calendar with numbers ticking down the days till Madison's execution. She turned a couple of pages, brought the calendar to November where the eighth was circled in black. Madison's death day. How strange, Cass thought, to actually know the day and time of your own death. To be able to count down the hours.

"And this . . ." Mariah pulled out a scrapbook, one of several lined up on a bookshelf next to the bed, and started paging through a chronicle of Madison's "accomplishments"—newspaper clippings of every murder he'd ever confessed to, starting with Geneva Williams, a nineteen-year-old prostitute killed in Colorado Springs almost ten years before. The sort of trophy book Cass would have imagined was more often kept by the killers themselves than their girlfriends.

"Did Madison put this together?" she asked, turning page after page of appalling headlines. *Woman Trussed and Killed in Motel Room. Prostitute Maimed and Murdered.*

"No, I did. After we knew we loved each other and were gonna stay together, I went to the newspaper archives of all the places where Madison had killed and made copies and set everything up in chronological order." She looked down at her hands, almost blushing. "I realize it's nothing to be proud of. I don't mean it like I'm boasting of my husband's 'accomplishments.' I know what he did was horrible and I feel for the families of those poor women. But—"

"You love him anyway."

"That's not why I keep the scrapbook, though." She looked up at Cass, big dark eyes swelling with tears. "People who can kill the way Madison did are different than other people. It's not like war, where you're doing it for your country, or in self-defense, where you're doing it to stay alive. You hear somebody get mad and say, 'Oh, I'd like to murder him,' but you know they don't mean it, they'd never do it. Or even you take a guy catches his wife with another man and kills both of 'em, he wouldn't have killed under any other circumstances and the law even recognizes that—calls it a crime of passion."

"The victims aren't any less dead."

"No, but my point is, however terrible a thing it is, at least there's an explanation. You say, well, he did it in a fit of rage, he did it out of jealousy."

"But somebody like Madison, he does it for what? Pleasure?"

"I asked him one time," said Mariah, "and he said no, it wasn't for pleasure, even though there was the sexual element involved. He raped most of them first. That wasn't why he did it, though, not for the sex, although everybody thinks it was for sex. He did it out of curiosity, he said, to see what it would feel like to watch them die and he did it because . . . he could."

"And you don't find that disgusting? Horrifying?"

"I find it scary, but kind of intriguing, too. I mean, look, Madison breaks the most cardinal rule of society and religion, not just don't kill, but don't kill without a damn good reason, and he does it without guilt or remorse, not caring what society thinks or what the consequences might be."

"Not giving a damn about his victims," said Cass. There was about an inch of Bloody Mary left in her glass. She pushed it away and stood up. "I should be getting out of here."

"Five minutes," said Mariah. "I'll put something on."

While Mariah was getting dressed, Cass wandered back into the living room for another look at the painting over the fireplace. She still found Madison's eyes disturbing and Mariah's expression incongruously come-hither, but now she finally realized why the painting seemed familiar.

Taking a few steps in the direction of the bedroom, she called out, "Hey, Mariah, this painting . . . how were you and Madison able to pose for it?"

Mariah came back in the room, tugging up the zipper of her jeans over a cream-colored blouse and fluffing her hair. "Oh, we couldn't pose for it, of course. I gave the artist a photo I liked of me and one of Madison and she painted it like we were together. I think I look a little plump, but it's great of Madison."

"The artist's a woman?"

"Yeah."

"What's her name?"

"Raven Sterling."

"I knew her," said Cass. "She was murdered, right?"

"Yeah. One more reason why you ought to carry a gun."

Cass studied the painting. "When was this done?"

Mariah scrunched her face up in thought. "Well, it was about a year after Madison and I got married, and I thought we ought to have a painting of us for the house, 'specially in case Madison got a pardon and was able to come home. So that was a little over three years ago, and it took her—oh, maybe six months to finish it, I'd say. Then about a year later, I picked up the paper and found out she'd been murdered. Just like CharLee. Couldn't fuckin' believe it."

"Were you friends?"

Mariah gave an odd little grimace, like she'd smelled something unpleasant. "Me and Raven? Well, no, I mean, I got nothin' against 'em, you know, to each her own and all that, but I'd never be friends with . . . you know, those kind of people."

"You mean born-again Christians?"

Mariah rolled her eyes. "Hell no, I mean fruits. Dykes. Lesbos."

"Raven wasn't a lesbian."

Mariah put her hands on her hips. "Sure, she was, she wasn't even in the closet about it. All out in the open. That was the only problem—her *girl*friend, this big bull dyke chick would come along with her whenever she and I needed to discuss money or how she wanted me and Madison to look or whatever. She'd wear these tiny little tank tops and it was obvious her tits had never seen the inside of a bra.

"And talk about jealous, she was worse than a guy! I got the impression she wouldn't let Raven out of her sight, and heaven help the man or woman who laid a hand on Raven." Mariah shook her head, chuckled. "Matter of fact, first thing I thought when I read she'd been murdered was the girlfriend musta done it. The cops are all running around looking for a guy and wouldn't you just bet was a woman did it."

"The girlfriend, what was her name?"

Mariah tilted her head, considered it a minute. "Erika. No, no that's wrong. Erin. See, I never really talked to her. She was so bitchy. Never opened her mouth, just sat there guzzling beer while Raven and I talked. Like she was keeping an eye on her property."

Chapter 15

The woman who finally barked into the phone at the Sterling residence identified herself as Crystal, the domestic manager. In addition to her title, she had an Australian accent and a lousy attitude. From the sound of the TV blaring in the background, she also had a fondness for American soaps. She said that Kenny and Bonnie were away until the middle of the week and couldn't be reached, but when Cass persisted, she finally agreed to pass a message on to Kenny, punctuating every other syllable with a sigh to indicate the magnitude of the imposition.

While she waited for Kenny to call back, Cass took a steaming hot shower and shampooed her hair twice, less from necessity than the fear that the odor of lunch meat and unwashed flesh from the car she'd been held in might still cling to her.

Getting out of the shower, she heard the distinctive growl of a Harley's engine, and her heart did a quick flip-flop. Clutching a towel around her, she rushed to the window and peeked out from behind the shade. A red Harley driven by a bearded blond man in fringed leathers was pulling into the lot. His ponytailed girl-friend with matching blond hair and fringed jacket held on to his waist. Cass relaxed and moved away from the window.

Kenny called while she was brewing a cup of coffee

to counteract the lingering buzz of Mariah's Bloody Marys. He sounded so uncharacteristically jovial that she wondered if he'd had a few Bloody Marys himself.

"Where are you?" asked Cass.

"The Broadmoor. You know it?"

She was pleased to be able to say that she did, though not from firsthand experience. "Yeah, that old hotel in Colorado Springs. Very elegant and upper-crust."

"Very good, Cass. Spoken like one of their brochures."

"I'll drive up tomorrow morning. We need to talk."

His good mood evaporated. "Now hold on a minute, there's no need for you to come up here. Besides, you'll miss a visiting day with Jack."

"He isn't going anywhere."

"What's this about?"

"We'll talk when I get up there tomorrow, Kenny. Say midmorning? In the main lobby?"

"If I can," he said, with a tone of petulance so similar to Crystal's that Cass wondered if the housekeeper had copied it from her employer. "But I don't like to be kept waiting, especially when whatever it is could be discussed on the phone. If you don't see me in the lobby, I'll be somewhere on the grounds."

She was going to ask him to be more specific about what that meant, but the line went dead.

The replacement car that the rental company provided her with was an upgrade from the Caprice to a Lincoln Town Car, a sleek pewter machine that hugged the road like a calfskin glove and whisked her to Colorado Springs in under an hour. Signs for Garden of the Gods, Seven Falls, and the Broadmoor Hotel led her through an upscale residential area of stately brick and Tudor houses that opened into the grounds of the hotel, just after ten o'clock.

Turning into the spacious, tree-flanked driveway that led up to the hotel, she could feel a battalion of tiny butterflies doing aerial maneuvers in her stomach. She hated to admit it, but this much conspicuous class made her nervous.

The grande dame of nineteenth-century Colorado resorts, the hotel exuded elegance and grandeur. It also reeked of wealth, both old and nouveau. It was the kind of place Cass had been brought up to believe she could never belong and shouldn't want to belong in the first place—that the only way a Lumetto could wind up in such a posh palace would be folding sheets and vacuuming floors or scamming some rich mark out of his trust fund.

She'd had this kind of jitters before, though, walking into the offices of some tony Manhattan magazine or joining Philip for cocktails at the Oak Room. Just old shit, ancient baggage, she reminded herself. It would dissipate like bad air if she ignored it.

And, for the most part, it did. After turning over her keys to an embarrassingly obsequious valet parking attendant, she went through a revolving door into a high-ceilinged, well-appointed lobby that mimicked an English hunting lodge with its heavy oaken decor and dog and pheasant hunting scenes on the walls.

She made two complete tours of the lobby, checking out the gift shop and bar and the second-floor breakfast room overlooking the lake. No sign of Kenny.

Returning to the front desk, she tried to wheedle Kenny and Bonnie's room number from a thin-faced young woman with full, berry-red lips and café au lait skin. No room number was forthcoming, but the woman gave her a handwritten note in Kenny's unmistakably chunky block print: SKEET SHOOTING ON THE LAWN.

Cass got directions from the desk clerk and headed out to explore the grounds—acres of shamrock-green golf fairway flanked by newer, more recently built wings that were smaller replicas of the main building. The skeet-shooting range was at the end of a short, cobbled walkway bordered with boxbush hedges and flowers that appeared to have been chosen for their colors: dazzling beds of burgundy, lavender, and royal-blue pansies, zinnias bright as a fistful of lollipops.

When she finally heard it, the shooting was surprisingly muffled, as though in this rarified atmosphere, even gunshots remained discreet. An object arced across the sky above the tree line. There was a gunshot and the clay bird exploded.

A moment later, she walked from between the box-bushes and came upon Kenny, squinting into the sunlight, face red as a slab of underdone beef. He was holding a short-barreled shotgun, aiming at clay birds that were fired two at a time from a pair of towers about sixty yards apart. Eight stations were marked off on a semicircle between the towers.

Kenny was standing at number four, taking the longest shots from a position perpendicular to the field. He wore khaki shorts, a blue polo shirt, and white deck shoes with no socks. Sweat left wet trails down the sides of his face and neck and into his open collar.

She heard a click and saw another clay pigeon streak like a fragment of bone across the blue bowl of sky. For a tenth of a second, Kenny tracked the target with his shotgun. Then he fired. There was an explosion and the target shattered and fell away, only to be replaced by another flying the same trajectory from the other tower. Kenny tracked and fired, and it too was obliterated. The next three shots hit the target, but then his timing got off, and the following four made the trip across the sky untouched. When the birds stopped, he lowered the shotgun and noticed Cass for the first time.

"So you actually made the drive? I thought you might change your mind."

"Is that why you didn't bother waiting for me in the lobby?"

He ignored the question and sighted down the shotgun at an imaginary target before tucking the gun under his arm, barrel aimed at the ground.

"Ever shoot skeet?"

"No. My dad used to say if you couldn't fry it, bake it, or stuff it, it wasn't worth the ammo to bring it down."

"But you're not your father."

"God forbid." She was trying for sarcasm, but it came out sounding more scared than smart-ass.

Kenny offered the gun. "It's a Briley twelve gauge. Bought it just for skeet. Give it a try."

"I don't think so."

"You don't shoot?" He sounded almost shocked at the idea, the way another man might react at the thought of a woman who disdained makeup and child-rearing. "Ought to learn then. A woman needs to be able to defend herself."

She caught a slight contraction of his muscles as he said it, wondered how many times he might have offered the same advice to Raven.

"I didn't say I don't know *how* to use a gun. I grew up around them, and I actually used to be a pretty good shot. But I don't *like* to shoot."

"You live in New York City and don't own a gun? Not even one of those silver-handled little twenty-twos designed for ladies to tote in their purses?"

"Hate to disappoint you, Kenny, but some New Yorkers go for months at a time without having to resort to firearms. I haven't fired a gun in years."

"No time like the present."

"No thanks, Kenny. We need to talk."

"Give me a minute then." He bent down and packed the shotgun in its case, much like a classical violinist might lovingly put away his instrument, Cass thought.

When he straightened, a look of apprehension crossed his broad features, then something else she couldn't quite identify—anticipation, hope? "You found out something? Jack said something incriminating? I knew it. Cocky son of a bitch, I knew he'd start running his mouth sooner or later."

"This isn't about Jack. It's about Raven."

"Well?"

"I need to know who Erin was. How she figured in Raven's life."

"Erin?"

She could see the anger rise in his face, a dark flush that crept like a heat rash up the broad slabs of his cheekbones. The blood pulsed in a vein at his temple.

"Did that bitch get in touch with you?"

"No, but I want to find her. Who is she? Where does she live?"

Kenny glared down at her. The sensation was far from pleasant, a beefy, florid-faced man towering over her, a case with a weapon in it at his feet. "Let's walk," he said finally, picking up the shotgun case.

They left the fairway and walked up a grassy embankment to a paved walkway that circled the lake behind the hotel. Swans and wild ducks glided across the water like small, feathered boats; joggers and those enjoying an afternoon stroll trod the path. Others lunched under umbrellas on the outdoor patio. The entire scene was one of repose and posh gentility and harkened back, Cass thought, to an era that at least in retrospect seemed gentler and more tranquil.

They passed an elderly couple sharing a bench by the lakeside. The silver-haired woman was breaking up bread and tossing it to a bevy of chattering ducks. The man snoozed, his mouth partly open.

Cass said, "Just for the record, I have to ask this. Was Raven gay?"

"What are you now, a reporter?" He made a snorting sound, a combination of chastisement and dismissal. "That question's ridiculous."

"Why? The world's full of gay people. Why couldn't one of them have been your daughter? Or is it just impossible for you to grasp the possibility of something so entirely beyond your control?"

His eyes narrowed to surgical slits as he glanced around them. They were nowhere near anyone else, but he hissed, "Keep your voice down. You want people to hear?"

"I want *you* to hear me, and I don't think you do. Was she a lesbian? A bisexual?"

"Raven had too many boyfriends to count. You were her roommate. You ought to know."

"She had boyfriends, that doesn't mean she didn't also have relationships with women now and then."

He walked faster. "Which, even if it were true, wouldn't mean she was a lesbian."

"What would it mean?"

"That she was young, she was experimenting, kicking her heels up. Nothing wrong with that," he added, angry now, challenging her to disagree.

Cass lengthened her stride to keep up. "Why didn't you tell me about Erin in the first place?"

"For what reason? She's not important. Just a nuisance. Irrelevant."

"C'mon, Kenny, I don't buy that. If Raven and this woman were lovers, then Erin might know something about her death. If Jack murdered Raven, then finding out she had a lesbian relationship might have pushed him over the edge. He doesn't strike me as being exceptionally p.c. That might be the motive. On the other hand, how do we know this Erin woman isn't the killer herself? Did the police interview her? Do they know where she was the night Raven was killed?"

They strode on a few paces, Kenny staring straight ahead. "Are you even listening to me?"

He glanced at his Rolex. Cass saw the glitter of diamonds outlining the large, Roman-numeraled face. "Bonnie's getting some kind of mud treatment and a shiatsu massage. She'll be out in another half hour. I'll talk to you until she shows up, but not a moment longer. I don't want her to know anything about this. It would devastate her."

Remembering the intense protectiveness Bonnie

had shown toward her husband at their last meeting, Cass said, "I think you underestimate your wife."

"Be that as it may. She isn't to know about Erin. Ever. Do you understand?"

"Are you saying that Raven confided in you about her personal life, rather than her mother?"

"No." The word came out a bark. "Hardly. I didn't know this woman Erin existed until about three months after Raven was killed. Right out of the blue she shows up at the house one afternoon." He chuckled mirthlessly, shook his head. "We don't get many visitors, unannounced ones anyway, and the way she looked, the way she was dressed, I had an awful moment when I thought maybe she was some indiscretion from *my* past turning up, some bimbo from a topless joint I'd given my card to when I was too looped to know better. Wish that'd been all there was to it."

"She told you she was Raven's lover?"

"No, actually she phrased it a little differently. She introduced herself as the daughter-in-law I'd never met. This, when I was still beside myself with grief. I just about keeled over, which I think was the reaction she wanted."

"Had you met her before at the funeral?"

"She said she didn't attend." He cocked a salt-and-pepper eyebrow. "Strange, huh? Claimed my daughter was the great love of her life, but she didn't show up for the funeral."

They were on the far side of the lake now, where a wooden bridge led out to a tiny, tree-covered island, an oasis within an oasis. Cass liked the peaceful look of the two shaded, wrought-iron benches facing the shore. Only one bench was presently occupied—by a mallard duck with its beak tucked under a wing—and she headed toward the unoccupied one.

"So if Erin didn't bother to come to the funeral, why show up at your house months later?"

"She said she wanted some things of Raven's. Noth-

ing specific or particularly expensive, just keepsakes.
Some photographs, jewelry she said she'd given Raven
over the years. A favorite book or two. What she
wanted wasn't unreasonable—if she'd introduced herself as a friend, I wouldn't have given it a second
thought."

"But the daughter-in-law bit—?"

"That was bullshit, she was just trying for shock
value. Thank God Bonnie wasn't at home to have
heard it."

"That still doesn't explain why she waited so long
to come forward."

"Well, supposedly—" He stopped to lean on the
bridge, squinting at a trio of swans sailing toward
shore like origami creations. "If you believe her story,
she had some kind of breakdown when Raven was
killed. Went on a drinking and drugging spree and
ended up in a twenty-eight-day rehab in Denver. The
shrinks there convinced her that part of her substance
abuse problem was having had to keep quiet about
her relationship with my daughter, which—again supposedly—had been going on off and on ever since
Raven lived in L.A. Get it all out in the open, they
said, confront the homophobic old bastard with his
Catholic school values and tell him what's what. And
fuck it if Raven would have wanted it kept secret,
she's dead."

"So Erin tells you everything."

"Tells me enough."

"You sound dubious. You didn't believe her?"

"Oh, the part about being locked up in rehab, I've
no trouble believing, although I'm not sure it took. I
think she was half in the bag when she came to the
house, that's how she got up her courage. And maybe
she and Raven did have a little fling, maybe when
Raven was drunk or something. But a relationship of
five years duration that Bonnie and I didn't know
about? That I doubt. That I seriously fucking doubt."

"And all she came for was to get a few keepsakes—

opening a whole new window into the world of Raven's sexuality was just incidental?"

"How would I know what her true motives were? Maybe it really was something she thought would be therapeutic. It was a long time ago and thank God I haven't seen or spoken to the woman since." He turned and marched toward the island.

"Kenny, was Erin by any chance—?" She was practically jogging now to keep up. The bench-sitting mallard untucked its wing and jumped down to the ground, clacking as it splashed into the water.

"—the person who told you Jack tried to rape Raven when she wouldn't sleep with him? You said it was someone undesirable, someone she wouldn't normally have associated with. Were you talking about Erin?"

"Yes." He slowed down, right shoulder slumping as though dragged down by the weight of the shotgun. "She told me Raven said Jack got physical with her one night in his car, that he basically dumped her out in the middle of nowhere when she wouldn't do what he wanted."

"Why didn't you tell me?"

Still a pace or two ahead, he swung around so sharply that they almost collided. "Because I didn't hire you to play detective, I hired you to find out whether or not O'Doul killed my daughter."

"It amounts to the same thing."

"No, it doesn't. I know O'Doul killed her—I'm absolutely convinced of it. It's just a matter of getting him to admit it."

The anguish underneath the anger in his voice was so palpable that Cass felt a surge of compassion. "He may never admit to anything," she said softly. "Maybe if I keep playing the role of his girlfriend, one day he'll have a pang of conscience or an attack of braggadocio. But maybe not. I've been thinking that if I can look at some other angles, come at it from a few different directions, then maybe I can learn something.

So why don't you tell me how I can find this woman? For starters, what's her last name?"

He exhaled wearily, jowls sagging. "O'Malley. She said she worked for some river-rafting outfit in town. Don't remember the name, if she even told me. She's a guide."

"A rafting guide," said Cass. "Yeah, that would ring true. Raven loved excitement, anything with an adrenaline high. I can see her being attracted to someone who ran rivers for a living."

His head jerked up. "What in blazes are you talking about? We don't even know for sure if what that woman said was true. She could have been lying."

"Claiming a relationship where none existed. Why? So you'd give her a photo or two of Raven, a few trinkets? That doesn't make sense."

"Unless something did happen, but it was a onetime aberration, something of no consequence to Raven, but important enough to Erin that she started building fantasies." He spoke faster, warming to this theory and to prevent Cass from interrupting. "Men used to become obsessed with Raven—it happened even when she was in high school—they'd go out with her one time and kiss her good night, then think they were in a relationship with her, that they were lovers, for God's sake, come mooning around for weeks after. No reason it couldn't have happened that way with this goddamn dyke." He thrust his neck forward. "Why the hell are you looking at me like that?"

"I never realized what a bigot you are."

"What's that supposed to mean?"

"You're more upset by the idea that Raven may have had a relationship with a long-time female lover than the fact that she's dead."

"My daughter wasn't one of—those people." He glared at her, gripping the bridge rail with huge, worn hands that had turned grayish-white at the knuckles. "She was a wonderful Christian woman, not some kind of—of pervert."

"That's what you think gays and lesbians are—perverts?"

He turned and hissed through gritted teeth, "What would you call them? Look in the Bible!"

"Well, screw the Bible!" It came out louder than she'd intended. Some joggers passing on the path beyond the bridge turned to stare. "And screw you, too, Kenny! You didn't deserve to have a daughter like Raven."

"For God's sake, what're you getting so upset about?"

All she could think about was her brother Tony, somewhere out there in a world full of people like Kenny, people whose bigotry was so deeply ingrained and accepted that it seemed to them as natural as breathing. People who didn't even have enough humility to be ashamed of their bigotry toward anything or anyone that was different, but flaunted it, wore their stupidity like a badge.

She waved him away. "I'm outta here."

Anger propelled her across the bridge and halfway around the lake again, headed back to the main building before he caught up with her, puffing. "What's the matter with you? I don't understand. Why're you so goddamned easily offended?"

She shook her head, mimed a slap to the forehead. "Right *there*. The fact that you don't even get why I'm pissed off. You think because I'm straight I don't have gays and lesbians in my life that I care about, that I love? That you can just blithely go about your bigoted business and then explain it away with that self-righteous shit that it's not really you who's condemning them, it's in the Bible, so it's God? I got news for you, Kenny. I may not know much about God, but I do know this—she don't operate that way."

He snorted at her choice of pronouns, but said nothing. They walked in silence a few steps, Cass thinking about Tony, wondering where he was and what he was doing, hoping nobody like Kenny—or worse—was making his life hell.

"What did you mean just now?" Kenny said.

She was so engrossed in her thoughts it took her a few seconds to realize he was talking. "About what?"

"That I didn't deserve to have a daughter like Raven." His voice was different now, absent the bullying growl. "You mean because I'm intolerant of homosexuality I couldn't have been a good father?"

"I meant that, given your attitude, if Raven was gay or bisexual, she could hardly have told you, could she? She'd have had to keep secrets. If she really wanted to win your favor, she might have even been tempted to join something like the Church of Good Hope."

"Bonnie and I weren't thrilled when she joined that church," he said quickly. "She was brought up in the Catholic faith and we'd hoped that she'd find her way back to it. The Church of Good Hope might not have been our choice, but we thought at least she was on the right track. She was looking for God again."

"But instead she found Jack."

His jaw muscles were working, like something had lodged in his throat. "Then it's my fault she's dead."

"Look, I didn't mean literally—"

He talked over her in a monotone, looking down at his feet, at the pristinely swept path. "There was a time, a couple of years after she moved back here from L.A., when Raven seemed so unhappy. She was talking of moving away, maybe trying California again. Bonnie and I didn't want that. We wanted her to stay here. I urged her to go back to the church, the Catholic church, of course, but when that didn't seem to suit her, I suggested she shop around. Find something that fit her needs better."

He stopped, took a harsh quavering breath. "I was actually hoping she'd meet someone. A nice young man who might want a family. She was past thirty and Bonnie and I thought it was time she settled down and got married. We both wanted grandchildren." He looked at Cass as though searching for some kind of absolution. "Is that so terrible? Wanting grandchildren and a happy life for your child?"

She wanted to say, *no, Kenny, it's not*, but something mean and niggardly inside her kept her lips sealed, condemning him silently.

They were approaching the main building when a female voice, just a little too exuberant to convey genuine pleasure, yoohoo'd from one of the umbrella-covered tables on the patio. Bonnie lifted a Nautilus-trim arm, waved them over. She wore a snug-fitting white sundress and a strand of ceramic beads a shade or two lighter than her tan. The mane of wild hair was tamed today, folded at the nape of her neck in a sleek, henna'd coil, and her skin glowed, perhaps from the effects of the massage and mud treatment or the glass of rosé she was drinking. She looked loofah'd and languid and only a smidgen annoyed to see Cass strolling with her husband.

"Cass, honey, what are *you* doing here?" Her eyebrows arched with concern. "Has something happened? Did Jack tell you anything?"

"No, Bonnie, no dramatic confessions, I'm sorry to say. I just needed a change of scenery and decided to drive up. Kenny and I were going over where I stand with Jack."

"Which would be where exactly?" said Bonnie. She was still smiling, but sipped her wine through collagen-plumped lips so taut they quivered.

"I'm not sure," said Cass. "It takes time. I have to win his trust."

"Well, pull up a chair," said Bonnie, "and tell me more about this folie à deux you and my husband are engaged in. God knows I could use a good laugh." She reached into her Yves St. Laurent tote bag and extracted a gold cigarette case from which she withdrew a cheroot. Kenny produced a lighter and she leaned toward him.

"How was the massage?" said Kenny, seeming more docile in the presence of his wife.

"Delicious," said Bonnie, "except the little masseuse babbled like a brook the entire time. Doesn't anyone appreciate the value of silence these days?" She drew on the cheroot, exhaled clove-flavored smoke in Cass's direction. "Really, dear, how can you stand going inside that awful prison day after day? It can't be clean, not with all those foul people confined there. You could catch some disease."

"I take very shallow breaths," said Cass, sniffling as the fumes from the cigarette reached her.

Bonnie sucked on the cheroot, leaving a vermilion stain on the brown tip. "Make fun of me, go ahead. My daughter used to do the same thing."

"I'm sorry," said Cass, then erupted in a fit of sneezing that was only contained when Kenny handed her a napkin and she blew her nose heartily. Somewhat recovered, she went on, "You're right, Bonnie, it's no fun going inside a prison even for five minutes. God only knows how people stand it who have to spend years."

"You hear her?" said Bonnie, sending her husband a look that could have drilled holes in steel. "She knows what she's talking about."

"Nobody said this was going to be easy for Cass," said Kenny, "going into the prison, small-talking with scum."

Cass fanned Bonnie's cigarette smoke away from her face, and said irritably, "Not to mention the thug that's following me around."

Bonnie's head snapped around. "What thug?"

"There's a guy on a motorcycle who's been tailing me. The other day he picked me up in his car and it got a little rough."

If Bonnie'd puffed any harder, Cass thought the cheroot would have disappeared down her throat. "Picked you up in his car? How could such a thing happen? You just got in a car with a strange man? What were you thinking?"

"It's a long story," said Cass, wishing now that she'd

never started it. "I had some car trouble. The guy picked me up. He wanted to scare me, that's all. I'm sure it was somebody Jack sent to keep an eye on me, make sure nothing's going on behind his back. At least that's the only explanation I can think of."

"Good Lord," said Bonnie, "he could have raped you. Murdered you." She turned to Kenny, as though he were entirely to blame. "You see where this insanity is leading, don't you? She's going to get hurt. Then you'll have one more thing on your conscience."

"Bonnie, will you please—be—quiet. Cass is a grown woman. She can look out for herself."

The old Kenny talking now, his voice like chips of stone. Bonnie retreated.

"Look, nothing happened. He didn't hurt me," said Cass, concerned that she was going to be the cause of a fight. Bonnie's look of pampered well-being had disappeared as fast as her wine, and Kenny was breathing heavily. "He was just some goon Jack put up to following me. I'm certain of that."

"That's it then," said Kenny, "I'm getting you a gun."

"No gun," said Cass. "If I change my mind about that, you'll be the first one I call." She redirected a curl of blue smoke with a wave, amazed and annoyed that, as a smoker herself since the age of fourteen, the cheroots could affect her so powerfully. "Actually now that we've talked, I'm going to drive back to Canon City. I'm going to start looking for an apartment."

Kenny seemed relieved. "Good, good, then you're going to stay here for a while. Find something nice, something comfortable. And don't forget to send me the receipt for whatever it costs you."

"Don't worry, I will." She pushed her chair back and stood up.

"Wait," said Bonnie, "you didn't say whether or not you called the police after this man picked you up? You did call them, didn't you?"

"I thought about it and decided not to. If Jack's

behind it—and I'm sure he is—I can get him to pull the guy off."

"I'm getting you a gun," Kenny blustered. "Not calling the cops, that's ridiculous."

"On the contrary," said Bonnie, "Cass is a woman who knows the value of silence. And as you just said, she can take care of herself."

On her way back into Canon City, Cass drove past the prison and saw a long line of cars turning into the parking lot. She checked her watch. Visiting hours were just starting.

She wavered for a second, knowing Jack would be expecting her, almost tempted to swing around the block and drive through the gates, but the memory of her encounter with the thug in the white Camaro ended any such impulse. It made her furious to think he had the gall to try to control her from inside the prison—and gave her some idea of what Melinda must have been up against in a marriage to such a man.

It was a battle of wills, a matter of control, she decided. And while she could pretend to accede to Jack in some areas—looking for an apartment, attending the Church of Good Hope—she couldn't afford to teach him that it was okay to use friends on the outside to bully her into towing some kind of imaginary "line." She had to teach him a lesson—that if he tried to intimidate her on the outside, that was it. He just wouldn't see her.

At least not until she felt he'd been sufficiently punished for what he'd had done to her.

But had he? persisted a nagging voice.

She answered herself out loud. "Of course he did. Why the hell else would somebody be following me unless Jack put them up to it?"

As she said it, she automatically glanced in the rearview mirror, half expecting to see the Harley or the Camaro. The only vehicle behind her was a minivan driven by a woman with kids bouncing around like trampoline artists in the backseat.

Satisfied with her decision not to see Jack that day, she bought a paper, consulted the ads for furnished apartments, and visited a few. She found precious little to choose from—most of the places she did see were almost as poorly furnished and depressing as her room at the Mountain View.

An ad under furnished houses caught her eye—a two-bedroom house west of Canon City in the subdivision of Cotopaxi. She called the number and spoke to a woman who said she was renting the place for a sister traveling in the British Isles. She was at the house now and gave Cass directions to an address on Burnt Mill Lane.

Twenty minutes later, she drove up to a small, rustic stone house with a garden in front and a protective wall of trees in back that provided privacy from neighboring houses. She knew this was it. Even inside, where the rooms reeked as a result of the elderly owner's fondness for sachets and cloying perfumes, the place exuded warmth and coziness.

"She has cats," explained the tiny, wizened sister, a Mrs. Brill, "and she was always afraid there'd be an odor from the litter boxes. Now that I'm keeping the cats, I think their smell is a lot better than all this damned lilac."

Cass smiled and asked about a lease.

"By the month," said Mrs. Brill, "plus one month's deposit when you move in." She squinted at Cass through her bifocals. "You cook much?"

"Not if I can help it."

"Good, because the kitchen's tiny. Not a lot of room for fancy gadgets."

"I think it'll be fine."

She wrote a check for a month's rent plus a deposit, shook Mrs. Brill's hand, and departed feeling a sense of elation rare in her life since coming to Canon City. Even the prospect of gardening buoyed her spirits.

The phone was ringing when she opened the door. She picked it up—

You have a collect call, the automated voice began. —and slammed it back down.

It started to ring again almost immediately.

Dammit!

She lifted the receiver and hung up again.

And again, it started to ring.

"Cass, c'mon, please!" She heard Jack's voice over the automated one. Frustrated, shaking a cigarette out of the pack and fumbling around for a lighter, she accepted the call.

"Where are you? Why didn't you come to see me?"

"Why would I *want* to come to see you considering how you treated me last time?"

They were both angry and speaking over each other.

He won—mostly because she had to pause to get the cigarette lit and then exhale the smoke—and kept talking.

"Look, I'm sorry. What're you so angry about? Why aren't you taking my calls?"

"Have you got somebody stalking me?"

"*What?*"

"Did you get some friend of yours to keep an eye on me and report back to you what I do, where I go?"

She could hear him muttering under his breath, maybe holding the phone away from him, thinking she wouldn't hear. Then: "Cass, honey, I swear to Christ I don't know what you're talking about. There's nobody following you."

Briefly she told him about her encounter with the guy in the Camaro the day before and gave a description.

When she finished there was a long pause before Jack said, "I dunno. Tattoos, beard, drives a Harley— that could be half a dozen guys I used to run with."

"How about the white Camaro? Does that narrow it down?"

"Coulda been stolen. That'd be the smart thing to

do, you know, borrow a car someplace to go after you in, then drop it off later or take it somewhere, sell it for parts."

The idea that the car she'd been picked up in might have been stolen just for that purpose hadn't even occurred to Cass, and it angered her that Jack offered it up as obvious, as though car theft and kidnapping were normal.

"If you're not behind this, then explain why some guy I've never met in my life is keeping tabs on who I talk to, where I go?"

"I don't know. Who *have* you been talking to?"

"Make him leave me alone or I swear I'll never come see you again."

"Jesus, how can I make anybody leave you alone when I'm locked up in here?"

"The same way you got him to stalk me—call him up and tell him to lay the fuck off or—"

"Or what?"

"Or I swear, Jack, I'll make him regret it. I don't know what I'll do to this guy, but I'll make him sorry he ever got himself mixed up in my life."

She could tell he was fighting not to laugh, which only made her angrier. "Now you're talking crazy. Plus you're pissing me off. If we're gonna have a fight, I want to do it in person. So you get your pretty ass in the car and come down here right—"

She hung up while he was still talking, was amazed and infuriated when it rang again so fast she wondered how he could have possibly had time to redial.

Lunging for the receiver, she grabbed it and, without waiting for the recorded voice to begin, yelled, "Goddammit, leave me alone!"

There was a beat of silence. "Bad day?" asked Shep.

"Shep?"

"Usually it takes two or three dates before a woman starts screaming at me to leave her alone. Tell me, was it something I said?"

"I'm sorry. I thought you were someone else."

"It wouldn't be O'Doul, would it?" He sounded amused.

"It doesn't matter. I'm sorry I yelled at you."

"It *was* O'Doul. Lovers' quarrel? Well, platonic lovers anyway."

"Hey," she cut him off, "enough already! You want me to yell at you for real?"

"No way. You sound like one tough lady. Can we start over?"

"Yeah, let's."

"All right then. Hello, Cass."

"Hi, Shep."

"I waited to hear from you, but you didn't call."

"What?" She ground her cigarette out, braced the phone between her cheek and shoulder while she lit another. "Was I supposed to—"

"Your last words to me—'I'll call you'—remember?"

"Hey, I was going to."

"That's what all the girls say."

She plopped down on the bed, stretched her feet out. He had a nice voice, smooth but just gritty enough to imply a certain bedroom prowess. She kicked off her shoes, wiggled her toes, and wondered what he looked like with his clothes off.

"I would've called you, you didn't give me time."

"That's okay, you can make it up to me."

"And how would I do that?"

"You good with a camera?"

"I know how to point and click."

"Great. I'm going camping day after tomorrow. Come with me and take my picture when I catch a monster trout."

She laughed out loud. "That's the favor? You want me to immortalize you holding a fish?"

"Hey, it's catch and release only. I've got albums with nothing but me and some of Colorado's best-looking trout."

"That sounds pretty tame. I've known guys who kept photo albums of themselves and their conquests, but it sure wasn't trout."

"Does that mean you'll go?"

She blew smoke at the ceiling, thinking she had no business planning fishing trips, that she ought to be tracking down Erin O'Malley for starters. Still, though, Shep was a detective and probably could provide information on Raven's death or Melinda's if she questioned him carefully. And, hell, he did have great arms.

"Tell you what, can I let you know? I'd like to go, but I'm not sure. How about if I call you tomorrow?"

"You mean you want to wait and see if you make up with Jack?"

"No, it means I've got other things to do here in Canon City besides visit Jack."

"Okay, sorry. You got my phone number. If you decide to come along, I've got extra gear, so you won't need to bring anything."

"Sounds good."

"But don't leave me hanging. Remember I know where you live."

She laughed. "Okay, fair enough.

But after she hung up, before she started looking up whitewater rafting companies in the phone book, she went over and slid the chain across the motel-room door.

After all, Shep Loomis wasn't the only one who knew where she lived.

Chapter 16

When she found no Erin O'Malleys or E. O'Malleys listed in the phone book, Cass began calling a lengthy list of whitewater rafting companies.

To judge from the number listed in the Yellow Pages, half of Canon City's unincarcerated population worked as river guides. She called half a dozen before being told that an Erin O'Malley worked for the Big Thrills Rafting Company located between Salida and Canon City.

"But see, she took a month's leave of absence," the laid-back-sounding dude on the phone went on to inform her. "She's in Switzerland visiting a rich aunt. She stands to inherit big time."

"Oh," said Cass, a bit taken aback by this unsolicited information but interested nonetheless. "That's disappointing. I'd really wanted to talk to her. Any idea when she'll be back?"

"She left it kind of, you know, open-ended? Like how long she stays depends on how things go with the rich relative, know what I'm saying?"

"Got'cha."

"I guess you could talk to her sister, though. She'd maybe have, like, more information." There was a pause. She could hear papers being shuffled. "I've got her phone number someplace around here. Hang on a sec." More background noise, including a file cabinet being opened. "Sorry, guess it's not here. But you could look them up in the phone book."

"Under Erin O'Malley?"

"No, Joan. The sister's name's Joan Trent."

Cass thanked him and started to hang up.

"Except—?"

"Yeah?"

A leer had crept into the stoned-sounding voice. "Except, you know, I don't think they're really sisters, know what I'm saying?"

There were two Joan Trents and a J. Trent listed in the phone book. Cass called all of them. J. Trent, who turned out to be Janet, sounded frail and elderly and had never heard of Erin O'Malley. The second number was answered by a man who identified himself as the husband of Joanie Trent, who was at work. The second Joan Trent was listed along with an address on IvyWild Road, but when Cass called, a recorded voice said the phone had been disconnected. She checked the address on her map, found it halfway between Canon City and the Royal Gorge exit, and decided to drop in.

A pale pink-gray hue, more like a somber dawn than a sunset, bathed the western sky as she drove toward the gorge. The sun dragged tendrils of brown, like smeared mascara, toward the horizon. Highway 23 was just over five miles out of town, a stretch of flat, two-lane black top running north past a couple of dairy farms and a defunct dude ranch with an empty corral and boarded-up iron gates. Farther on, IvyWild Road, unpaved and circuitous as its name implied, intersected 23 at a hodgepodge collection of mailboxes, one of which was marked with an address and the names O'Malley/Trent.

The house was the first one on the road, a turn-of-the-last-century farmhouse with a wraparound porch and broad bay windows. There was a silo in need of a paint job out back and two multistory birdhouses in the front yard, the avian equivalent of a Hyatt Hotel. To the west, a handsome stand of cottonwoods cast brown, amoeba-shaped shadows.

Cass parked next to the avian high-rises and got out of the car. As soon as her door slammed, a pair of dogs came bounding around the side of the house, a golden retriever and a bigger-boned beast who looked like some sort of shepherd/rottweiler combination. Both seemed as delighted to have company as kids who'd spotted an ice cream truck pulling into the drive.

The woman who came to the door in response to Cass's knock seemed a good deal less thrilled than the dogs were at having a visitor. She had short, mahogany-brown hair cut in a functional style, harried-looking gray eyes, and a broad, open face whose underlying sweetness contradicted the initial impression of a plain young woman who would become homely with time. She was holding a Tupperware bowl full of ice cubes in one hand, a towel in the other.

"Yes?"

She cracked the door open and the dogs bounded past her, careening on a narrow throw rug in the hallway inside. "Guys wait!" she called after them as though yelling at a couple of kids, but they were long gone. She sighed and turned back to Cass.

"Joan Trent?"

"That's right."

"I'm looking for Erin O'Malley. I understand she lives here?"

A heartbeat of hesitation before the tentative admission, "That's right, but—" Joan Trent seemed flustered. She kept looking at the bowl of ice cubes. "Erin's not here right now."

"You mean she just stepped out for a few minutes? If that's the case, I can wait."

"No, no, I mean she's out of the country."

"For how long?"

"It's really indefinite. I'm sorry, who did you say you are?"

Cass held out a hand, introduced herself. The other woman's handshake was firm and strong, the skin cold from holding the bowl of ice. "If you'd like to leave a message for Erin, I can try and get it to her."

"I'll leave my phone number," said Cass. "By the way, I did try to call before I came by, but your phone's been disconnected."

"Disconnected? Really?" Joan Trent's head shot up as though this was the first she knew of it. Her lips pursed tightly together and two deep horizontal grooves appeared between her eyebrows. "I guess someone forgot to pay the bill again," she said tightly.

"Well, maybe when Erin gets back she can give me a call from a pay phone. Have you got something to write with?"

The woman stared at the bowl of melting ice cubes and the washcloth in her hands as though uncertain how they'd gotten there. "Uh, yeah, sure," she said distractedly. "Hold on."

She started to move away from the door when, from farther back in the house, a woman's voice, querulous and strident, screeched, "Jesus, Joan, I'm in pain here! What the hell are you doing? Where's the goddamn ice? And put the dogs out for Christ's sake! They're driving me crazy!"

"That wouldn't by any chance be Erin?" asked Cass.

Joan rolled her eyes in exasperation. She looked like a downtrodden housewife beset by a bullying mate. "I'm sorry. Please, can't you just leave?"

"Dammit, Joan, are you so stupid you can't even crack a goddamn ice tray? Bring me the fucking ice!"

Joan Trent winced at the scolding tone. Her front teeth gnawed a chapped lower lip.

"Goddammit, Joan!"

"May I?" said Cass.

Joan shrugged and thrust the bowl and the towel at Cass.

"First door on your right. Don't say I didn't warn you."

As Cass walked into the bedroom, the blond woman on the bed lunged for the nightstand, grabbed a pair of tortoiseshell sunglasses, and slapped them onto her face. The fact that she was naked didn't seem to concern her. It wasn't her body she wanted to hide, but the twin shiners.

"Who the hell are you?"

"I'm sorry if I'm catching you at a bad time," said Cass, reaching past the two dogs to put the towel and the ice on the nightstand, "but I believe you wanted these."

"Joan! Joan, what the hell is this, letting strangers wander in here?" The woman grabbed a sheet and tugged it up over substantial breasts. Her hair, cut in layers and streaked toffee-blond, fell past freckled shoulders that were tanned to a deep, lifeguard bronze. She looked muscular and resoundingly fit and, in spite of the black eyes—or maybe because of them—combative.

"Erin O'Malley?" asked Cass.

The woman gave a curt, fierce nod.

"I'm Cass Lumetto. I'm—"

"I don't give a shit who you are!"

"—a friend of Raven Sterling's."

Even with her eyes hidden behind the dark glasses, Cass could tell the woman's demeanor changed from arrogance and hostility to a kind of guarded wariness. Her full mouth set in a sullen line. She glanced toward the bathroom and said, "I have a rule about letting people see me naked if I haven't seen them naked first. So unless you're prepared to strip, how about looking inside there and handing me my robe."

Cass found a white terry-cloth robe on a hook behind the door. The dogs thumped their tails and made the trip with her from bathroom to bed as though it were an adventure, trying to sniff out her life history from the scents on her body and clothes.

Despite what she'd said about not letting strangers see her naked, Erin slid out of bed and stood up as Cass brought her the robe, showing off an all-over tan, a body with minuscule amounts of fat, and several interesting-looking tattoos positioned like way points to mark off strategic locations. She knotted the robe around her and climbed back into bed, plumping the pillows behind her and leaning into them with a sigh. "You say you were a friend of Raven's—did you really mean friend or was that just a euphemism for lover?"

"I meant friend—as in friend." She took a seat on the only piece of furniture in the room other than the bed, a green velvet ottoman covered with enough dog hair to stuff a small pillow. "Why? Is the distinction important?"

"Just wanted to save myself the effort of sizing you up as competition, even if it's shallow and meaning-less. Now we can just talk and I don't have to try to figure out which one of us has better tits." She reached for the ice cubes, took her glasses off, and applied a cube to each puffy eye. "You'll have to excuse me," she said, wincing. "These hurt like a bitch."

"Car accident?" said Cass.

"Blepharoplasty. Upper and lower. I had the best cosmetic surgeon in Colorado Springs, but she's sure as hell chintzy with the pain pills." She beckoned to Cass. "Lean over a second. Lower your lids. Hmmmmmm. Yep, I don't see any sag in the uppers, but give it a couple more years you'll definitely be a candidate for getting the lowers fixed. You've got just a hint of those pesky fat pouches that make for those oh-so-attractive bags. It's genetic." She grinned. "Don't worry, they just make an incision, suck the fat out, suture you up, and you're better than new. Well, after a couple of weeks anyway."

"This is fascinating," said Cass, "but fat pads under my eyes aren't really my top priority at the moment."

"Oh, really? A woman of depth?"

"Isn't there a rich aunt you're supposed to be visiting in Switzerland?"

Erin shrugged and flicked the remains of the ice cubes back into the bowl. "Yes, and when I come back to work, everyone will say isn't it amazing how much good the trip did her, how well rested she looks." She dangled a hand in the bowl and wiggled her fingers, making the melting ice tinkle softly. "So why did you take the trouble to come here? What do you want?"

"Just to talk to you. I want to find out what was going on in Raven's life before she died."

"You a detective?"

"No."

"Then why do you care?"

"Well, for starters, I was Raven's roommate in college and we were close at the time. We drifted over the years, but—"

"Were you in love with her?"

"No. I cared about her, though. But what I want now is to learn more about this church she joined, the one where she met Jack O'Doul, the Church of Good Hope."

Erin's eyes narrowed and Cass could see the red, weeping surgical scars outlining the upper lids. The eyes themselves were a striking deep blue, almost lilac. "Yeah, it's the Church of Good Hope, all right—all of them hoping to get laid. What a nest of wackos!"

"Did you ever go there with her?"

"You kidding? That'd be kind of like an African-American attending a KKK rally, wouldn't it? Anyway, Raven must've figured I was a doomed soul, she never invited me. We broke up right after she started attending."

"Her idea?"

The bruised lilac eyes shifted a bit. "Let's say it was mutual—she thought she was going to hell if she continued her muff-diving ways. And after she dumped me, I felt like I was in hell anyway."

Cass petted the retriever, who climbed onto the ottoman next to her and laid its head in her lap. "You must have loved her a great deal."

Erin looked at the door. "Close that, will you?"

Cass leaned back and gave it a nudge with her hand. Out of the corner of the eye she saw a flash of movement. Joan, caught eavesdropping, stepping back from the door.

"Sure I loved her," said Erin. "We were together five years. I left a good job in California—I was a stockbroker, making big bucks—to follow her here. But make no mistake about it, she loved me, too. In the end she realized just how bad she'd fucked up, and she tried to make it up to me."

"Why would she join an outfit like the Church of Good Hope in the first place? What appeal did it have for her? Was it Jack?"

"Oh, Christ, no," said Erin, reapplying the ice. "It was her father. She adored the old prick, God only knows why, and she wanted to please him. You know, meet a nice young Republican, settle down, squeeze out a few rugrats so the old man'd have somebody to bounce on his knee come Christmastime. Trouble was, Raven didn't know the meaning of the word *moderate*. If she wasn't going to be a free-living, hell-raising lesbian artist, then she'd reinvent her virginity, give up humping dykes for thumping the Bible, defend the values of chastity and marriage or chastity in marriage or whatever the fuck." She grabbed the towel, blotted the front of her robe where the ice had dripped down her neck.

"But she lost interest didn't she?" Cass said. "One of the women at the church knew Raven and said she basically told Reverend Butterworth he could shove it."

"And probably added that she's burning in hell because of it, right?" Erin said, rolling her swollen eyes. "That's how those people think. They're God's chosen and everyone else's on the celestial shit list."

"So what happened that changed Raven's mind about the church?"

"They let her down, showed their true colors, that's what happened. Raven took the crap they were peddling seriously—she was trying to live it, for Christ's sake—then she found out they were hypocrites, just paying lip service."

"The people I've met who're connected with the church seem sincere," said Cass, remembering her conversations with Opal and with Linda Lomax.

"I'm talking about Jack O'Doul and that witch who's married to the fat fuck in charge," said Erin. "Viola or whatever her name is."

"Fiona."

"Yeah, whatever, they both fucked Raven over royally. She said in the beginning Jack came off like a complete gentleman. He told her he was divorced and, yeah, he'd had some trouble with the law before he found God, but that was in the past. So they'd go out on these little preteen-type dates where they held hands and drank milkshakes and said praise God a lot until I guess Jack got a beer or two in him and decided enough was enough and it was time she put out. And when she reminded him about the born again's favorite commandments, Thou Shalt Not Fuck Before Marriage and Thou Shalt Never Fuck For Fun, he threw her out of his car on a dark road in the middle of nowhere."

"Pretty traumatic."

"That's not the half of it. She finally gets a lift back to town, but she's so upset she doesn't want to be alone, and she can't come to me, 'cause we're broken up, right? So she goes to the Butterworths' house, 'cause she thinks these folks are her friends. The fat fuck is out on some spiritual mission, but Fiona's home and you know what she does when Raven tells her what happened, when she's just walked three miles in the dark and hitched a ride with some trucker who coulda turned out to be as big an asshole as Jack?''

"I've got a pretty good idea."

"She puts the moves on her," said Erin. "The wife of the minister of this gays-are-damned fundamentalist fruitcake church and she's got her hand between Raven's legs, pretty much the way Jack did an hour or two earlier and she's not even guilty about it. She spouts some bullshit about the flesh being weak and they'll get on their knees and ask God for forgiveness—after they finish fucking, that is, and Raven says something like thanks but no thanks, Born-Again Bitch, I'm outta here."

She glanced toward the door and lowered her voice. "She called me from a pay phone and I came and got her. We spent the night together, making up for lost time. She kept telling me how sorry she was that she'd left me, that she'd been a fool to get caught up with that bunch of straight hypocrites who wouldn't know a spiritual life from a porn show. She told me she was through trying to live her life to please Daddy, that she'd learned something from all this. She was going to live exactly the way she wanted to, to be who she was and to hell with what the old man thought of it or whether or not he cut her off without a dime."

"Sounds like a pretty dramatic about-face."

"Well, she'd got her eyes opened the hard way. But there's more. She wanted us to get married. Go to Vermont for a lesbian wedding and then fly off to Paris. If Daddy wanted grandkids, we'd adopt. If he decided to cut her off without a penny, we'd say fuck you and live off her trust fund for as long as we could. And that was how it was gonna be, that was our dream—except somebody killed her before any of it could come true."

For the first time since she'd started speaking, real emotion undercut the veneer of flippancy in Erin's voice. Sadness dark as the bruises around her eyes freighted her voice. She swallowed hard and looked toward the door as though expecting Joan to barge through it. Cass could see the muscles in her throat working.

"After she came to you and said she wanted to get back together, how long after that was it when she was killed?"

"We got back together on a Tuesday," Erin said. Liquid—either tears or ice water from the melting ice cubes, Cass couldn't tell which—slid along her cheeks. "She was murdered on Friday. How's that for a short reconciliation?"

"Raven's father said you weren't at the funeral?"

She shook her head. "I was too drunk to walk, let alone pay my respects. But the cops talked to me later—they found some of my letters in Raven's apartment, trying to get her to come back to me—so that made me a suspect till they found out I was out of town on an overnight rafting trip when she was killed.

"I told them about Jack kicking her out of his car a few nights before and that he was the person they ought to talk to. They said they already had, that he had an alibi for that night."

"So I heard," said Cass. "But I'm curious about something. Why did you wait more than three months before you went to Kenny with that information. He said you ended up in rehab."

"That's right. I mean, you gotta understand it was like some lousy cruel twist in a movie or something. Girl loses girl, girl gets girl back, girl loses girl again forever. I truly loved Raven. She was"—her eyes flicked to the door again—"like nobody I've ever known, straight or lesbian. Beautiful and irreverent and exciting. She'd had a lot of lovers and a lot of disappointments and she was looking for a better way to live. Not just to please the old man, although that was certainly part of it, but because she wasn't happy with her life. She thought maybe cozying up to God was the answer, after all. That all that bullshit she'd been fed as a kid, say your prayers, follow Jesus, and be a good little girl, maybe that was the way after all. I told her it's not that simple. Spirituality isn't that neat, but she'd lived without rules for so long, I think she needed them. At least to try them out for a while."

"So what do you think," said Cass. "Alibi or not, do you think Jack killed her?"

Erin leaned back, smoothing the sheets out in front of her. She had strong, long-fingered hands that looked older than the rest of her. "A poor white trash redneck with a hard-on and no place to put it? Sure, I think there's a good chance he did it, no matter what the police think. I mean this is the same guy killed his wife, right, just a few months after that. I remember seeing his picture in the paper when he got arrested and thinking, shit, that's the guy, that's the guy who threw her out of his car.

"On the other hand, though, Raven told me he called her the next day to apologize, that he was crying he was so remorseful. Said it would never have happened if he hadn't been drinking." Her lips curled in a small, sad smile. "But then all drunks say that, don't they? I know I always do."

"And who's to say he wasn't drinking the night Raven was murdered," said Cass. "He could have gone to her apartment, maybe with the best of intentions, maybe planning to apologize, then things got out of hand."

"Yeah, I thought that, too," Erin said. "Except—I always wondered about the other guy, too. The one she never wanted to talk about."

Cass looked up from scratching the dog behind the ears. "What other guy?"

"The guy she was dating before Jack. You didn't know?"

"I told you I'm not a detective. Fill me in."

"See, the whole time she was involved in that church was maybe six, seven months and she just went out with Jack for a few weeks right at the end. But there was someone else she got involved with who I think she was serious about, but he wasn't into her born-again stuff."

"And she wasn't supposed to date outside the church?"

"No, getting hooked up with nonbelievers, people headed for hell, that was a big no-no. But she could date other fundamentalists or even a nonbeliever—as long as he eventually came around, saw the light, and joined up with Jesus."

"And this guy wouldn't go for it?"

"Oh, she worked on him, I know she did. But when push come to shove and she told him she couldn't see him again unless he found Jesus, well—at least I guess he wasn't a hypocrite. He could've pretended to go along just to keep seeing her—I know a lot of people who would have—but he wasn't that kind of guy. Supposedly, anyway."

"She told you all this but not the guy's name, what he did, anything at all?"

"I had to pull it out of her, the little bit of information that I got," Erin said. "See, she was trying not to have anything to do with me, afraid of temptation, I guess, but now and then she'd get lonely or it'd be some occasion, like my birthday, and we'd get together for a drink and I'd get a tidbit or two. The one time she talked about this guy was when it was already over and then she called him Mr. Wrong. She wouldn't tell me his name or what he did, just that when it fell apart it was because he refused to join up with Jesus. She was upset about it, too, said she wasn't going to risk getting involved with anyone outside the church again. So after that was when she took up with Jack." Erin blotted her eyes carefully. "From Mr. Wrong to Mr. Psycho."

"Maybe," said Cass, "but I'd sure like to know more about this other guy."

"Believe me, if I'd known more about him, I'd've

told the cops." Her voice was starting to sound softer
and a little slurred. Cass guessed that behind the dark
glasses, the swollen eyelids were starting to close.
"Goddamn pain medicine's finally kickin' in. You better leave."

"Thanks for your help." Cass rummaged a piece of
paper and a pen out of her purse, printed the phone
number of the motel and her room number. "If you
think of anything else . . ."

"Yeah, sure."

She laid the paper on the nightstand and got up
to leave.

"One thing more," Erin said, when she was almost
at the door. Cass turned back. "Don't know if it matters, but—they didn't sleep together. Her and this guy,
they never got it on. I could tell she regretted it. Like
if she'd known it wasn't going to work out, she might
have bent the rules a little bit."

The drive home took Cass past the Pioneer Café,
so she stopped and had huevos rancheros, sitting at a
table near the window so she could keep an eye out
for a black Harley or a suspicious-looking Camaro. If
she was being stalked, though, it was by nothing more
menacing than an especially persistent mosquito who
seemed to find her arm every bit as delectable as she
did the Key lime pie she had for dessert.

After the meal, she got out her notepad and smoked
a cigarette while making a list comparing Kenny's
story with Erin's and adding some thoughts of her
own about the mystery guy Raven had supposedly
dated prior to Jack.

According to both Kenny and Erin—as well as what
Cass herself had observed when she knew her in col-
lege—Raven was a woman who inspired obsession.
Had this man been immune?

Perhaps, since he'd refused to compromise his beliefs for her. Or maybe he'd just hidden it better.
Maybe the knowledge that Raven valued her religious

beliefs more than their relationship had eaten away at him after they split up. Maybe he'd decided to drop in on her.

On the other hand, maybe there was no mystery man at all. Maybe Erin had made him up in order to throw suspicion off herself. She jotted down a note reminding her to try to check out that rafting trip Erin claimed to have been on.

On the way home, satisfied that no one was following her, she let her thoughts drift back to Jack. Realistically, he was still her only suspect—everything else was just so much speculation.

I wonder if Jack knows anything about this guy, she thought. *And how can I find out without seeming overly interested in a woman I supposedly never even met?*

For that matter, were she and Jack even speaking to each other? Since that last visit, Cass hadn't been back nor had she accepted Jack's calls—half a dozen of them over a two-day period. She reminded herself that she wasn't just mad at him for siccing the Camaro creep on her—and deny it all he wanted, she was still sure that's what was going on—she was in a battle for control. Macho as Jack might be, the fact remained that he was on the inside and she was free. She could choose whether or not to visit, whether or not to accept his collect calls, which were exorbitantly expensive anyway—some sort of rip-off perpetrated by the State on the inmates' families, Jack had said. Once he realized she wouldn't tolerate abusive behavior, he'd have more respect for her. Then, hopefully, their relationship could proceed.

At the motel, she stopped in at the desk to ask about messages and to pay for another night's stay before moving into her new place. The night clerk, a corpulent woman in sweats and flip-flops with an abundance of fine facial down, took her money, wrote out a receipt, and told her she'd had five collect calls from the prison that afternoon.

She handed Cass the receipt and said with a woebe-gone air, "I usta date one a them cons years ago and I can tell you, honey, it ain't worth it. You're a young woman—find ya somebody can keep you warm at night, put a roof over your head."

"One of these days," said Cass, smiling at her, wanting to tell her not to worry, this wasn't what it appeared to be.

But later that night, on the verge of sleep, she found the woman's words unaccountably depressing. Leaving Jack out of the picture, the fact remained she didn't have anyone to keep her warm at night, either here or in New York, and the only person putting a roof over her head was *her*.

Maybe I should give Philip a call, she thought drowsily, reminding herself of the two-hour time difference. It was almost one o'clock in New York but Philip, if he was true to his old habits, rarely went to bed before two. Still, a middle-of-the-night phone call smacks of desperation, she thought just before falling asleep.

The phone woke her from a light, troubled sleep. A glance at the digital clock by the bed told her it was just after five a.m.

Galvanized by the thought of an emergency, she flung her arm out and grabbed for the phone, succeeded in knocking the entire apparatus to the floor where, even before she picked it up, she could hear the familiar tinny recording asking her if she'd accept a collect call.

Her first reaction was how the hell dare Jack wake her up like this, followed by an impulse to slam the phone down and yank the cord out of the wall. Then her head cleared enough for her to wonder how Jack had gotten out of his cell and received permission to use the phone at this hour anyway. A little nibble of fear chased through her and she accepted the call.

"Cass, honey, thank you, thank you for taking the call."

His voice sounded like rust being scraped off an old fender. Nothing arrogant now. Just raw fear and guilt and—something else—humility.

"Jack, what is it? What's wrong?"

"It's Twyla. She got hit by a car, but I only just found out last night." He started to cry. "They don't know if she's gonna make it."

Chapter 17

Climbing the brick steps to the Canon City Memorial Hospital, Cass felt a sense of apprehension not unlike what she experienced when going into the prison. In both cases she was a volunteer, entering with the knowledge that she was free to leave at any time, yet her stomach flip-flopped with apprehension, and she sucked on her cigarette so hard the smoke felt as if it were singeing her ribs.

A nurse at the information booth told her Twyla O'Doul was on the third floor in ICU. Her look implied that Cass could be there, too, in about twenty years if she didn't give up the cigarettes. She crushed out the one she'd just lit in an ashtray by the elevator and resolved to puff her way through the rest of the pack as soon as she left.

She took a wrong turn in one of the upstairs corridors, doubled back to an intersection of three different hallways, and was looking for someone to direct her when she heard a pained female voice that was unmistakably Angela's saying, "What are we gonna do? Do you have any idea how much this is gonna cost?"

"Fuck yeah," a male voice that could only have been Parker retorted. "I got an idea. And you know what? I'm gonna go get a beer."

"This time of the morning?"

"Goddamn, yes, what the hell else you expect me to do?"

A moment later, Parker careened out of a door up ahead, stopped, straightened, then continued walking with the exaggerated care of a man not entirely sure if the floor would still be in the same place when he took his next step. He passed Cass without a hint of recognition. She turned in time to see him list into a wall, right himself, then take the next corner at a ninety-degree angle, like a drunk doing an impersonation of a cadet in a military parade.

Inside the waiting room, Cass found Angela curled on a small, flower-print sofa. She wore a badly rumpled gold smock, frayed cutoffs, and sneakers that looked like they'd done a few hundred laps around a very dusty track. A single pink curler nestled from beneath the dark hair near the nape of her neck. When she looked up, her eyes were blood-rimmed, more glazed than her bleary-eyed husband's.

She looked at Cass and said bitterly, "You believe him? I think his ma gave birth to him in a barroom and nursed him on ninety proof milk." She inhaled violently. "You're here, so I guess somebody musta gave Jack my message."

Cass nodded and took a seat next to her. "He called this morning."

"It was late when I phoned the prison," said Angela, "so I didn't know if he'd get the message."

"Jack said Twyla was hit on Saturday, but he only just found out last night. He called me as soon as he could get a C.O. to let him use the phone. Did you call right away when it happened and there was a delay in getting him the message?"

"No, I waited till the next day," said Angela, looking sheepish. "Parker didn't think I should call him at all, but—well, her getting hit, it was mentioned in the paper and on the local news. Didn't seem right Jack should hear about it that way."

"He said it was bad," said Cass. "How's she doing now?"

"Well, she was awake for a while after they brought

her in, but yesterday she went unconscious again and she hasn't woke up."

"How did it happen?" said Cass, although remembering the chaos of the Parker home, it was easy to guess.

"She was playing outside about nine, ten o'clock at night—wasn't supposed to be out that late, but you know how kids are. A car comes around the corner. I didn't see it, but the guy claims he wasn't goin' more than twenty-five miles an hour, and Twyla runs out from behind the Suburban. He didn't have no chance to swerve or stop, he said, she was just there and he hit her."

She pulled a wadded clump of tissues out of her purse and dabbed at her eyes.

"So anyway, the car hits her and, believe it or not, that's not so bad—the guy musta been tellin' the truth about goin' the speed limit, because all she's got is some scrapes and a—what did they call it—greenstick fracture in her right arm. But her head hit the curb, that's what did the real damage. She's unconscious. If there's bleeding underneath the skull, they might have to operate and if it's real bad, she might even—die."

Angela said that last word like a prayer, so soft and ripe with terror that it filled the room like frost.

"Who's keeping your other kids?"

"Neighbor's got 'em." Her eyes filled with tears again. "I feel like I'm goin' crazy. Those things I said about Parker a minute ago, that was wrong. It's just that he's half out of his mind, too, but the way he deals with his pain, he tries to drown it in booze."

"I saw him on the way out," Cass said. "It looked like he was doing a pretty good job."

"He loves Twyla, too, even if she ain't his. But he don't know how to deal with what's happened. I mean, we don't even have insurance. Even if Twyla comes through this okay, we'll be in debt for the rest of our lives." She shook her head. "Oh, damn, why did this have to happen? It's all my fault."

"Angela," said Cass, trying to comfort her, "I just want you to know you did the right thing calling the prison to let Jack know what happened."

"Oh, God," whimpered Angela, "you don't understand. I didn't have no choice but to call him—it was because of him, no, because of me that Twyla got hurt."

"I don't understand."

"Ever since you came by the other day, Twyla's been just hateful mean, willful as she could be. She wanted me to take her to see Jack or let you take her. She wouldn't let up about it neither and it was driving me crazy. Last night when I told her to cut the TV off and go to bed, she starts in on me again, wanting to know why she can't see her dad, why can't she go to the prison, and we got into it pretty bad. Parker had just got home and I wanted things peaceful, so I hollered at her to go up to bed before I took the hairbrush to her and instead she hollers that if I won't take her, she's gonna go see her dad by herself and she runs out the door."

"And into the street?"

"I couldn't stop her," said Angela miserably. "What the hell do you do, how do you stop a kid like that? Reba started yelling about something and I turned around to tend to her. Next thing I knew I heard the tires squeal."

"I'm so sorry, Angela."

"You tell Jack when you see him it wasn't my fault. I love that little girl, I just couldn't stop her when she run out the door."

"He won't blame you, Angela. He just wants to know she's gonna be all right." She found a box of tissues on an end table across the room and handed it to Angela, who snatched a handful and blew her nose loudly.

"You gonna go see Jack?"

"Later today."

"Well, this is between you and me—I don't want Parker to know, but if Twyla comes out of this okay, if she makes it, I'm gonna let you take her to see him. That's the deal I made with God. Let Twyla be okay and I'll let her see her dad."

"Angela, that's wonderful. Thank you."

"Just remember I'm not doing this for Jack. I had my way, they'd take him where he belongs—to Death Row—today and he'd never see another sunrise. I'm doing this for Twyla, nobody else."

"I want to talk to one of the doctors before I leave here, okay? That way I'll have a clearer idea what to tell Jack. Who'd be the best person for me to talk to?"

"There was an old bowlegged guy with hair coming out of his ears and a black girl didn't look hardly old enough to be out of high school. If they told me their names, I was too rattled. I don't remember."

"I'll find out," Cass said. She gave Angela's limp hand a squeeze.

The slack hand gripped back with surprising force. "You're a good lady, Cass. And it's probably on account of all the pills that they gave me that I feel like it's okay to hand out free advice but please—no matter how much you love Jack O'Doul or think you love him or think he's sexy or whatever it is—you get away from him, you understand me?"

Cass nodded, but Angela wasn't finished. She held on tight.

"Lemme tell you something—you're prob'ly thinkin' that Parker don't look like much of a husband and wondering why I stay with him, but before Parker I married a man whose soul was as black as Jack O'Doul's. He'd beat me up, lock me inside the house, and rip the phone out of the wall; he once punched me in the belly so hard I had a miscarriage. Wherever I run to, sooner or later, there he'd be. Once he tracked me all the way up to Sturgis, put a knife to my throat, and told me the next time I left I was dead."

"But you got away?" said Cass.

"Yeah, and you know why? 'Cause I got lucky. Real

lucky. He's out with some buddies fishing one day. It's hot and he takes a notion to jump off the side of the boat into the lake. He's got a wad of gum in his mouth and when his head hits the water, a wave smacks him in the face. The gum goes down wrong, blocks his windpipe, he can't yell so he can't call for help, and he drowns. Just like that." She snapped her fingers. "Just like that, I'm free."

"Why are you telling me this, Angela?"

"Because if it weren't for the grace of God and a stick of Wrigley's Spearmint, I'd either be dead or still running from that man today. It was a one in a trillion chance—like winning the abused women's lottery— and I lucked out. But you, Cass, your troubles are behind bars. Jack can't come after you. Just get in your car and drive back to wherever you came from and stay there. Don't answer his letters and don't take his calls. Let it be like a bad dream."

"Angela, you gotta trust me on this one. I'll know when it's the right time to leave." She touched a finger to the forgotten curler dangling from the woman's hair. "You've got a curler here."

"I do?" With an impatient gesture she tore the plastic roller out, plucking several strands of hair with it. Cass got the impression she wished Jack could be yanked out of the picture as easily. "Even knowing that man killed my sister, you still have faith in him, don't you?"

"I do." Cass swallowed hard. She didn't like lying to this woman whose pain was so raw, didn't like pretending to be the kind of woman who'd fall for a convicted murderer. Yet the more uncomfortable she became with her assumed role, the more determined she felt to learn the truth about Raven's death.

"Melinda believed in him, too, and look where it got her," said Angela. "Even after he slapped her around, she thought he'd change. She had so much faith in that church of hers, thought that might change him." She tossed the curler onto the floor, let it roll. "Even after she saw the photos of him and that woman, she still believed he might change."

Cass looked up. "What photos?"

"The ones of Jack with his other girlfriend—the one he was seeing while he was still married to Melinda."

"Was this woman's name Raven?"

"I don't know if Melinda ever said. If she even knew. But the one in the photos had long dark hair, darker than mine and straight. Beautiful woman. Like a model."

"How did Melinda get photographs? Did she follow Jack?"

"No, she hired a P.I. Well, she didn't hire him exactly—she agreed to do a trade—she'd clean his office and answer the phone for a few days." She sniffed, wiped at her eyes. "You ask me though the guy wasn't much of a detective. I saw the photos and they weren't much."

"You mean they weren't very clear, out of focus, or what?"

"Oh, no, they were clear as day. They just didn't show a whole lot in the way of skin, know what I mean? Two of 'em just playin' kissy-face was all. But I guess they showed enough, 'cause they sure broke Melinda's heart when she seen 'em."

"Wait," said Cass, "I thought Melinda had moved in with you and Parker, because Jack had been violent with her. The domestic violence stuff, that was on record, so what would she have needed with photographs? If she wanted grounds for divorce or to get custody of Twyla, I'd say she had plenty."

"She didn't want the photos to use against Jack in court. She just wanted to know if he was up to anything before she thought about moving back in with him or if he was stayin' sober and not seein' other women like he claimed. See, Jack wanted her back. He told her he was turning his life around with the help of that minister, that old guy with the name like the candy bar—Butternut or whoever he was. In the end, though, the damn pictures cost her her life."

"What do you mean?"

"The photos were the reason she went back to the house the night she was killed. She'd forgotten to take them when she and Twyla come over to my house, and she was afraid Jack would find them and be furious."

"So? What difference would that make?"

"You don't know Jack's temper, do you? He's a dangerous man. Melinda had a restraining order against him, but she knew if he ever found out she'd had somebody spying on him, that wouldn't be worth the paper it was printed on. He'd come after her."

"Is that why she had a gun with her? To protect herself in case Jack came home?"

"Of course." Angela bowed her head and curled into an even tighter knot on the sofa. "And I was the one who gave her the damn gun, who insisted she take it with her if she was going over there. If I hadn'ta give her that gun she might be alive today. Jack might've beat her, but there wouldn't have been no gun lying around for him to kill her with."

"Melinda and Jack didn't own any guns of their own?"

"Jack was a convicted felon, had done time for assault and for car theft when he was in his early twenties, so he couldn't own a gun, least not legally. Melinda, she was scared of guns. I had to force her to take this one."

"But didn't she know she could get caught? That Jack could walk in on her at any time?"

Angela's head jerked up and she fixed Cass with eyes so puffy and slitted that it was like staring into a pair of coin slots. "Why're you asking all this? You in love with Jack or you doin' research on him?"

"I'm sorry, Angela," said Cass, realizing she'd made

a mistake by slipping into the role of a reporter in front of Angela. "I didn't mean to pry."

"No, no, you've got a right to know this stuff. I mean, you're involved with him now. 'Sides, the more you know about what you're getting yourself into, the more chance you'll decide to back out."

"I won't back out, Angela. I'm in love with him."

"Your choice, then, whatever. But you asked if Melinda didn't know she'd get caught and the answer was no, she'd already called around and found out Jack was at the Dark Horse with some of his buddies. Once Jack got started drinking, believe me, he never failed to close the place down, so there was no reason for her to think he'd be home before two."

"So he left the bar early?"

"No, according to the bartender, he left right at last call."

"I'm surprised Melinda didn't realize he'd be getting home."

Angela shrugged. "Maybe she didn't keep track of the time. Maybe he'd found the photos and gotten rid of them, and she spent the time trying to find them. Or maybe he just drove faster than usual. Who the hell knows?"

"So you figure he walked in on her?"

"Yeah, that's how I see it. He comes in drunk and catches her—he sees the photos of him and this other woman, and he goes nuts. Goddamn gun is right there, so he shoots her with it."

"Well, yeah, maybe," said Cass, trying to keep the excitement out of her voice, "but if that's what happened, I can't help but wonder—where are the pictures?"

Angela blinked and blew her nose into the soggy wad. "Huh?"

"The photos? I know the gun was left at the scene— Jack told me it had his prints on it—but the photos, what happened to them?"

"I don't know."

"But Melinda went back to the house to get them, right? She told you that?"

"Yeah, of course. I remember 'cause I tried to talk her out of going over there."

"And you know the photos existed? You saw them?"

"Sure I saw them. What are you saying? That my sister was a liar?"

"Of course not. But if the photos were right there, if that's what Jack and Melinda were fighting about, then what happened to them?"

Angela frowned. "I don't see what this has to do with—"

"All I'm saying is that if Jack killed Melinda in a blackout and was so panicked that he walked out of the house and left the murder weapon, it seems funny he still had the presence of mind to get rid of photos of him and another woman."

A woman who'd been murdered just a couple of months earlier, she thought.

"You can't never tell what a drunk's gonna do," said Angela.

"So either Jack found the photos when he came home and caught Melinda," said Cass, unable to stop herself from thinking out loud, "or Jack never saw the photos at all."

"Well, maybe they was arguing over something else."

"Maybe," said Cass, "but what if somebody else murdered Melinda, wiped his or her prints off the gun and left it behind, but took the photos. That would explain why Melinda was still in the house when Jack left the bar at the usual time. Because when he got home, she was already dead."

"No!" said Angela. "Don't you even think that! Jack O'Doul murdered my sister. Don't you dare suggest different."

Angela's eyes suddenly clocked to the left, and her

face took on an expression of desperate longing and fear. A squat, gnomish doctor with tufts of gray hair sprouting out at either side of an otherwise hairless dome and the bowlegged gait of an old-timey western saloon keeper ambled into the room, swallowed visibly, and said almost apologetically, "Mrs. Dunn? You're Twyla's guardian? There's something . . . well, it's a bit unusual, can I speak with you in private?"

Angela's already doughy complexion paled even further. Mutely, she got up and followed the doctor outside into the hall.

"I'll wait for you," Cass called after her, but found herself too nervous to sit by herself in the waiting room. She kept thinking about the photos. From Angela's description, they had to have been of Raven and Jack. So where the hell were they? Maybe Melinda had gotten to the pictures and destroyed them or hidden them before Jack got home and killed her? Or had someone other than Jack taken them, maybe the same person who'd murdered Melinda?

She started to leave, caught up in her thoughts, then remembered there was something important she hadn't asked Angela yet and wandered out into the hall.

At the nurses' station midway down the corridor she talked to a willowy woman with a lilting Jamaican accent and skin as blue-black as a starless sky, who introduced herself as Dr. Peabody and told her that Twyla was still unconscious.

"She was awake for a while, when she first got here, but then slipped into the coma again. Unfortunately, that happens sometimes with this kind of injury." She gave Cass a questioning look. "Are you family?"

"I'm a friend of Twyla's dad."

"She asked for him, you know—when she was awake. Does he live out of town? He should really be here."

"I'm afraid he can't be. He's in prison." She went on before Dr. Peabody could react to this. "I don't understand, why, if Twyla came out of the coma once, she became unconscious again?"

"It's called an intracranial hemorrhage. That means there's bleeding on the surface of the brain inside the skull, which creates intracranial pressure. It isn't acute enough to warrant surgery yet, but—"

"It may come to that?"

"Possibly. We can only wait and see how she does, if she comes out of the coma. If not, then surgery's the only option."

Feeling she knew little more than before, Cass paced to the end of the hall and was standing in front of the elevator, contemplating going downstairs for a cigarette, when she saw Angela walking toward her. Her face was buried in a nest full of tissues. Her fleshy shoulders shuddered convulsively.

Fearing the worst, Cass rushed toward her. "Angela, what's happened?"

Tears streamed down Angela's face. "I don't believe it, it's like a miracle."

"You mean she's okay? She woke up?"

"Like we have a guardian angel, Parker and me."

"What are you talking about?"

Angela plucked at her hair as though trying to gather her thoughts from the snarled locks. "I have to find where Parker's gone drinking. I have to tell him."

She started for the elevator. Cass grabbed her wrist and physically stopped her. "Tell me what's happened—did Twyla wake up?"

"No," said Angela, her smile wilting a bit. "No, but the hospital bill—everything's been paid for to this point, even the ambulance ride, with more money put into escrow. That's when—"

"I know what escrow is," said Cass, "but who did it?"

"Our guardian angel," said Angela, her eyes misting. "The same one who give us the money for the car and the TV set." She looked at Cass, rolled her eyes. "What, you didn't think we bought those on what Parker brings in?"

Not for a minute, Cass started to say but restrained herself.

"I gotta go," said Angela, pushing past her. "I gotta find Parker, let him know we don't have to worry about no hospital bills. He don't make a lot of money, you know, and it shames him. That's why he drinks. This way, whatever happens to Twyla, he can hold his head up. Knowin' it won't look like we can't pay our own way."

"Angela, wait, I forgot to ask you—"

The elevator door opened. Angela hurried in.

"The name of the P.I. Melinda used—what was it?"

"I can't recall," said Angela as the doors started to close. "The first name, though, all I remember was Melinda laughing about it. Said it was some kinda cow."

Chapter 18

Sometimes, ministering to the souls of his flock could wear a man down. Butterworth walked in the wilderness, seeking redemption and solace. Around his shoulder swung a rawhide canteen and in his back pocket was tucked a small, white leather-bound Bible. In his right hand, he swung the silver-handled walking stick that had brought down Otis Dawes.

A thought startling in its lack of humility struck him—that he was not unlike Saint Anthony. Anthony, too, was often called to journey into the wilderness, where the Devil used the stark landscape and awe-provoking vistas as a background upon which to proffer up temptations.

Since his violent encounter with Otis Dawes, he'd found himself obsessing about the man, alternately worrying that he had been seriously injured and fearing that he'd show up with a gun to exact retribution. He didn't think Dawes was the type who'd go to the police, because that would violate his macho image, but neither could he imagine he'd be able to let the incident go.

Nor had Fiona said anything to indicate she was aware of what had taken place between her husband and her lover.

Yet Butterworth could not forget that he had used violence against Dawes for no other reason than that the man angered him. Hurt his pride and affronted his male ego. His attack had been completely devoid of any charitable motive, any desire to attain the higher good. Revenge, pure and simple, had driven him.

To quiet the turmoil in his mind, Butterworth was indulging one of his favorite pastimes, rumination combined with hiking the rugged hill country to the north of the city. Hiking, however, was perhaps too auspicious a term for Butterworth's gently rolling locomotion. It suggested a more strenuous covering of terrain than a man of Butterworth's age and girth could readily sustain. Meandering was more like it. Butterworth had been walking for several hours now, and he was achingly tired in both body and spirit. Though he was headed back in the general direction of his vehicle, he was no longer capable of hurrying.

Lunch rumbled sourly in Butterworth's belly as he meandered—the chicken from the chicken fried steak he'd dined on earlier appeared to be experiencing a resurrection of its own, such was the gassy roiling and cramping in his belly. A fatty serving of grease-soaked hen and a measly portion of wilted collard greens at the Pioneer Café had been the last thing on his mind when he'd set aside his work in the church office at noon, bade good day to the church secretary, an elderly volunteer who chirpily addressed him as Reverend B., and ambled across the street to partake of one of Fiona's mouthwatering repasts.

What he'd found was a warmed over meat loaf casserole and a note telling him she had to run out for a few hours. Which meant, of course, that Otis had taken the afternoon off and some motel bed would soon be needing a new set of springs.

Briefly Butterworth had contemplated getting in the car to search for his wife, but to what avail? Dawes was digging himself a hole straight to hell with his dick, which was exactly what the wastrel deserved.

Fiona, God love her, was saved by the blood of our Lord Jesus Christ and would be forgiven her sins. She had only to ask.

And she would ask—contrition after the fact was one thing Butterworth knew he could count on, a full account of the sordid details, phrased in the gutter language she'd learned as a teenage whore, and Butterworth would listen and weep with her and, ultimately, forgive.

In the meantime, he had a weakness of the flesh of his own to attend to—hence the hasty trip to the Pioneer and the flirtation with gluttony followed by the gastrointestinal price he was paying now.

Incipient flatulence notwithstanding, as he walked, he envisioned himself like St. Anthony, a godly man besieged by temptations on every side, a man who had followed steadfastly the path of God despite all manner of iniquities flung in his face.

He prayed aloud, "Forgive me, Lord, for I have sinned. I've entertained un-Christian thoughts toward my wife and harbored hate and resentment toward her lover. Worse, I've used violence for its own sake, not to further a greater good. I've indulged in gluttony and vainglorious behavior. I have fallen victim to sloth and have sinned at times in order to rescue souls that would otherwise have fallen to Satan."

Huffing for breath, he crested a small ridge and paused, gazing out over a basin of red, sun-scorched earth where pale, sinuous fingers of heat shimmered up toward a low bank of anvil-shaped clouds, their flat bellies dusted with ocher. "Give me a sign, Lord," he whispered. "Give me a sign that You forgive me my failings."

He waited, but the air seemed as motionless as the inside of a tomb. In all creation, nothing but Butterworth himself seemed to breathe.

"Please, Lord, give me a sign that I did the right thing."

He waited, while sleek clouds shaped like Scud missiles scrubbed the top of the butte and the silence intensified into a great soundless percussion and then, feeling weary as some modern-day Methuselah, the arthritic knee hampering his descent, he continued down the other side of the ridge.

Seared by a sun that fell over him like hot rain, he spied an outcropping of rocks a few hundred yards away and ambled toward it, pausing at the midway point to gulp water from his canteen. The rocks overlapped in layers like ancient waves in a petrified sea, the upper ones casting pools of shade over the lower.

He eased himself heavily onto one of the broad stones, clutching the cane in his right hand and setting the left hand on the smooth, cool surface of the rock.

Within inches of his fingers, concealed in the crevices between the rocks, something stirred.

He felt a whisper of air against the back of his wrist.

Heard the rattle.

His body stiffened into a kind of living rigor mortis. Only his eyes moved, clocking to the limits of his peripheral vision. The rattler was within six inches of his right hand, its elegant, spade-shaped little head poised atop gleaming black coils. Angry or frightened, its rattles going full tilt, tiny black-beady eyes piercing Butterworth in a way that seemed knowing, malevolent, a fitting prelude to the fangs.

"No, please," Butterworth heard himself implore someone—God or the Devil or the reptile itself.

The snake didn't strike, but neither did it retreat, so they sat there, reptile and minister, locked in a silent, sweaty standoff. The sun slid to the west, nudging into the shade in which Butterworth sat. Sweat poured down his corpulent body. A tic invaded one eye, causing him to blink spastically, uncontrollably. He wondered if the rattler would notice the movement and be lured to strike, imagined the thrust of the fangs burying into his eye.

Lord help me, he prayed silently. *If you want me to continue to serve you, deliver me from this fate.*

Sweat-drenched and motionless, he held his position while a terrible urgency churned in his bowels. He clamped his buttocks together and prayed not to fart.

What felt like five sweltering hours compressed into five minutes passed. The rattlesnake's tongue flicked out as it uncoiled and moved to a rock outside striking distance of Butterworth's fingers.

Slowly, furtively, like a thief palming gems from a jewelry case, Butterworth withdrew his hand. He stared at the snake, which was now blithely sunning itself on the adjacent stone. Relief quivered through him. He lifted his eyes to the sky and thanked God for having spared him. There was so much more work to be done, he thought God was telling him. That was why he'd been saved.

He reached the trailhead feeling bedraggled, but spiritually vindicated, and drove back to town with his foot on the floor, anxious only for a hot bath and the comfort of bed.

He dragged himself up the front steps, but before he could reach for the door, Fiona opened it for him. She wore a flowing white cotton dress that revealed as much as it concealed and high-heeled ankle-strap sandals. Her long hair was contained in a single braid slung over one shoulder. A strange smile toyed at the corners of her mouth.

Whatever game she was playing, he had no zest for it now as he barreled past her with a curt greeting and charged for the stairs.

"I know what you did, Claude."

If she'd shot an arrow into his neck, he could not have halted more suddenly. The air froze in his lungs. His bowels filled with knives, ripping him from the inside.

"You *know*?"

"Everything, Claude."

He still didn't turn around. He couldn't look at her. "Dear God. You have to listen to me, Fiona, hear my explanation. What God demands of us isn't always easy or tender or even merciful. Remember when God asked Isaac to sacrifice his son . . ."

"Oh, for God's sake, Claude, don't start quoting the Bible." She came up behind him and put her arms around his waist, then ran them up to his chest. "Otis called this afternoon and said we can't see each other anymore. I admit I was upset at first, but then he told me what you did. I couldn't believe it. I'm so proud of you, Claude. For once, you acted like a man and hit Otis with something besides Scripture."

"Fiona, I . . ."

"Shut up, Claude." She rubbed against him like an amorous lynx. "I realized today you're more of a man than I thought. And that maybe I owe you an apology for the way I've behaved. Maybe I owe you respect. What do you think, Claude? You want to give it another try?"

He was beyond speech, his body thrilling to her touch, but his mind elsewhere entirely, whirling like a dozen amphetamine-stoked dervishes. Tears welled dangerously behind his eyes and his voice sounded strange and choked to him when he said, "Fiona, I've been walking the entire afternoon. I need a shower."

Her hands remained relentless, caressing, probing. "That's all right, Claude. I need one, too. Come on, let's bathe together. We haven't done that in God only knows how long."

She took him by the hand and preceded him up the stairs.

Chapter 19

A kind of cow.

Cass's finger scrolled down the list of private investigators in the Canon City phone book. There were more than she'd have expected for a city this size, but then maybe when prison was a county's industry, there was more incentive to find reasons to lock people up.

Her finger came to a stop.

Angus Platt.

Angus. Like the cow.

She dialed the number and got a recording, left her name and number and hung up. The phone rang again almost immediately and she answered, thinking the P.I. might have been screening his calls.

When a female voice said, "Where you been all morning? I called twice," she felt a twinge of irritation.

"Mariah? What's up?"

"That's what I want to know. Didn't see you at visiting hour yesterday or the day before. Did something happen between you and Jack?"

"Things are okay between Jack and me, but something happened all right." Briefly she filled Mariah in on Twyla's accident. "Jack said he'd rather I spent time at the hospital than coming to see him. Plus I've been looking at places to live."

"Find anything?"

"Actually, yes. A house I can rent by the month

while the owner's away. It's a ways out—almost to Cotopaxi—but it has a view of a lake and a garden."

"Well, Jack ought to be tickled pink now that it sounds like you'll be staying around for a while."

"Looks that way," she said, struggling to put some enthusiasm into her voice.

"You let me know when you move in. I'll come over and help you."

"That's sweet of you, Mariah, but I don't have much stuff. I can probably fit it all into my car in one trip."

"Well, whatever," said Mariah. "You don't want help, that's up to you. I'm just glad you're getting out of that motel. It's not safe. Look what happened to CharLee. Ever since she was murdered, I can't hardly sleep. I have nightmares that someone's crawling in my window, standing over the bed, and I wake up just drenched in sweat, shaking. God, I wish they'd find the son of a bitch who killed her."

"Whoever it was, he's probably miles away from here by now," said Cass, wishing she really believed that.

Mariah didn't seem to believe it, either. "It was that guy she was dancing with that night who killed her. And *he's* still around. I saw him the other night at a bar cozying up to some floozie."

"If he'd done it, Mariah, I think he would have been arrested by now."

"Maybe, maybe not. I don't have a whole lotta faith in Canon City's finest. Anyway, speaking of floozies and bars"—she giggled—"I thought maybe we could get together later on for a little barhopping. Have a few beers and check out what's bending over the pool table."

Cass glanced at her watch. There was still plenty of time for her to drive down to Florence and try to catch Angus Primm in his office, then swing back by the hospital before she went home. "Actually I was just going out the door. I'm not sure what time I'll be home."

"Call me when you get back then."

Cass was amazed at the woman's persistence. "To tell you the truth, I'm probably going to be tired when I get back."

"Tired, sure."

"And, you know, barhopping's not really my thing," she went on, hating that she felt the need to justify herself. "I'm not a big drinker."

"Plus you got a boyfriend who's gonna be around for a while."

For a second, Cass didn't get it. Then Mariah filled the silence by saying, "You know what day this is?"

"Uh, sure, it's the fifteenth, no, the sixteenth, right?"

"That's not what I mean." An urgency—completely absent only a moment before—infused Mariah's voice. "Ninety-eight days, Cass. Ninety-eight days till Madison takes the needle."

She struggled to think of something to say that was even remotely comforting. Came up with the very inadequate, "I know that's got to be hard, Mariah. I can't even imagine—"

"No, you *can't* imagine," said Mariah, cutting her off.

"I guess you're right. Maybe the appeals—"

"Madison's exhausted his appeals. It's over. Ninety-eight days and that's it. The State murders him."

She sobbed quietly. Cass listened, helpless, unable to think what to say that could possibly offer comfort. Finally she heard Mariah take a great gulp of air and say in a small voice, "I'm sorry. I shouldn't fall apart like that. I've got to go now, Cass. I'm sorry for putting you through that."

She hung up before Cass could say anything else.

The conversation left her feeling depressed and helpless, wanting only to get out of the motel room that, after talking to Mariah, was starting to feel as cramped as a cell. What must it be like, she wondered, to tick off the days until someone you love dies? And she felt guilty and small for having criticized Mariah in her heart only moments earlier—if getting drunk and trolling for men eased the pain of waiting for Madison's execution, who was she to judge?

All Cass knew about the town of Florence, thirty miles to the southeast of Canon City, was that it housed the Federal Correctional Complex, a cluster of four prisons incarcerating twenty-nine hundred inmates at four different security levels. Lower level felons whose crimes were committed without weapons ended up at the Prison Camp, the lowest security level institution at the complex. At the opposite end of the criminal spectrum, the most notorious felons, criminals like Ted Kaczynski and Tim McVeigh, were confined at the Administrative Maximum Penitentiary or "Super Max." Here security was stringent and many inmates spent twenty-three hours a day locked in their cells. Any movement around the prison was with double escort and restraints.

Cruising past the grim-looking facility as she drove into Florence, she was reminded of the fact that half the jobs in Fremont County stemmed from the corrections industry and that Fremont was the only county in Colorado that could claim an Escaped Inmate Hotline.

A.P. Investigating Services was tucked away so discreetly on the second floor of a modest strip mall that Cass began to think she might need the services of a P.I. just to locate it. The street address listed in the phone book actually turned out to be the adjacent side street, and the only signs out front advertising commerce were those for the Homeopathic Herb Center, a bleak-looking faux Tudor pub called MacRay's Billiards and Brews, a tattoo parlor, Laundromat, and a pawnshop.

Finally, cruising around the block for the third time, she saw a small sign, barely readable at a distance, stuck in a window on the second floor of the pub, accessible by an outside stairway. She parked the car

and, a few minutes later, was in the office of Angus
Platt, an apple-cheeked, fortyish man who seemed so
surprised to have a visitor walk in unannounced that
he almost choked on the sundae he was wolfing down
from a Dairy Queen cup. Hastily wiping at his lips
with a paper napkin, he pushed the ice cream away
as though not sure how it had gotten on his desk in
the first place. He looked so guilty that Cass wondered
if he was cheating on a diet.

"Mr. Platt?"

"That would be me." He blinked round, almost owl-
ish brown eyes.

"Sorry to barge in. Please don't let me interrupt
your lunch."

He pushed the sundae away again with his finger-
tips. " 'Sokay, I'm better off without it. I quit smoking
the other week, and so far I've gained five pounds."

"At least you won't die of lung cancer."

"No, just complications from the triple bypass when
they're trying to scrape all the crap out of my arter-
ies." He steepled his fingers in front of his face, looked
her up and down. "Do we know each other?"

"Not really."

"Well, then that must be rectified. Please sit down."

She took the only seat available, a desk chair on
rollers that squeaked mightily when she lowered herself into it. Platt couldn't seem to resist another spoon-
ful of sundae, so she took the opportunity to look
around.

Besides the desk he was sitting behind, his office
consisted of an old-fashioned rolltop desk in one corner, a minifridge, and a file cabinet festooned with
Post-its. Above the file cabinet was a framed poster
of a speedboat coming around the turn in a race, a
huge roostertail of water extending out in its wake.
Platt himself was so tidy as to look out of place in his
environment. He wore relaxed fit denim jeans and a
soft-looking leather vest over a crisp blue shirt.

"You'll have to excuse me, my secretary's out sick

this week," he said. "Otherwise I'd have remembered we had an appointment, Ms.—?"

"Cass Lumetto. And we didn't have an appointment. I called, but nobody was in. My call wasn't returned, so here I am."

"Well, you're in luck"—he turned the page of what might have been a day planner—"I don't have anything scheduled at the moment." He laughed. "Actually I don't have anything scheduled for the rest of the day. I was thinking about taking the afternoon off and heading out to do a little mountain biking."

"I won't keep you then." She crossed her legs, taking note of the effort he seemed to exert to keep his eyes on her face.

"No, no, take your time." He cleared away some stacks of paper, making space on the desk for his elbows. "Where did you hear about me?"

He looked so eager that she didn't have the heart to repeat Angela's remark about the cow, but simply said, "I understand you had a client named Melinda O'Doul. She was murdered a little over a year ago."

"Yes, of course, I remember. The husband did it." He combed a hand through his hair. "Melinda was a nice lady, but her life was really f— really screwed up."

"How did you know her?"

"I met her through a temp agency. I was between secretaries and I needed somebody who could come in part-time, put in a few hours a week filing and answering the phone, that kind of thing. She was smart, punctual. When I heard about what happened to her, I was just—" He rapped his knuckles on the edge of the desk, paused for a second, then went on, "How exactly do *you* know Melinda?"

"I never met her," said Cass. "Her sister Angela told me you did some work for her. That it was barter."

"Well, yeah, Melinda didn't have much money. I told her she could come by and clean the office, if she wanted to pay me back, but of course she never got around to it. Seemed like all her time was taken up with husband problems.''

"Angela says you took some pictures of Melinda's husband with another woman.''

"Yeah, that's right.''

"I wonder if you got the woman's name?''

"No. But even if I did, that's confidential. Why do you want to know?''

"I had a friend named Raven Sterling who was murdered shortly after she stopped seeing Jack. No one was ever charged in her murder, but it would have been right around the time you were doing surveillance on Jack. He had an alibi for the night my friend was killed, but . . .''

"You're not convinced. Well, considering that he murdered his wife, I don't blame you for having suspicions. But if the police say he had an alibi—?''

"I don't have much faith in the woman who claims that she was with Jack the night Raven was killed.''

"I see.''

"If you have copies of the photos you took or even negatives and I could take a look, I could tell you right off if it was Raven.''

"What happened to the photos I gave Melinda?''

"That's something I'd like to know myself. But, as I was saying, if you still have the negatives, I'd really like to take a look at them.''

"I can't do that, I'm afraid. Client privilege.''

"Even if the client's dead?''

He was looking at her legs again. She uncrossed and then recrossed them, so that the denim skirt she was wearing rode up a half inch or so. Platt made the hair-combing gesture again. "I'm sorry, Ms. Lumetto, I can't do that.''

She smiled to indicate no hard feelings and tried another tack. "Angela said the photos were . . . I guess you'd say tame. Would you agree?''

"Compared to the kind of stuff I usually get? Absolutely. Had a guy the other week was making it with his girlfriend on the golf course—you'd be amazed how creative people can get when it comes to where they have sex—anyway, yeah, Jack and this woman didn't do anything very hot and heavy far as I could tell. They'd park for a while out in front of the woman's house when he brought her home sometimes. I got a few shots of them making out, but all hands seemed to be on deck, if that's what you mean."

"For how long were you doing surveillance?"

"Just a few nights. Melinda just wanted to know if he was seeing somebody." He shook his head. "She was a good person. She said she knew she and Jack had problems, but she was sure they could work things out."

"It's sad, all right," said Cass.

"If I'd had any idea your friend was in real danger, though, I would have . . ." He seemed to reconsider what he was about to say and trailed off.

"Would have what?"

"Oh, hell, I don't know. Maybe broken Jack's legs, whatever it took."

He didn't seem to be kidding, and Cass was surprised. He sounded more like the guys her father used to hang out with than someone supposedly on the side of the law.

Perhaps anxious to change the mood, Platt tapped his fingers on the desktop and glanced at his watch. "It's almost three. What say we move the cocktail hour up a bit?"

Alcohol on top of ice cream? she wondered. "No, thanks, I'll pass."

"Ah, but you haven't had one of my cocktails." He stood up from behind the desk—he was shorter than she'd realized, no more than five six, and wore black snakeskin boots. Going over to the rolltop desk, he opened it up to reveal the tools of a bartender's trade: shaker, strainer, jiggers, and a variety of highball, lowball, and long-stemmed cocktail glasses.

From the minifridge, he pulled out an ice tray and

what appeared to be a variety of fruit juices, then went through the boozer's ritual of measuring/shaking/stirring/tasting before pouring the concoction into a fluted glass.

He took a sip, held the liquid in his mouth a moment before swallowing. "Sure I can't interest you in one of these?"

"There's no alcohol in that, is there?"

"Does it matter to you?"

"No, but I'm curious."

He lifted an eyebrow. "Alas, no. Smoking's not the only thing I've given up, although that's a more recent deprivation. I haven't had a drink of alcohol in, let's see, two years, eight months, seventeen days. I'm an alkie—correction, a recovering alkie—if you haven't already figured that."

"Why the bartending equipment?"

"If I can't have the booze, at least I can still enjoy the ritual. The ritual's as big a part of the addiction as the buzz. So I decided to hang on to the cocktail hour and all its accoutrements. It gives me a sense of civilization in the midst of chaos."

"Which is probably a good idea in your line of work."

"Actually, most of the time, my line of work's pretty mind-bogglingly boring. After you've watched the first few dozen cheating spouses get it on with somebody else's husband or wife and after you've spied on the same number of permanently incapacitated accident victims killing their opponent on the racquetball court or doing double black diamond runs up at Keystone . . . well, it starts to feel like being forced to watch reruns of a TV show that was boring the first time around."

"Yet you basically worked for Melinda for free?"

"Like I said, she was a nice lady." He sipped his drink so reverently Cass wondered if he was imagining the bite of bourbon under the sweet taste of the juice. "Guess I always hoped she'd realize her old man was scum and, well, see things differently."

He trailed off again. It was the second time he'd done that, which brought Cass's mind back to an earlier part of their conversation.

"If you'd known my friend Raven was in danger when she was seeing Jack, you said you'd have broken his legs. But before that, I got an idea you were thinking something else. What else would you have done?"

This time when he stared at her, it wasn't at her legs. He gave a small smile and tilted his glass slightly. Cass had the impression of a man playing charades at a party, doing 007 with a martini in his hand. "Well, I guess I would've taken pictures of the other guy while I was at it."

"*Other* guy?"

He set the drink aside and leaned forward, steepling his hands again. "Lemme ask you something, Ms. Lumetto. This friend of yours, can you think of any reason somebody would have been tailing *her*?"

"Not that I know of. You think somebody was?"

"In retrospect, well . . . yeah, yes, I think so."

"And you didn't find this odd? Maybe worth reporting to the police?"

"Odd, yes, but I just assumed the guy, the person, was tailing Jack. From everything Melinda told me about Jack, he seemed like the kind of guy who runs with the wrong crowd, never learned to play well with others, and ends up making enemies, either by ripping off some of his buddies or screwing their girlfriends and wives. And you gotta remember I wasn't really interested in the woman Jack was seeing, only the fact that he *was* seeing her and how serious it seemed to be."

"Serious meaning was he spending the night?"

"Exactly. And he wasn't. Least not unless he came back later and climbed in a window. He'd walk her to her door, she'd let him have a good night kiss, and that was it."

"The person you thought was tailing Jack, did you get a look at him?"

Platt finger-combed his hair again and shook his head. "I couldn't even tell you if it was a man or a big woman, although I assumed it was a man. Whoever it was wore a baseball cap and drove a black Ford pickup truck. I didn't get the license number—"

Cass groaned and made a conscious effort not to roll her eyes.

"—but I was able to see the writing on the side of the truck. See, it was a company vehicle. The name on the side was GRD Construction Company."

"That's great," said Cass, pulling out her notebook and pen.

"Yeah, but it won't do you any good."

"Why not?"

He looked indignant. "Well, I'm not stupid, for God's sake. I tried to find it, of course, but there was no GRD Construction Company in the phone book. I even called the local builders association—they never heard of any such company. Then I did a statewide check of business names, but nothing turned up there, either."

"Oh." She jotted the name down on a scrap of paper anyway and tucked it in her purse. "So how often did you see the truck? And where?"

"Well, let's see. Once it was around the corner at your friend's house when Jack brought her home. Once it showed up after I was already there. And once I saw it outside an Italian joint where the two of 'em were eating dinner. I coulda got the license number that time, 'cause of the lights in the parking lot, but whoever it was drove away before I could get close enough."

"That's it?"

"That's it. Melinda just wanted to know if he was dating anybody. I told her he was and showed her the pictures. That was the last I heard about Melinda till I picked up the paper one day and she was dead."

"You must have read about Raven in the papers? You never connected her with Jack?"

"Like I said, Melinda didn't care *who* he was seeing, just whether or not he *was* seeing someone. Till you showed up today, I never knew the woman's name." He drained his drink, shoved his chair back, and went to make a refill. "I gotta tell you, Cass Lumetto, you've made my day more interesting, but you've also given me a lot to think about." He held up the bottle of cranberry juice. "Guess I'll make this one a double."

Chapter 20

On the way back from Florence, Cass stopped by the hospital. There'd been no change in Twyla's condition. Angela was there, but so distraught and exhausted that there was little point trying to talk to her. Angela did say she'd accepted a collect call from Jack earlier in the day and had updated him on Twyla. By that point, it was too late for Cass to visit the prison, so she stopped at a Mexican restaurant for a plate of *carne asada* and fried rice and then headed home.

The conversation with Angus Platt ran through her head in circles, much like the trio of small children racing around the table next to hers like Indians circling a wagon. Erin had told her there was a "mystery man" whom Raven dated prior to Jack. Was this the guy in the GRD Construction Truck? For that matter, why couldn't it have been Erin herself in the truck? Or maybe Platt's original assessment had been correct, that the driver of the truck was actually watching Jack.

Platt said he'd done a statewide search and found no GRD Construction, but maybe the company was based somewhere else—she made a mental note to do a computer search for states bordering Colorado.

It was dark by the time she pulled into the parking lot of the Mountain View. A couple of kids still splashing about in the pool were being shooed out by their mom, some late check-ins were unloading luggage from a Honda Civic with California tags.

She got out her key, unlocked the door, and went in, automatically reaching over to flick on the lamp to the right of the door. No light. Setting her purse on the table, she leaned down to check the cord, thinking maybe the maid had accidentally pulled it out while she was vacuuming.

As she bent over, something slammed into the back of her skull. Pain exploded all the way to her teeth. She collapsed forward, knocking over the lamp as she tried to catch herself on the table. *Scream* she willed herself, *scream*, but her jaw—her entire body—was clenched against the pain. She slid sideways, and the table came down with her, crashing onto the floor.

A second blow missed her head and glanced off her shoulder—an unspeakable pain somehow worse than the first. She thought she was being stabbed—it galvanized rather than numbed her, and she screamed, a long animal keening that to her own ears sounded pitifully strangled.

The attacker grabbed her hair and twisted her head back. Her mouth dropped open. She heard someone shouting her name, banging on the door to the room. Then she was hit again, a blow that came from above, but seemed to open up a trapdoor underneath her, plunging her through the floor into a liquid darkness full of gyrating, pinwheeling lights.

"Stay still. Don't try to get up."

She opened her eyes on a world that swirled like a TV screen gone kaflooey, then slowly righted itself. She was on the floor, on her back. Shep Loomis was bending over her, looking into her face. If the expression on his face was meant to reassure her, he failed badly.

"What happened?" She tried to get up, paid the price. A stabbing pain seemed to rend her skull like a cleaver. She lay down again. "Someone hit me. Who—?"

"Whoever it was went out the back window when I banged on the door. I didn't get a look at the guy, but I called it in. A couple of squad cars and an ambulance are on the way over."

"I don't need an ambulance."

"Yes, you do."

"No, really, I—"

"Shhh, c'mon, don't argue."

She reached back and felt her head. No blood that she could find, but a king-sized lump was already forming. Her tongue felt like it had been dipped in tar.

The cops who arrived checked the room and asked her questions while she was being put in the ambulance. Shep rode with her. He explained how he'd waited all day for her to call to let him know about the fly-fishing trip, leaving messages for her that didn't get returned. He'd told himself the smart thing to do would be to forget it and take off without her, but instead he'd stopped by on his way out of town, hoping to catch her and give her a piece of his mind about how he felt about being stood up.

"At least that's what I told myself I was going to do. Actually I was hoping I could get you to change your mind at the last minute."

"I'm sorry I forgot about the fishing trip."

"And I'd say I'm sorry I was so persistent about you coming with me, except I probably saved your life."

When they got to the hospital, she said, "Look, you don't have to stay, you know. You've got a fishing trip planned."

"Forget it. At least not till I know you're okay."

As it turned out, she was okay—more or less. A bad bump on the head and a deep bruise on one shoulder. The doctor told her she'd be sore and achy and wanted her to spend the night in the hospital, but Cass had had enough of hospitals for one day and after she'd been thoroughly probed and prodded, asked what year it was often enough she was tempted to lie just for variety's sake, she said she was going to go home.

Shep was waiting in the reception area when she came out a little after eleven o'clock. He shut the cell phone he'd been talking into and jumped to his feet. "Whoa, where are you going?"

"Home. All I want to do is sleep."

"Not by yourself you're not."

She gave him a mock glare. "A little pushy, aren't you?"

"You know what I mean. If you won't stay here at the hospital, come over to my house. You can have the bed and I'll sleep on the sofa."

"I just want to go back to the motel."

"Where you were attacked? How do you know the guy's not coming back?"

She sighed. "I guess that means the cops didn't find anybody?"

"Not yet, no. The fact that you didn't see anything, that you couldn't give a description makes it tough."

He held the door for her and kept an arm under her elbow, almost carrying her, as they crossed the hospital lobby and went outside. The night sky was silent and vast and seemed to offer up space for the anger that was building within her.

"I did give a description," she said finally. "I told the cops about the guy on the Harley, the one who picked me up in the white Camaro after he sabotaged my rental car."

"Yeah, I know," Shep said, "I called one of the cops you talked to and he read me the report. The problem is you didn't actually see the person who attacked you. The guy you say has been following you, there's no proof that was him in your motel room tonight."

"And you don't find that just a bit coincidental that

someone's been following me, that this same person picked me up in his car and practically kidnapped me, and now I'm attacked in my motel room."

"I was going to ask you about that, the incident in Red Canyon Park. Why didn't you report it at the time?"

"It was stupid of me," she snapped.

"No argument there. So why didn't you?"

"I thought I could handle it on my own."

He shook his head. "Well, I hope what happened tonight convinces you otherwise. You're lucky you weren't killed. And for the record, yes, of course I think there's probably a connection between this incident and the guy you say's been tailing you. On the other hand, we can't just assume that either. Who knows, maybe you've got a knack for making enemies."

"Thanks for the reassurance."

They reached Shep's car. He held the door for her and she climbed up, and he went around the other side and got in.

"In my motel room, did anything appear to have been taken?" Cass asked as he started the car. "The laptop and portable CD player were the only things worth stealing."

"The cops on the scene said nothing appeared to have been touched. The perp got in through the back window, came in the bathroom. He'd removed the lightbulb from the lamp, the one you were trying to turn on when he conked you. If he was in there to steal something or to vandalize, all he had to do was go back out the window when he heard you come in. But he didn't. He stood behind the door, waiting for you to come in."

"Jesus, an ambush."

"So it would seem."

"I don't get it," said Cass. "The guy who's been following me, I figured it was somebody Jack asked to keep an eye on me. I can't see Jack telling him to beat me up, though, especially when I haven't been cheating on him."

Shep gave her a look. "Don't get pissed, but you're being naive. For these cons, controlling their women is a huge thing. On the outside, they terrorize the women themselves, just like Jack terrorized Melinda before he finally killed her. They get sent away, they find someone else to do it."

"If I'd had a gun—" she said, thinking out loud, remembering her conversation with Kenny at the Broadmoor.

"—he'd have gotten it away from you and you might have a hole through your head instead of a knot on it." He cleared his throat, appeared to debate the wisdom of what he was going to say next. "The guy who killed your friend CharLee, he didn't steal anything out of her room either."

"CharLee was strangled," said Cass.

"Yeah, that was the cause of death. But she was also whacked over the head from behind and—this is between you and me now, it can't find its way to the press—?"

"Sure."

"Some of these guys, the really sickest fucks of all— the ones that if I had the chance, I'd stick the needle in their arms myself—they take trophies, souvenirs, so they can intensify the memory of the killing. Body parts sometimes. Or hair, swatches of pubic hair. In CharLee's case, it was—well, forget it, I'm not trying to scare you but—"

"You're trying to scare the hell out of me and succeeding," Cass said. "You think whoever killed CharLee may have tried to kill me, too."

"There are some similarities in the style of the attack."

"Jesus." They rode in silence a few minutes before pulling up in front of the Mountain View.

Shep said, "I'm not leaving you alone. Your choice is whether you want my company here or at my place or I could drop you off at a friend's."

She weighed her options, which seemed pretty limited. She could call Opal or Mariah, which would almost surely mean waking them up at this hour or, in Mariah's case, possibly interrupting another tryst. Cass didn't want to risk that again, and besides, the idea of spending the night in Mariah's house-turned-shrine to a serial killer didn't really appeal to her.

"You can stay here," she said finally, "if you don't mind sleeping on the floor."

"No problem. Much as I hate to admit it, it wouldn't be the first time."

"And I think I would like to come along with you on that fishing trip tomorrow—if the offer still stands."

He looked surprised. "Of course it still stands."

"Good," she said. They got out of the car and walked to the room. She handed him the key. "This didn't work out so well the last time I tried it. You want to go first?"

"Gladly."

A few minutes later, she was lying in bed when Shep came out of the bathroom and lay down on the pallet he'd made up for himself next to the door. Exhausted as she was, she found herself thinking about his forearms. It *had* been a long time.

Forget it, she thought. *I'm too tired.*

Her last thought, though, before sleep overtook her, wasn't of the man sleeping a few feet away but the one lurking somewhere outside. Hoping he'd come back one night and try again.

Thinking she'd be ready for him this time.

Promise.

Chapter 21

Sometime during the night, the pain pills they'd given her at the hospital wore off and a headache began zigzagging its way through her dreams like a maniac pursuing her with a hatchet. Her mind tried to retreat into deeper unconsciousness, but the pain drove her upward into a light, fretful half sleep where dream and memory merged into a terrible facsimile of a night twenty-some years earlier.

Her father was bending over the bed, shaking her, saying, "Wake up, baby. We're gonna take off. Big adventure. Whole new life waiting for us."

Without waiting for her to react to this startling news, he grabbed her up, crushing her to his chest, and ran out into the hall. Her mother was waiting by the front door, bundled in a thick coat, her face as white as the snow banked up on the windowsills. She was holding Cass's brother Tony, who was waking up now, starting to cry.

"We can't just *leave*," she kept repeating, as though some physical impediment prevented their departure, "We got family here. We can't just *leave*."

While her mother moaned, her father chattered, "Better for us, you'll see. Be a better life. Look at it like an adventure."

The baby started to wail now and Cass struggled in her father's arms, not understanding, not liking the sound of this at all, *great adventure, new start*, something very bad was happening, her father sugarcoating everything, patting himself on the back as always while he tore up their lives.

Her father dashed to the closet, grabbed Cass's coat and his own, put her down, and started bundling her up for the subzero cold outside the Detroit apartment building.

Her mother was crying now, the smooth contours of her face cracking like old porcelain. "We can't just leave, Johnny! We got no place to go. Where we gonna go?" and Johnny yelling back, "Someplace, we'll go someplace. New start, new adventure. We sure as shit can't stay here." He finished buttoning Cass's coat, swept her up in his arms, and strode toward the door, nudging her mother and brother out ahead of them toward the car.

But once in the car, hunched over the steering wheel, her father seemed to tire of the cheery patter and hissed through his teeth, "Fuckin' Liano bastard. I shoulda known I couldn't trust him, I shoulda fuckin' known."

Oh, fuck.

Her eyes snapped open, and she didn't breathe, listening for some reaction from Shep, sure that she'd yelled out in her sleep. The old nightmare again—how many years now since she'd last suffered through that one?—the dream of flight-in-the-night before the people her father owed money to came with silencers on their weapons and their consciences.

Anthony Liano had been Johnny's gambling partner in a high-stakes poker game that traveled around the city. Both men skimmed money off the top, but Johnny'd gotten greedy and started taking enough money to attract the wrong kind of attention. Seeing a chance to have the business to himself, Anthony had gone to the mob boss and ratted Johnny out.

When Johnny found out Anthony had betrayed him, there'd been only time to grab what they could and take off in the middle of the night. Cass still remembered it with a kind of horrified awe—the departure had been so sudden, radical, and unexpected it had felt to her for years that a part of her, a remnant of herself had been left behind in the eastside apartment house.

Sunlight filtered from behind the edges of the curtains. She sat up, wincing at the dull ache at the back of her head. Shep was gone, the sheet and blanket he'd been sleeping on neatly folded and placed on top of the dresser. A note next to them read, *Gone to get real coffee. Back soon.*

Real was underlined. Apparently Shep shared her sentiments about motel-room instant coffee.

She got up and went into the bathroom, swallowed a couple more pain pills from the bottle on the sink, then took the hottest shower she could stand. By the time she came out, wearing shorts and a long-sleeved khaki shirt, Shep was stirring sugar into a large foam cup. A second cup with the lid on sat on the table next to a small mound of sugar packets and half-and-half.

"How're you feeling this morning?" he said.

"Like I got whacked over the head. But better now that I've had my shower." She lifted the lid off the second coffee cup and took a sip. "Better still once I get some caffeine in my system."

"I didn't know how you like your coffee," he said. "Hope I brought enough of everything."

"Actually I take it black," said Cass. "But thanks for covering all the contingencies."

"I try."

"I have a favor to ask."

"Shoot."

"I have something I need to do this morning before the fishing trip, but I don't want to hold you up. How about if you give me directions and go on ahead? Then I'll drive out and join you this afternoon."

She read his face: *No,* as the muscles in his eyebrows stiffened slightly, a subtle, almost imperceptible gesture.

"We could do that, I guess. Where I go is kind of out of the way. It's called Owl Creek Campgrounds. There's a turn you'll have to look for at an old Amoco station that's been out of business for years and then about a half-mile hike down from the parking lot at the trailhead. I'll draw you a map."

He found a menu for a take-out service on top of the TV, turned it over, and started furiously scribbling directions.

Cass said, "Is something wrong?"

"No. If you need to go ask Jack for permission, that's your business."

"Hey!" She set her coffee down so hard it sloshed onto the tabletop. "What is it with you?"

He held his hands up. "I don't know. I'm sorry. I just don't like the guy, that's all."

"Well, this has nothing to do with *the guy*. I'm not going to see Jack this morning. For the record, visiting hours aren't even until afternoon—I couldn't go if I wanted to: I've got something I need to take care of, and I need to do it alone. But I would like to go fishing—if you still want me to."

"Of course I do." He handed her the directions. "All that make sense?"

"I'll find you," she said. "You got extra flies or do I need to stop at a bait store?"

"Plenty of everything. Just pick up whatever you want to drink. I've got a Coleman stove. We can grill hamburgers."

"Sounds good."

But she must have sounded dubious, because he put his hand on her arm, looked into her eyes, and said, "Look, don't worry. I'm not a nutcase. We're gonna have a good time. And we're gonna get whoever it was who attacked you."

"I believe you." She kissed him and was impressed by how good it felt, after the events of the night before, to get a jolt of adrenaline not precipitated by pain or fear. "I'll see you this afternoon."

After he left, she watched from the window until he pulled out of the parking lot, then went to the phone and called Kenny.

Bonnie answered, sounding strained when she recognized Cass's voice. She seemed to make an effort to warm up, though, wanting to know what Cass was "up to" today. For lack of anything better to say, Cass described her plans to go fly-fishing. Innocuous as the conversation with Bonnie seemed, after only a few minutes, she felt drained and headachy, as though she were being grilled by an expert interrogator.

When Kenny finally came on the phone, she didn't mince words. "I've changed my mind. That gun you said you could get me the other day? Does the offer still stand?"

Cass made a quick trip to the Sterling ranch, then dropped off the rental car and got a ride over to the repair shop to pick up the Duchess. A couple of hours later, she turned onto a dirt road at the weed-infested remains of an Amoco station thirty miles east of Canon City and drove south, bouncing over ruts as big as speed bumps, through a forest of cottonwoods and oaks. She passed a woman on horseback and a couple of backpackers plodding along like beleaguered mules under their burden of camping gear.

Just as Shep had described it, the road climbed steeply, then leveled out and curved to the left, where about a dozen vehicles were crowded into a small parking area. Shep's car wasn't among them, but she figured one of several SUV and offroad vehicles parked here was probably his. Rather than try to squeeze her own vehicle in among the others, she pulled off onto the shoulder of the road, set the parking brake, slipped on her backpack, and set off down the trail.

Although Shep's directions indicated it was less than a mile, the path was rock-strewn and steep, and she was grateful to have worn hiking boots. Halfway down she could hear the water of the Arkansas River, which progressed from a faraway humming to the loud, rhythmic slapping of water on stone.

Closer to the water, she saw a couple of men wearing waders and wide-brimmed hats, who were casting their lines. She walked north along the riverbank, as Shep had directed, and finally spotted him about a half mile farther down. His back was to her and he stood in knee-deep water, wearing rubber waders and a hat that was little different from the other fishermen she'd seen, but recognizable to her by the jut of his shoulders and by body language—he had a way of moving, both on land and in the river, that suggested a man in the habit of having people get out of his way, a self-assurance that both annoyed and aroused her.

He's probably conceited as hell once you get to know him, she thought.

She stood there on the bank upstream from him, watching him cast out his line and play it in, then wade a little farther on and cast again, and wondered if she could afford to make her life more complicated by sleeping with him. Decided she might just have to take the chance.

While she watched, he caught a small trout, netted it, and used a hemostat to remove the hook. Her eyes followed his hands, the flow and rhythm of his movements. If she'd been making a fishing documentary, there'd have been a close-up of his hands cupping the netted fish, dislodging the hook, then lowering the shimmery, slick creature back into the water. Perhaps a brief caressing of the camera on his forearms and butt.

But then, she thought, that would be a very different kind of documentary.

"Hey, there," she called out.

He straightened and turned around, waved at her with a surprised-looking grin. For the first time, it occurred to her that he hadn't really believed she'd come, that he'd thought whatever "errands" required her to be in Canon City were just an excuse not to show up at all and that he was pleased to have been proven wrong.

Good, she thought as he waded out of the river to meet her, *a good start.*

A few minutes later, outfitted in waders that came up to her hips and a fishing vest with pockets containing an assortment of flies, she was working the river downstream from him. She cast toward the pockets of slower-moving water near the banks, places where trout were most likely to float facing the current, feeding on whatever floated downstream.

Like many serious fly-fishermen, they were silent, but they developed a rhythm, working a section of river for a time before moving on, keeping a distance of about ten yards between them. In the first hour, Cass caught two small cutthroat trout, which she held aloft to show Shep before releasing them back into the stream. He caught only a few small brown river trout for the first half of the afternoon, then made up for it by reeling in a beautiful rainbow trout. Cass rushed to the bank, grabbed the Polaroid, and snapped the classic photo of man and fish.

That night, after it appeared that everyone else fishing the river had packed up their gear and left, they cooked hamburgers over the Coleman stove, drank Miller Lite, and watched a fingernail moon rise up like a sated half smile from the limbs of the trees. The mosquitoes started to pester them, but at least the ants stayed away, so they sprayed themselves with insect repellent and considered themselves lucky.

"Is there something wrong with this picture?" said Shep, biting into a burger. "We spend the day catching fish that we throw back and then eat ground beef for dinner."

"I kind of like that," said Cass. "That way I don't have to feel guilty about killing fish."

"Only about killing cows."

"Yes, but not by my own hand. And I do feel guilty

about the cows. I'm just not ready to turn vegetarian yet. I like meat too much."

"My ex-wife's a vegetarian. I tried it for a while, but I couldn't pass a steakhouse without salivating and I had dreams about prime rib—I lasted about eight months and caved."

"Eight months is a pretty long time. How long did the marriage last?"

"Not a lot longer. I think I was more ready for marriage than my wife was, but she was—what's that word her therapist used, codependent?—and she didn't want to disappoint me by not being the happy homemaker type I'd envisioned. So she acted out her resentments by fooling around behind my back instead." He slugged back some beer. "I'm sorry, I shouldn't be telling you this. Nothing less romantic than a guy whining about the ex-wife who did him wrong."

"No, it's interesting."

"The whining?"

"That's a guy word, *whining*. Women do the same thing and call it expressing our feelings."

"I'll have to remember that. What about you, ever been married?"

"No."

"Ever come close?"

"There was a guy in New York I was seeing, but— I don't know—the chemistry wasn't right. I mean, mostly, it wasn't *there*. He was a good person and a friend but that was it, and that didn't seem like enough. To get married to somebody, to commit your whole life to that one person, shouldn't there be passion?"

"I'd like to think so. But then you see relationships where there *is* a lot of passion—too much passion maybe—because it drives people to do crazy stuff— stalking, battering, murder—all in the name of passion. They get love twisted around. They still call it love, but in reality it's anything but. It's ownership. Egomania. Possession."

"When you put it that way," Cass said, "bland sounds almost appealing."

"Almost, that's the key word there. For you, I don't think bland's ever going to be appealing." He reached past her, grabbed the mayonnaise, and spread a liberal amount on top of a second burger. "What about you and O'Doul? What's the deal there? I'm sorry, but I've just never understood it, this thing some women have for convicts. Now, a woman falls in love with a guy on the outside and he screws up and goes to prison and she stays loyal to him and waits, that I can see. I can even find something in it to admire. But she meets him when he's already in prison for twenty years or for life and she still falls in love, I don't get that. I just don't."

"I'm not in love with Jack," said Cass. "I never said I was."

He leaned back and stared at the moon, as though some answer might be written on its sliver of face. Finally, he said, "Well, I don't know about your being in love with him or not. But I'd be willing to bet sure as shit he's in love with you."

"I hope not."

"Why's that?"

"Because it isn't that way."

"You just like him? You like cons? You just happen to prefer Canon City to New York? Sorry, Cass, I don't buy it."

"Can we just drop it?" A note of strain had crept into her voice. "The last thing I want to talk about right now is Jack."

"Fair enough. Let's talk about something more uplifting. Fishing, for example. You're pretty good at it. Where'd you learn?"

"My father was into it. When we still lived in Detroit and my brother and I were little, the whole family would drive up to Houghton Lake, rent a cabin, and my father and his buddies would fish. Then after we moved to Denver—I was seven or eight then—he'd take us fishing up in Estes Park in the summer. It was a great time. The best time I remember from my childhood."

" 'Cause you were outdoors?"

" 'Cause I didn't feel like something terrible was about to happen, like a big dark wave getting ready to break over our heads. In Detroit that was how it felt all the time, and in Denver, it wasn't much better."

"I don't get it," said Shep. "What was going on?"

"My father," said Cass, "led what you could call an interesting life. He ran with the wrong people, did a couple of years in prison when I was four or five. He liked the ponies and the action in Vegas—still does—every now and then it'd all catch up to him, the debts and the double crosses and whatever the latest scam was, and we'd have to change our address—fast. I still have nightmares about gangster types showing up in the middle of the night. Taking my father away, like in a *Godfather* movie. That never actually happened, but I was always afraid it would."

"Jesus," said Shep. "My old man used to get drunk on the weekends, and I thought *that* was bad."

"It wasn't all bad," said Cass, trying to lighten the mood. "My mother was great, really loving and kind. Her big weakness was not being able to imagine a life without my father. When she found out she had cancer, I think, in a way, she was actually relieved to know she'd go before he did. Johnny screwed up our lives big time, but he did teach me and my brother some useful things—"

"Whoa, you call your dad Johnny?"

"Yeah, kinda weird, isn't it? But that's what I called him after he came back from prison, and he didn't seem to mind. I think he thought it was cute, this little kid saying stuff like, 'Johnny, will you read me a bedtime story. Johnny, buy me a Coke.' "

"Anyway, you were saying?"

"He taught me practical things, you know, how to change a tire, how to fly-fish."

"Which is more than most of the women I've dated know how to do."

He sounded so much like a typical disgruntled male that she felt a little put-off. "You sound like you've been through a bunch."

"Not at all. Mostly blind dates set up by well-meaning friends at the station. Most of them didn't go anywhere. And the ones that *did* go somewhere or that I hoped would go somewhere—well, then the woman didn't always feel the same way about me."

"Want to talk about any of them?"

"Like you want to talk about Jack."

She grinned, feeling somehow relieved. "Fair enough."

"I will say this, though."

"What?"

"When I saw you at the Abbey the other day, I got a little worried. I don't mean to offend you, but when I was growing up, I knew a few guys who were Catholic. They were always bitching and moaning that they couldn't get any, that Catholic girls don't like sex. But then when they *did* have sex, even solo sex, they went running to confession, because they were sure they were going to hell."

"But it didn't stop them from having sex, did it?"

"No, it just kept them going to confession."

"Which is what I suspect the Catholic girls were doing, too. I know I was. Besides, you know what they say about confession. It's—"

"Good for the soul."

She smacked an itch on her thigh. "The mosquitoes are drinking up this bug spray like it's happy hour." She glanced toward the tent and decided to take a chance. "Want to go back to the tent? Maybe give me something to have to confess to?"

A couple of hours later, listening to a fox yipping somewhere on the other side of the river, she remembered their discussion of passion earlier and thought he was wrong to think there could ever be too much. He stirred and turned toward her again, and she smiled in the darkness and reached for him.

Never too much.

Chapter 22

She awoke to the chill of the predawn dark and the sound of Shep's breathing beside her. An unfamiliar, but somehow comforting sensation. More familiar—and less welcome—was the realization that she had to pee, which meant scrounging around for her T-shirt and shorts, unzipping the tent flap and crawling outside, then pulling on her clothes, grabbing her daypack, and heading up the trail toward a stand of bushes. She peed, stuffed the used toilet tissue in a Ziploc bag in her daypack for future disposal, and decided to hike down the trail toward the river.

A herd of mule deer were wading across as she approached. She froze, watching their graceful, almost balletic procession, while the eastern sky grew paler and clouds bunched above the rock-ribbed mesa to the west.

Coffee would be nice, she thought. Even better, a Starbucks about fifty yards up the trail. Laughing at herself, a New Yorker at heart still attached to her creature comforts, she headed back toward the campsite. Beyond the tent, sunlight glanced blindingly off the grillwork of Shep's vehicle. She knew he'd driven down, rather than leaving it at the trailhead with the others, but it had been dark the night before when they'd started dinner, and all she'd really seen was the shape of a vehicle parked at the end of the jeep trail.

Now she could see that the vehicle was a black Ford

pickup truck. When she got a few yards closer, the way the light was striking the side revealed something else. She blinked, thinking that what she was seeing had to be an optical illusion. She was still half-asleep maybe, seeing things.

She moved closer, hesitant, as though the pickup were a large and potentially vicious animal. At one time, a stencil had been used on the door of the truck and then removed, leaving behind a residue. The layer of dust highlighted the outline of that residue in the manner of fingerprint powder. When the light struck the surface just right, the outline of the letters was legible.

GRD CONSTRUCTION. With a phone number printed underneath.

The same truck Angus Platt had spotted tailing Jack and Raven.

Don't do this, she thought, *there's an explanation,* but she couldn't think of what it could be.

She stood there a full minute, staring at the faint outline of the lettering. Gooseflesh scurried along her arms. Her breathing seemed to fill the forest.

She looked back toward the tent. Shep still hadn't stirred. She thought of trying to act as though nothing had happened, but knew her nervousness would give her away. Besides, what if he wanted to make love again? She couldn't let him touch her now. Not unless there was a reasonable explanation for why he'd been spying on Jack and Raven.

Slinging her daypack over her shoulder, she headed up the trail she'd hiked down the day before. She knew when Shep woke up and couldn't find her, he'd start to search, but when he saw her car was missing, too, he'd know she wasn't lost, just *gone*.

Part of her mind kept insisting there was an explanation—she knew Shep disliked Jack. Maybe he'd been keeping an eye on him for some reason. That didn't make sense, though. Until he murdered Melinda, Jack's criminal career might have been lengthy and sordid, but it surely didn't include the kind of high-profile crimes that would get a detective assigned to stakeout. Besides, according to Angus Platt, the person in the Ford pickup hadn't appeared to be tailing Jack, but Raven.

Twenty minutes later, dripping with sweat, she arrived back at the trailhead where she'd left her car. Yesterday, there'd been a dozen or more vehicles parked here. This morning the only car she saw was her own.

She started to cross the dirt parking area, then halted suddenly and ducked back into the trees. A man had suddenly emerged into view from the other side of her car. He wore grubby-looking jeans, a black T-shirt with printing on the front, and a white bandanna knotted around his neck. Even at a distance, she had no trouble identifying him as the creep in the Camaro. He was trying to break into her car. *Again.*

Stepping farther back into the trees, she watched him pull a pry bar from inside his jacket and probe for a crack in a window. He worked like someone for whom breaking into vehicles was second nature. A moment later, the driver's side door popped open. Camaro started to slide in, then must have realized there wasn't enough space between the seat and the wheel to accommodate his bulk. He reached down and adjusted the seat setting, then got in, leaned over, and started fiddling with the glove compartment.

Squatting down, Cass slid off her daypack and unzipped it, removed the .44 she'd gotten from Kenny, reshouldered the pack, and loped across the parking area toward the car.

Camaro was still leaning sideways, peering into the glove box as he pawed through the few items inside—maps, a first-aid kit, sun lotion, and extra sunglasses.

She crept to the car, approaching from behind, and put the .44 up to the window so close that the barrel pinged off the glass.

"What the hell are you doing?" she said.

He saw the gun and jerked back, then lunged for the driver's side door, but she was racing around to the front of the car even as he was trying to climb out and met him with the gun pointed at his jaw. He slammed the door and fell back into the seat.

"I should blow your head off."

He put a hand up, seemed to realize how foolish that looked in the face of a bullet and tried to lower it, but the hand wouldn't go down. It stayed there, ready to ward off a shot.

"Put the fucking gun down."

"Oh, I will. As soon as the cops get here. Till then, I don't think so."

He glanced around, realized there was no one else in sight—just her and him—and his bravado seemed to come back. He wasn't going to die today. Wasn't even going to get arrested probably. All he had to do was get the gun away from this woman, who probably didn't know how to use it anyway. She could see the thoughts ticking behind his eyes, could read them in the subtle change in his expression—from horror to bemused contempt.

"How you planning to call the cops? Mental telepathy?"

"I had a cell phone once, but some scumbag stole it. Then he sent it back to me looking like it had been through a trash compactor."

"Lucky it was only a cell phone. Coulda been your spine."

"Roll down the window."

"Huh?"

"Roll it down and toss out your wallet."

"What the fuck—you robbin' me now?"

"Just give me your driver's license. I want to see who you are."

He bared his teeth, muttered, "Bitch."

"*Do it*. Don't make me take it off your dead body."

She hoped she sounded believable. Evidently she

did because he pulled out his wallet and, a moment layer, lowered the window and gave her the license.

She took a step back and studied it while keeping the gun trained on him. *Grady Post, age 34, six feet, two hundred and five.* An address in Penrose. She memorized it before tossing the license back to him.

"What're you gonna do now?" he said.

The truth was she wasn't sure. "Just sit there and shut up."

"You can't shoot me, you know. It'd be murder. Breakin' into a car, that's hardly even a fuckin' misdemeanor."

"Yeah? What about assault? Vandalizing my car? What about damn near cracking my skull?" She could feel her fury gathering strength as she imagined him in her motel room, looming over her. "What were you gonna do to me if you hadn't been interrupted? Just leave? I don't think so."

"I don't got no idea what the fuck you're talkin' about."

"Well, think real hard. While you're at it, what about CharLee St. John?"

"Never heard of him. Matter of fact, I'm startin' to get bored with this shit." He made a move toward the door.

She raised the gun and lowered her voice. "Sit . . . the fuck . . . down." He did.

She stepped to the side, careful to stay out of range of the door, in case he suddenly swung it open. "What I want to know is how you found me here. What'd you do, follow me out here yesterday, then come back this morning? What made you think I'd still be here?"

"Like I said, I got no idea what you're talking about. All you can prove is that I was sitting in your car. Maybe you left it unlocked, huh? Maybe I was tired and wanted someplace to sit down."

"You were gonna steal my car."

He shrugged his huge shoulders and snickered. "Prove it."

"Well, for starters, there's a pry bar with your fingerprints on it that you used to break into the car."

He stared at her through slitted eyes, then suddenly laughed, shook his head. "You think you're pretty damn smart, don't you? New York writer bitch. Think you're pretty sophisticated, huh? You don't know nothin'. You don't even see what's right in front of your face."

"Shut up and turn around in the seat. Face forward."

"What, you don't wanna talk no more?"

"We're gonna sit here and wait."

"Huh?"

"This is a popular spot. People are gonna start showing up to go fishing. First one that does, I'll send him to call the police."

That smirk again. "What if nobody shows up?"

"Then you're gonna have a long hot wait."

"Fuck you," he muttered, but he sat back in the seat, put his hands behind his head, and closed his eyes.

Cass moved back a few feet and took a seat on the ground, cross-legged, facing the car. A half hour passed, then an hour. The sun climbed, and there was no shade around for either her or the man in the car. She thought about Shep, a half mile away. Surely he was awake by now. Would he come looking for her?

She thought about making Camaro get out of her car and marching him back down the trail to the campsite. With Shep there to help her, he'd be easy to control. They could tie him up, throw him in the back of Shep's truck, and cart him off to jail.

But did she still trust Shep? If he was the man stalking Raven, did that mean he was also the killer? Not necessarily. On the other hand, just because he was a cop didn't mean he was exempt from flipping out, having a psycho dark side, did it? She knew sometimes the stress of police work, dealing with the lowest element of life, pushed cops over the edge. If Shep was one of those . . .

Camaro leaned out the window and banged on the side of the door. "Hey, I'm dying in here. I'm burning up."

"Relax. Take a nap."

"Fuck that, I'm dehydrating. I'll die."

He was exaggerating, of course. It wasn't *that* hot, not yet, but the sun was rising and, even with all the windows open, she couldn't leave him sitting in the sun indefinitely.

She made a decision. "Get out of the car."

"About fucking time."

He got out, making a great show of wiping the sweat from his forehead. He had a broad, fleshy torso that managed to look hard and blubbery at the same time, like the fat had been layered on over rippling slabs of muscle. A tattoo of a spiderweb covered one bicep. A naked woman pranced across a forearm. The black T-shirt he was wearing read: *Never trust anything that bleeds for five days and doesn't die.*

Cass gestured with the gun. "Walk ahead of me— slowly—to the trailhead. We're going for a hike."

"What're you gonna do?"

His questions were starting to annoy her. "I'm gonna shoot you and dump your body in the river."

"Yeah, sure you are." He walked ahead of her to the edge of the woods, stopped to stretch, then looked around at some jays having a cussing contest on a branch overhead. Just a guy enjoying a fine summer's day, going for a walk in the woods.

"I don't think I'm going to play anymore," he said. "This is as far as I go."

He spun around on the balls of his feet and lunged for her like a fullback going for a tackling dummy. She sidestepped and swung the gun at his head. Metal and flesh collided with a meaty thwack. He looked stunned, disbelief as much as pain contorting his fea-

tures. She took advantage of the second's hesitation
and cracked him across the temple. This time he
sagged and went down, blood streaming from a gash at
his hairline. She stood over him, gun raised to deliver
another blow if he moved.

"Cass? Cass, is that you?"

Shep was about ten yards away, climbing up the
trail from the river. He saw the man on the ground
and the gun and broke into a run.

"Jesus, what happened? What's going on?"

"This is the guy—the guy who's been stalking me,
who broke into my motel room."

Camaro groaned and covered his face. Blood seeped
between his splayed fingers. Shep stared first at her,
then at him. He shook his head. "C'mon, let's get this
guy to a hospital. You can explain on the way. I don't
know what the story is, but I have a feeling it's going
to be good."

A few hours later, after the man Cass hit had been
stitched up at the hospital and taken to jail, Cass was
sitting in a Burger King across from the police station,
eating French fries and thanking God that she wasn't
behind bars. The police had seized her gun, which was
unregistered, and which she wasn't licensed to carry.
She'd told them that she'd brought it with her from
New York, claiming to have driven out instead of
flown, and was carrying it for protection since the murder of her friend, CharLee St. John. Only Shep's inter-
vention on her behalf and the fact that the cops
seemed genuinely delighted by the number she'd done
on Post's head had kept her from being arrested.

She was reflecting on her good fortune, hoping that
it would hold, when she saw Shep walk in. He glanced
around till he spotted her, then came over and sat
down. "You're not going to like this," he said.

She found it difficult meeting his eyes. The memory
of the residue of letters stenciled on the door of his
truck kept intruding into her thoughts. She selected

the greasiest-looking French fry of the bunch, swirled it in a puddle of mayonnaise for a little additional fat, and popped it into her mouth.

"Did the cops change their mind about the gun and send you to arrest me?"

"Not yet, but that still doesn't mean you're not in trouble."

"Me? What did I do?"

"Will you just listen a minute? That guy you smacked, his name's Grady Post. A minor league scumbag-around-town with an arrest record of petty crimes as long as my"—she still wasn't looking at him, but he must have sensed that the vibes coming off her weren't positive and amended the sentence to—"real long. He moved to Canon City from South Bend, Indiana, six years ago, got work here at a machine shop. Bounced around from one job to another over the years. Sounds like a hard-core alkie. Has been eighty-sixed from all the local bars. The guys at the station say Paulie's Pit in Florence is the only bar in Fremont County where he's still welcome. And—this is the good part—turns out he and your buddy O'Doul had jail sentences that overlapped a few years back. Post for car theft, O'Doul for his usual drunk and disorderly. They weren't cellmates, but they might know each other from there."

She stopped scarfing fries long enough to take a sip of the chocolate shake and said, "So which part of this am I not going to like? I got the bad guy, didn't I? So far, it all sounds pretty good."

"Well, let's see . . . there's the part where Post says he's going to charge you with assault with a deadly weapon and sue you for bodily damage and mental distress—I wouldn't worry too much about that, though—with his record he's looking at two to three years on the car theft charge alone, so the D.A.'s got some leverage to use to persuade him he's not as angry at you as he thinks."

"And?"

"There's the fact that he's got an ironclad alibi for the other night when you were attacked."

For the first time, she stopped eating. Looked up at him. There was more concern and confusion in his face than she wanted to see. He looked the way she *felt*.

"How ironclad's ironclad? What's he got, some friends willing to swear he was with them at a bar? Something like that?"

"Try a couple of cops who hauled him downtown for questioning about a backhoe that disappeared from a construction site right around the time he got into a beef with his boss last spring. They picked him up at four-thirty that afternoon and didn't let him go until eleven that night. So there's no way, no possible way, he was lurking in your motel room."

"But he's in jail now?"

"For the moment."

"What do you mean, for the moment?"

"He'll be arraigned before a judge this afternoon. The judge will set a trial date, but in the meantime, he'll probably get out on bond."

She started to speak, but he held up a hand, kept talking. "Believe me, he's going to think twice, though, before he comes near you again. He knows about all the charges alleged against him for harassing you and—"

"Alleged?"

"You can't prove anything. He admits he picked you up when you were hitchhiking, but he claims you came on to him, that you offered him sex in exchange for a ride, then changed your mind when he didn't want to pay you."

"What? Jesus, Shep, you don't—"

"Of course, I don't believe it, and neither does anybody else. But it's still your word against his. And as far as the vandalism to your Eldorado and the rental car—"

She was starting to feel sick. "I can't prove anything."

"Exactly."

"So Grady Post walks, and in the meantime, someone else is out to get me."

"Not a personal attack on you necessarily. It could have been random."

"Like CharLee St. John?" Her voice rose. At the table behind them, some kids blowing soda at each other through their straws turned to stare at her.

"I know it's frustrating, but I just want you to know—" He reached for her hand and she pulled away.

He looked surprised. "What's wrong? You're just upset in general or did I do something?"

"You're always ready to think you did something wrong. Why is that? Where's all that guilt coming from?"

"It's not guilt. It's just a habit I've got of always waiting for the other shoe to fall. No matter how good things seem when the relationship starts out, sooner or later it always does."

"And I suppose you have nothing to do with that?"

"Jesus, Cass, what's wrong? I thought things were great with us. Now all of a sudden you act like I'm the enemy. At least fill me in—if you're angry at me about something, tell me what it is."

She stared at the fries in their puddle of mayo and felt the cold finger of paranoia drag along her spine. Shep had "rescued" her by appearing at just the right moment to frighten off whoever'd attacked her. She'd just accepted that as a given. But what if there'd never been an attacker at all? What if there'd only been Shep?

She looked up at him, trying to banish all memory of the previous night, embarrassed at how quickly she'd been ready to indulge in expectation and romantic fantasy. No time for that now. He was right, she should say what was on her mind.

"Your truck," she said coolly, "it used to have letters stenciled on the side that read GRD Construction. This morning when the sun was hitting it, I could see the residue left by the stencil. What's GRD Construction? And why did you have the name and phone number removed?"

"GRD Construction was my brother-in-law Frank's business out in Provo, Utah, before he retired. I liked the truck, so he gave me a good deal on it. As far as having the name taken off, what would you expect me to do? Drive around advertising a company I don't work for that doesn't even exist anymore?"

"So you're saying that when you bought the truck, you had the name removed right away. Like a few days after you bought it?"

"I don't remember exactly when I had it removed. Why, is it important? What difference does it make when I had the name taken off?"

"I want to know if you kept the name on for some reason. Like for doing undercover work. Cops do that all the time, don't they? Hide out in a van or a truck with some kind of logo on the side while they wait for a drug deal to go down or a convenience store to get robbed?"

He'd been dragging a French fry through the mayonnaise and had it halfway to his mouth. Now he stopped. "Sounds to me like you watch too much TV. What are you getting at?"

"Just one more question. Did you have Raven Sterling under surveillance? Except under surveillance is a police term, isn't it, and maybe that's not what we're talking about here. So let me rephrase that. Were you stalking her?"

"Stalking her?" He stared at her, then looked quickly away, but not before Cass thought she saw fear, like a fleeting shadow, cross his face. "Why would you ask such a thing? Where's this coming from?"

"Jack told me where he claims he was the night

Raven Sterling was murdered. Now why don't you tell me where you were."

"You think that I would . . . Jesus, Cass, you think I'm capable of *murder*?"

"I didn't say that, you did. Just tell me where you were."

"I can't do that."

"Why not?"

He shifted in his seat, adjusted his collar, and seemed to find something fascinating about the condiment counter. As hard as it was not to say anything, she waited him out.

Finally he met her eyes. "I'm sorry, Cass. But if you don't trust me, then whatever I say about where I was that night, you'll never believe me anyway. So it won't make any difference. You'll always have doubts."

"Try me."

"I can't."

"Then maybe you need to have more faith in *me*."

He scraped his chair back. "I wish it didn't have to be like this, Cass. I'm sorry, I really am. But I don't think that there's anything more to say."

Chapter 23

After the incident with Post and the fight with Shep, Cass wanted nothing more than to pack up her suitcases and take the next plane back to New York. For the first time since she'd arrived in Colorado, though, she wasn't really free to leave. The police had confiscated her gun and were running a check on it, and she was the only witness against Grady Post when he went to trial for breaking into her car. And, in spite of what Shep had told her, she was still convinced it was Post who'd been waiting for her in her room that night, if only she could find some way to prove it.

Exhausted and dispirited, she went back to the motel, where she called the hospital to inquire about Twyla. Her condition was unchanged, a nurse told her. Cass's heart sank, thinking of the bleak future the little girl faced even if she pulled through this and of her father, waiting in prison for word of a child he might never again see alive.

She hadn't visited Jack for three days now, and if he'd been calling her, he must be wondering why she was never in the room to take his calls. Any news about Twyla, she figured he must be getting from Angela. He might be so furious with her at this point, he wouldn't even want to see her again, but she was too tired to worry about it. She put the chain on the door, unplugged the phone, and fell asleep with her clothes on.

Once during the night, she was frightened awake by a nightmare in which she was being chased by a truck with ghostly initials stenciled on the side and she spent a few frantic seconds trying to locate the gun before she remembered she no longer had one.

She stayed awake the rest of the night, waiting for dawn, trying to decide what she'd tell Jack about her latest encounter with Post. She decided to tell him nothing—if Jack was behind this, he'd be hearing about it from Post himself before long. At that point, he'd have to decide whether to confront her, thus admitting his involvement with Post, or let it go. It was possible, too, she decided, that Jack could have asked Post just to keep an eye on her, but that Post himself was a loose cannon who'd initiated the rough stuff.

With that in mind, she dressed later that morning for a reunion of sorts—her first visit to Jack in seventy-two hours, which in the life of a convict must seem like a month. She put on her tightest jeans, the ones that always got her looks when she wore them in New York, slingback heels, and a sheer turquoise blouse with a lace camisole underneath.

Even the male guards took a second look when she passed through the metal detector and started down the long corridor to the visiting room.

One of the C.O.s had sent word to Jack that he had a visitor, so he was there waiting for her when she arrived. At first she thought the look on his face was his delight at seeing her. Then she realized such joy couldn't possibly be the result of her visit, sheer turquoise blouse notwithstanding.

He held out his arms to her. "God, but I got the greatest news in the world this morning!" He wrapped her in his arms and buried his face in her hair. "I may be doing life in prison, but I'm the luckiest man alive! The warden just sent a C.O. to tell me Angela called. Twyla's awake, and she's talking. The doctors say she's gonna be okay. Hell, I been in here praying my ass off, and God musta heard."

"That's wonderful," said Cass, feeling a genuine sense of relief. They held each other a long time, the first embrace they'd ever had where Cass's affection wasn't feigned.

"Angela told me she'd keep her word, too, about letting Twyla come visit. She said it may be only a few weeks till you'll be able to bring Twyla here."

"That's great," said Cass, although this time, to her own ears at least, her enthusiasm sounded forced. Letting Jack think she was his girlfriend was one thing; allowing his daughter to believe the same thing was another.

He held her hands and looked into her eyes, studying her so intently that she looked away, feeling flustered. He was handsome in a way that Shep wasn't, she thought, a kind of masculine good looks that few men could pull off, because it verged too close to being pretty. The cornsilk hair, the pale blue eyes, a mouth that could be either sensuous or belligerent, depending on his mood.

"I missed you," he said. "You were so great to go over to the hospital and check on Twyla. And I know why you didn't come see me these last few days and why you weren't answering your phone."

"You do?"

"Yeah, I acted like a jerk and you had to teach me a lesson. I don't blame you, the way I treated you when you come here last time. So, from now on, you come to visit when you want to or not at all, if you don't. *If* you still want to see me, that is. I gotta know, 'cause it's drivin' me crazy—are you tired of me already? Having second thoughts 'bout being involved with a con? It's all right, if you do," he added quickly. "I understand."

"I missed you, too, Jack," she said. "And yes, of course, I want to keep seeing you."

"All right then!" A whoop of delight exploded out of him. "Then I truly am the luckiest man in the world." Then something seemed to tick across his mind, and his face grew somber again. He pulled away from her and led her over to a table, where they sat down.

"That guy you say has been followin' you? He give you any more trouble? You don't still think I'd be behind somethin' like that, do you? 'Cause I'd never do that to you, darlin'. You ought to know that."

He sounded so sincere she was almost frightened. What if he was telling the truth? What if Post was some nut operating from his own delusional motives?

"I believe you, Jack. And I'm sorry I jumped to conclusions. That wasn't fair. Forgive me?"

He cupped her face in his hands, kissed her mouth. "Course I do, darlin'. But what changed your mind?"

She took a breath and gave him the answer she'd been rehearsing in her head. "Well, partly because the cops finally nabbed the guy—he was trying to break into my car again—but, mostly"—here she tried for her most ingratiating smile—"because I thought about it, and I just couldn't see you doing something like that to me. You want me to like it here in Canon City, not terrorize me, so I move away."

"What's this guy's name anyway?"

"Grady Post. He's been in jail a few times and hangs out in the local bars. Ever heard of him?"

He shook his head. "Doesn't ring any bells. I don't get it, though. Why was this guy after you?"

"That's a good question."

"What'd you do, flirt with him or something? Lead him on?" He glanced down at her blouse. "You wear somethin' sexy like this around town and catch this guy's eye?"

Once again, she was amazed by the sudden change in him. One minute he was being protective and concerned for her well-being, the next implying that she'd asked for it.

"Of course I didn't flirt with him. I'm scared to death of him."

"Son of a bitch." Light glinted in his pupils like

knife points. He seemed excited, almost happy to find a focus for his anger. "Goddamn, he's lucky I'm locked up in here or I swear to God, I'd put him in the ground."

"Look, forget it," said Cass, gripping his upper arm and snuggling closer. "Let's talk about something else. I got some news I think you'll like."

"Yeah?"

"I found a place to live."

"You did? That's terrific! Where at?"

"It's a house out near Cotopaxi."

He frowned. "I figured you'd be getting an apartment. And Cotopaxi, that's kinda far out, ain't it?"

"A little ways out of town, but I like it."

"Can you—you know, can you afford this? I mean, you don't have work yet?"

"I'll find work, don't worry about that. Besides, I have some savings. I'll be fine."

"If you say so."

"Just be happy I found a place."

"I am, darlin'."

He kissed her and she kissed him back, feeling an ache of guilt in her stomach. She thought of Kenny, who would have told her that the end justifies the means. If Jack had murdered Raven, what difference did it matter if she deceived him to get that information? On the other hand, what if he hadn't?

She tried to make her mind blank, to relax into the ardor of Jack's kiss. The plastic chairs weren't conducive to cuddling, but they did their best, going at it like teenagers in the backseat of a car. Every now and then, she'd have a flashback to her lovemaking with Shep and she'd force the image out of her mind. She tried not to feel guilty or weepy and discovered she was feeling something else entirely—turned on. Maybe Shep—or the adrenaline thrill of holding Post at gunpoint—had got her juices flowing, but if she and Jack hadn't been in a room with fifty other people, she would have been tempted to play the part of his girl-friend for real.

As it was, they necked for a while until she pushed him gently away and said, "I need to ask you a question."

"Yeah? What is it, darlin'? You gonna propose?"

"I'm serious, Jack."

"I'm serious, too."

"It's about—something I heard recently."

"Can't believe everything you hear, darlin'."

"Something I heard Fiona Butterworth say."

"Shit." He rolled his eyes. "Lord love that woman, but she does talk, don't she?"

Cass had rehearsed this conversation in her mind and felt comfortable with it. She wasn't lying, so there wasn't anything to remember—Fiona had volunteered information about her affair with Jack.

"Look," said, squeezing Jack's hand and looking into his eyes to show she wasn't angry, "I like Fiona, too. And whatever you and she did before we got together, that's none of my business. But she is a married woman and if you and she had an affair—"

He looked away, gave a quick, glum nod. "Yeah, darlin', I can't deny it. I am a sinful man, and I did sleep with Fiona Butterworth. I've asked the Lord's forgiveness, though, and I know Fiona has, too. We're both deeply sorry."

Cass suppressed the impulse to tell Jack just how sorry Fiona was as far as temptations of the flesh and said, "She told me you were with her the night that other woman, Raven Sterling, was murdered. She told the cops that, too. Is it the truth?"

"Are you asking did Fiona say that to provide me with an alibi?"

"Well, did she?"

He gave a hoarse, short laugh. "Hey, this is great. You're asking did I boink the reverend's wife or did I—maybe—murder this other lady? Murderer or adulterer? Which will it be?"

"Jack, please—"

"No, no, I'm not mad, darlin'. You got a right to ask. But I tell you, you spend enough time in the joint, your sense of humor gets kinda twisted, and it does pinch my funny bone, what you're asking. Anyway, the truth—yes, darlin', I did spend the night you're talking about with Fiona, part of that night anyway."

"Only *part* of the night?"

"Well, we were at my place, and she had to go home to her husband, of course, so it wasn't no more than a couple of hours."

"Melinda and you were split up then?"

"We were on the outs again, yeah, and she'd moved back in with Angela. So Fiona came to my place and then left, but it was"—he glanced toward the wall clock as though searching its face for an answer—"oh, pretty late, almost midnight."

Fiona had said she told the police the same thing, that she and Jack were together until almost midnight, too late for him to have killed Raven if the coroner's estimate of time of her death was correct.

"So after Fiona left, what happened? It was late. Did you go to bed after that?"

He pulled a face as though she'd said something laughable. "Hell, no, any time before midnight's just the shank of the evening as my old man used to say. What I did was I got dressed and headed up the street to the Dark Horse."

"So people saw you there, right?"

"No, nobody saw me, 'cause I never made it."

"Why not?"

"I got the sh—pardon me, darlin'—I got the crap beat out of me. I ran into some asshole and we got into a scrape. I'd've kicked his ass from here to kingdom come, but I was already three sheets to the wind from the wine I'd drank with Fiona, so you couldn't exactly call it a fair fight. When I come to, I was lying in an alley with blood all over my face in a world of pain. It was a warm night, and I felt pretty poorly, as you can imagine, so I just slept where I lay the rest of the night."

"In the alley?"

"Yeah." He slid his arm back around her and tilted her chin to face him. "You don't believe me, do you?"

"I don't know what to believe."

"Well, you believed I murdered my wife and you wrote letters to me anyhow, you come all this way to meet me, left your job and your life in New York. Would one more murder really make that much difference? Or maybe it would." The sarcasm twisted his mouth into a savage smile. "Maybe you figure, now one murder, anybody could commit one murder, but two is a trend or a habit or something. Two murders is just one away from being another Madison Raines, is that what you're thinking?"

"No, Jack."

"Well, what then? Why all these questions about where I was the night that woman was killed? Hell, I only went out with her a few times. Never even slept with her, you want to know the truth. I'm gettin' tired of talkin' about this. You want to be jealous of somebody, be jealous of Melinda. She's the one give me my daughter."

A shiver rippled across his shoulders. "You okay?" said Cass.

"What I just said, about Melinda givin' me my daughter, I take that back. God gave me Twyla, and He's the one give her back to me. I don't ever want to forget that." He squeezed her against him. "Know something? Even if I never get out of here, even if I die in here, I feel at peace with it now. Before Twyla got hit, I never thought I could say that. But as long as I got my little girl"—he gave her a kiss—"and as long as I got my other girl, I guess, all said 'n' done, I'm a lucky man."

Cass felt her heart sink. His faith in her—and in their future together—weighed on her like a basket of stones.

There was a beat of silence during which she searched for something to say.

"You *are* my other girl, aren't you?" said Jack. "Or have you changed your mind already? You want to go back to New York? Back to your old boyfriend?"

She shook her head, more in reaction to her inner distress than to reassure him. "I'm moving into my new place, aren't I?" It came out sounding angry and defensive.

"Somethin' the matter, darlin'? You're not happy about moving out of the Mountain View?"

She almost laughed. "No, actually the sooner I get out of there, the better."

"Then why aren't you excited?"

She groped for words—a way to warn him against getting so serious while at the same time giving nothing away.

"I know what the problem is," he said.

Her eyes widened. "You do?"

"Yeah," he said, looking somber, "I think I do. You're an honest woman, Cass, I knew that the first time I saw you. You can't abide lying."

She felt the skin start to creep at the back of her neck. How could he know? Was it something she'd said?

"What I told you earlier, honey, it weren't all exactly the truth."

"What do you mean?" Sweat started to trickle down her temples.

"I lied, but—this has got to stay between you and me now, okay?"

"Of course."

"I lied about the time Fiona left my place the night that girl was killed. Fiona lied to the cops, too. It wasn't almost midnight when she left. That'd been the case, Reverend Butterworth woulda known for sure something was up. It was just about nine-thirty when she left. But the rest of the story's true, I swear to God. I did head for a bar and I did get beat up, and I did spend the night in an alley. But you see why Fiona and me had to lie, don't you, honey? Otherwise . . ."

"Otherwise, you would've been a suspect in Raven's murder."

"Which I didn't have nothin' to do with." He stared deeply into her eyes and caressed her cheek, gently, with the backs of his fingers. It was all she could do to allow him to touch her. "You know I'm telling you the truth, don't you, darlin'?"

She nodded, feeling numb.

He pulled her to him and kissed her, hard and deeply. When he broke the embrace, she was gasping, but not from arousal.

"And you understand why you can't tell anyone else. Not ever, okay?"

Again, she nodded.

"I'd better go, Jack."

"You just got here."

"I know, but the new place I'm moving into, I want to pick out some new things. To make it feel more like mine. You know, drapes, sheets and pillowcases, a throw rug or two."

"Girl stuff, you mean."

"Yeah, girl stuff."

"Okay, fine, just make sure I don't find out you bought no satin sheets. Just regular old cotton's fine, 'less I get paroled outta here."

She managed a smile. "Cotton it shall be."

As she headed for the doorway along with a few other early-departing visitors, she saw Opal and hurried to catch up to her. She saw at once that something was wrong. Opal's eyes were swollen and red-rimmed.

Her first thought was that Frank had been turned down for parole or transferred to a prison in some other part of the country. "Opal? Is something wrong?"

"Oh, Cass, I just got through telling Frank the news, and I was too upset to stay any longer. I just want to go home and be alone for a while."

"What is it?"

"Oh, honey, it's terrible. Linda Lomax called just when I was leaving the house to come see Frank. Some fishermen found Judd's body in the river last night. He'd been camping. They think he must've been trying to wade across and got caught in the current and drowned."

Chapter 24

A memorial service for Judd Lomax was held two days later, early Thursday afternoon. Cass woke up at dawn and spent the early part of the morning moving out of the Mountain View Motel and into the house in Cotopaxi, a move that was accomplished with almost embarrassing ease. Everything she'd brought with her could fit into the Duchess's roomy backseat and trunk with room left over for a few bags of groceries, as well as the gardening gloves and tools and a few other purchases she'd bought on a whim at the hardware store next to the supermarket.

She was grateful, though, to have something to occupy her before the memorial service. For whatever reason, Judd's death had affected her more powerfully than she would have anticipated. It made her think of her brother Tony, who was older than Judd, but shared with him a certain physical similarity—that same tall, wiry frame—and an attraction to faraway places and exotic philosophies that their father had sometimes derided until Cass would have to leave the room, ashamed and furious.

Tony hadn't gone off to join the Peace Corps—he'd simply disappeared. The last Cass had heard from him was three years ago. She'd received a letter at Christmas, postmarked Anchorage, Alaska. No return address. Brief and to the point as a Zen haiku. He'd said he loved her, but felt a clean break with his family was the best thing for right now. Unfortunately, that included his older sister. She still remembered his closing line: *From this point on, my family will be one of choice and not of origin.*

Had Tony found his family of choice by now? she wondered. Was he happy? Safe? Or had he so completely divorced himself from his original family that he could be dead, drowned in some fast-running river, without her or her father ever having been notified?

To get her mind off the brother she hadn't seen in five years, she put on the gardening gloves as soon as she got home and set about weeding the flower beds on either side of the walk. The hot sun flailed at her back and shoulders. Within minutes, she was dripping with sweat. Far from uprooting at a tug, the weeds stubbornly fought back. Her hands, more accustomed to typing at a computer keyboard than struggling with weeds, quickly tired.

Half an hour later, with only a tiny portion of the work accomplished, she was happy to be interrupted by the sound of a car pulling up. She straightened up, back cracking, and saw Opal and Mariah getting out of Opal's Ford Taurus.

She knew Opal would be going to Judd's memorial service later, but right now she was dressed much like Mariah, in jeans and a loose-fitting T-shirt. Only the puffiness around the eyes and haggard lines bracketing her mouth betrayed her.

"Great place!" exclaimed Mariah, bounding up the walk ahead of Opal, who proceeded at a more demure pace, carrying an armful of red roses.

"For your new house," she said, handing the flowers to Cass. Moisture glimmered in the corners of her eyes. "I stopped by the florist's this morning to get flowers for Linda and Jim. Thought I might as well buy flowers for a happy occasion as well as a sad one."

Cass thanked her, moved by the gesture from a woman whose primary link to her was that they both had a man behind bars.

"You take the day off from work?" she asked.

"Yeah. I could've taken just the half day to go to the memorial service, but I figured I wouldn't be any use to them out on the road today anyhow, way I'm feeling. Frank suggested I just take a sick day."

Mariah was appraising the outside of the house. "How much rent you paying on this place?"

"Too much."

"No, seriously."

"Seriously too much."

Mariah put her hands on her hips. "You got money or something? Nice place like this and you still don't have a job?"

"My father sent me some money," Cass lied. "He was worried about me staying in a motel."

"Well, must be nice. All my old man ever gave me was grief."

"Come on inside. I'll give you the grand tour. It should take all of five minutes."

Carrying the flowers, Cass went to the door and gave it a shove with her hip. When that failed she twisted the knob and realized, with a little sting of irritation, that she was locked out.

"I can't believe it. I already did this once today and had to climb in a window."

"What?" asked Opal.

"I'm used to doors that only lock if you use a key. I just locked myself out."

"Back door?" asked Mariah.

"Locked. But I'm prepared this time."

She handed the flowers to Opal, bent down, and turned over one of the rocks bordering the flower bed, where she'd put a spare key. Then she opened the door for Opal and Mariah, replaced the key, and joined the other women inside.

"Have a look around while I put the roses in water."

Mariah wrinkled her nose. "What's that smell?"

"Oh, the owner has a thing for sachets."

"Smells like old farts."

Opal shot her a look.

"Oh, don't mind me," said Mariah. "I'm in a bad mood. We just came from the prison and I didn't get to see Madison. Some bitch guard claimed he spit on her when she walked past his cell."

"Nobody's in a good mood this morning," said Opal.

"Why's that?" said Mariah. "You got to see Frank. And Cass could've visited Jack if she hadn't been too busy with her new house."

Opal rolled her eyes and Cass busied herself searching the kitchen cabinets for a vase. "Are you forgetting that Cass and I are going to a memorial service this afternoon?"

"Oh, yeah," Mariah said, sounding disinterested, "I read about it in the paper. That kid who drowned."

"Judd Lomax," said Opal.

"Whoever."

"Come on," said Cass. "Let me show you the house."

Mariah followed grudgingly, but Opal made up for her lack of enthusiasm by oohing and ahhing over the fireplace in the bedroom and the Jacuzzi tub as well as the few personal touches Cass had added—a black-and-white poster of Paris's Montmartre lit by gas lamps on a foggy day and a Tiffany-style lamp in the shape of a dragonfly.

The two women visited a little longer, avoiding the topic of Judd and concentrating primarily on prison gossip passed along by their men. Predictably, Mariah gave the countdown to Madison's execution and started to cry. When Cass gave her a tissue, she blotted her eyes, sat up straighter, and announced, "I've made a decision. If nothing happens to stop Madison's death, I'm not going to go to the execution."

Opal looked relieved. "Honey, that's probably best," but Cass picked up a note of foreboding in Mariah's voice and kept silent.

"I'm going to stay home and wait until midnight—close as I can get to the moment that Madison dies—and I'm gonna shoot myself."

Opal flinched. "My God, don't say that!"

"You don't mean that," said Cass, resorting to a cliché and thinking instantly that she didn't know if Mariah meant it or not, that she very well might be serious. "Madison wouldn't want you to do that."

"Suicide's a mortal sin," said Opal. "You'll go to hell."

"Yeah, sure. Hell's right here on earth, didn't you know that?"

"I don't like this kind of talk," said Opal, standing up like a schoolteacher about to address a rowdy class. "First a wonderful young man dies in some stupid accident and now you're talking about taking your own life. I can't stand it. Come on, Mariah, let's go. I'll drop you off at your house." She turned to Cass. "I'll see you at the church in a bit, honey. Or you want me to swing by and pick you up? I don't mind."

"Thanks, but how about if I meet you there?"

"I'll save you a seat."

"Enjoy your new place," said Mariah, sounding for all the world as though the conversation of a few moments earlier had never taken place. "Keep those doors locked. Remember what happened to CharLee."

"See you later," said Opal and half dragged Mariah out the door. As they went down the walk, Cass heard her chiding the other woman, "Now what'd you go and say that for? You'll scare her."

Although she rarely drank during the day, after her guests left, Cass took a beer from the refrigerator and went out onto the back stoop, which was shaded this time of the day. She sat on the top step and looked at the stand of birch trees and elms that backed up to the property, wondering if this had been a bad choice of homes, if she wouldn't be more secure in an apartment complex with people coming and going all day.

Still, she decided she was glad she had rented the

place. The air of deep peacefulness reminded her of Houghton Lake in Michigan, the place her family had gone fishing when she was a child. For some reason, she never remembered feeling afraid when they were at the lake. It had been as though an invisible wall surrounded that world, as though none of their problems could follow them there. Thinking back on it, she found her naiveté startling, even for a child.

Then her thoughts strayed to Jack and his admission that he and Fiona had both lied about the time they'd spent together the night Raven was killed. Did that mean he was guilty? But if that was the case, why would he bother telling her the truth about the time? Would he conceal a murder, but have scruples about telling the truth in other areas? Or was his "confession" just a smoke screen to conceal a deeper guilt?

Pondering Jack's motivations was confusing enough, but trying to figure out Shep was downright maddening. She *liked* him. Hell, she'd spent the night with him. But if there was some good reason for him to have been tailing either Raven or Jack, why wouldn't he tell her about it?

Still turning the questions in her head, she went back inside—locking the back door as per Mariah's instructions—stripped out of her gardening clothes, threw them into a wicker hamper, and got into the shower. A feeling of listlessness dogged her, and she found herself lingering under the soothing beat of the water. By the time she got out of the shower, dried her hair, and put on the only remotely funereal outfit she had— a navy-blue skirt and white blouse that, in her eyes at least, made her look like a flight attendant for a regional airline—she was in danger of running late for the start of the service.

Judging from the full parking lot at the church and the difficulty Cass had finding a parking spot on the street, Judd Lomax had been a popular young man. Dozens of friends from his high school were in atten-

dance as well as a few who'd flown and driven in from
Salt Lake City, where Judd had attended college. The
plain little Church of Good Hope was so resplendent
with flowers that Reverend Butterworth had to pick
his way gingerly among them, the protuberant belly
preceding him as he navigated his way around huge
wreaths and horseshoes of blossoms.

Opal had already arrived, of course, and Cass
squeezed in beside her.

One by one, people got up to share their memories
of Judd. A gawky long-haired boy with a barely con-
trolled stutter spoke of playing ice hockey with Judd
when the two were in high school together. A frail-
looking, white-haired old woman who'd been Judd's
third-grade teacher reminisced about his artistic talent
and interest in Civil War history.

Judd's older sister, a heavyset redhead who'd flown
in from Houston with her husband and daughter,
spoke about her brother in a tiny, halting voice that
was difficult to hear. She declared his death to be the
will of God and closed by reading the Twenty-third
Psalm, which she said was Judd's favorite passage.

Then Jim Lomax approached the podium. He wore
a suit so stiff and sharply creased he might have been
crowbarred into it and walked like a man with explo-
sives duct-taped up his ass. His face flushed, his voice
raspy, he said only that Judd had been a good son,
undeserving of such an early and unexpected death.

If he felt any guilt for having thrown Judd out of
the house only a few days earlier, he said nothing to
indicate it.

Linda Lomax said nothing, but tucked her head
back into her husband's shoulder the instant he returned to the pew and sobbed throughout the service.
How could she stand to touch her husband, Cass wondered, if what Opal had told her was true? And how
could all these people who claimed to have known
and loved Judd stand up, one after the other, and

proclaim his devotion to fundamentalist Christianity when, from everything she could gather, the last weeks of his life had been spent renouncing it?

Finally, when everyone else who wanted to speak had done so, Butterworth lumbered back up to the pulpit and gripped it as though the strength of his hands alone was holding him erect. Some of the children by now had grown tired and fractious, fidgeting and whispering—he cleared his throat and let his sharp, blazing eyes rove the room, searching out miscreants. When the children realized he was waiting for them to get quiet, all became pindrop still.

"Even in the most incomprehensible tragedies, God is merciful," Butterworth said, "for He sends us lessons. And the lesson here, in Judd Lomax's untimely and horrific death, is that as Christians, never, not for one second, dare we stray from the path of salvation, for it is just in that instant of spiritual lassitude that death may strike and if it strikes at a time, however brief, when we no longer love and trust and honor the Lord, then we are damned for all eternity, as surely as if we'd never walked the path of righteousness at all.

"In Judd Lomax's last days, he underwent a test of his faith, a trial," Butterworth went on. "The Devil was tempting him mightily and his parents and friends were concerned for him, and I was concerned for him. There were times, in fact, when I feared deeply for this young man's soul."

"What's he saying?" said Cass, although she thought she knew. She glanced at Opal, who was listening raptly, gazing at Butterworth with a look of glassy-eyed adoration that she generally reserved for Frank.

Tears streamed from the minister's eyes. He started to speak, but his voice broke, and he took a swallow of water from a glass at the podium before starting again. "Imagine it if you will, here you have a young man raised in a fine Christian family, a faithful churchgoer, a young man who in his short life had been a devoted servant of Jesus Christ, and yet even he was so sorely and grievously tempted by the workings of Satan that he actually gave thought to renouncing his faith.

"Imagine, if you will, the implications of that." His voice dropped to a whisper that filled the church.

"But I am hear to tell you, friends, that Satan was foiled, the Evil One was denied his prize, which was the very soul and salvation of our Judd. I feel confident Judd saw the light before the end and that he died embracing Jesus."

Butterworth's mighty voice boomed outward until the very church seemed too small to contain it. Its rich basso profundo thundered with resonance and power worthy of a Shakespearean play. Sitting so close to the pulpit, buffeted by the force of that voice, Cass tried to imagine what it would be like if she no longer spoke English, if she had no idea what Butterworth was actually saying, but could only hear the thunder and the power of it. She decided the experience would be compelling, possibly even moving—if only she were unable to understand the words.

"So think on this, every one of you. When your time comes, as it could come at any moment or any day—for God does not abide by our schedules—are you saved as Judd Lomax was saved? Or are you risking your immortal soul by flirting with temptation, sitting on the spiritual fence as it were? Are you headed for heaven or are you traveling the road to damnation?"

Cass muttered something under her breath that was sufficiently profane for Opal to look round and stare.

A few minutes later, the service ended and the mourners began filing out.

Butterworth, walking solemnly and slowly, left first, followed by Fiona shepherding the Lomax family. Then the rest of the church emptied out. People milled about on the lawn or headed back to their cars. Others clustered protectively around Linda and Jim.

Cass lit a cigarette and leaned against the side of the church, waiting for a chance to say a brief word to Linda. She didn't know the woman well, but she liked her and couldn't even begin to comprehend the magnitude of her and her family's loss.

Butterworth approached her, hand extended, and nodded a greeting. "Cass, thank you for being here. Even though you only knew Judd a short time, I can see you share our pain."

She felt her frustration overflowing. "What you said in there, you know what, it was bullshit."

Butterworth stopped and blinked at her, apparently as startled by what Cass had said as Cass was herself. But there was no going back now and she realized—belatedly—that she hadn't been lingering in hopes of speaking to Linda at all, but with a vague thought of unleashing her anger at Butterworth.

"What did you say?"

"I said that was bullshit. If there's a heaven, I'm sure Judd is there now, but not because of some non-sense about giving his soul to Jesus."

Butterworth glared down at her from his great height, his trio of chins overlapping like dollops of pudding. "What are you saying? I thought you were a Christian?"

"Your brand of Christianity has nothing to do with God or Jesus or loving thy neighbor, it's nothing but a holier than thou club based on fear. And if Jesus was anything like the kind of loving, truly holy person I believe him to be, then I'm sure he loathes the crap you're preaching even more than I do."

"You don't know what you're saying." He made a fly-swatting gesture with his hand and tried to steer himself away, but she was quicker on her feet and got in front of him, blocking his way.

"How dare you dismiss me like a child."

"Because you're behaving like one."

His condescension infuriated her. *Stop, enough already,* her mind commanded, but she'd been holding her anger back for so long, playing the part of Jack's adoring little girlfriend, that now it overflowed her.

Butterworth saw the fury in her face and seemed to back off. "Forgive me, I didn't mean to make light of your concerns." His eyes darted in their deeply set sockets, trying to make eye contact with Fiona, but she was on the other side of the lawn now, getting into the car with the Lomaxes. "Perhaps we can sit down some other time and discuss this with the seriousness it deserves."

Someone hailed him from across the lawn. He looked up and saw several members of the congregation coming toward him, and moved away like a great ship changing course.

Cass watched his lumbering retreat, experiencing the cathartic relief of anger and, at the same time, appalled by what she had just done and how she'd explain her outburst to Jack, who was sure to hear about it.

Fuck it, she thought, *I said what I had to*, and headed back to her car.

Chapter 25

When Cass got home, there were two calls on her machine. One was a hang-up and she figured this was from Jack, since the automated voice that asked the recipient if they'd accept a collect call usually cut off automatically if a machine picked up.

The second was from Shep, letting her know that Grady Post had made bail and was back on the streets. Sounding conciliatory, he asked her to call him on his cell phone as soon as possible.

The news about Post was upsetting but not unexpected. As far as hearing from Shep, she wasn't sure whether to be annoyed, flattered, or frightened that he'd gotten her new number so fast, until she remembered the obvious—she'd given it to him that night at Owl Creek Campground.

Finally, after arguing with herself over whether or not to return his call, she decided to see what he had to say.

He answered the phone with a curt hello, then brightened considerably when she spoke. "Cass, I'm glad you called."

"I almost didn't."

"You don't sound so good."

"I'm not. I just came from Judd Lomax's memorial service."

There was a pause. She wondered if he could possibly have had the audacity to think she was depressed over *him*?

"The boy who drowned. Yeah, I heard about that. Terrible."

"The service was pretty terrible, too. I practically got into a shouting match with the minister. I was so angry by what he said in his eulogy that I made a complete fool of myself."

"You don't know how happy I am to hear you say that."

"And why's that?"

"Because it makes it easier for me to say the same thing. I got defensive with you the other day and acted—well, I acted badly. You had every right to ask what you did, but you caught me off guard. I just wasn't up to answering. Now I'd like to, if you still want to hear it."

When she didn't answer right away, he added, "If you're not rushing off someplace, that is?"

She thought a moment and said, "Actually, I think what I'd like to do is go to a bar. I could use a drink."

"You and me both. How about the bar at the hotel on Main?"

"I was in the mood for something a little seedier. Say, Paulie's Pit in Florence?"

"Paulie's Pit? You gotta be kidding. You walk in the door, you need a tetanus shot when you leave."

"You're not up for it?"

"I didn't say that."

" 'Cause if you're not, I could go by myself."

"Forget it. You're not going there alone."

At Cass's insistence, they took separate vehicles to Florence. She told herself that she was only being practical, since one of them might want to leave before the other. What she really wanted, of course, was to keep a safe distance between them.

She found Paulie's Pit without difficulty, arriving there well ahead of Shep who, unlike her, was probably observing the speed limit. The building was impossible to miss—it sat about a hundred yards back from the road in what looked, literally, like the middle of nowhere, a flat stretch of sand and scrub on the outskirts of Florence. Paulie's was the only thing that could remotely qualify as a landmark. A low, ramshackle building that looked like it had been added to many times, by builders of widely varying skills, it squatted froglike on a macadam lily pond, surrounded by pickup trucks and bikes.

Judging from its condition, the macadam surrounding the building must have been poured around the turn of the previous century. One especially deep hole was blocked off with a sawhorse, but there were plenty of other, smaller craters that gave the impression the area had been recently bombarded with a shower of meteorites.

Cass parked her car and ventured inside without waiting for Shep to arrive. The interior of the Pit was stark and cavernous, the floor covered in sawdust, walls bedecked with an assortment of plaques commemorating various sports victories, everything from bowling competitions to beer-chugging contests. The air stank of cheap beer and poor personal hygiene. Five men sat hunched over their drinks at widely spaced intervals at the bar. A couple more shot pool at a table next to the door. The way they turned to stare when she came through the door made her wonder if she'd forgotten to zip or button something strategic.

The bartender was a beefy-looking blond woman with basset-hound jowls and biceps, forearms, and mustache that hinted at serious steroid use. The deep scars zigzagging her hairline suggested she'd been on the wrong end of a broken bottle at some time in her life. She gave Cass a long, woeful look and said, "Need directions, honey?"

"No, honey, what I need is a beer," said Cass. She laid a ten on the bar, paid for the beer, and gave the woman a five-dollar tip, which still didn't elicit a smile but at least erased part of the sneer.

When Shep came through the door a few minutes later—all heads swiveling once again—Cass waved him over to the booth where she was sitting. She'd already drunk most of her beer and the start of a buzz was taking the edge off the headache that had started back at the church.

"Your driving reminds me of someone."

"Mario Andretti?"

"No, *me*, before I totaled a brand-new Corvette and busted my leg up when I wiped out on a curve near Durango a few years ago."

Cass shrugged. "I haven't totaled any cars."

"Not yet."

"Yet?"

"There's always yet."

"Is this a lecture?"

"That wouldn't be a good idea, would it?"

"Probably not."

"Then I'm not lecturing. Just observing." He picked up a plastic-covered menu that was speckled red with something Cass hoped was ketchup, glanced over it, and put it back down. "I'm hungry, but I don't know for what."

"Yeah, I know that feeling. But I know what I want at the moment." Did she imagine it or did his expression change just slightly? "Another beer."

"Stay there, I'll get two." He got up and went to the bar, chatted briefly with one of the men there, and came back with a pair of chilled longnecks.

"You know him?" said Cass.

"I know most of the guys here."

"You do?"

"Sure. You do police work, you get real familiar with the people who hang out at your finer drinking and dining establishments." He glanced over at the pool table and made eye contact with a rangy, bearded fellow whose skinny arms displayed the handiwork of a half-dozen jailhouse tattoo artists. The man's thin mouth turned down and his crooked nose twitched, as though he'd just smelled something nasty. Cass thought she'd never seen so much poison shoot from such tiny eyes.

"That's Tommy Pritchard," Shep said. "I arrested him back in '91 for assault with a deadly weapon. He tried to amputate his brother-in-law's arm with an ax right out there in the parking lot."

"Jesus." Now she was really hoping the stuff on the menu was ketchup. "Nice guy."

"And the bartender there, that's Fat Sallie. She and I go way back. She used to run Paulie's Pit with her boyfriend till they had a lovers' quarrel one night and she shot him in the spine. She got fifteen years and served seven. Then she got out, married the dude, and now she runs the bar for him."

"The same boyfriend she shot?"

"Well, he needed help. He's a paraplegic. Sallie takes care of him."

Cass took a swig from the longneck. "Talk about instant karma."

Behind her, the door swung open and a couple of guys in paint-splattered work bibs sauntered in. Cass twisted around to check them out, turned back to her beer. A few seconds later, when a similarly clad guy who appeared to be a buddy of the first two came into the bar, she did the same thing.

Shep said, "Don't tell me you're one of those people who can't sit with their back to a door?"

"Of course not."

"Because we could switch seats, that way you wouldn't risk straining your neck."

"Forget it."

"No, you're looking for someone. Who?"

"Hey, lay off. Maybe I'm just checking to make sure the next person through the door isn't carrying an ax or a pistol. Anyway, I thought you had something to say to me."

He leaned forward and lowered his voice. "I'm taking a big chance here, you know that? I'm going to tell you the truth and just hope you don't use it against me. And hope it doesn't change things between us."

"I think they're already changed."

He straightened up as though he'd been slapped. "Then let's change them back. I only ask one thing, that you let me tell you the whole story. Don't jump up and leave the way I did the other day. And don't judge until you've heard me out."

She gave no response and he went on. "You wanted to know where I was the night Raven was murdered. I was at her apartment that night. But when I left there, she was alive, I swear to God she was."

She tipped the beer to her mouth, stalling for time so that, when she spoke, her voice wouldn't betray the shock she was feeling. "You never told anyone about this?"

"How could I? How does it look, for God's sake? I left her apartment around eight o'clock. Forensics said she was killed sometime between eight and midnight. You think anyone's going to believe I didn't do it?"

"Yet I'm supposed to believe you didn't."

"All I'm asking is that you hear me out."

"You were sleeping with her?" She couldn't believe she was asking him this, didn't want to believe how much it mattered to her, but it did.

He shook his head. A muscle in her jaw that she hadn't even realized she'd been clenching released, and then he said, "No, but not because I didn't want to."

She stiffened and reached for her beer. "How'd you meet her?"

"My sister saw some of her work in a gallery down in Santa Fe. She thought we could get Raven to do a portrait of Mom and Dad for their wedding anniversary, so I called her and then stopped by her studio. It turned out she couldn't have it done by the time we wanted, so my sister found someone else, but that was how we started going out together."

"What happened? Why didn't it work out?"

"Her obsession with religion, of course. We used to argue about it. I said she was being brainwashed, that God wouldn't have made two sexes if He didn't expect us to have sex and that she was just plain crazy to let these people at the Church of Good Hope dictate whether or not we could make love. And then I'd start to wonder if maybe she was just using her religious beliefs as an excuse not to go to bed with me, that she didn't really want to in the first place, and it was convenient to blame God, because God said she couldn't."

"Were you in love with her?" She tried to pose the question casually and hoped he didn't hear the tension in her voice.

"I don't know . . . I thought I was, but the sexual abstinence thing was driving me crazy. I'm not against marriage, I was married once, I told you, but I couldn't conceive of marrying a woman I'd never slept with and at the same time I couldn't conceive of just walking away from her, either."

"So you were thinking of marrying her?"

"Possibly. If I had to." He saw the look on Cass's face, raised a preemptive hand. "That's not how it sounds, don't get me wrong, I wanted to marry Raven—if that time came—but in my world, you spend a year or two getting to know each other, in all kinds of ways, but especially sexually, maybe moving in together, and then, then if everything's worked out okay to that point, *then* you get married."

"Which wasn't the way Raven saw it."

"To put it mildly. She wasn't just holding out for marriage, she also told me she couldn't even consider marrying a man who wasn't a born-again Christian. I didn't have to join the Church of Good Hope—that was the only slack she cut me—but I did have to accept the fundamentalist faith."

He sipped his beer and redirected the smoke from

Cass's cigarette. She exhaled the next puff at the ceiling—mostly—so that only a little went in his face.

"I remember asking her at the time how the hell was I going to do this, will myself to accept a belief system I didn't believe. I couldn't see how I could do it without being the worst kind of hypocrite. And she'd say just give it a chance, open your heart to Jesus, that kind of thing. But the problem was no matter how much I wanted her or loved her, I couldn't shut down my brain for her. I could say two plus two equals five if that's what she wanted to hear, but I couldn't make myself believe it was true."

"So you broke up," said Cass, remembering what Erin had told her. "And that was when she started dating Jack."

"Yeah. And I was afraid for her. I know how that sounds, like condescending male bullshit and maybe it is, but I know O'Doul, I've arrested him a half-dozen times. To imagine a dirtbag like that with someone like Raven"—he looked up—"or someone like you, drove me fucking nuts. So there were a few nights, yeah, I did watch. I'd just bought my brother-in-law's truck—Raven had never seen it—so keeping the GRD decal on the side didn't seem like such a bad idea. I followed them a few nights and then—I'm not proud of this—I hung out at Raven's apartment to see if all those religious scruples were as strong when it came to keeping Jack out of her bed as they had been with me."

"And were they?"

"So far as I know she never even let him come in with her, which was good because I swear to God I don't know what I'd've done if she'd let down her guard with him after everything I—"

"After you were a good boy and played by her rules."

"Something like that, yeah."

"And the night she was murdered? Why'd you go back?"

He shut his eyes and tilted his head back. For an agnostic, he looked remarkably like a man praying. "I'm ashamed to tell you the reason, but I went back to cave. To tell her I'd changed my mind, I was ready to sign up."

"You'd decided maybe two plus two equals five after all."

He shrugged. "Something like that."

"So you went to her place to tell her you were willing to do it her way, that you'd embrace Jesus if it meant you got to embrace her, the whole nine yards."

Cass knew the rest of this story—or thought she did anyway—from what Erin had told her, but she wanted to hear Shep's version of it. And hoped the telling of it made him squirm.

"She wasn't interested in getting back together, she had—other things going on at this point," he said quickly and Cass realized whether from tact or a desire to save face or both he'd decided to omit Raven's bisexual nature from the story. "She was disillusioned with men and said Jack was the cause. I'd been right to be afraid for her. O'Doul had run true to form. He wanted sex and when she wouldn't put out for him, he drove her out into the middle of nowhere and threw her out of his car."

He couldn't keep the bitterness out of his voice as he added, "That's the kind of man you're involved with, Cass, just so you know."

"Funny, up till now I thought I was involved with you."

He looked startled. She went on before he could speak. "You were at her apartment—you didn't see or hear anything while you were there to make you think she was in any danger?"

"If I had, you think I'd've left?"

"When did you leave?"

"About eight o'clock. It wasn't that long of a conversation. I mean, I came there to ask for another chance and I find out O'Doul's no longer in the picture, but she still doesn't want anything to do with me. She'd found other—"

"Someone else?"

"She wasn't interested in seeing me anymore, born again or otherwise, that was the long and short of it. So yeah, I left, because I was upset and I didn't want her to know how upset and—I did something that was probably crazy and definitely immoral, but it seemed the right thing to do at the time." He picked up his beer, put it down without drinking. "This is the part that gets tricky, Cass. When I tell you what I did after I left Raven's, you may not want to see me anymore, either. Assuming you even do now."

"Let me make that decision."

"I couldn't blame myself for losing this woman that, at the time anyway, I thought I loved. I blamed O'Doul, because his behavior hadn't just made her scared of him, it had made her scared of all men. Including me.

"So I cruised around looking for him till I spotted his car just a block away from the Church of Good Hope. He was on foot, headed up the street toward the Dark Horse. I told him I wanted to talk to him. My intention . . . I swear to God my intention was just to scare him . . . but he was drunk out of his mind. He didn't even knew who I was. We walked into an alley and next thing I know, he unzips himself and takes a piss all over my boots. I lost it. I beat him up pretty bad."

"So that's what Box Car was talking about that day at the Pioneer. About you having piss on your boots."

"Yeah, he was passed out in the alley, but he must've woke up in time to see O'Doul mistaking me for a urinal."

"So that's why you were so sure Jack didn't kill Raven. Because he was too beat-up?"

"Exactly. I went back, oh, around midnight, because I started to worry, what if O'Doul died? What if he was already dead when I left him there? So I went back to the alley and he was propped up against the brick wall with Box Car and they were sharing a bottle."

"You're sure there's no way Jack could have gotten it together enough to go over to Raven's place after you beat him?"

"No way. He spent the night in that alley."

"And Fiona Butterworth lied about the time to give him an alibi that would sound better than he was drunk in an alley."

"I figured as much. I think they did have an affair and Jack had paid her a little visit earlier in the evening—that was why his car was parked near the church. They had some drinks and a quickie, but I think they both lied about the time."

"Yeah, Jack admitted they did." Shep looked surprised. She went on, "Weren't you afraid Jack would go to the police?"

He shrugged. "I knew he wouldn't. It was my word against his that he didn't assault me first. And he did, in a way, when he peed on me. As far as Box Car, he wouldn't make much of a witness."

She thought about that a minute, the inequities of such a situation, where a man like Shep could exercise a little vigilantism and a man like Jack had to take it. She thought about the anger that always seemed to burn just under the surface of Jack's skin and wondered if that was where it came from.

Finally she said, "You never told anyone any of this?"

"How could I? You've got a dead woman that I was involved with, a woman who rejected me, and I'm at her apartment the night that she's murdered. Who'd believe that, Cass? Would you? Or, I get O'Doul to testify that I couldn't have been murdering my ex-girlfriend because I was too busy beating him senseless—that might clear me of the murder charge, but I go to prison for assault. Either way, I'm fucked."

"I see what you mean."

They sat in silence for a moment. Cass lit another cigarette. Shep stared out the window at the derelict pack of cars and pickup trucks parked outside. Finally he said, "So where does that leave us, Cass? You don't have to answer that now if you don't want to. If I give you some time maybe . . . ?"

She sighed and looked at him, not wanting to say that she believed him and forgave him, because she wasn't sure if that belief was based on her gut instinct that he was telling the truth or because, deep down, she knew that she was just as guilty of twisting morality to suit her purposes. That the urge to rationalize his actions was based in part on her desire to justify her own. The realization sank like a stone to the pit of her stomach and for a second it cut off her breath.

He was looking at her expectantly. "Well?"

"I know what I want to say. I want to say I understand what you did and I can live with it. I know a lot of people would've lost their temper with Jack under the circumstances you describe—assuming that's how it happened. On the other hand, I can't help thinking that you're a police officer, and you *can't* sink to the level of acting like a thug. So what am I supposed to say about *us*, Shep? I don't know. I think I need some time."

"I understand. Maybe later if—"

Before he could finish, the door opened again behind her, and she twisted around to see who was coming in.

"By the way," Shep said, a note of scorn creeping into his voice, "you're wasting your time hanging out in this dump. He's not coming in."

"Huh?"

"He's not coming."

"What are you talking about?"

"Grady Post. The reason we're sitting here in this toxic waste dump. He's not coming in."

"And why would that be of interest to me?" She jabbed out her cigarette, lit another one, and blew a long column of smoke into the gray smog at the ceiling.

"Because for some reason that I can't even begin to fathom, you think you want some kind of confrontation with this guy. That's why you wanted to come here to the only bar in Fremont County that'll still serve him." He ran a hand through his hair. "Believe me, Cass, the last thing you want is a confrontation with this guy. He's sick and he's dangerous, and you were lucky you came out on top last time."

This time she didn't even try to pretend he was wrong. "So how do you know he's not coming? The message you left on my machine, you said he got out on bond."

"That was true—when I left the message. But he was picked up again a couple of hours ago on an outstanding warrant the cops missed the first time. The judge wants him off the streets, so she set bail at twenty-five thousand. No way can Post pay that. He's gonna be off the streets for a very long time."

Chapter 26

After leaving Shep at Paulie's Pit, Cass tried to process everything Shep had told her about his relationship with Raven, but found it overwhelming. Instead she concentrated on her plan for that night, getting out her map and doing a little reconnaissance work before going home.

After the depressing motel room at the Mountain View, the house on Burnt Mill Lane felt like the Taj Mahal. No matter that the former occupant had a fetish for sachets and the place smelled like the perfume department at Saks. She opened up all the windows, then sprayed liberally with pine-scented air freshener she'd picked up at the grocery.

Her answering machine showed three calls, two hang-ups that she guessed were collect calls from Jack and a message from Mariah, saying she was at home and would Cass please call her back.

There was no way she could return the calls from Jack—she'd have to wait until he tried her again—but she did call Mariah, more out of guilt than the desire to talk to her. She hoped, in fact, Mariah wouldn't be home, but she answered on the second ring, sounding irritated.

"How'd the funeral go?"

"It was a memorial service. The funeral hasn't been scheduled yet."

Mariah sighed deeply. "Wonder what kinda funeral Madison will have."

"Try not to think about that, Mariah." She tried not to sound condescending. From Mariah's message, she'd thought something was wrong, but apparently all the woman wanted was to unload more of her sorrow. At the same time, Cass felt guilty for feeling uncharitable toward a person so obviously troubled.

"You thought I was kidding, didn't you?"

For a second, Cass didn't know what she meant. "About what?"

"What I said about killing myself the night Madison dies."

"I don't know if you're kidding or not, Mariah, but I think you need help. Madison's being executed for a reason—all those women he killed. Don't let him make you one of his victims."

"You don't understand what it's like."

"No, you're right. I don't. I can't begin to imagine what it's like for you. But I know suicide's not the answer."

"Then what is?"

The question hung in the air like a challenge. Cass found herself speechless. What to say to a person like this?

"Have you tried therapy? It's understandable you're depressed, but—"

Mariah cut her off. "Only kinda therapy's ever worked for me's either at the bottom of a bottle or between a guy's legs. That answer your question?"

"Loud and clear."

"Look, Cass, the reason I asked you to call, I know you're not into the bar scene, but I thought maybe you could use some company—what with going to that boy's funeral and all. I know I sure could. How about I bring over a bottle of wine and a couple of joints. We can have some girl talk just the two of us?"

Even if she hadn't planned an adventure of her own,

the last thing Cass wanted was to spend an evening with Mariah.

"I already have plans for tonight. Maybe another time?"

"Sure."

They chatted a few more minutes, Mariah updating Cass on Madison's latest, slim hope for appeal, before Cass ended the conversation, feeling drained. Obviously Mariah was lonely and eager for friendship. The feeling wasn't reciprocal, but Cass didn't want to cut the woman off completely. Mariah seemed to be an expert at getting Madison to confide in her—Cass figured there was a lot she could learn from her.

Rather than continue to analyze the other woman, she decided to do something more productive—went for a run, ate an early, light dinner, and then waited impatiently for night to come.

In midsummer the Colorado daylight lingered far into the evening. Cass thought the night would never come, but when it did, she felt she had prepared herself, mentally and physically, for what she was going to do. She put on black tights and running shoes and an extra-large black T-shirt, the darkest item she could find to pair with the tights, from a long-ago Grateful Dead concert. She added a belt to the T-shirt to keep it from billowing out around her, tied her hair back, and tucked it up under a dark blue baseball cap. The results, when she appraised herself in the mirror, were pretty good—she could either be a cat burglar or, if this were New York City, a dancer headed out to audition for a part where a certain air of androgyny was required.

Earlier that afternoon, after parting company with Shep, she'd found Grady Post's street on the map and then done a test run to make sure that she'd be able to locate the address she'd read on his driver's license. It had turned out to be one of half a dozen white clapboard cottages just off a county road, a few hundred yards from the Willows Bend Trailer Park on the opposite side of the road.

From the looks of the places, Cass figured they'd originally been rented out as summer cabins but fallen into such disrepair that they now served as lodging for whoever would have them. The fact that the black Harley was parked in full view gave her a start at first, until she remembered Shep said that Grady must have had someone drop him off at her car. With Grady in jail, it made sense that the bike would still be there although the Camaro, she noted, was gone—probably either impounded or sitting wherever Post had left it when he'd been rearrested.

In the dark, she missed the dirt turnoff, but realized she'd gone past it when she saw the lighted sign for the Willow Bend Trailer Park. In one of many identical-looking lanes, all of which bore the name of some type of tree, she found a parking spot in front of a white double-wide with a satellite dish and incongruously out-of-season Christmas lights blinking around the front door. She jogged back to the main road, crossed the street, and slowed to a walk as she approached the row of cottages.

To judge from the absence of vehicles and generally deserted appearance, Cass guessed that three of the cottages, two in the middle and one at the end, were vacant. A TV was on in the front room of another one, where she could see a heavyset woman slumped in a recliner with a drink in one hand. The cabin next to that was dark, but a Mazda with a trailer pulling what looked like some kind of fishing boat attested that the place was occupied.

Then there was Grady's place. A light was on above the door, and she could see a lamp on in a front room. Well, why not; after all Grady hadn't known he was going to be nailed on the outstanding warrant and could reasonably have left a light on the last time he went out.

And since he'd expected to be coming home, wasn't it possible he'd left the door unlocked as well?

She walked to the front door and tried it, but found Post was more conscientious about locking up than turning off the lights. The window that looked in on the kitchen was locked, too, as were a couple of others in the back of the house.

The kitchen window seemed to offer the easiest access, so she returned to it, grateful that the volume on the fat woman's TV set was turned up loud enough to mask the sound of glass breaking when she wrapped her hand in the hem of her T-shirt and used a rock to punch out the lower half of the pane.

Reaching inside, she twisted the latch and lifted the window, then crawled through and dropped to the floor.

She looked around. Post wasn't much of a housekeeper. No surprise there. Not into cooking, either. The stovetop, compared to most of the other surfaces in the room, appeared almost pristine, untouched by any fleck of grease or dribble of stew.

A glance at the overflowing garbage can in the corner told her his eating habits—Hefty Man microwave meals, an empty tub that had held Häagen-Dazs ice cream, crumpled cellophane snack bags, and a small mountain of empty beer cans.

On top of that, the kitchen reeked of beer and cigarettes and another vaguely sweetish odor, some sort of perfume perhaps, she thought, with oriental highlights. She couldn't imagine Post wearing an aftershave that carried such a scent nor did she readily imagine it dabbed behind the ears of a woman likely to be his girlfriend.

Still, the scent was definitely there, so she made a mental note of it and moved on.

The adjacent living room contained more spillover from the kitchen, beer cans on a scarred faux marble coffee table, an empty pizza box resting on top of a TV. Bookshelves adjacent to the TV contained titles that Cass was in too big a hurry to scan closely, but she did notice—with some surprise—a couple of books on recovery from alcohol and drug addiction and some recent self-help titles that would not have been out of place in her own library.

The lamp that had been left burning sat on an end table with a couple of drawers, which she opened in hopes of finding a day planner or address book. In the top one, she found a phone book and a stack of dog-earred *TV Guide*s. The second, deeper drawer contained half a dozen manila folders, which she leafed through quickly: court and D.O.C. documents and trial transcripts from Post's numerous arrests over the years. Odd, she thought, that he'd hang on to this stuff, but maybe he took a certain macho pride in it. The material was interesting in a lurid way, but she could find nothing in Post's criminal past to indicate a history of stalking and no indication of any links to Jack O'Doul.

When she finished reading, she stacked the folders in the order that she'd found them and returned them to the drawer.

Across from a closed door that she guessed led to a bedroom sat a cheap metal desk piled with newspapers, magazines, and a black plastic ashtray of the type found in inexpensive motel rooms, overflowing with cigarette butts. Nothing of interest there—she learned only what she'd have already guessed, that he favored those magazines where the centerfold was a split beaver shot and others devoted to firearms and "America's top ten tattoo artists."

She squatted to check out the drawers. The top one contained a shoe box full of unpaid bills, an assortment of canceled checks for mundane items like rent and utilities, a postcard from a buddy spending the summer riding his bike across Canada.

Below that was a photo album that told her nothing beyond the fact that Post enjoyed having his picture taken in semipornographic poses with his women friends. There was also a collection of letters, bound together with a rubberband, most of which had been written by his mother and sister while he was incarcerated.

She read just enough to know the letters wouldn't tell her anything and felt guilty with even this modest amount of snooping. The guy was scum, but he had a mom and sister who cared about him enough to write to him in jail and he cared about them enough to save their letters.

C'mon, find something that tells me something, she thought.

The second drawer was empty, the third contained only a pipe, a bag full of marijuana that was mostly seeds and stems, and half a dozen bottles of prescription painkillers.

As she stood up from inspecting the desk, she realized she was about to sneeze and automatically put a finger under her nose to try to cut off the urge. She sneezed anyway, causing some of the ash to disperse in a fine cloud of foul dust, like toxic dandelion fluff.

Leaning over the desk as she sneezed, she noticed that among the white, unfiltered butts were a couple of darker ones.

A woman's voice from behind the closed door called out, "Hey, what're you doing out there?"

Her breath stopped. She stood rigid as if someone were holding a knife to her eyes.

The voice came again, raspy and petulant, "Hey, why don't you bring me a beer?"

Jesus. She cursed herself for stupidity. It had never occurred to her that anyone besides Grady Post might be in the house.

Cass's heart was thundering so wildly she was sure the woman behind the door must hear it as clearly as her sneeze. She started back the way she had come.

"Hey?" The voice sounded annoyed now, maybe a little frightened. "Grady, that you?"

Cass heard rustling and the creaking of bedsprings,

the woman getting up out of bed, coming to investigate.

She ran for the front door and yanked the knob, forgetting in her panic that it was locked. She fumbled with the bolt, twisted it back. The bedroom door was opening.

"Who's there?"

She threw the front door open.

Behind her, the woman came into the living room, and let out a startled screech.

Cass glanced behind her and saw the woman, who was naked, with shoulder-length brown hair and a square face contorted with rage.

"Who the fuck are you? You sneakin' in here to see Grady? You that bastard's fucking whore?"

Cass slammed the door, turned to run and collided with Grady Post, who was carrying a twelve-pack in each hand. He threw the beer aside, grabbed Cass, and muscled her back inside the house.

Before she could scream, he clamped a hand across her mouth and wrapped the other arm in a viselike grip around her waist.

"Hey, SheriAnn, look what I got?" he called out in a voice that managed to combine venom and mirth.

The brunette came bounding across the room, her pancake breasts flopping against her rib cage. Her teeth were wide-spaced and bovine, gray as tombstones. She fixed Cass with a bleary, bloodshot gaze.

"Who the hell is this? What's she doin' in here?"

"The bitch's name's Cass," said Post, "and as far as what's she doin' in here, I damn well intend to find out." He jerked his head toward the door. "Put some goddamn clothes on and go grab those twelve-packs 'fore the fuckin' kids from the trailer park get 'em. I need a drink."

"A-fuckin'-men to that," said SheriAnn and started toward the door.

"Grab my goddamn shirt before you go out there," said Post. As he said it, his hold on Cass's mouth loosened slightly. She caught one of his fingers and bit down until the skin popped under her teeth. Post made a hissing sound. His hand came away from her mouth, but he maintained a crushing hold on her midsection. She kicked backward, trying to hit a knee, but the blow was off center and didn't come close to taking him off his feet.

"Fucking bitch." His arm around her waist suddenly loosened. She wrenched free, but he caught her and spun her and was there to meet her with a backhanded blow whose power was doubled by her own momentum turning her into it.

The world upended. She glimpsed a corner of ceiling and then her head thunked against the floor. Red dots danced at the edge of her vision. Absurdly they reminded her of the cinnamon candies she used to eat as a child.

Before she could get her breath back, Post's boot caught her in the small of the back—a bright, breathtaking pain that wrenched a scream from her.

SheriAnn stomped back into the living room wearing a man's shirt buttoned wrong. "Jesus, make her shut up!"

Post grabbed a pillow off the sofa and smashed it down on Cass's face.

The world went airless and black. She struggled to free herself, but he was much stronger and easily held the pillow in place. Her lungs ached for air. She heard him yell, "Quick, get somethin' to tie her with!"

The pillow came off. Post hauled her to her feet while SheriAnn grabbed her arms and tied them behind her.

He glared into her face. She thought he was going to hit her again and braced for the blow, but instead he wrenched her mouth open. Her jaw snapped back into place with an agonizing pop as he stuffed a wad of cloth into her mouth and tied a bandanna around her face to keep it there.

"That oughta shut you up." He examined his hand. "Jesus, bitch, you better not have AIDS."

SheriAnn disappeared into the kitchen and came back with a beer. "She broke the window to get in. There's glass all over the fucking floor."

"Oughta make her pick it all up—with her teeth."

"Who the hell is she?" She popped the top on the beer, chugged some down. "Hey, wait a minute." The fresh infusion of alcohol seemed to be jogging her mental faculties. "That's the bitch with the Eldorado—where I dropped you off at that trailhead the other—"

"Shut up!" bellowed Post.

"So what the fuck are you gonna do with her?"

"I'm not sure, but I think I got an idea. I just gotta wait a little bit."

He shoved Cass ahead of him into the hallway with the desk, opened the closet, and shoved her inside with the jackets and boots, then slammed the door. She heard him pushing the desk across the floor, using it to block the door in case she had any ideas about kicking her way out.

The darkness inside the closet was absolute, the air stuffy and sour. She felt as if she were locked inside a tomb.

Maybe this will be my tomb, she thought, fighting the rising panic. *Maybe I'll never get out of here.*

She sank to the floor, trying to rest and get her wits about her. She knew the worst thing she could do was give in to panic, but she was close to that now, felt it thrumming through her body like a swift, icy current.

Someone will come, she told herself. *Someone heard me scream.*

There were other people in some of the cottages, she reminded herself. Someone might have heard her screams and called the police. Maybe even someone in the trailer park across the street, because in the still air, sounds would carry.

But would anyone really help her?

There were some neighborhoods where screams weren't that uncommon—Cass knew because she'd spent part of her childhood in one—and this might be just such a place. Maybe around here domestic violence was the norm. And maybe the people who might have heard her scream wouldn't want to risk involvement with someone like Grady Post.

Right now, she decided, her biggest task was breathing. With her mouth blocked and adrenaline racing, the sensation of suffocation was unbearable. She forced herself to relax and take long, slow breaths through her nose.

The pain in her jaw was acute—as if two strong people had grabbed hold of either side and tried to split it in two like a wishbone—and made worse by the wad of cloth keeping her mouth open.

She tried to keep track of the time, which passed with excruciating slowness. She knew she'd entered the house around ten and spent twenty minutes or so inside before being caught. She also estimated she'd been inside the closet almost three hours. That would make it close to two in the morning.

Now that they'd subdued their intruder, Post and his girlfriend seemed to be back to business as usual. She could hear the TV blasting and the occasional drunken whoop in response to something on the screen.

He's waiting for something, she thought, *but what? For the girlfriend to leave?* But being the polite host didn't seem to be Post's style. Surely if he wanted SheriAnn out, he'd just tell her to go.

Abruptly she heard the TV turned off. The front door opened and closed. A few seconds later, she heard the Harley revving. *He's leaving,* she thought. *But why?* As soon as she thought it, a worse idea came to her. *He's going to get some friends, to bring them back here with him . . .*

The thought had barely had time to sink in, though, when Post cut the engine again, and she heard him clomp back inside. The closet door opened. Light stabbed at her eyes.

Post leaned into the closet, a nasty grin stretching his face. "Thought I forgot about you, didn't you? Well, don't worry, our night's a long way from bein' over. Fact is, it's just begun."

Chapter 27

Post hustled her to her feet and prodded her outside. She prayed for someone who'd call the police at the sight of a woman, bound and gagged, being pushed around the side of a house, but the night was silent and still. The only witness to her nightmare was a rabbit that sat, ears twitching, under a shrub in the yard. The Harley was now parked around the back of the cottage. SheriAnn stood beside it holding a helmet. She pushed the helmet down over Cass's head.

Post flipped up the plastic visor. "Now we can do this easy or we can do this hard, but I suggest you make it easy, 'cause otherwise you could get hurt real bad. I'm gonna set you down on the bike there and SheriAnn's gonna tie your hands to the sissybar. You try to kick me, you struggle, I'll choke you out."

He put a hand under the helmet and gripped her throat. There was a terrifying sense of suffocation, and her legs started to fail. The next thing she knew she was being set down on the back of the Harley, which was tilted sideways on its kickstand. Post sat backward on the bike, straddling her, his thighs wrapping her own, while SheriAnn worked from behind. She untied Cass's wrists, then quickly tied them again to the sissybar, the metal bar attached to the back of the bike to provide back support for a second rider.

"You ever ride on a motorcycle?" Post asked. "Just shake your head, yes or no."

She shook her head *yes*.

"Then you know how this works. You decide to freak out back there, start kicking, throwing your weight back and forth, you won't get loose, but you *will* make me roll the bike. I'll be thrown off, and I may not get hurt too bad. You're wearing a helmet, but you'll be dragged under the bike with both your arms dislocated. Then the bike will probably fall on top of you."

He slapped some goggles onto his face and leaned into her. She got a faceful of warm, beery breath. "Try something like that and I swear, if the crash doesn't kill you, I will. Understand?"

He mounted the bike and righted it, then revved the motor and roared off into the night.

On a normal bike ride, Cass would have gripped the sides of the sissybar for balance or held on to the driver's waist. Being tied to the sissybar didn't allow her leverage for shifting her weight with the bike. Too much of a shift and she could slide off the seat, flip the bike, and be dragged by her hands. So instead she sat stiffly, muscles clenched with the effort of maintaining her position.

A car passed them coming in the opposite direction. She wondered if someone in the vehicle would see her bound hands, but knew it was virtually hopeless. The helmet concealed the gag in her mouth, and in the darkness, the position of her arms would just give the impression that she was holding on to the sissybar.

Perhaps purposely, Post had neglected to lower her visor. Without night glasses, like the ones he was wearing, there was nothing to protect her eyes from the wind. She was constantly trying to blink away tears just to see where they were going.

In spite of what Post had told her about making him flip the bike, she considered doing just that. Dying in a bike crash was one of the worst ways she could think of to go, but it might beat whatever Post had in mind for her. On the other hand, realistically, did she have the nerve to try to topple a motorcycle going sixty miles an hour?

No, realistically, she didn't.

Maybe he's just going to drop me off someplace in the middle of nowhere, she thought, *try to teach me a lesson.* She concentrated on paying attention to where they were going, so if Post stranded her somewhere, she'd have a better chance of finding her way back.

He was heading back toward Canon City, then turned east toward Florence. She wasn't expecting that. She'd expected him to be taking her somewhere remote, maybe onto one of the dirt roads that snaked up into the hills. The bike wouldn't maneuver so well on a dirt road, of course, but Post seemed to be an experienced rider and probably wouldn't worry about the terrain.

After the first car that passed them, Cass saw no more vehicles. The road stretched into what looked like utter blackness under a sky that loomed above like a black, inverted dome, barren of moon or stars.

Who'll miss me? she thought frantically. *Not Shep, after the way I ended things. Mariah might call, but she'd figure I was just unavailable. Jack would notice my absence and be angry, but what could he do? If Post killed me or left me injured someplace where I might die of thirst, there'd be no one to report me missing.*

To distract herself from such dispiriting thoughts, she tried to wiggle her jaw back and forth. The entire lower half of her face felt numb. She could barely see for the wind-stung tears in her eyes. The next thing she knew, the bike turned sharply, slowed, and bounced over a bump in the macadam.

She opened her eyes, wondering at first why everything looked so familiar and yet so strange. Then she realized they were in the parking lot of Paulie's Pit, the very bar where she and Shep had drunk longnecks that afternoon—what felt like a hundred years ago. Now the sprawling parking lot was utterly deserted and the building dark. Only a weak light over the front door cast a single sickly cone of yellow light.

Post drove the bike around back of the bar, cut the motor, hit the kickstand, and dismounted.

He lifted the helmet off Cass's head and hung it on one of the handlebars, then untied the gag around her mouth and pulled out the cloth. Air had never tasted so good. She took in great gulps of it.

"You can scream out here if you want to, but I wouldn't bother," Post said. "There's nobody for miles."

He went behind her and untied her wrists. She rubbed them together, trying to get the circulation back.

"C'mon," he said, "I know where Fat Sallie keeps a spare key. We're going inside."

He grabbed her upper arm and started to pull her up off the bike.

"Give me a minute." She put her head down and kept rubbing her arms. "I don't feel so good. I think I'm going to throw up."

"Puke all you want to. Just don't fucking throw up on the bike."

"What are we doing here?" She knew she shouldn't ask and might not want to know, but the question popped out of her anyway.

Post appeared gratified that she'd asked. He leered down at her. "Remember that deal a few years back with the chick who got banged on a pool table. They made a movie out of it. I always kinda envied those guys who fucked her that way, wondered what it musta been like. There's a couple of pool tables in there. Now I get to find out."

"If you know where the spare key is, why didn't you bring SheriAnn here?"

He chuckled darkly. "Who's sayin' I haven't? But SheriAnn's already been fucked every way 'cept standin' up under the bed. And anyway, ain't as much fun if they like it."

She realized that now that the circulation was coming back, her hands were starting to shake. She clenched her fingers together so he wouldn't see. "Why are you doing this?"

"How 'bout you answer that question for *me*? Why did you break into my place? Why were you looking through my stuff? What the hell were you hoping to find?"

"An explanation for why you've been stalking me."

"So, Miss Smart New York Bitch—you find anything?"

She couldn't look him in the face and lie—she was afraid her eyes would give her away—so she lowered her head and said, "No."

"That's what I figured. C'mon, get off the bike." He grabbed her by the upper arm, hoisted her off.

If he takes me in there, I'm dead, she thought. *I'll never get out again.*

"Wait, think about what you're doing. So far you really haven't done anything but teach me a lesson for breaking into your place. Let me go now and we'll call it even. But if you take it further, you're the first person the cops are going to look for. You'll go to prison for the rest of your life."

Too late, she realized—from the look on his face—that was the wrong thing to say. "I'm not going to no fucking prison—ever. I've been to prison and I know what it's like. Christ, I'm out on bond now. I'm fucked anyway if I stay in Colorado. After I settle the score with you, I'm outta here. Heading for Mexico. They catch me, they catch me, I'll blow my head off. But I ain't goin' back to no prison." His grip on her arm tightened. "C'mon, no more bullshit. We're goin' inside. Have some fun."

"Give me a minute. I'm gonna be sick."

She bent over and started to retch, her face directly over his boots, and he took a step back. She turned away and put one hand on the handlebars, leaning on them as though for support.

"You puke on that bike, I swear I'll make you lick it off."

Her hand was next to the helmet he'd hung over the bars. She knew she'd get one chance only. She grabbed the helmet and swung it backward, all her weight going into the swing as her body pivoted. Its heft caught him full in the face. She heard cartilage crunch. A gout of blood shot from his nose. As he grabbed for her, she swung the helmet forward, but he blocked it. The helmet bounced off his shoulder and tore free from her hand, crashing onto the macadam behind him.

She ran. Her aim was to get as far from Paulie's Pit as she could and hide in the darkness. She thought about running toward the road, but no cars had gone by since they'd arrived—she'd been listening—so the odds of one coming by just when she needed it were too small to risk running that way.

Where to go? She tried to remember what the parking lot had looked like in daylight, when she'd been there only hours before. She remembered it was vast, sprawling like a football field around the sorry-looking squat building. Beyond that was nothing, no houses, no businesses. Just what appeared to be miles of scrub and rocky, wind-blasted terrain.

Within seconds, she was out of range of the weak light over the door and plunged into total darkness. Running blind. Her breath screamed in her ears—he had to hear it.

But where was he? She risked a glance backward, didn't see him. Was it possible the blow to the nose had actually stopped him? That he was giving up?

She kept running.

The bike's engine started to rev. A cone of light, like a huge hook yanking back the protective darkness, illuminated the area just behind her. *He was coming after her on the bike.*

She darted to the left, hoping to make it off the

paved area into the scrub where he'd have more trouble following, but he'd already spotted her. Roaring like an enraged animal, the bike bore down on her.

There was no place to go, nothing to hide behind. The high beams of the Harley lit up the area around her, the roar of the motor so thunderous now she could feel it inside her body, vibrating through her flesh, booming against her heart.

She zigzagged, and he missed her and roared past, and she turned and ran the opposite way, but he came around her this time, cutting in front, missing her on purpose but coming so close that a spray of gravel bit into her face and arms.

She got a glimpse of his face. He was laughing, lips stretched wide in a malevolent grin, even as blood poured from his crushed nose. This was a game, she realized. He knew he could run her down on foot easily, but he wanted to do it this way. Run her in circles, terrorize her with the bike, herding her as if she were an errant sheep and he a motorized Border collie.

The headlights swept over and passed her. Temporarily blinded, she changed direction again, found herself running back toward the bar.

Post swerved the bike into a screeching curve and came back for another pass. Over the roar of the motor, she could hear him whooping with glee. He was loving this.

She never saw the thing she hit, only knew that her hip smashed into a hard, waist-high object that then crashed to the ground. The impact threw her off balance. She tripped and rolled, realized she'd plowed into the sawhorse she'd seen in the parking lot that afternoon. It was set up to mark the gaping hole in the pavement.

Getting to her feet, she grabbed a leg of the sawhorse as the motorcycle came at her again. It was heavy and she wondered if she could swing it effectively. This time his aim was wide, and he roared past her ten feet away. Apparently he hadn't seen her fall and had misjudged her position in the lot.

He slowed the bike, looking around as he made the turn, then saw her again and came back, howling vengeance as he gunned the engine. When he passed within reach, she heaved the sawhorse at the wheels of the bike, but the horse was heavy and unwieldy, and he swerved around it.

She started running again. Heard him screaming behind her and the sound of the bike growing louder.

She raced toward the unpaved open space beyond the parking lot. It had to be close, she told herself.

And then what? He'd leave the bike and chase her on foot—that had probably been his intention all along. Pursuing her on the bike was an impulse thing, borne of drunken hilarity, an adventure he could regale his barroom buddies with in years to come.

Her foot went into a hole—the same one that had previously been guarded by the sawhorse—she was going the wrong way, running back toward the Pit.

She turned and saw Post coming back at her for another pass, and she jumped to the side, as though trying to dodge him. He was standing up on the bike pedals, looking around for her. She screamed for help to get his attention, and he aimed the bike at her and gunned it.

Come on, come on, she thought, but the bike missed the hole by inches as he braked and swerved toward her. His arm came out like he was signaling for a turn. He was trying to hit her as he went past. She grabbed for his arm, thinking to pull him off balance and capsize the bike. He was moving too fast. She missed, and his fist thumped off her elbow. Pain surged up her arm.

Try it again, she told herself.

This time she raced after Post, waving her arms, screaming. Wanting him to think she had lost it, trying to distract him from everything else but her screams.

He curved into a turn and came at her. She hurtled the gaping hole in the pavement and sprinted. The bike's front wheel hit the hole in the macadam just as Post was picking up speed.

She heard the bike scream into a skid and whirled around. The Harley went airborne in a shower of gravel, high beams cutting a yellow swath through the night sky, Post somersaulting over the handlebars.

Then came the screech of metal meeting macadam in a constellation of sparks and shattering glass, the thump of Post's body slamming down farther off. No helmet, thought Cass, and no leather gear. No sound, either, except for the rasp of her own breathing.

She ran to the edge of the asphalt and crouched in the darkness. Despite the warmth of the evening, she was shivering, drenched in cold sweat. After a few seconds, she heard Post moan and moved in the direction of the sound.

Was he trying to trick her? She knew that was a possibility, but she'd also seen him vault off the bike, heard him crash. She had to take the chance.

She found him sprawled on his back about twenty feet past the crumpled motorcycle, illuminated by one of the bike's beams that remained intact. One leg bloody and broken, bone protruding through a jagged tear in the jeans. Blood seeped from his nose and his scalp.

His eyes were open, but she wasn't sure if he was seeing anything or not.

She strolled over and nudged him in the ribs with her toe. "Grady, can you hear me? Grady?"

No response.

"I think I know who put you up to this, Grady. Now I want to know why. Tell me what I want to know and I *might* call an ambulance."

His eyes rolled back. Not hearing her, going into shock.

She tried one more time. "You piece of shit, you were gonna rape me. Probably kill me. You know what I oughta do? I oughta do what my father would do if somebody fucked with him this bad—find a big rock and bash in your skull."

For all the response she got, she might as well have been singing a lullaby.

"Fuck you," said Cass. "I'm gonna go find a rock."

She turned and walked back to the road. The few rocks she encountered, she kicked out of her path.

Around four in the morning, she hitched a ride with a trucker hauling a load up to Colorado Springs. Her story was she'd rolled her motorcycle and needed to get back to the Willow Bend Trailer Park where she had friends who'd help her get the bike to a mechanic.

The trucker looked at her bruised jaw and torn, dirty clothing and shook his head. "Lady, you don't need a mechanic. You need a hospital. Were you wearing a helmet?"

"As a matter of fact, I was."

He looked satisfied. "Well, then that's what saved your life. Can't be too careful with motorcycles. Them things are dangerous."

She had him drop her off at the trailer park, got her car, and drove back to Canon City, where she called the cops from a pay phone and reported an injured man in the parking lot at Paulie's Pit. When the dispatcher asked her for details, she hung up.

At home, just looking in the mirror required a huge effort of will. What she saw dismayed her—she was covered in scrapes and bruises. Her jaw was swollen and her back ached from where Post had kicked her. She even imagined that she could still smell, ever so faintly, the sweetish scent of Bonnie Sterling's cheroots on her clothes, making her want to sneeze.

She ran the water as hot as she could stand it and showered until the water turned tepid, turning it over in her mind. She was now sure it was Bonnie Sterling who had been in Post's apartment and put him up to stalking her, and she could only think of one reason why.

She desperately wanted to sleep, but she couldn't—it was better, she'd decided, to catch Bonnie and Kenny completely off guard by showing up in the middle of the night, waking them up from what might be the last good night's sleep they would have in a very long time.

Chapter 28

Kenny loomed in the doorway, barefoot, wearing a pair of blue pajama bottoms. Oily sweat beaded his temples and glistened off saggy, deeply tanned pecs. Strands of hair poked out from his head in unruly directions. In his right hand, he held a small, black-handled pistol.

He squinted down at her. "Cass, what's happened? What are you doing here?"

A few feet behind him, Bonnie peered out fearfully over her husband's shoulder, like a child peeking through her own fingers. She wore a peach-colored gown and matching slippers with a row of rhinestones across her peach-painted toes. When she saw it was Cass at the door, she let out a breath.

"Jesus Christ," said Kenny, setting the gun aside, "you scared the shit out of us. It's—what—five in the morning?"

Emboldened now that she knew they weren't being menaced by an intruder, Bonnie said, "What on earth is it? Couldn't it have waited?"

"No, it couldn't," said Cass. She took a step closer, so the porch light illuminated the cut and scrapes on her arms and her bruised, swollen jaw.

"My God, what happened?" said Bonnie. "Have you been in an accident?"

"In a manner of speaking, yeah."

"Well, come in," said Kenny. "Do you want me to drive you to the hospital?"

"No hospitals," she said, walking inside, "but I could do with a glass of water."

Bonnie hurried to comply. "Put some Scotch in it," Kenny yelled.

They crossed the cushiony carpet into the formal living room next to the entrance hall, the one that looked more like the posh lobby of an exclusive Santa Fe lodge than a private residence. Waist-high pottery urns and bright Navajo rugs against pale ocher walls. Cass lowered her aching, exhausted body into the deep lap of the chair.

Bonnie brought a tumbler of what looked like water. Cass sniffed it and found it reeking of Scotch. She set it aside.

Bonnie seated herself on the sofa next to Kenny. Her small mouth was pinched tight, and her well-manicured fingers left indentations in the fabric of her gown.

"Did you find something out about Raven?" asked Kenny. "Is that why you're here?"

"No, it isn't. In fact, I don't think Jack killed Raven, although at this point I'm still not sure who did. What I do know, though, is that he didn't kill Melinda." She paused for effect and then added, "The only question now is which one of you two *did*."

There was stunned silence. Bonnie's eyes clocked to the left, toward her husband. Kenny lurched upward as if he were getting ready to hurl himself out of his seat, then stiffened and sat straight again.

"Is this some kind of joke?" said Bonnie. Crumpling a fistful of orange fabric, she turned to her husband. "You see? Didn't I tell you she doesn't know what she's doing? You paid her all that money, and *this* is what she comes up with. Didn't I tell you it was a waste of time?"

Kenny ignored her, his granite face as frozen and

expressionless as something excavated on Easter Island. "That's a helluva accusation you're making. You'd better be able to back it up."

"You still haven't answered my question," said Cass, "but I've got a bet going with myself. I think it was Bonnie who shot Melinda. Bonnie's the one who hired Grady Post to harass me, to beat me up and run me out of town, so that seems to make the most sense. I won't count what happened tonight, because I went to Grady's place and broke in, and he caught me. I figure tonight he was off the clock, practicing thuggery on his own time. But all the rest of it, Bonnie, you were behind."

"She doesn't know what she's talking about," said Bonnie. "I don't know any Grady Post. This is ridiculous."

"Explain what you're talking about," Kenny said. "Who is Grady Post and why the hell would you think my wife has anything to do with you being stalked?"

"Remember when I changed my mind about having the gun? It was because I'd been attacked in my motel room and my car had been vandalized—twice. Well, the guy got arrested. His name's Grady Post. I'd never seen him before in my life, but he knew I was a writer from New York and he knew where to find me, at a remote campsite, the day after you gave me the gun."

"So?" said Kenny. "You already said he'd been following you."

"He didn't follow me to the campsite. He already knew I was there. And after I got to thinking about it, I realized I hadn't even told you where I was going. The only person I'd told was Bonnie, when we were on the phone."

"The kind of person who'd do these things, he'd be someone Jack knew," said Kenny. "You told me you thought Jack was behind it when we talked at the Broadmoor that day."

"At first, yeah, I did think it was Jack working behind the scenes, but not anymore. Even if Post did know Jack, that would explain him knowing I'm from New York, but not that I'm a writer. You and I agreed at the beginning it would be better if Jack thought I'd worked as a secretary. That way, he wouldn't get paranoid that I was doing research or something. You and Bonnie are the only people here who know what I really do. And as far as the camping trip, I never told Jack I was going anywhere, let alone what trailhead I'd be parked at. The only one who could have possibly told Post where I'd be was Bonnie."

"I'm telling you I don't know any Grady Post," said Bonnie. "I think you missed your calling, Cass. Your talent's wasted writing magazine articles. With an imagination like yours, you should be writing fiction."

"You bailed him out of jail, didn't you?"

"I tell you I don't know what you're talking about."

Cass took a sip of her drink. "You went to Post's trailer yesterday—my guess is to pay him off for his efforts to steal my car or to pay him in advance for whatever his next trick was going to be. You smoked two cigarettes while you were there. I found them in the ashtray. Hand-rolled cheroots with red lipstick on them."

Bonnie appeared unfazed. "Much as I'd like to think my tastes are unique, I'm not the only one in the world who smokes cheroots."

"With the Gudang Garam label? C'mon, Bonnie, you think Post and his friends smoke those?"

"I've heard enough of this nonsense. I think you should leave."

Kenny cleared his throat. "Wait. I want to hear her out."

Cass said, "Grady Post's bail was set so high there's no way he could have paid it. You paid the bail for him or got your lawyer to pay it—the latter's my guess. Either way, the money had to come from somewhere, and your bank records can be subpoenaed."

Bonnie jerked to her feet. "This is a joke. I want you out of here—now."

"That's enough," said Kenny. His voice was soft but imbued with authority. "Nobody bolts out of here 'less I say so." His eyes locked with Bonnie's, and a look passed between them that caused Bonnie to lower her head and slump back down on the sofa, defeated-looking.

"Is what she says true?" Kenny said. "Did you pay somebody to scare Cass?"

"Why would I do that?"

"You know damn well why you'd do it." He exhaled a long breath, the unsure, wheezy breath of a much older man. His cheeks deflated, and he seemed to get smaller, shed bulk. Along his clenched jaw, small muscles roiled like ball bearings under the skin.

"Look at me, Bonnie. Did you go behind my back, set something up to undermine everything I was trying to do? Christ, woman, don't sit there and lie."

An abrupt, silent flood of tears streamed down Bonnie's cheeks. "I was only trying to protect you—from yourself. From your own goddamned scruples."

"Scruples?" Her use of the word seemed to appall him.

She looked up, face blanched to the whiteness of linen. "You had no business bringing her here! To do what? What difference does it make whether or not Jack killed Raven? She's dead! Whoever did it, finding out won't bring her back."

"But not finding out could mean an innocent man's sitting in prison," Kenny said. He looked at Cass. "You lost your bet, I'm afraid. I was the one . . . I killed Melinda. My wife didn't have anything to do with it."

Bonnie let out a moan. "You idiot. You goddamned idiot. You know what you just did? You just destroyed everything, our whole lives."

"I think," said Kenny, "I destroyed everything a long time ago."

"Tell me the truth," said Cass, "all of it. You killed Melinda. Why?"

Kenny's face showed no expression, but the muscles in his jaw had begun to twitch. "Not on purpose. Good Christ, of course I didn't kill her on purpose." He turned to Bonnie. "Get me a drink, will you?" He looked at Cass's glass. "Something stronger than what you got her."

She looked up, tearful and surprised. "A drink? You just threw away everything we've worked for together, and you expect me to bring you a drink?"

"Do as I ask, won't you?"

"Please, don't do this, Kenny. It's her word against ours. Nothing's lost yet. We can keep our life just as it is. Nothing has to change."

He sighed. "You just don't understand, do you? It already changed. Everything changed when I killed that woman."

Bonnie clenched her fists and shut her eyes tightly. After a moment, she got up and disappeared into the hall.

Kenny turned back to Cass. "The night Melinda was shot I went to Jack's house. That woman—the one you insisted you wanted to meet—Jesus, I can't think straight, her name—"

"Erin O'Malley."

"Erin, yeah. I already told you this part. She came here that afternoon, half in the bag, wanting some mementoes of Raven's. She went on a rant about O'Doul. Told me things I hadn't known before about how he treated my daughter, how he abused her. By the time she left I was beside myself. I'd been drinking already and I had a few more—I suppose you know where this is going—"

"You went to Jack's house to confront him. He wasn't home, so you broke in."

"That sty he lived in wasn't even locked—I walked in the back door." He gave a raw, choked-sounding laugh. "Not that it matters. Under the circumstances."

"So you waited for him in his house?"

Bonnie swished back into the room, a tumbler of

clear liquid in her hand, and handed it to Kenny. No ice. He gulped down half.

"I waited, yes. Snooped around a bit. There was a packet of photos hidden at the bottom of an upstairs drawer that showed O'Doul and Raven together. Making out, I suppose you'd say. I didn't want that scumbag to have anything to remind him of my daughter, so I took them.

"Then I hid where I could see both the front and back doors and I waited. I expected O'Doul to come in any minute, probably tanked to the gills.

"I heard someone come in the front door, using a key. The house was dark, you understand, and my eyes aren't what they used to be. I saw a person O'Doul's height, wearing a baseball cap and baggy pants, and some kind of parka—a man's parka, heavy, plaid. This person started upstairs. I shouted something like, 'Look at me, you son of a bitch,' and as the person turned around, at that point, I saw the gun. It was coming up, and I figured O'Doul was going to shoot me where I stood. I lunged and we struggled and I got the gun . . ." He kept massaging his knees with both hands, over and over as if he were polishing twin doorknobs. "I suppose I could say that it went off by accident, just one of those things. I'm not sure. I swear to God I didn't pull the trigger, but it went off while we were struggling."

"And it turned out to be Melinda."

"The shot from the gun blew her hat off and her hair fell out. I was stunned. I couldn't move. I just kept staring at her, like if I just stood there long enough, it would turn out to be O'Doul there on the floor. Then I thought maybe she was still alive, but I checked her—the shot had gone through her eye."

"Then what?"

He looked up, anguish etched in his face. "What could I do? She was dead, killed with her own gun. I wiped my prints off and put it back on the floor beside her. I didn't know what else to do."

"You left knowing Jack would come home and find her."

"I hoped the cops would think it was a suicide, that this was her way of punishing Jack. It never occurred to me he'd come home in a blackout, pick up the gun, and figure he was the one who shot her.

"So, you see the logic of it—I knew all along O'Doul didn't belong in prison for killing Melinda. Trying to find out if he'd murdered Raven was just a way for me to know if he belonged in prison anyway— even if it was a different murder from the one he got convicted of."

"Which you felt let you off the hook as far as Melinda's death? If Jack killed your daughter, but got away with it, then he was getting what he deserved by being in prison, even if it was for a murder he didn't commit?"

"Yes, that's how I saw it." He turned toward Bonnie. "How *we* saw it."

"And at the same time you felt guilty about depriving Twyla O'Doul of her mother. So you sent money anonymously to the Dunns? Is that it? I don't know how you found out about Twyla's accident so quickly, but you sent money to cover her hospital bills, too, didn't you?"

Kenny nodded. "Soon as I noticed Bonnie was trying to stop me from reading the morning paper, I knew something was up. So I turned on the radio and heard about it from there. I had to do something, didn't I? None of this was that little girl's fault."

"So how do I figure into this little charade? You went to all this trouble and expense to get me to come out here to try to prove Jack guilty of Raven's murder and absolve you of your guilt?"

"Something like that, yes," said Kenny. "I was so sure, so *sure* Jack killed her . . ."

"But he didn't," said Cass, "yet he's the one sitting in prison. What're you going to do about that, Kenny?"

"I made that decision a long time ago—what I'd do if it came to this."

Bonnie's head jerked up. "No, that's out of the question!"

He sighed tiredly. "What choice do I have?"

Color rose furiously in Bonnie's pallid cheeks. "I can't stand this! I can't stay here and watch you throw our lives away! I won't!"

She rushed out of the room, fists working at the sides of her head, digging into her temples like a possessed woman trying to drive out her demons.

Cass was starting to get a creepy feeling in the bottom of her stomach. "The decision you say you made—what are you talking about?"

"In spite of what you may be thinking, I'm not entirely a man without honor," Kenny said. "I'd hoped—prayed, even—to avoid having to take responsibility for Melinda's death and face the consequences. I guess I'd talked myself into believing it would never come to this. In a way, I'm almost glad it's over. At least now I don't have to live with the uncertainty of whether or not I'm going to prison any longer."

He walked across the room to the phone and handed it to Cass. "You dial the police, give them my name, and then hand the phone back to me. That way you'll know I'm not pulling some trick, calling in a confession to Dial-A-Prayer."

His voice broke and his eyes filled with tears. Cass realized she was crying herself as she took the phone out of his hand. There was no victory in this. Only tragedy.

She started to dial 9-1-1.

Upstairs they heard a gun fire.

For an instant neither of them moved. Then Kenny yelled "Bonnie!" and bolted for the stairs.

Cass's eyes went to the .22 Kenny'd lain on the table—it was still there, but she knew there were other guns in the house. She started to follow him up the stairs and then stopped in her tracks. It was the sound that stopped her—an ululating cry of abject distress that at first filled her with relief—she thought it could only be coming from a female throat. Then the timbre changed and she realized it was Kenny.

"Jesus," she whispered and sank down onto the bottom stair, cradling her head in her hands.

Chapter 29

The desk sergeant at police headquarters was named Griese, a lean, crooked-nosed man with a tight, churlish mouth and flat, unsurprisable-looking eyes. He listened to Cass repeat the story she'd already told to the officers who showed up in response to Kenny's frantic call.

"So Mrs. Sterling went upstairs. You heard the gunshot. You ran upstairs and found her dead."

"Not exactly."

"Which part not exactly."

Cass closed her eyes, trying to block out the images. This was the hardest part. "I mean, she wasn't dead. She didn't die right away. I don't know how . . . I mean, she must've put the gun right up to her head, but . . . she still had a pulse. I felt it myself when . . . when Kenny ran downstairs to call the ambulance, but . . ." She took a deep breath, remembering the ruined face, the eyes that were open and glazed, but not, she thought, completely unconscious. Eyes that still, somehow, *knew* where she was, what was happening.

"Go on, Ms. Lumetto."

"She died before the ambulance got there. I was with her. Kenny was downstairs on the phone. The whole thing . . . it was over in three or four minutes."

"And this was right after Mr. Sterling had confessed

to killing Melinda O'Doul. She shot herself in reaction
to finding out her husband was a murderer."

She hesitated. She could tell the truth, which was
that Bonnie had known everything from the beginning, that she'd killed herself because she couldn't face
what her life would be like once the truth was known.
She could add that Bonnie'd hired Grady Post to terrorize her and explain why, in Bonnie's mind, that had
been necessary. She decided to stick with the basics.

"As far as I know, yes, she committed suicide because she'd just heard her husband confess that he'd
accidentally killed Melinda O'Doul and let her husband take the blame for her murder."

The sergeant wrinkled his lopsided nose and shuffled some papers. He looked at her for so long without
blinking that she wondered if he'd fallen asleep with
his eyes open.

"Tell me again why you think Kenny Sterling would
have confessed after all this time, Ms. Lumetto. Why
to you and why today?"

She'd been anticipating this question. Even though
she knew she was only buying time, that the true connection between her and the Sterlings would come out
eventually, she decided to try to keep it simple.

"Kenny and Bonnie are friends of mine. I drove out
to see them, because I was upset about a relationship
I have with Jack O'Doul, the man who went to prison
for the murder Kenny confessed to. All I can think is
that when Kenny heard me talking about how horrible
it is for Jack in prison, what a nightmare it's been for
him and me both, his conscience got to him. He knew
he'd sent an innocent man to prison, and he broke
down."

She waited, trusting her version of events would
match more or less with Kenny's. She didn't think
either of them wanted to get into the deception involving Jack and the murder of Raven.

The sergeant still hadn't blinked. "Were you aware

the Sterlings had a daughter, Raven, who was murdered last year?"

"I knew that, yes."

"And that Kenny Sterling considered Jack O'Doul a suspect in his daughter's death? He used to come down here, ranting and raving. I personally once had him arrested and held overnight because he threatened to punch out my lights, told me I couldn't find my ass with a shit detector."

She was so exhausted that a hint of a smile crossed her lips. "No, I wasn't aware of that."

"Quite a coincidence, though, wouldn't you say? You being friends with the Sterlings and yet involved with the same guy who they believed murdered their daughter?"

"It would seem so." There was a beat of quiet. Cass said, "Do I need to get a lawyer?"

"Not yet, Ms. Lumetto, but I wouldn't leave town."

Two more detectives, including Shep's partner, Detective Munez, interviewed her. Finally, in the early afternoon, she was at last told she was free to go.

She was leaving the station when Shep came running up the steps. When he saw her, he stopped as though he'd run into a wall.

"Well, you got what you wanted. Munez filled me in. O'Doul's going to be a free man."

"How soon will that be?"

"Can't wait, can you?"

"That's not what I meant."

"What *did* you mean?"

"That I'm happy an innocent man is going to go free. Surely you can say the same thing."

He stared at her a moment, then reached out and touched the bruise on her face. "What happened here?"

"I fell down."

"Down what? An elevator shaft? I don't know, Cass, it's a funny thing. A woman phoned in a tip last night that a man was badly hurt in the parking lot of

Paulie's Pit. Turned out to be Grady Post. Apparently he'd been roaring around the parking lot, drunk out of his mind, and rolled his bike. He smashed himself up pretty bad. You wouldn't happen to know anything about that, would you?"

"Do we have to talk about this now? I've been here answering questions since seven o'clock this morning. I'm exhausted."

"That makes two of us."

"I don't understand."

"You think I could sleep last night after the way things ended between us?"

"After what you told me about you and Raven— you understand why that's something I need to get past. Not just the part about your following her. Knowing Jack's history with women, I can understand that. But the fact that you were *there*, at her apartment, the night that she was murdered, and yet you didn't tell anyone . . ."

"I thought I explained that, Cass. If there'd been *anything* that I'd seen that would have helped find her killer, I'd have come forward. But there wasn't anything." A pair of cops coming up the stairs greeted Shep. He nodded to them, then turned back to Cass. "Tell me the truth. Is this really about Raven or is it because O'Doul's getting out of prison? Because there's nothing now to stop you from being with him?"

"Jack's getting out has nothing to do with us."

He grimaced. "Yeah, right. I believe that like I believe you fell down and that you had nothing to do with Post winding up in I.C.U. I've been truthful with you, Cass. Why can't you be truthful with me?"

She started to say something, then realized she couldn't tell Shep just *part* of the truth. She had to either tell him the whole story of why she'd gotten involved with Jack or tell him nothing at all.

"I just . . ."

He stood there, looking hopeful, waiting for her to

go on. When it hit her that his willingness to divulge the truth was greater than her own, she felt ashamed, hypocritical.

"I'm tired, Shep. I'm going home."

She started down the steps.

"Cass?"

She turned around.

"I don't want it to turn out like this. When I told you the truth the other day, I took a helluva risk, but I'd hoped you could find something to admire in my honesty, if not in my actions. I took that risk because I had hopes for us. I still do. If you'll just meet me halfway, that is."

She felt a weariness descending on her that exceeded even her physical exhaustion. She'd had hopes, too.

"I gotta go now, Shep. I'm sorry."

She walked away quickly, afraid he'd call after her again, both relieved and disappointed when he didn't.

She got home, exhausted and depressed, in the early afternoon. Part of her knew she should feel glad for her part in vindicating Jack, but at what a terrible price—Raven's idyllic family that she'd once envied long ago had been destroyed, with Bonnie dead and Kenny facing prison.

Then, before she could grow too maudlin, she reminded herself that Kenny had set all this in motion. It was Kenny who'd sought her out, Kenny who'd planted the seeds for his own exposure. And she thought of Raven and her relationship with Shep and felt a twinge of bitterness that she tried to pretend was something other than what it was, pure jealousy. In college Raven had always been prettier, sexier, more sought after. Now, fifteen years later, she was exerting the same power even from the grave.

Too many thoughts and emotions poured through her mind too fast. She finally collapsed into bed with her clothes on and slept until seven, when a collect call from Jack woke her up. She accepted the call and was gratified to hear Jack's voice, giddy with jubilation. "Cass, you'll never believe what's happened! My lawyer just left here! They found the guy who murdered Melinda. Turned out it was the father of that woman I used to date. He confessed, Cass. He confessed he did it! I'm a free man!"

"That's wonderful, Jack. I'm so happy for you."

"My lawyer says I'll be out in just a few days. We can be together."

She was silent.

"What's wrong? Aren't you happy I'll be getting out? We can be together, have a life together. Don't you want that?"

"This is all happening so fast, Jack. Of course I'm happy for you, it's just that—"

"Oh, I get it. You *wanted* a boyfriend behind bars because it was easier that way. Now I'm gonna be a free man, so all of a sudden you're scared."

The doorbell rang like an answered prayer, loud enough that she hoped Jack heard it over the phone.

"We need to discuss this in person, Jack. I'm sorry, but I've got to go now."

They hung up simultaneously.

The doorbell rang again, more insistently. Probably cops with more questions, she thought.

She peered out through the peephole, breathed a sigh of relief when she saw who was there, and opened the door. "Reverend Butterworth?"

"I'm sorry to bother you, Cass. May I come in?"

"Sure." She stood back from the door and he lumbered in, looking weary, almost forlorn. He sat down on the couch with a loud crunching of springs and took in Cass's disheveled appearance with an expression of consternation. "I'm sorry—did I wake you?" He glanced at his watch as if to confirm that it was not an inappropriate hour for a visit. "It's only a bit after seven."

"I didn't sleep last night, so I took a nap."

"Oh, I'm sorry," he apologized again. "Opal Brady

was kind enough to give me your address. I hope you don't mind my dropping in?"

"No, it's okay. I was just going to make some coffee. Would you like a cup?"

"I'm afraid I can't take the caffeine. Tea perhaps?" She shook her head. "Sorry. I don't have any."

There was a moment of awkward silence. Cass wondered if he'd talked to Jack and knew about Kenny Sterling's confession. She thought maybe Jack had even asked him to come here, but what he said as she got out the coffeepot was, "I just came from Linda and Jim's house."

Cass flinched inwardly. She'd been so absorbed in her own personal drama of the last twenty-four hours that the death of Judd Lomax hadn't even entered her mind. She'd forgotten, in fact, that he was dead. Now, as it came back to her, she felt a pang of guilt and dismay at how quickly her own situation could eclipse everything else.

"How are they doing?"

"Bearing up bravely, I'd say, considering their terrible loss. Linda's burden is especially great. She blames herself for not having objected when Jim ordered Judd out of the house. I reminded her that she was only being a good wife and obeying the dictates of her husband as Scripture tells her to do."

Cass bit back a retort. *Let it go*, she told herself, but she could feel her blood heating up along with the water in the coffeepot.

There was silence again. She started to share the good news about Jack just to give them something to talk about, then decided that was Jack's news and he should tell Butterworth himself.

"I'm weary this evening," the minister said unexpectedly. "I spent most of the afternoon hiking. I do hike quite a bit, you know. It surprises people"—he patted his ample belly—"that I actually get out and exercise, but I find it helps me to think. And to talk to God."

"Solitude can be very healing," Cass said as she poured a mug of coffee for herself and came back into the living room and sat down across from Butterworth. "Actually, Reverend, after the other day at Judd's funeral, I had intended to call you or stop by the church."

"Really?" He looked so pleased that she could only assume he expected an apology, so without giving him a chance to speak, she continued, "I can't offer you an apology, because I meant what I said, but I do regret the setting. Judd's funeral wasn't the place for me to start an argument. I have a temper. I'm sorry that I let it get the better of me."

Butterworth's face seemed to deflate as though his head were a balloon she'd just stuck with a pin. He stared at his hands. "I'm sorry, too, Cass. Truly sorry."

"Is that why you're here? Because of the other day?"

"Well, no . . . I mean, yes, in a sense I suppose, but no . . . what I really came for was to tell you . . . before you read it in the paper or hear about it on the news, that is . . . there's been a new development regarding Judd's death, I'm afraid. The Lomaxes told me that the police want to do an autopsy. They say his death may not have been an accident."

"Someone *killed* him?"

Butterworth seemed to look past her as he spoke, as if he were reading from a TelePrompTer somewhere over her shoulder. "Apparently there was no water in his lungs, which means his head injuries occurred before he either fell or was thrown into the water. He didn't drown because his skull was fractured, as the coroner thought at first. Apparently, he was already dead when he hit the water."

"My God, that's horrible."

Cass was trying to absorb this new shock and at the same time put her own thoughts together. Why would Butterworth come to her house to tell her about Judd when there were so many in the congregation much closer to the Lomaxes than she was? Had Jack heard about what happened at the funeral and encouraged Butterworth to visit and attempt a reconciliation? Or was this something that, for some reason, the minister had decided to do on his own? Either way, the visit struck her as exceedingly odd.

"The police want Linda and Jim to delay the funeral a few days, so more tests can be done," Butterworth went on. "As you can imagine, they're both in shock. Judd was well loved. Dearly loved. That someone could do this . . . it's just . . ."

He brushed tears out of his eyes.

"So the police think Judd was attacked while he was camping and then dragged or carried to the river and thrown in? Wouldn't there be footprints? Tracks?"

"He was killed on stony ground," said Butterworth. "Besides even if there were prints left by the killer, by now there'd be those of other people, too—hikers, fishermen. I believe it's called compromising the crime scene."

He pronounced the last words carefully, as though speaking a foreign language.

"Was there any motive as far as the police know? Did Judd have enemies?"

"None. He was well loved," Butterworth repeated. With that, he lapsed into silence again.

Cass sipped her coffee. It was strong and sent a welcome jolt of caffeine through her. Now that she was more awake, though, the headache that had bothered her earlier was coming back. She found her mind drifting to the bottle of Tylenol in the medicine cabinet. How long was Butterworth going to stay? she wondered. Should she simply ask him to leave?

"You know Jack's worried about you," said Butterworth, catching her off guard as he veered off in another direction. "As am I. I felt it was only right that I tell him some of what you said the other day. Your lack of faith, your belief that the Bible is open for interpretation, that I gather you do not consider it the literal word of God."

"Did Jack—"

He put a hand up to stop her from going on. "No, my coming here wasn't Jack's idea. I'm here strictly on my own. I want to talk to you, Cass. I have to believe that if you truly understood what's at stake here, your own immortal soul, you'd at least be open to discussion. I think—"

Now it was Cass's turn to interrupt. "Hold on, Reverend Butterworth. This is all a little too much, okay? First you tell me the police think Judd was murdered and I'm trying to absorb that. Now you want to discuss theology. The last twenty-four hours have been *extremely* rough on me. This just isn't the time."

"When *would* be a good time?"

She exhaled in exasperation. The guy just wouldn't give up. "Look, Reverend, I don't want to be rude, but if I want to hear you speak about your conception of God, I'll be in church Sunday morning. Front row center. Is that fair enough?"

She drained her coffee and went back to the kitchen for a refill, hoping that her standing up would prompt him to do the same. Her head was really hurting now. She wanted to go back to bed. To be alone.

Instead, he planted his hands on his knees and said in the same matter-of-fact voice in which he'd earlier asked if she had any tea, "You are destined to burn in hell, Cass Lumetto."

She didn't know whether to be outraged or to burst out laughing. The laughter won. When she could contain herself, she said, "*That's* what you came here to tell me?"

"This is not a joke. It concerns your soul."

"Why don't you let me worry about my soul, and you worry about yours."

"You mock me," said Butterworth. "That shows the depth of your ignorance. We are talking about *hell*, Cass Lumetto."

"No, *you're* the one who's talking about hell. It seems to be your favorite subject." She poured her coffee and started searching for a pack of cigarettes. "I don't like being rude, but I'm going to have to ask you to leave."

"But we're discussing something vital—"

"No, we're not."

"—to your salvation."

She found the pack in a drawer, shook out a cigarette, then realized that she didn't have a lighter.

In the living room, Butterworth was saying, "If you'd just pray with me—"

Ignoring him, she turned on a pilot light on top of the stove. An orange and blue flame hissed up.

"—and get down on your knees and ask God in His mercy to forgive—"

She leaned forward to touch her cigarette to the flame, then stopped suddenly, the cigarette falling unlit to the floor, when a question that she should have noticed earlier, that she might have noticed if she hadn't been so dead tired, clicked in her mind.

"Reverend Butterworth? How did you know the ground was stony where Judd went into the river?"

He was standing at the door now—on his way out, she hoped—but instead he turned the bolt to lock it from inside and came back across the living room, advancing toward her with that peculiar, rolling gait that suggested a great ship listing to starboard. His eyes gleamed, but not with tears. When he reached the sofa, he laid the cane across it, and kept approaching.

"Cass, my child . . ."

"Did you just lock the front door?"

"There's no need to be afraid. I only want us to pray."

"Hold on." Her voice rose. "I want you to leave—*now*."

He held his hands out, palms up beseechingly, and said in his most avuncular tone, "Be still, child."

"Stop calling me child."

"Come pray with me for your salvation."

"I'm telling you to leave."

"And leave I will, in due time."

He crept forward, taking steps so small perhaps he thought she wouldn't notice that he moved at all, that he was still advancing.

"Why did you lock the front door?"

"You're imagining things. It wasn't tightly shut. I only closed it."

He took another step toward her, apparently intent on boxing her into the kitchen. She tried to dart past him, but her movement was hampered by the narrow space. His hand shot out and snagged her T-shirt.

"Don't scream," he said.

"What are you doing?"

"Only looking out for you when you refuse to look out for yourself."

He gripped her by the shoulders and bore down, using his weight to force her to her knees. She reached up and grabbed one of his little fingers, twisting until it popped and wobbled in the socket. He grunted with pain, shoved her onto the floor, and lowered his bulk onto her chest. His face loomed over hers, gravity pulling the loose flesh into grotesque creases and folds, like cooling tallow.

"Please don't scream."

She tried to nod an assent. She couldn't have screamed anyway with his weight on her.

"I don't want to do it this way, Cass. I wanted to give you more time. I thought perhaps being with Jack would help you see the light. But the police came to my house this morning asking questions. My time may be running out. That leaves me no choice. If I don't save you now, you are *damned*."

His knees ground into her shoulders. She tried to speak, but was only able to cough. She banged her hands on the floor next to his knees and shook her head from side to side.

"Scary when you can't breathe, isn't it?" He adjusted his weight so a little more went onto his legs, allowing her rib cage to rise. "There, is that better?"

She nodded weakly.

"Good. Are you ready to pray with me now?"

"No."

His face took on a new severity. He shook his head, jowls flapping. "Must you make this difficult? Must you conspire with Satan to bring about your own damnation?"

He put his weight back on her chest, pressing the air from her.

To Cass, floating in and out of consciousness, the torture seemed like an endless, drug-induced nightmare. Sometimes she could hear Butterworth talking and even her own voice answering, other times there was only an enormous white roar in her head, a roar that faded into silence and blackness. Sometimes she was aware of dreams, during those interludes when she lost consciousness. She dreamed she was at a carnival full of fierce and terrifying rides—spinning teacups that generated a centrifugal force so powerful her ribs were snapped and driven through her spine, water slides that ended in gaping pits filled with cotton candy, deep and sweet and smothering.

Sometimes the minister's voice drifted eerily through the dreams. She caught words—*Jesus* and *Savior*, *forgiveness* and *sin*. The carnival spun away like a nightmarish merry-go-round and was replaced by the church of her childhood. She stood at the rear, studying the backs of people's heads, looking for her mother and father, knowing if she found them, she'd be able to breathe again.

"Open your eyes, child, and look into the face of a sinner."

Air seeped mercifully into her lungs, and she came back to a reality more terrible than her oxygen-starved dreams. Opening her eyes, she saw something hidious looming over her, a woman crimson-faced and blotchy-skinned, eyes compressed to bleary slits, an ugly turquoise vein worming its way up one temple into the strands of sweat-soaked blond hair.

"The face of a sinner is ugly, isn't it?" Butterworth said.

She blinked and realized she was looking at herself. While she was passed out, he'd left her long enough to remove the oval mirror from the wall and position it above her face.

"A sinner. What you see is a sinner. Destined for hell!"

"Get . . . off. I . . . can't . . . breathe."

Concern creased his greasy forehead. He shifted his weight slightly and set the mirror aside, leaning it up against the wall behind him. She was able to draw a full breath. Her head stopped spinning. The white roar in her ears drained away.

"Let me sit up."

"Sit up?" Her request seemed to astonish him. "What for?"

"I can't pray lying down. I need to pray on my knees."

He considered it. "All right. Remember you mustn't scream."

She wondered who he thought would hear her if she did. The truth was she felt well beyond screaming. She didn't know how long she'd been lying there, blinking in and out of consciousness while he deprived her of air, but something had pounded the back of her head like a gavel and her ribs felt like they'd been used as a trampoline by a gang of sadistic children.

He helped her to her knees, so she was facing him. The deep folds in his flesh were slick with sweat. His breath smelled of some sugary confection, cinnamon and vanilla.

Cass's voice was a hoarse croack. "You murdered Judd."

He looked affronted. "I saved Judd's soul from Satan. He died a Christian."

"You bastard!"

"Hush!" His fingers dug bruisingly into her arms. "I saved Judd's soul, just as I've saved the souls of other good people who succumbed to the blandishments of evil. I brought them back into the fold."

"How many have you brought back into the fold? Was Raven Sterling one of them?"

"Raven?" His eyes clocked to the side and he focused his gaze behind her again, as though he were watching his past deeds replayed on a TV screen. "Satan came so close to claiming her." He held up a thumb and forefinger a half inch apart. "This close. But I snatched her away just in time. I saved her." He stared down at Cass pensively. "As I will save you."

"Think about what you're saying, Reverend! Think about what killing me will do to Jack! Please, you can't do this!"

"Repeat after me," he said calmly. "I accept Jesus Christ as my Lord and my Savior."

"And then what?"

He smiled benignly. "Then everything will be all right."

She searched his eyes, trying to fathom the evil she knew must be there, but what she found was only emptiness and disconnection, as if he'd become transfixed by the mindless tick-tock of some inner metronome and become permanently hypnotized.

"What you're doing, Reverend Butterworth, it was done in the Inquisition. Torturing people to get them to accept the teachings of the church, then killing them before they could go back on their vows. Killing people in order to save them. It's not what God wants. God hates what you're doing."

"Enough!" he roared, shaking her so that her head snapped back and forth like a newborn's. "Repeat what I say!"

She kept silent. Shook her head like a child refusing medicine.

Butterworth glared at her, sweaty and vexed. His pink mouth knotted in a cupid's bow pout.

Maybe this hadn't happened before, she thought. Maybe Butterworth's victims had always done what he'd asked, trying to save their own lives. But that was the trick, the catch-22. Once they claimed to have accepted Jesus, once their "souls" were no longer in danger, their bodies were dead meat.

"You're throwing your soul away," intoned Butterworth. "You're trading a moment of fear and discomfort for an eternity writhing in hell."

She shook her head. "Let me go. If you kill me, the police will find out. Then they'll link you to Judd, if they haven't already. You'll be ruined. Sent to prison. Your congregation will be without a spiritual leader, Fiona will be without a husband."

"Sinner!" he hissed. "Who are you to lecture *me*?" He planted his hand in her sternum and shoved, and she toppled straight backward, crying "No, please" even as he climbed on top of her and settled his bulk on her stomach. "I accept Jesus Christ as my Lord and Savior," he commanded. "Say it!"

Tears of pain filled her eyes. "No, no."

He repeated himself, inching forward on her torso so that his weight now was riding her chest. The air left her lungs in a long, wheezing whoosh. The white roar hummed in her ears like a cyclone. It spread into her skull, growing louder and sharper, its encroachment preceding the darkness.

"Say it," he prodded her. "Say it and you'll be saved."

I say it and you kill me, she thought, but she figured he was going to kill her anyway. What choice did he have?

She shut her eyes and went limp, pretending to be passed out, hoping he'd take some of his weight off her chest. He did, but in doing so, shifted his bulk more to one side than the other. She felt a sharp, internal crack. A bolt of pain careened through her torso.

"Jesus, my ribs!"

"Thou shalt not take the name of the Lord thy God in vain," he said, straddling her again.

"Get off mè. Please, I'll do what you want."

His lips wrinkled into an unappealing smile. "Forgive me if I appear to be a doubting Thomas, but you've shown little interest in your own salvation to this point."

"If I accept Jesus Christ, will you give me another chance? Will you let me prove my sincerity to change?"

"Just *say* what I told you to say," ordered Butterworth.

"And you'll let me live?"

She'd meant to placate him, but her words had just the opposite effect. Butterworth's brow accordioned into angry furrows. His cheeks puffed out with rage.

"Live? You want to live? That's all you care about, isn't it—your miserable existence in the body? You don't care if you're saved or not—only that you *live!*"

"Who's going to save you, Reverend Butterworth?"

He looked bemused. "I'm already saved."

He reset his weight on her chest. Her lungs were full of knives, her ribs on fire.

She heard a loud crack and thought it was the sound of more ribs breaking. Butterworth's eyes widened in amazement. His hands began to paw the air as though he were groping his way up an invisible wall before he shuddered and toppled sideways. His head slammed the floor and he rolled onto his back, blood pluming out of his nostrils.

A blizzard of sound filled Cass's head. The last thing she saw was a figure standing in the darkened doorway holding a gun.

Chapter 30

Cass opened her eyes to a vision so strange that for a moment she thought she was dreaming. A dark-haired woman in denim shorts and a baggy green T-shirt was leaning over Butterworth, brandishing a small, silver-plated handgun.

Butterworth snorted blood and thumped the floor with his feet. He moaned and tried to sit up, but got his shoulders up only a few inches before flopping back down.

The woman kept the gun trained on his head as she stepped over his legs and cast a quick, sideways glance at Cass. Cass saw pasty skin and piercing, close-set dark eyes.

"Mariah!"

Mariah flashed a triumphant, gray-toothed grin. "And I'll bet you thought I was nuts when I said I never leave my house without protection. Good thing I stopped by. Looks like you wouldn't have lasted much longer."

Cass raised herself up onto her elbows, felt the floor turn to Jell-O as a wave of dizziness washed over her. "How'd you get in?"

Another grin, this time so broad the laugh lines framing it resembled scars. "I saw where you keep your spare key, remember?"

"Thank God."

"Thank God is right. Talk about good fucking fortune. Synchronicity, that's what it is." Her eyes, almost avian in their dark quickness, darted back to Cass. "Bet you didn't think I knew big words like that?"

Cass had been focusing all her energy on not passing out. She missed most of what Mariah was saying. Something about synchronicity. *Synchronicity, yeah, no shit.*

Mariah squatted down and gave Cass a sharp slap in the face. "Hey, don't go passing out on me now. I need to know what was going down here when Good Samaritan Mariah arrived in the nick of time and came to the rescue. What was it? The man of God stopped by for a heavenly blow job and you told him to stick his dick up his holier-'n-thou ass? What?"

Cass took a deep breath, marshaling her strength. The floor did one last Jell-O jiggle and then solidified. "He came here to kill me. To save me. To kill me and save me. It's the same thing to him."

"Sick fuck," said Mariah.

"He killed Raven Sterling, too, and Judd Lomax. Who knows how many others. There's a phone in the hall. Call the cops."

"Looks like you could use an ambulance, too. How bad are you hurt?"

"Broken ribs, I think."

"He rape you?"

"No."

She frowned. "Old goat prob'ly couldn't get it up."

Butterworth gave a groan like a great bell tolling. One leg began to jitter. His left foot thumped the floor.

Mariah glared down at him. "Shut the fuck up!" To Cass, she said, "Hon, you might want to cover your ears."

Before Cass could register the implications of the warning, Mariah took a step back from Butterworth's body and fired a shot into the great mound of belly. Cass shrieked. Butterworth screamed and jerked upward, flailing his arms. His feet twitched. Then he lay still.

"Jesus," said Cass, "you didn't have to do that!"

"Yeah, I did."

Mariah reached down and lifted Butterworth's wrist with one hand, checked his pulse.

Cass's ears were ringing. "Leave him alone. Call the police."

Mariah made a tsk-tsk sound deep in her throat. "He's a tough old bird, ain't he? He's still breathing. See you in hell, you sick fuck." Dropping the minister's wrist, she stepped back, squinted, and fired a shot between his eyes. Butterworth's forehead collapsed. Blood beaded in the hair inside his ears.

Mariah toed his head to the side and peered down. "No exit wound. That's good for your floor. With such a small caliber weapon, the bullet just bounces around inside for a while, turns everything to purée." Seeing Cass's expression, she said, "Don't look so shocked. He had it coming, didn't he?"

"Jesus, Mariah, what have you done?"

"Done the world a fucking favor, I'd say."

"He may have killed other people besides Raven and Judd. He might have confessed."

Mariah tilted her head, deep in thought. "You make a good point. He probably did kill other people. Who knows, he might've even killed CharLee."

"Let the police figure that out," said Cass. She tried to get to her feet, but was brought to her knees by a paralyzing pain in her rib cage. "I need an ambulance, Mariah. I'm hurt."

"Okay, just stay where you are. Phone's in the bedroom, you said?"

"Yeah."

"I'll call for help."

Cass inched backward until she could lean against the wall. The pain in her ribs was excruciating. She had visions of bone splinters skewering her heart. The paramedics would be here soon, she told herself.

She smelled the sharp, coppery odor of Butterworth's blood. Beneath the bloody wound to his forehead, the minister's eyes were open and staring, his mouth forming a small "o" of surprise. She turned her head to the side to avoid looking at him. The mirror Butterworth had held up for her rested against the opposite wall. She could see her face in it, blanched white as talcum powder, angry red blotches on her forehead and cheeks. A face that looked like it had been made up at a mortuary.

In the next room, she could hear Mariah giving the address to the police, urging them to send an ambulance quickly. *Thank God,* she thought.

She wrapped her arms around her midsection, rocking herself gently, like an autistic child. It was so painful to breathe. If it weren't for the pain, she could almost sleep. She was so achingly tired.

Her eyes flicked to the mirror again. She saw part of Mariah's bare legs, then the phone cord dangling off the edge of the hall table. Had Butterworth unplugged the phone? There were only two phones in the house, the one in the hall and another in the bedroom. But Mariah was in the hall now. What was she talking on—a cell phone?

"Yes, there's one person shot and someone else injured," she was saying. "Please come as quick as you can."

Cass took a deep breath, braced herself against the wall, and pushed herself to a standing position. A glint of silver caught her eye—the handle of Butterworth's cane that was propped against the sofa. She took a halting step toward it.

Mariah called from the other room, "Help's on the way."

Cass took another faltering step, her eyes fixed on the cane. Something shifted inside her, bone scraping bone. She felt her heart stutter and realized she had to stop moving or risk passing out from the pain.

Mariah came back into the room. She was still carrying the gun, but she had put on Cass's green gardening gloves. Seeing Cass on her feet, she snapped, "Hey, what are you doing?"

Cass forced herself forward.

"Come *lie down*."

Cass reached the sofa just as her legs gave out. As she sagged onto the arm of the sofa, her hand closed on the cane. She leaned her weight on it, put up a mental barrier against the pain, and took a few hobbling steps toward the kitchen.

"Where're you going?"

"I need a drink of water."

"You don't need any water. Trust me."

Cass reached the door to the kitchen, a few feet from the stove. The burner where she'd tried to light a cigarette—what felt like a lifetime ago—still crackled with flame. She leaned against the wall to get her breath. Staring at Mariah's gloved hands, she felt a sick, stomach-roiling terror. "You didn't call anyone, did you?"

Mariah's mouth twisted peevishly. "Now don't go getting all paranoid. I was using my cell phone."

"You have a cell phone? Show it to me."

Maria shrugged. "Sure. Hang on a sec." She laid the gun down on the coffee table, but instead of producing a phone, she crouched next to Butterworth's body, unfastened his belt, and started pulling it through the loops.

"You ask me, you know, I think this dickhead killed CharLee," she said conversationally. "Maybe even bragged about it before I shot him. Might've bragged about killing other women, too."

"Mariah, what are you talking about? Why the gloves?"

"I'm just picturing what I tell the cops happened here. How I arrived too late to stop him from strangling you, how he would've killed me, too, if I hadn't shot him. How he mutilated you the same way he did CharLee and some of those women that Madison's been accused of killing."

"Jesus, Mariah, this is about Madison?"

"Everything in my life is about Madison. He *is* my life. I really thought that if CharLee turned up murdered, the cops would realize there was another killer at work—that it wasn't just Madison—but apparently one dead woman wasn't enough. There has to be more."

"You're saying you murdered CharLee to save Madison?"

Mariah pulled the belt free. Coiling it in her gloved hands, she stood up and started toward Cass. "It's not crazy. Madison has a unique M.O. that nobody knows about except him and the police. And me. He takes trophies. The little toe of each foot. Bet your buddy the detective didn't tell you that, did he—that two of her toes were gone? It's what I'll do with you, too. *After* you're dead, if you're lucky."

"Madison will still die. The only difference is you'll be getting the needle with him."

"This was meant to be," said Mariah. "Talk about synchro-fucking-nicity. I'd thought about killing you if I got the chance, but I never dreamed I'd have it handed to me on a silver platter. This fat fuck set it all up for me. Talk about luck!"

She advanced on Cass, eyes dancing with a murderous elation. "I wish I could just shoot you, hon. But I can't do that, 'cause I'm not the one who murdered you. It was the crazy preacher who played 'This Little Piggy' while he snipped off your toes."

Cass leaned her weight on the cane, trying to steady herself. With each heartbeat, the pain in her ribs seemed to sharpen. "You asked if he'd raped me. Because you were hoping he had, right? So there'd be semen. The cops said there was semen on CharLee's body, but not inside her. Is that what all the fuss about condoms was about that day at your house? You were trying to collect semen?"

Mariah laughed as though particularly pleased with herself. "Hey, a girl needs a hobby, right? What the cops found on CharLee was jism I'd kept frozen till I needed it. Too bad I didn't bring any with me today, but I was just stopping by for a friendly visit. Had no idea if I wanted to kill you, I'd have to stand in line."

She raised the belt. "Be a good girl and this can be over with fast."

Cass ducked and drove the handle of the cane up through the looped belt, into Mariah's lip and through her front teeth. Mariah grunted and spat out blood. She dropped the belt and came at Cass with her fists. Cass flipped the cane so that the hooked end snagged her ankle.

Off balance, Mariah stumbled forward. Cass grabbed her hair and let her body weight shove Mariah toward the stove. The effort sent red agony ripping through her ribs. Pain blinded her, but she kept her weight on Mariah's head, forcing her face toward the fire.

Mariah howled as one side of her face hit the burner. Her hair caught fire. She bucked wildly, breaking Cass's hold and throwing her backward into the wall. The impact jarred Cass's broken ribs. Her chest felt full of knives.

Mariah bolted back into the living room, flapping at the fire with her arms. She dropped to the floor, rolling and writhing while flames crowned her head and tongued at her eyes.

Putting her weight on the cane, Cass crept past Mariah in small, excruciating steps. By the time Mariah had extinguished her burning hair, one side of her face was a scarlet mess, and Cass was pointing the gun at her head.

Chapter 31

I want things to be different, Shep was saying. *Forget any of this ever happened. When you get out of the hospital, we'll sit down and decide how we'll do this, whether you'll stay in Canon City or I'll move to New York. Either way it's okay with me. I just want us to be together.*

I want that, too.

She smiled in her sleep, making her dry lips crack at one corner and bleed. The pain woke her up and she looked around, confused and disoriented when she realized no one was sitting there by the side of the bed, that Shep didn't have her hand cupped in his.

The dream had seemed so real—as real as a couple of hours ago when he'd shown up at her hospital room with an armload of flowers, as real as the smell of the roses that now permeated the room. He'd been distressed about her injuries and the ordeal she'd been through, but along with the concern and caring for her, she'd also felt an unmistakable distance. When he'd told her he was taking a leave of absence to spend some time with his sister and her husband in Utah, she'd had to pretend that the tears welling up in her eyes were due to the pain she still felt when her medication wore off.

While she was still adjusting to the gap between the dream and reality, a nurse stuck her head into the room. "You've got a visitor."

"Who—?"

But the nurse had already ducked back out into the hall.

She heard the sound of boots approaching and sat up straighter, fussing with the neck of her nightgown until she realized that any attempt to primp was ridiculous. With broken ribs and possible internal damage, she looked and felt like the survivor of a train wreck. Trying to look sexy was beyond futile.

"Cass?"

She hadn't expected the visitor to be Jack—she'd already convinced herself it was Shep coming back—and had to fight not to show her disappointment.

He smiled as he came in, brushing his lips across hers, and sat down in a chair next to the bed. His blond hair was cut short, and he looked freshly shaven.

"Funny, huh," he said, "me visiting you for a change?"

"You look good. I've never seen you with short hair."

"Yeah, I'm just getting used to it myself. My lawyer said it might be a good move if I want to get custody of Twyla."

"Are Angela and Parker going to contest it?"

"I doubt it. They're both kinda in shock at the moment. Me being on the outside and that Sterling guy being the one who murdered Melinda. He's going away for a long time, so I hear. Anyway, Angela's going to keep Twyla for the time being. Till I can get a job and save up some money to make a good home for her. And guess what, honey?"

"What?"

"I quit drinking! Almost a week out of the can and I ain't been near a bar, haven't taken a drink of anything stronger than soda. Tell you the truth, it feels so good to be free that I don't even miss it. I figure it's drinking been the cause of all my problems. I always thought I had to drink 'cause I had so many problems. Never realized I had so many problems because I drank. I'm a changed man, honey. I mean it."

"Jack, that's wonderful. Good for you."

"Something else that I'm gonna start doing is making amends. It may take a while, but I'll do what I can—pay back the people I owe money to little by little, apologize to the people I've mouthed off to and lied to and got into fistfights with over the years. I've been a real jerk all my life and I'm only just starting to realize it."

"You've got a lot of good in you, Jack. I know that."

He seemed embarrassed, reaching over to brush back a stray lock of her hair. "How about you? You got banged up pretty bad, huh? How're you doing?"

"Better than when I first got here. My ribs are healing, but the doctors want to keep me here a couple more days for observation. What about you?"

"Oh, I'm free to leave at any time."

She laughed and then winced. "Jesus, don't make me laugh. I mean, what're you gonna do now that you're free?"

"Well, I'm crashing at a buddy's house for the time being. Next thing, I guess, is to see about finding some carpentry work and start getting my life back on track now that—" His voice broke, and his face reddened. He took a deep breath.

"What is it?"

"Shit, I keep thinking about Reverend Butterworth. About what the cops told me, what I heard on the news—that not only did he try to kill you, but the prints they found at Judd's campsite matched his shoes and there was blood in his truck that matched with Judd's. Now they're trying to link him to Raven's death, too."

"He admitted to me that he killed her, Jack."

"Jesus God, I loved that man. I respected him. Now it's like everything he said was a lie. He wasn't fighting Satan, he *was* Satan."

"Or maybe he was just sick."

He was silent awhile. "You know what that wife of his did?"

"Fiona? No."

"Soon as she found out the reverend was dead, she took her stuff and moved in with some roofer guy. She's a whore, no two ways about it."

"That's a little harsh, isn't it?"

"Oh, I don't think so, no. You know why? 'Cause before she moved in with the roofer, she called me. Told me I could come live in her house, sleep in the Reverend Butterworth's bed. With her. I told her I'd as soon stay in the damn prison—better quality of people there—thank you very much."

"This has devastated a lot of people," said Cass. "Opal stopped by the other day. She's in shock. She lost her minister and her best friend Mariah the same day."

"Mariah, yeah, saw on the news that she's still in a burn unit up in Denver. By the time she goes to trial, Madison will be dead. Can't happen soon enough in my book—I hear he admitted he knew Mariah killed Luthor's girlfriend CharLee and that she was planning to kill other women, too. Way I see it, Madison probably knew her copying his crimes wouldn't save him, but he was getting off on hearing her tell him about her plans."

"I could believe that."

"Hey, look, though, I didn't come here to talk about them two." He leaned forward, taking her hand in much the same way Shep had held it in the dream. "I know our last conversation didn't go so good. Sounded like you weren't exactly thrilled I was getting out. Was I wrong about that? Are you gonna stay here in Canon City and try getting to know me as a free man instead of a guy behind bars? Or are you gonna take off?"

She'd been waiting for this, dreading it. "I've given it a lot of thought, Jack. I'm going back to New York."

"Yeah, well, after everything that's happened, guess I can't blame you. But—" He gripped her hand even tighter. She thought she saw tears in his eyes. "I've given things a lot of thought, too, and I need to say this. Keep an open mind on me. Give me a chance to build a life out here, to prove I'm different now. Man doesn't go through everything I've been through and not change. He either gets worse or he gets better. I've changed for the better, Cass. Let me prove that to you."

She started to speak, but he put a finger across her lips. "Wait. Don't say anything now. Just think about it. You loved me once, when I was in prison, I know you did. That was different, it was safer for you, because I was on the inside. If I prove to you that I've changed, think you could try loving me again? Try to make something together?"

For a moment, she found herself imagining Shep saying those words. She felt tears welling up.

"At least keep the door open," he said. "Let me write once in a while, let you know how I'm doing. Maybe one day I can come out to New York, get a hotel room, you and me have a cup of coffee somewhere and talk over old times. See if maybe there might still be a chance for us."

She didn't speak. He kissed her hard and headed out into the hall, closing the door behind him.

Epilogue

Dear Cass,

Guess you thought you'd be hearing from me before now, but I been a busy man. And I can honestly say I am a changed man. First thing I did after seeing you in the hospital that day was go out and get a job and work my tail off to save up some money and make a decent life. Found me a new church to go to and stayed out of the bars and strip clubs like they was poison. I started making my amends to people, too—even made peace with Angela and Parker.

Forgiveness is an amazing thing.

Other week, I drove up to Buena Vista, where Ken Sterling's doing his fifteen to twenty-five. Wanted to tell him how sorry I was about what happened to Raven and that I'd honestly cared for her, but couldn't show it proper 'cause I was drinking at the time. He looked like hell, I don't mind telling you. And after I finished talking, he broke down crying and begged my forgiveness for having killed Melinda, and I cried, too, and we hugged like we was family.

And I forgave him, too.

But not you, Cass.

Because he slipped and gave it all away. That it was all a scam and he was paying you to pretend to be my girlfriend.

I heard that, my heart stopped and then it froze to ice. I went out and bought a quart of Johnny Walker and I got in my car.

Right now I got a six-pack on the front seat and a map of New York City on the dash with your street circled in red. By the time you get this, I may be ready to come knocking on your door in that nice apartment building I've been watching you go in and out of for a couple days now.

Or maybe I won't knock.

I can forgive a lot of things, Cass.

But you, I thought you loved me once, and now I know it was all a goddamned lie.

You made a fool of me.

And that I won't forgive.

ONYX

USA Today Bestselling Author
LARRY BROOKS

DARKNESS BOUND

BOUND IN PLEASURE

Two strangers meet. A woman without inhibitions...a
man without limits...for a private game between two
consenting adults...

BOUND IN PAIN

They indulge every secret fantasy. But one of them has
a secret yet to be shared...

BOUND IN DARKNESS

Now the real games are about to begin...

0-451-40945-0

To order call: 1-800-788-6262

S331

NAILED

Lucy Taylor

"Nailed opens in a bar, but what happens to protagonist Matt Engstrom, is more like a bar brawl. He's assailed from every point of the compass, and author Lucy Taylor has done a fine job of keeping the reader as off-balance as her hero under siege. A genuinely different, edgy kind of mystery."
—Jeremiah Healy, author of *Spiral* and *The Only Good Lawyer*

Matt Engstrom has a successful construction business, a son he raises on his own, and a past that's about to come full circle. He's not going to know what hit him...

"Lucy Taylor's writing is filled with a richness of place and a precise attention to detail."
—*Cemetary Dance*

0-451-40990-6

To order call: 1-800-788-6262

S500/taylor